W9-AWM-873

Double Prey

Books by Steven F. Havill

The Posadas County Mysteries
Heartshot
Bitter Recoil
Twice Buried
Before She Dies
Privileged to Kill
Prolonged Exposure
Out of Season
Dead Weight
Bag Limit
Red, Green, or Murder
Scavengers
A Discount for Death
Convenient Disposal
Statute of Limitations
Final Payment
The Fourth Time is Murder
Double Prey

The Dr. Thomas Parks Novels
Race for the Dying
Comes a Time for Burning

Other Novels
The Killer
The Worst Enemy
LeadFire
TimberBlood

Double Prey

A Posadas County Mystery

Steven F. Havill

Poisoned Pen Press

Poisoned
Pen
Press

Copyright © 2011 by Steven F. Havill

First Edition

10 9 8 7 6 5 4 3 2 1

Library of Congress Catalog Card Number: 2010932086

ISBN: 9781590587829   Hardcover
       9781590587843   Trade Paperback

Poisoned Pen Press
6962 E. First Ave., Ste. 103
Scottsdale, AZ 85251
www.poisonedpenpress.com
info@poisonedpenpress.com

Printed in the United States of America

For Kathleen

Acknowledgments

The author would like to extend special thanks to Frank Cimino, Peter Egetenmeir, Clint Henson, David Pasquale, and Ryan Walker.

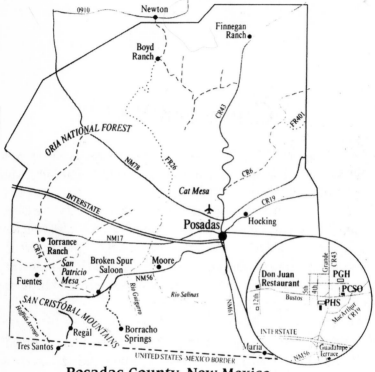

Posadas County, New Mexico

Chapter One

Carla Champlin's voice had taken on real urgency. "Your son is running over this way," she said. "The other boy is down on the ground. Now I just don't know *what...*"

Traffic was light, only a single on-coming car at the intersection of Bustos and Grande. Estelle flipped on the grill wiggle-waggles, ran the red light, and accelerated hard to continue west bound on Bustos. At Eighth, she turned south. In a moment she could see the open prairie, an expanse of tans and browns bordering the Eighth Street cul-de-sac.

A dirt two-track had been carved into the desert by scores of dirt bikes, motorcycles, and four wheelers that had jumped to the open lot from Eighth Street. Estelle eased the county car over the worn, crumbling curb. Off to the left, she could see Carla, arms waving commands. A tiny figure sprinted away from the old woman back toward the arroyo, racing a beeline through the scrub to intersect the patrol car's path. To the right, just back from the arroyo's edge, the other boy was hunkered on his elbows and knees, head down near the ground.

"PCS, three ten."

"Go ahead, three ten."

"I need an ambulance at this location ASAP. It may be a snake bite. One juvenile." Little Francisco was sprinting in high gear now, and Estelle realized that the loud pounding was her own heart.

2 Steven F. Havill

"Ten four. Say the location again."

"The south end of Eighth Street, out by the arroyo."

"Ten four."

The dirt two track wandered toward the houses on Carla's street. Estelle braked hard, sliding the county car to a stop. By the time she had climbed out, her son was within easy earshot.

"Butch got something in his eye!" the little boy called.

Estelle looked hard at her son, the nine-year-old so lanky now that his bones poked at the lightweight, white linen Mexican shirt that his grandmother had given him.

"Show me." She strode after the boy as he dashed back toward his friend.

"We found a snake," Francisco called over his shoulder.

And sure enough, they had. The creature writhed in slow motion under a broken clump of creosote bush, rattles sounding like a short-circuited electrical gadget. With both hands covering his face, Butch Romero was curled into a crying, whimpering, cursing ball, crumpled so that the crown of his head dug into the gravel and sand. Estelle glanced quickly at the battered reptile, guessed that it wasn't going anywhere with most of its own head pulped, and sank to her knees beside the tortured boy.

"Butch, you'll be okay." She took his shoulders, feeling the trembling that racked his wiry body. He yelped and thrashed, hands tearing at his face. His mouth gaped, a strand of drool soaking his chin. Hugging him close, she caught one of his hands. "Come on, now. Let me see."

The boy wailed something incomprehensible, leaning his weight against Estelle. As if the flashes of pain were punching him in the gut, he kept ducking his head and twisting. The undersheriff maneuvered her hand across his right arm, and she could feel the knotted muscles like small bands of steel. The fourteen-year-old was no more than five-foot-two and ninety pounds, but he was a tough little kid.

All the while talking gently into the boy's ear, she worked her arm across Butch's chest until she hugged him tightly, pinning his upper arms. "You're going to be all right. You have to stop digging at your eyes. Come on." Still he fought her with a desperate strength that was astonishing. At one point he jerked his head back, his hard skull cracking Estelle on the cheek. She flinched and tightened her bear hug. In the distance, she heard a siren.

"*Hijo,* run over and wave them in," she said. "Butch, hang in there, now. You're going to be all right. Help is on the way." She still had no idea what the extent of his injuries could be. Struggling would make matters worse, so she settled for the tight hug, trying to hold him still.

Still whispering to the boy, she turned her head and watched the progress of the big diesel EMT rig as it waddled up over the curb at the end of Eighth. The ambulance left the two track and pursued Francisco, making its own road across the scrub-covered lot. It turned in a wide circle at the last moment.

Doyle Maestas climbed out of the truck and took two seconds both to survey the area and watch where he stepped, taking in the undersheriff and the apparent victim. He pulled a field case out of one of the storage compartments on the side of the truck, by that time joined by his partner, Matty Finnegan.

"What do we have?" Matty knelt by Estelle. "Oh, jeez, here we go." She caught sight of the battered snake. "Butchie, we're going to help you now. You hang in there." She inclined her head and looked at Estelle. "You have a good hold?" The undersheriff nodded.

"Butchie, you have to move your hands," Matty said.

"You want the sedative?" Maestas asked.

"We're going to need it. Here, take his right hand." With Estelle locking his upper arms, and one EMT on each lower limb, they were able to force the boy's hands down. "Butch, can you tell me what happened?"

"In my eye," the boy sobbed, finally saying something coherent. "My right eye."

"You have his arms?" Matty asked, and when Doyle nodded, she gently took his head in both hands, gripping him on each cheek, her fingers under his ears, thumbs on the crests of his cheek bones. The eye was already discolored, and a massive flood of tears poured down his face. Butch spasmed. "Well, you have *something* there, old man." She turned to look at the discarded electric Weed Whacker. "Now that's something I haven't seen before. You were teasing the snake with that trimmer?"

Butch howled something incomprehensible.

"Okay. I'm going to cover that eye so you don't injure it any more. You're going to help me do that, my man. All right?" In an instant, she'd found a large white eye cup in the bag, and with a few deft wraps had secured it over the injured eye, taping it around his head.

"Gurney?" Doyle asked.

"You betcha," Matty replied. "We're going to need the belts. Nobody's going to get an I.V. in him the way he's bouncing around." She looked over at the snake again as she rose to her feet. "Coon tail, right?"

"Yes." Estelle turned so that she could see her son. "Francisco, what happened?"

"We went looking for snakes," the nine-year-old said.

"With a trimmer?" The western diamondback was arguably the largest, most dangerous rattler in the southwest, doubly so because of its enormous venom supply and aggressive habits.

"It kinda worked," Francisco said. "We got it cornered, and then Butch was gonna cut its head off with the Weed Whacker. It kept striking at it."

"So we've got some of *that* in the eye," Doyle said. "Envenomed, you think?"

"Most likely," Matty said. "We're going to want that I.V., and get him on some Versed to calm him down. Butch, we're going to give you a little happy juice, all right? You're going to help us do that by trying your best to hold still."

Estelle looked around for her son, who stood with his hands clasped tightly under his chin. "*Hijo,* get the shovel out of my car. You know where the trunk release is. Be careful when you do it."

Doyle returned with the gurney while Matty popped the I.V. package out of the sterile packaging. "Butch, I'm going to give you a little shot to kill the pain, all right? You just try to hold still now." She had the needle in before he could react, and taped it securely in place.

In a moment, with the help of the fast-acting sedative, they were able to coax Butch Romero onto the gurney. He thrashed a bit, but finally they were able to secure his arms and legs, and then his head. With the boy trussed and wrapped, Doyle started a saline I.V., and in a moment their cargo was in the ambulance.

"Just another day's work in paradise," Doyle cracked as they boarded the vehicle. "Talk to you later, sheriff. Odds are good that he'll be flyin' out to University. We have antivenom at the hospital to start with, but your hubby isn't going to want to mess with that eye. Butch's mom at home?"

"I'll find her," Estelle said. "I'll bring her to the hospital."

"You got it."

Estelle reached out a hand for her son's bony shoulder and gave it a little shake, keeping her hold until the heavy ambulance had maneuvered away. "Thank you," she said, taking the shovel from him.

The diamondback was a full sixty inches long, its compliment of rattles showing that it had endured a good many seasons before running into an incomprehensible enemy. With a deft, sharp whack of the spade, Estelle cut off the mangled head, setting off a renewed thrashing as the powerful body tried to tie itself into knots. Francisco watched with eyes wide.

She handed him the spade and pointed. "We'll bury him right there. Dig a good hole." He set to work without question, and Estelle walked back to the car. She selected one of the heavy clear plastic evidence bags from her briefcase, along with a brown paper bag. By the time she returned to the site, Francisco had excavated an impressive hole.

The undersheriff used the edge of the shovel to flip the remains of the snake's head into the plastic bag. The trimmer's high speed spinning nylon string had been an effective weapon, macerating and then tearing out much of the rattler's mouth tissue. One fang was still in place, but the other had been torn free...and apparently was pegged in Butch Romero's eye. She slipped the evidence bag inside the brown sack. The snake's now limp body slid into the hole, and Estelle spaded the dirt back in to cover it.

"Butch said his dad *grills* 'em," Francisco offered.

"Not this one, *hijo*. The snakes don't know that coming into town is the most dangerous place for them."

"What do you do with the head?" he asked.

"In case the doctors need it, *hijo*." She nodded at the string trimmer. "You fetch that so you can give it back to Butch's mom. We need to go talk to her now." The little boy nodded soberly.

"I'm sorry, *mamá*."

"So am I." She followed him back toward the car, watching the grace of his movements, the dark intensity of him. It would be so much easier if children could be cocooned until they reached twenty-one, she thought.

Chapter Two

Francisco watched his mother complete the entry in her patrol log. His hands were clasped between his knees, and he remained silent, trying to stay out of the way. The log entry she wrote didn't reflect the alarm in Carla Champlin's voice when she had called.

"Estelle, I'm so sorry to bother you." Carla, the retired Posadas postmistress, had picked up a quaver in her voice as age chased her, but she had still managed to sound authoritative. Undersheriff Estelle Reyes-Guzman pictured the elderly woman, scarecrow-thin, standing in her kitchen with the receiver of the old-fashioned black wall phone pressed to her ear, face pursed with disapproval. Carla disapproved of most things.

"Carla, how are you?" Estelle pulled the county car into gear. "Are you calling from home?" If Estelle had stood on the top front step of her own home on Twelfth Street back in Posadas, she would have been able to see the white roof of Carla's neat little bungalow across the open patch of undisturbed prairie beyond Christman's arroyo. As it was, when Carla called the undersheriff's car had been parked on the shoulder of New Mexico State 78, seven miles from the village. The passenger seat was covered with file folders as Estelle found a quiet afternoon to peruse job applications and make calls to references. The sun was warm, and to keep herself awake, she'd changed locations from time to time, from one end of the small county to another, watching the traffic, the ranch kids on four wheelers, the patrons of the rural saloons as they took an afternoon brew break.

Carla had tracked her down, preferring a direct call to going through Sheriff's Department dispatch.

"Well, *I'm* just fine," Carla had said. "And of course I'm home. But listen. I'm watching a couple of hoodlums out beyond the arroyo, and I *don't* like what I'm seeing."

"What are you seeing, Mrs. Champlin?" She knew that *hoodlums* was a favorite Carla-ism for *children.* If children were seen or heard doing anything more disruptive than stamp collecting, they were *hoodlums.*

"Listen," the woman said again, as if Estelle might not be, "at first I couldn't see what they were doing, but I found my binoculars, and I just don't like this at all. They're over by the arroyo, and they're playing with a *snake,* for heaven's sakes. And it's a *big* snake. My gosh."

It's not illegal for boys to play with snakes, Estelle almost said.

"Now, one of them has one of those whacker things…one of those Weed Whackers? That's what they're using, for heaven's sake."

Estelle turned onto the highway. She accelerated eastbound, at the same time trying to conjure a mental image of what Carla might be watching.

"It's Butch Romero," Carla reported.

"Ah, Butch." Estelle's amusement turned into apprehension. The skinny kid with enough imp in him for ten hoodlums lived just two doors west of the Guzmans on Twelfth Street. He out-Tom Sawyered Tom Sawyer by a quantum leap.

"Your little angel is with him."

"Francisco, you mean?"

"That's *exactly* who I mean. And oh, now they've gone down into the arroyo. I can't see what they're doing. But this can't be good. I really think you should…oh, here they are again. You know, they're right *at the edge.*"

Christman's arroyo was no more than twelve feet deep at its most precipitous, but the edge could crumble, depositing the hoodlums at the gravel bottom under half a ton of desert sand.

Estelle took a deep breath. Kids played along arroyos all the time. Not a single rain cloud graced the southwest at the moment, so there was no danger of a fast-moving headwall of water sweeping them away. Kids played with snakes all the time, too—hopefully learning early on which were the dangerous species. If Butch had elected to go hunting with a trimmer, its nylon string flailing, then he wasn't after garter snakes. Estelle could imagine a dozen ways that such an absurd expedition might turn tragic.

"I'll swing by, Carla. I'm about five miles out, so it'll be a few minutes."

"Come right down Eighth Street," the post mistress commanded. "That's the closest. Oh, my, there he goes…"

"Stay on the line, Carla," Estelle said, and palmed the mike. "PCS, three ten."

Dispatcher Ernie Wheeler responded instantly. "Go ahead, three ten."

"I'll be ten-six at Eighth and Christman's Arroyo with a juvenile complaint," Estelle said. Two minutes later, she took the curve that joined County Road 43 with the State Highway, inbound on what would turn into Bustos Avenue. "Carla, are you still there?"

Yes, she had been, watching the two boys lure trouble. From the arroyo to Carla Champlins' was a mere hundred yards. Close enough for her to become alarmed and call, a call that brought Estelle to the scene and kept bad from being even worse.

Estelle closed her log book, and then keyed the mike.

"PCS, three-ten will be ten-six at 402 South Twelfth Street." Confirmation came immediately, and she racked the mike and looked across at her son. "So. Hunting snakes with a Weed Whacker. Butch does that a lot, *hijo?*" She started the car and backed out to the two-track, careful to avoid the larger clumps of cacti.

The little boy hunched his thin shoulders against the shoulder harness. "He said it was fun."

"Ah, and so we see how fun it is. For both the snake and for Butch, *¿no?* The snake gets his head chopped off and is buried in a shallow grave in the desert. Butch gets to go to the hospital to see if they can save his eye. And if there's venom from the snake, maybe his life. Fun, *¿no?*"

"The snake didn't bite him," Francisco said. "How could there be venom?"

"Because the trimmer gouged out a chunk of the snake's mouth parts, *hijo.* The snake was mad to begin with, and feeling threatened. Lots of venom loaded, ready to go. If a fang flew into Butch's eye, then there's probably venom with it."

"Will he die?"

"We hope not." Her son did not need a sugar coating of this situation. She touched her own face by way of demonstration. "But eyes are close to the brain, *hijo.* That's a bad place for venom."

The boy looked off into the distance, and Estelle felt the odd mixture of emotions—relief that the flying fang hadn't struck her son, anger at Butch Romero for initiating such a stupid stunt, and finally sympathy for both boys and what they would endure.

"This will be expensive, won't it?" Francisco asked quietly.

"*Hijo, hijo, hijo,*" Estelle sighed, impressed nevertheless… from little boy playing with snakes to the precocious nine year-old that he was, seeing into the complications. Life had been so much simpler before the great, wide world had started to beckon her sons. "Yes. It will be expensive."

"Do you know how much?"

"I don't know, *hijo.* But a lot, I bet. Paying *that* will be fun, too." She glanced across at him. She could see that the little boy was miserable. Estelle hesitated, but now was the time to say it, now when she had his attention. "You always have to *think, hijo,*" she said. "*Before,* not just afterward." She reached across and patted his leg. "I'm glad you didn't let Carlos go with you." Francisco and his little brother were usually inseparable.

"He doesn't like snakes," Francisco said.

"Ah. Well, maybe you and Butch won't after this, either." The car thumped down onto the asphalt of Eighth Street. "How was school today?"

"It was okay." He sounded grateful for the change of subject.

"You still don't like Mr. Reynolds?"

"He's okay. He wastes a lot of time."

Estelle kept a straight face. The concept of a nine-year-old who might be concerned with wasted time was something that would challenge first-year teacher Marv Reynolds, she suspected.

The drive back to Twelfth Street took only a moment, and as she pulled up to the curb in front of her own home, she saw Tata Romero on her hands and knees in the front yard two doors down the street, the sun hot on her back, grubbing around a spectacular bed of red hot pokers, the tall, homely flowers that thrived under the blistering sun. The house across the street had blocked her view of the field beyond. She had no inkling of the episode.

"Take the trimmer, *hijo*." Estelle touched the remote trunk release. "And then you go keep your brother company until I come home. And *hijo,*" she added, and waited until he was looking at her, "you stay in the yard when you get home."

He nodded soberly, and set off down the rough sidewalk with the trimmer. Estelle followed. Tata Romero saw them coming and eased out of the flower bed.

"Butch and I borrowed this, Mrs. Romero," Francisco said. "Do you want me to put it back in the shed?"

"Well, hi, *hijo,*" Tata said. "Yes, that would be nice. Thank you." She stood up and brushed her knees. "Estelle, how are you these days? Here we live two doors down, and we never get to see much of you. The boys have been doing yard work for you?" She dusted her gardening gloves together.

"I wish that were the case, Tata. Butch and my son were over in the field by the arroyo. They were teasing a rattlesnake with the Weed Whacker."

"Oh, for heaven's sakes," Tata exclaimed, and it was clear that her assumption was that some sort of mild delinquency was afoot...neither of the Romero boys, Butch or his older brother Freddy, were strangers to that. And then she realized that neither son was part of the equation here. She craned her neck, looking down the street. "And now where *is* the young man?" she asked sternly.

"Tata, the EMTs took him to the hospital. He suffered an eye injury."

"Oh, my gosh. The snake bit him?" Her face drained of color, and she looked after Francisco's retreating figure as the little boy trudged back toward his own home. "What has he gotten into now…"

"The trimmer line struck the snake in the head. I think that maybe a piece of fang, or maybe a piece of jaw bone…something… something struck Butch in the right eye. They'll do a preliminary assessment here and administer the anti-venom if they have to, but the EMTs tell me that it's likely they'll want to fly him to University Hospital in Albuquerque if there is significant damage to the eye."

Tata raised a hand to cover her mouth.

"Let me drive you to the hospital," Estelle said. "Then I'll stop by the dealership and have George come down to be with you."

"I need my purse." Tata turned toward the house. She stopped. "Will he lose the eye?"

"I don't know, Tata. They'll have news for us at the hospital."

The woman nodded and hurried into the house. Estelle waited on the sidewalk, and then escorted Tata back to the county car.

"How did you find out?" Tata settled into the car, looking apprehensively at the racked shotgun, the computer that invaded her knee space, the radios, all the other clutter of Estelle's mobile office.

"One of the neighbors saw the two boys playing out by the arroyo and was worried that they had cornered a snake. She was watching them through binoculars. She called me to check."

"Oh, my. These boys." *These boys,* Estelle thought, and she could inventory all the toys and gadgets that the two Romero brothers, cherished in their pursuit of their own adrenaline rushes. The Romeros' fleet grew by the season—motorcycles, four wheelers, even now a powered skateboard that enchanted her sons. The idea of a cocoon around her own two little boys grew more appealing with every week. Estelle relished the beginning of school, when the day's activities separated the three boys, Francisco now in fourth grade, Butch a freshman, Freddy a senior.

"The caller saw Butch fall to his hands and knees, so she knew that he was hurt. By then I was just up here on Bustos. The EMTs were right behind me."

Tata heaved a great, shuddering sigh. "Oh, these kids. Francisco is all right?"

"Yes. He's fine. Scared, but fine." In a moment they swung into the driveway leading to the emergency room of Posadas General Hospital. Inside she handed Tata off to one of the ER nurses. "I'll send your husband over," she said. "And then I'll be right back." She squeezed the woman's hand.

Posadas Chrysler-Jeep was three minutes away, and Estelle made her way through the cluttered service area to where George Romero stood gazing at a diagnostic computer screen as if he didn't believe what it was telling him about the fancy sedan on the rack. He listened to Estelle, keeping an eye on the computer at the same time, then shook his head. "Christ," he said, obviously vexed. He finally looked directly at the undersheriff but said nothing, as if waiting for her to break the rest of the news.

"I dropped Tata at the hospital," Estelle said.

"Well, I'll see if I can break away," George said. "Is Freddy with her?"

"I haven't seen him, sir."

"Well, he's probably out burnin' up more gas," Romero said, and let it go at that. Without any further questions, he turned and stalked off toward the service manager's counter, adding over his shoulder, "I'll be over in a few minutes."

Estelle wanted nothing so much as to go home, but that would have to wait. Irma Sedillos, *nana* to the boys and a dear friend, would hear Francisco's version of events, and Estelle trusted Irma's instincts to say and do the right things. The Romeros, however, did not need to face a hospital staff without answers to their questions.

In another few minutes, she walked around the large ambulance that was parked near the emergency room entrance, its diesel engine rumbling gently.

Inside, she passed the small cubicle where the admission clerks worked.

"Mrs. Romero?"

One of the clerks looked up from the computer screen. "Oh, she's in the ER, sheriff."

A large hand on her shoulder startled her. Dr. Francis Guzman had padded up behind her without a sound.

"Airlift," her husband said, and Estelle groaned. "It left Cruces about five minutes ago, so we're getting him prepped for transfer here in a minute."

"How is he, *oso?*"

"*Por diós,*" Francis said. "If Butch didn't have bad luck, he wouldn't have any at all." He held up his right hand, index finger and thumb about half an inch apart. "He's got a fragment of rattlesnake fang like that, pegged right through his eyelid and into the cornea. And that's just the start. He got his grimy little hands into the act. Had to hurt like hell."

"Will they be able to save the eye?"

Francis shrugged. "I'm not a betting man, *querida.* They'll give it a shot. By the time we get up there, they'll have a team ready. They'll do what they can."

"You're flying up?"

"I don't think I need to. They have a good flight crew, and to tell the truth, there isn't a hell of a lot that I can do now. He's stable and sedated. The anti-toxin will either work or it won't. Matty said it was a Western Diamondback?"

"Yes."

"Lots of venom there, even when the delivery system is hacked up. No way to tell how much the boy actually got in his system. Maybe some, maybe none. But that's a dangerous place to be bitten."

Estelle felt the air pressure change, and turned to see George Romero slip through the automatic doors. The mechanic thrust his hands in his pockets, perhaps feeling out of place in this anti-septic setting with its hushed tones and air of medical *authority*. He shook hands with Dr. Guzman and nodded at Estelle.

"So what's the story?" A burly man, his pleasant face now looked as if he wanted to backhand someone—a wayward son, perhaps.

"We're about to transfer him to University Hospital in Albuquerque," Francis said. "There's a team waiting for him there."

"That's a six hour drive," Romero said.

"He'll be flying Medivac. We're about to take him out to the airport now. The plane will be here shortly."

"Jesus. So what's the deal, then? Estelle was saying that the boys were playing with a rattlesnake or something like that?"

"There's what looks like a fragment of the snake's fang embed-ded in the eyeball," Francis said. "That and other matter from the snake's mouth. It's a mess."

"So why can't you just pull it out? The fang, I mean."

Estelle shuddered at that thought.

"Well, it's not that simple," Francis said. "The fang is curved, for one thing, and we're not sure what damage it did on entrance. We don't know how much venom was involved, if any. And it must have hurt like hell, George." The physician made a fist and mimicked grinding it into his own eye. "Something like that happens, it's hard to leave it alone, so there's ancillary damage to consider as well. We flushed the hell out of it, but we'll let the ophthalmologists put it all together."

"Tata's going with him? On the airplane?"

"Yes."

"Well, that'll be okay, then. Can I talk to him?"

"He won't make much sense, George. We've pumped him full of enough sedative to keep him quiet. But I'll take you in. Let's see how he's doing before they pack him up for transfer."

George stopped just shy of the ER door and looked at Estelle. "What were they doing with the snake?"

"Teasing it with a Weed Whacker."

"Well, that's a new one," he said in wonder. "Freddy got his bare foot caught up in the big gas trimmer once. Just about skinned his toes down to bare bone. Blood and bits of stuff all over the inside of the garage. But an eye...now that's not so good."

"No sir, that's not so good." Estelle reached out and touched her husband on the sleeve. "I'll be home if you need me."

"You bet."

George thrust out his hand. "Thanks, neighbor." His grip was calloused and almost too hard. He turned and followed her husband into the ER.

Chapter Three

As if retreating to a more familiar, safe world, Francisco had settled at the piano. Estelle paused on the front step and listened. His scales sounded almost pensive as Francisco worked around the circle of key signatures. Not pushing for speed as he usually did, but working like a little human metronome set on *adagio*, he played through the sharps and then the flats, the minor and diminished keys, pushing each scale up and down through a full five octaves. The scales then blended into enormous chords that walked from one key signature to the next.

He stopped as his mother opened the front door. "Carlos is out back," he announced, apparently fearful that she would think he wasn't paying attention. Estelle could see through the sliding door of the dining room that led out into the back yard. Sure enough, six-year-old Carlos was industriously excavating another tier in his open pit mine, the over-burdened Tonka truck carrying a load to the tailings pile. "And Irma's making corn bread," the pianist added.

"That smells wonderful."

Francisco turned away from the keyboard. "Will Butch be okay?"

"He's going to Albuquerque, *hijo*. We'll see."

Irma Sedillos, Gayle Torrez's younger sister and the on-call *nana* for the two little boys, appeared around the foyer partition. "You've had a day, I hear," she said.

"Not *me* so much," the undersheriff replied. "The mighty hunters met their match, though."

"Is *papá* going to Albuquerque on the plane?" Francisco asked.

"No. He'll be home in a bit." She stepped into the kitchen. "What magic are you up to?" She hugged Irma's shoulders.

"Your mom wanted a chicken salad, so that's what you get," Irma replied. "By executive order, the salad has to be chilled, the chicken and green chile have to be hot." She grinned at Estelle. "And a message from *Padrino*," she continued. "He has a question for you." Irma frowned. "Is Butch going to be all right?"

"We're not sure yet. Nasty thing." She pointed at her own right eye. "The trimmer shot a fang right into his eye."

"Ay!" Irma shivered.

Estelle picked up the pile of mail along with the yellow Post-it note with Irma's exquisite handwriting. "*Padrino and jaguars,*" she read.

"He has a question about jaguars. He said that he remembered your great uncle talking about them."

"Reubén and jaguars? *Es muy curioso.* Is *Padrino* coming over for salad?"

"I told him that he should. But he grumbled something about health food."

"It has chile in it, though."

"I told him that. But you know how he is."

"*Oh, sí.* I know *exactly* how he is. I should call him and tell him not to be so fussy."

"He wondered if Bobby was coming back from Cruces this evening, and I told him that I thought so."

"Your brother-in-law won't stay in the city any longer than he has to." Estelle leafed through the rest of the mail, stopping at a fancy envelope with no stamp. She became aware that Irma was watching her.

"I brought that over with me," Irma said, and Estelle looked up, alerted by the quiet tone of the young woman's voice. The envelope was the sort one would expect with an invitation, and Estelle instantly knew what it was…hints had been in the air for some months. Once again, she was jolted by an odd mix of emotions—a euphoria for Irma, a deep, almost selfish sadness for herself and the family.

"Is this what I think it is?" Estelle asked. She held out her arms and encircled Irma in another hug, this one long and hard. "When?" Without releasing her hold, she slipped the invitation out of the envelope, reading it past Irma's right ear. "October sixteenth," she whispered. "Irma, that's wonderful."

Releasing the hug, Estelle contemplated the engraved wedding invitation. For eight years, Irma had helped what she called the *Guzman Corporación* avoid going bonkers with their impossible schedules: Francis the busy physician, now in clinic partnership with Dr. Alan Perrone, and Estelle the Undersheriff of Posadas County, on-call 24/7. Irma had become more than a well-paid *nana*—a dear friend now to Estelle's aging mother, to the little boys who had never known a household without her, and to the undersheriff herself.

"It will be a grand occasion." Estelle looked quickly at Irma, since the girl hadn't yet had a chance to offer her plans.

"Gayle is excited," Irma said. "She wants to put together the wedding of the century." She smiled wistfully. "Maybe something a *little* less grand than that, but Gary would like a nice traditional ceremony, and so would I. It's a chance to kinda catch up on what we all missed when Gayle and Bobby got married."

"You do it the way *you* want to," Estelle said. "No matter what, your *mamá* and *papá* would be very proud. And so are we. Anything I can do to help…"

"Gayle and Bobby will give us away," Irma said, then smiled. "Of course, Bobby doesn't know that yet. It'll be just like him to be the only one there who isn't in a tux."

"He'll behave." *Maybe* Sheriff Robert Torrez would consent… maybe.

Irma reached out and touched Estelle on the forearm. "If you'd be matron of honor?"

"I'm honored. Of course."

"And I'd really like to borrow Carlos as the ring bearer. He's the handsomest man in my life."

Estelle laughed. "He'll take the responsibility *very* seriously."

Irma took a deep breath, obviously relieved to have the whole affair out in the open. Gary Herrera, Irma's fiancé, would be relieved too, Estelle thought. His willingness to share his beloved with the *corporación* over the past three years had bordered on the saintly.

Out in the living room, Francisco had settled into Bach as the composer of choice for warm-ups. Irma stepped closer and lowered her voice. "Do you think he'd play for the wedding? May I ask him?"

"Of course you may, *querida.*" Estelle chuckled. "The real question is *what* he might play. You know how he is." Play-on-demand had always been a concept that had escaped Francisco. "You're as apt to get his famous Car Crash Composition as you are Schumann, Haydn, or Bach."

"I'll work on him," Irma said. "And…" She stopped, frowning at the cornbread. Nothing in the perfect pan of golden aromas warranted a frown—the crust was just so, neither too dark nor too light, only lightly fissured with small canyons to catch the melting butter. "Gary has been accepted into Stanford's MFA program."

"*¡Caramba!*" Estelle whispered in delight. She took her time pouring the tea water into her mug, unable *not* to think of all the ramifications of Stanford University…a long, long way from Posadas, New Mexico. "An MFA?"

"What he really wants to do is write screenplays. Teleplays, really."

"That's a side of him that I never realized," Estelle said. Gary Herrera, a popular middle-school math teacher and basketball coach, did not fit her image of a playwright, working in smoke, caffeine, and alcohol-laced solitude. "You two are going to become Californians, then? *Por dios,* I can't imagine."

Irma grimaced. "Well, for a while, anyway."

"When does he start at Stanford?"

"We're going out in June, right after school finishes. And you know the superintendent? Dr. Archer? He promised Gary an unlimited leave-of-absence. I'm so pleased about that. He'll have a job waiting for him if he wants it."

"Dr. Archer would be foolish not to. *Ay,* what an adventure for you two. And what about you, *querida?* What new vistas for you in California?"

"I would like to study Spanish," Irma said quickly, as if she had expected the question. "Historical Spanish. I talk to your mother, and she knows so much. I could listen to her all day." Estelle's expression was so blank that Irma plunged on. "Like Spain, centuries ago? Not street Spanglish…that's all I know."

Estelle slowly shook her head. "You've been with us for years now, *querida,* and why didn't I know that this was an interest of yours?"

"Well, I never talked about it, I mean except with your mom, Estelle. How could you know?"

"*Ay.* I sometimes feel as if I live on another planet."

Irma's eyes teared, and she wrapped her arms around Estelle. "We just need to do this," Irma whispered. "Gary and I. We'll be out there for two, maybe three years. Do I get a leave of absence too?"

"You always have a place in our family, Mrs. Herrera."

"Oh, not yet!"

Estelle squeezed her shoulders. "I was just trying the name on for size. It suits you."

"What is this conspiracy going on out here?" The voice that interrupted them was thin, fragile, little more than a croak. Teresa Reyes, bent over her aluminum walker, was so tiny that six year-old Carlos could look her straight in the eye when they stood face to face.

"October sixteenth," Estelle said. "The best holiday of the year."

"I know all about that," Teresa said, wrinkling her nose. "That Gary…he doesn't know how lucky he is."

"We'll all make sure he does, *mamá.*"

"You have a month and more to make plans," the old woman said, and it wasn't clear to whom she had addressed the remark. "Things are going to be different around here." She regarded her step-daughter sternly, black eyes bottomless. "It's an opportunity for you, Estellita."

Estelle held up both hands in surrender. Teresa was right, of course. Irma Sedillos, cheerful, bright, trustworthy—willing to be on-call, just as were both Francis and Estelle—would leave an enormous hole in the *corporación* with her leaving. Estelle realized that she had coped with the notion of Irma's eventual, inevitable leaving by *not* thinking about it. Now she had a deadline. Seven months after the wedding, the Herreras would move west.

For a few minutes she watched her youngest son playing outside the back door while, in the front room, Bach grew more complex. She nudged the door open and Carlos looked up. He wore a good deal of the excavation on his face. "Time to clean up for dinner, *hijo.*"

"*¡Mira!*" Carlos swept a hand grandly to include the road he'd been engineering up the side of the mine. A sand box would have been too simple. This excavation, where once there had been a struggling flower bed, sank deep enough that it had earned the name "burglar trap" from Dr. Francis. If the driver of the over-loaded Tonka was careful, the ore truck wouldn't plunge over the precipice—that had happened a time or two.

"How deep are you going?"

He regarded his work judiciously. "I think seven levels."

"*Ay, ¡caramba!* Such a grand mine." Carlos had been capti-vated during a stop at the Morenci open pit in Arizona during a family trip the previous summer. Now, with a little more work, he'd be able to sit in the bottom of his pit with his head level with the patio.

"I'll probably need a new truck," he mused, ever hopeful.

"Maybe so. Come on, now. Shut down the mine and clean up. *Nana* made cornbread for us."

"*Papá* is home!" Francisco bellowed from the living room, and Bach's *Invention* sped up to light speed, finishing with a resounding crash. For the next half hour, Estelle let the natural momentum of the meal draw them together. Dr. Guzman didn't allow the conversation to center on Butch Romero's misfortune, and Francisco's initial apprehension about what his father was going to say about the rattlesnake episode relaxed.

They talked about Irma's impending marriage and studies, but no one dwelled on what losing their *nana* would mean to the household. At one point, Estelle happened to glance across at her husband. Francis raised an eyebrow as if to say, "*and now what?*" But he didn't pursue the question.

"Did you see the paper?" he asked instead. He cut another square of cornbread and balanced it on the edge of his salad plate. He leaned back in his chair, scooped the mail and the newspaper off the counter, and shuffled through them quickly, seeing the note from *Padrino,* Bill Gastner. He tossed the rest of the mail back on the counter and folded the newspaper neatly, presenting one of the inside pages to Estelle.

The article included a photo showing Nate Underwood, a biology teacher at the high school, as he bent over an animal's skull, probe in hand. It was a surprisingly good picture, taken from table level so that the skull appeared large and impressive, with the teacher looming in the background. Frank Dayan, publisher and sometimes roving reporter for the *Posadas Register,* had triumphed this time in his struggles with the digital camera.

From the left, a student leaned over the skull as well, pointing a pencil at one heavy, blunt canine tooth.

"I heard about that," little Francisco said. He leaned over Estelle's elbow to look at the picture. "Freddy found that."

Skull of Rare Jaguar Found, the headline trumpeted. Estelle scanned the brief article. *A Sunday afternoon jaunt south of Borracho Springs ended with discovery of a jaguar skeleton by a local student. Intrepid explorer Frederico Romero, 18, said that the skeleton was found in the San Cristóbal mountains, in a small cave deep in Salazar Canyon within a few hundred yards of the crest.*

The rest of the article didn't add many details of the discovery's circumstances. Salazar Canyon was carved out of the north flank of the San Cristóbals, one of the few mountain ranges on the continent that ran east-west. Hunters like Sheriff

Bobby Torrez would know the mountain range and its various canyons intimately.

"I'd like to see that skull," her husband said. "Did *Padrino* have something to do with all this? I saw the note from him."

"Curiosity, at the least," Estelle replied. "Anything unusual, there he is, especially if it has something to do with local history. I'm guessing that curiosity has *Padrino* deep in his library, exploring. Irma tried to get him over for dinner, but he refused. I didn't think that there has been a jaguar sighting in this part of the country in generations."

"That's what the teacher said," Francis added, nodding at the newspaper.

She looked at the article again. *"At first, I thought it was a mountain lion skull," Romero reported. The high school senior added that, "But then I found a little patch of fur that was still attached to one of the hip bones." Biology teacher Nate Underwood agreed with his student's assessment.*

"The skull is much too heavy and broad to be a mountain lion," Underwood said. "The jaguar is an altogether different genus—a much bigger, heavier, more powerful cat." Underwood said that although now considered to be an endangered species throughout Mexico and Central America, the jaguar's original range included portions of the Southwestern United States, particularly areas near plentiful water.

"This animal might have died of old age," Underwood said. "The teeth are blunt and show lots of wear. One of the canines is broken off near the jaw-line as well. This big cat wasn't much of a hunter any more. That's one theory. There's some damage to the skull, too. It's hard to say what happened to him."

"*Curioso, ¿no?*" Estelle said, handing the paper to Francisco. "What was old *gato* doing this far north. You should walk over to the high school to see it tomorrow." Even as she said it, she remembered that the gulf of the parking lot between the elementary wing and the high school might as well have been the San Christóbals for younger students. They weren't allowed to wander about by themselves. "Maybe your teacher can take you over."

"How did he get way up there on the mountain?" the boy asked.

"Somebody chased him," Carlos offered.

"Or he might have just been tired, sick, old…that's as far as he was able to go before he found a comfortable place to call it quits," the boys' father said. "Nice view from up there. Lay on a nice warm rock and wait it out." He frowned judiciously at a piece of cornbread. "It's too bad that Freddy's younger brother didn't go exploring with him. It would have been more productive than chasing snakes."

Estelle saw little Francisco duck his head as if he'd been slapped. "I wonder what trail *Padrino* is following with all this," she said. "Maybe he remembers someone talking about jaguars years ago."

"They would have been rare then, too."

"Do they eat people?" Carlos asked.

"Not this one anymore, *hijo,*" Estelle said. "With teeth like that, he'd be lucky if he could catch a sick calf. Maybe that's what *Padrino* is thinking about. Maybe somebody down that way has complained about losing cattle."

"If they lost cattle, it wasn't because of this old guy," her husband laughed. "And that skeleton could have been lying in that cave for ten years…or more. Enough time for all the bugs and mice to pick it clean. If all of the skeleton is there, they should bring it out and get it mounted. That would make a rare display."

"Freddy might have been thinking along those lines," Estelle said. "I hope that Mr. Underwood told him that he can't just possess the carcass or skull of protected animals without permission from the Fish and Wildlife Service. Even the school would need permission."

Her eldest son wrinkled up his face. "Not even an old skull? That's silly."

"Well, it's like possessing eagle feathers," Estelle said. "They don't want those things on the open market. You start allowing that, and pretty soon you'd have a flood of things showing up at garage sales."

"I think that you could sell a jaguar skeleton in old Mexico for a good deal," Irma said. "If there's such a thing as a sacred cat, the jaguar is it."

Estelle nodded. "It's likely that the school will be able to cut a deal with the feds to keep it as part of their academic collection."

"If Freddy gives it to them," Francis amended. "Of course, now that he's gone public with it, what choice does he have?"

Chapter Four

The next morning, the last thing on Estelle Reyes-Guzman's mind was the old bones of a dead cat. The younger Romero brother who'd managed to peg himself in the eye with a charged rattlesnake fang was her immediate worry, since despite the rapid EMT response and the most advanced treatment, Butch Romero's case was proving a challenge. The optic nerve provided a short, direct, wide-open pathway to the brain. Whether the venom was delivered by an angry rattlesnake's strike or by the fragments flung by the plastic strings of the trimmer, the end result had been the same.

Irma Sedillos arrived at the house by five-thirty Friday morning, and her cheery punctuality reminded Estelle of what her family was about to lose. She became acutely aware of the family's dynamics that morning. Dr. Guzman left just before six to begin his hospital rounds, armed with fresh coffee and an enormous slice of butter-slathered banana bread. Youngest son Carlos was a snoozer, and dove his head under the pillow when Estelle kissed his forehead. Francisco had been awake for an hour, chaffing at the routine. He was forbidden to play the piano until Estelle's mother had awakened, and had settled for second best, sitting on the sofa with the unplugged electronic keyboard, playing silently with an intensity driven by the music that had accumulated in his head overnight. There would be time for a quick breakfast before the school bus picked them up at five minutes before eight.

A few moments after eight, Estelle headed out the door, fortified by her own share of fragrant banana bread and a full

Thermos of hot tea under her arm. Deputy Jackie Taber would have finished her shift plus an additional two hours of overtime, and the day and the county waited for the undersheriff.

As she prepared to pull out of her driveway, Estelle took a moment to review her log notes from the day before. She found George Romero's cell phone number and keyed it in. He answered on the second ring, his voice distorted by static and signal gaps. At that early hour, he might be in the motel's shower, or he might have spent a sleepless night at the hospital.

"...omero."

"George, this is Estelle, down in Posadas."

"Hey, let me call you back...a minute."

Estelle switched off and waited, eyes roaming the neighborhood. Two doors down, she saw neither George's late model Suburban nor Freddy's aging Dodge pickup.

In a moment, her phone came to life. "Guzman."

"Yeah, that's better," George Romero said. "What's going on, Estelle?"

"I know it's early, and I apologize for bothering you, sir. But I wanted to know how Butch is doing."

"Well, it isn't good. I don't know what the hell is coming next. He's lost the eye, I know that much. But I don't understand what they're doing now. I know that they're talkin' about some brain swelling that they're trying to get under control. We've been here pretty much all night."

"*Ay.* I'm sorry to hear that. Is there anything we can do for you at this end? Anything you or Tata need?"

"Some sleep," Romero replied. "Well, hey, there is something you can do, as a matter of fact. You know, yesterday, I couldn't find Freddy before I had to drive up here, so I left a note for him in the kitchen where he'd see it. I didn't want him driving up here in that rattletrap of his. There's nothing he can do up here anyway. Look, I tried to reach him last night on his cell, but no go. And hell, I tried around eleven, too. He should have been home. Probably out with Casey Prescott. You know how *that* little deal goes. I tried the house a few minutes ago, but no luck."

"You tried this morning?" She looked down the street again. "His truck isn't in the driveway at the moment."

"Yeah, just a few minutes ago. No dice, though. If he's where he's supposed to be, he'll be over at the school. I could call over there, but I don't want his phone going off in class. I guess I could call the office, but if you wanted to run on over? If you had the time? You could fill him in on what's goin' on, make sure he understands that I *don't* want him drivin' up here. Absolutely not. No way."

"I'll do that right now," Estelle said.

"Just tell him to sit tight, and have him give me a call when he has the chance."

"I'm on my way."

"Hey, thanks. I appreciate that. We'll keep you posted, Estelle. How's Francisco doing with all this?"

"He's upset, certainly. But he'll be all right. He's worried about Butch."

"Ain't we all. Maybe he'll learn something from all this."

"*Sin duda.*"

The drive to the high school's student parking lot just behind the football field was a matter of a few blocks. Posadas High School included fewer than two hundred students in grades nine through twelve, most of whom didn't drive to school. It took only a moment to cruise through the lot, looking for Freddy Romero's primer-gray, sixties vintage Dodge 4x4. The undersheriff circled the lot twice, then crossed through the teacher's parking area, finally parking on South Pershing Street in front of the school.

"PCS, three ten is ten-ten Posadas High School."

Dispatcher Gayle Torrez acknowledged that Estelle was on the road but subject to call, then added, "Be advised that the State Livestock Inspector is here." Estelle could hear Bill Gastner's gruff voice in the background. "He says there's no hurry as long as the coffee cake holds out. He wants to know if he can bring you a piece."

"That's negative. But I'll be about ten minutes."

In considerably less time than that, Estelle had learned from Donna Bates, the principal's secretary, that Freddy Romero was not in school that day.

"Wait for me out in the hall lounge, honey," Ms. Bates said to the student office aide who hovered too attentively, apparently impressed that the police should be visiting the school. As soon as the girl was out of earshot, Estelle made her request, and as Mrs. Bates prompted the computer, she added, "You know, just between you and me, Estelle, master Freddy's attendance record isn't absolutely stellar." She pointed with one heavily ringed finger to a bulletin board just inside the office door where the article, fresh from the *Posadas Register,* was tacked to the cork, joining the plethora of other recent newspaper photos and stories about student achievers.

"He's enjoying his celebrity status, I think. Sure enough, he isn't here enjoying school this lovely morning. He's probably out digging up more bones." She held up a hand as she tapped the computer keyboard with the other. "He wasn't in school yester-day afternoon, either. Morning, yes. Afternoon, no. I hope he's not in trouble again?" She tapped a key again and leaned closer to the screen. "His younger brother might be with him. Butch is absent this morning, too, in fact."

"And that's why I'm here," Estelle said. "Butch was injured late yesterday afternoon, ma'am. The family went with him when he was airlifted to Albuquerque, and no one is home at the moment. They had to leave before they were able to find Freddy and leave a message. If you happen to see the young man, perhaps you'd tell him to contact his dad?"

"My word, of course." The secretary jotted a quick note and stuck it to the corner of her desk calendar, shaking her head as she did so. "In this day and age, how could the folks not reach him on his phone? You know, most of the time, we curse those gosh darn things, but sometimes…"

"Apparently they couldn't last night, and Mr. Romero didn't want to bother Freddy in school."

"Well, we appreciate that, of course. But he could have called *me.* He knows that well enough. Now, will Butch be all right? What happened?"

"An unfortunate accident with a rattlesnake," Estelle replied.

"You're joking, Estelle."

"I wish I were."

"Oh, my. He was bitten?"

"In a manner of speaking. He was using a Weed Whacker and was struck in the eye with a fragment of snake fang when he was teasing the rattler."

Donna Bates recoiled back with a grimace. "Oh, for heaven's sakes," she gasped. "Now what next, you know? Honestly. Butch makes his older brother seem like a saint. But we just love 'em to death. Just love 'em." She looked as if she wanted to pursue the incident in every detail, but then she hesitated. "Ah, let me check one thing," she said, and scrolled to another computer file, leaning forward as she rested her chin on her hand. "Master Freddy is squiring Casey Prescott these days, by the way. *Much* too serious with each other, I may add. But that's the mom in me talking, I suppose." She frowned and she scanned the screen. "Let me see, now. Casey is one of our stars, so we know where *she* is. And right now, she's in Chemistry with Maryann Orosco. Room A-5. Let's ask her, you think?"

She nodded as if Estelle had said something, and then leaned across her desk. "Lola?" she called. "Will you run an errand for me?"

The student aide reappeared and favored Estelle with a radiant smile. The flash of teeth and braces lit her round, pleasant face.

Mrs. Bates handed her a small note. "Casey Prescott is in Ms. Orosco's class right now. Would you see if she can come to the office for a moment?"

Estelle watched through the partition window as Lola trooped out into the foyer, collected another student who lingered at the water fountain, and then disappeared down the hall.

"How are your boys?" Mrs. Barnes asked. "Don't the years fly by, though?"

"Yes, they do. It's a scary business sometimes."

"Oh, my, yes." Mrs. Barnes leaned back in her chair. "You said the Romeros went to Albuquerque yesterday afternoon?"

"Yes."

"And they couldn't reach Freddy all evening? Oh, boy. He's going to catch it. I know papa, and the only one with a worse temper is mama. You probably know all about that."

On occasion, the parental voices of either George or Tata Romero, or both, could be heard more than two doors away as they tried to discipline their two live wires.

In a moment, Lola returned in company with Casey Prescott. The attractive high school junior's expression was quizzical as she came into the office.

"Casey, you know Undersheriff Guzman?"

"Oh, sure." Casey flashed a quick smile at Estelle. "Hi." She offered a handshake, her grip strong, her hands warm and rough—a ranch kid's grip.

"Casey, we're trying to deliver a family message to Freddy Romero, but we haven't been able to cross paths with him this morning. His folks had to go out of town, and I wonder if you had a notion of where he might be?" The undersheriff didn't mention it was Donna Bates who had cheerfully offered the information about Casey Prescott and Freddy Romero's relationship.

"Freddy?" Casey asked.

"Yes."

"He's not in school this morning?" the girl asked Mrs. Bates, and her puzzlement sounded genuine.

"On vacation...*again*," the secretary said with disapproval.

"Well, when I see him, I'll let him know," Casey offered. She glanced at the undersheriff. "I didn't see him this morning." She grimaced and closed one eye, a funny face that was nevertheless attractive. No wonder Freddy was smitten, Estelle thought. "But sometimes he doesn't make it to accounting first thing," Casey continued, "and I had to go to the chem lab early to catch up on some stuff." She shrugged.

"You didn't see him yesterday afternoon or evening?" Estelle asked.

"No, ma'am. I went right home after school to help dad finish up some stuff. And then I had a *heap* of homework."

"He didn't call you? Or you, him?"

"No, ma'am."

Astounding, Estelle thought—there were still two teenagers left who didn't talk, text, or Twitter on the ubiquitous gadgets that grew from belts and pockets. "Have you tried calling him this morning?"

Casey glanced at Donna Bates shyly. A large poster out in the hallway featured a cell phone with a bold diagonal red slash across it.

"I couldn't reach him," she said. "But he was having trouble with his phone, anyway. I think that's what it is. At first, he thought it was the batteries, but I guess not. He was going to buy a new one."

"Ah. Well, if you see him, please ask him to call his folks," Estelle said. "How's chemistry going now?"

"I love it," Casey said with obvious passion.

"Then we don't want to keep you. Thanks for coming down."

"No problem. Thanks, Mrs. B." She smiled at Mrs. Bates and then left the office, slapping the plastic hall pass against her thigh as she hustled out of sight.

"She's a gem," the secretary said. "We can only hope that Freddy doesn't rub off on her entirely. I mean, the computer tells all." She ran a finger along the screen. "I mean, look at last week. Three days that young man missed on the first week of school. He's going to have his ten days before the end of September, and *then* where will he be?" The phone console at her elbow lit, and Estelle raised a hand in farewell as Donna Barnes lifted the receiver.

"If I see Freddy first, I'll have him call you," she said.

"That's not necessary," the undersheriff. "Just have him call his folks."

She left the school and less than two minutes later her county car turned into the parking lot behind the Public Safety Building. A pickup with state plates and livestock inspector's shields on the doors was parked in the spot reserved for Sheriff Robert Torrez.

Chapter Five

Former sheriff of Posadas County William K. Gastner stood under the row of framed photographs in the Public Safety Building's spacious foyer. He was examining the portrait of Eduardo Salcido, four sheriffs in the past. In the photo, Salcido was sitting behind his huge desk—the same desk that now graced undersheriff Estelle Reyes-Guzman's office—hands folded in front of him on the blotter, gazing directly into the camera. He reminded Estelle of a *patrón* waiting to hear complaints from the peasants.

Gastner turned as Estelle approached from the narrow passageway past the dispatcher's island. He tapped the corner of Salcido's portrait. "Way back in 1965. That's the first time I met him." The state livestock inspector's grin widened, and he ran a hand across the burdock of his salt and pepper hair. "And you know, this looks like it was taken on that very day. That's what he was doing when I came into his office for an interview, you know? Sitting there like the grand poobah."

"That's what he was doing when *I* interviewed," Estelle offered.

"A man of infinite good taste in his hires. And that was a long time ago." He stepped back and looked to his right, past the portraits of Martin Holman, himself, and the current sheriff, Robert Torrez. "What a rogue's gallery." He turned and regarded Estelle. "You're about settled on a new hire or two?"

"Yes. I think so. I was working on the applications yesterday and got sidetracked. One or two of the applicants look strong."

"The Veltri kid? It's always nice to hire local."

"He's on the list for sure."

"That's interesting. I half expected him to stay with the military."

"A homesick wife, I think."

"Ah…the wife. You have time for breakfast?" Gastner patted his ample girth. "I got a late start this morning, and the tank's empty."

"I'll keep you company, but Irma made sure I didn't skip out hungry."

"Ah. Speaking of Irma, an interesting thing came in the mail yesterday." Gastner looked at Estelle, one bushy eyebrow raised.

"A wedding invitation?"

He nodded. "It wasn't exclusive to me? I'm crushed."

"Mine was hand-delivered," Estelle said. "I knew it was coming someday, but I'm not ready for it."

"I can imagine."

"The wedding is only the tip of the iceberg, sir. She told me this morning that Gary has been accepted into an MFA program at Stanford. She's going to study Spanish out there."

"Well, my, my. Changes and rearranges. Happens, doesn't it." He followed her back through the offices, and they headed out the back door for the parking lot. "And that's easy to say, of course. What are you guys going to do?"

"I have absolutely no idea."

"Well, that's a start," Gastner chuckled. "Guess who else is finished."

"Finished?"

"Changed and rearranged. September thirtieth is my last day." He reached out and patted the fender of the state truck as they walked past it toward Estelle's county car. "And it feels absolutely wonderful."

"Something prompted this?" She paused at the door of her car as Gastner walked around to the other side. "Not that it's a bad thing, sir."

"Ah." He waved a hand with impatience. "You know, just too much nonsense. I got a notice here a day or two ago discussing electronic tagging, and everything else we're going to have to do to accommodate that. Jesus, it's just a goddamn cow, for Christ's sakes. It seems to me that we ought to be able to manage a god-damn cow without a digital infrastructure." He said the last two words with considerable distain. *disdain.*

"One would think so."

"You know, it's just because they can. No reason other than that. So I told 'em to hell with it. Next they'll think about implanting a GPS chip in each little calf ear. Nah, they can have it. I got things to do."

They settled in the car, and Estelle took a moment to clear with dispatch and make her log notations. "What's your next project?"

"I don't know why I'm so damned interested in history, but I am, so there it is. Did Irma pass on my message to you, by the way?"

Estelle nodded. "She mentioned your interest in the jaguar. And then I got side-tracked when I saw the wedding invitation. I should have called you, but I didn't."

He waved a hand in dismissal. "I wouldn't have answered anyway. I was out roaming. Did you see it?"

"It?"

"The jaguar skull."

"Not yet."

"I stopped by yesterday afternoon and what's-his-name, the teacher, showed it to me, along with all the measurements that they took. He and his class, I mean."

"Nathan Underwood."

"Yup. He says that they did a quickie class project with it, right there on the spot. Pictures, measurements, the whole nine yards. They're sending all the information to the Fish and Wildlife Service, and over to the university."

"They're going to need permission from the feds to keep it, no?"

"Underwood knows all about that. He's pretty sharp, I gotta say. Anyway, that got me thinking. Those cats haven't ever been common around here…just way too dry. They don't have *agua* in their name for nothing. And then I remember your great uncle talking about seeing one. If I hadn't known better, I would have thought he'd been in the sauce again. But if he says he saw one, then that's it. He saw one."

"Nothing about Reubén would surprise me," Estelle agreed.

"You still have his journal, I would hope?"

"*Sin duda.*"

"I'd like to look through that and find a date. I can't imagine him seeing a cat like that and *not* mentioning it in his diary."

"I'm sure he would. It's all in Spanish, you know."

"Ah, but I have access to a most accomplished translator," Gastner said. "All I'm after is the date, and that should be easy enough."

"Odd place for a big cat to show up," Estelle mused. "The Cristóbals aren't the most hospitable place in the best of times."

"For us. For an old kitty being chased, maybe just fine."

"You think chased?"

"I do. And caught. I'm no forensic specialist, but I know a bullet hole when I see it. The old guy's last moments weren't the most peaceful, I'd guess. Some bastard put a bullet in him." Bill Gastner touched his head just behind his right eye. "Didn't detonate the whole skull, so it wasn't a hi-powered rifle. Thirty-eight caliber or a little bigger."

Estelle looked across at her old friend.

"Interesting, eh?" Gastner said.

"Most," she replied. "Most people go through an entire lifetime and never see a big cat in the wild, much less up close and personal. And a *jaguar?* That's not even once in a lifetime."

"As far as I know, springs are few and far between up there, not that I've trekked it all. But Bobby has, and he's going to be interested in all this, I would think. He's going to want to know exactly where the Romero kid found it. I was going to ask the boy the same thing, but I got over there after school let out. Didn't catch him."

"You're not the only one," Estelle said, and briefly related the details of her afternoon.

"A fang in the eye. That's a new one on me. Freddy's probably cattin' about, no doubt. The fair Casey didn't know where he was?"

"She says not." That Bill Gastner knew the relationship between Casey Prescott and Freddy Romero didn't surprise Estelle. The former sheriff and short-time livestock inspector had known the Prescott family for decades. More a walking, breathing gazetteer than a busy-body, Gastner collected information and filed it away. As he cheerfully admitted, accessing those files in a time of need was the challenge.

"Well, maybe he's back out in the boonies," Gastner said, and reached out to rest a hand on the dash for support as they jounced over the first speed bump in the parking lot of the Don Juan de Oñate restaurant. "You make a find like that, and the site is an attraction. Pays to scout it out, see if you missed any thing."

Estelle pulled the car to an abrupt halt in the middle of the small parking lot, and Gastner looked across at her, puzzled.

"Yesterday, I saw a four-wheeler down at the Broken Spur," Estelle said. "Way, way in the distance. I had just pulled out on 56 from 14, and saw him swing off the shoulder of the highway, into the saloon's parking lot, then scoot out back, probably across the arroyo." She reached over and picked up the aluminum clipboard that contained her log. "Two-twenty, yesterday afternoon. I had stopped to make some notes after talking to some references, then saw the four-wheeler just after I pulled back out onto the highway."

"Could have been anybody," Gastner said.

"Could have been." She closed her eyes, trying to coax her mind to replay the bit of memory. She hadn't watched the four-wheeler because there had been no reason to. Now the incident was an amorphous blur, the details lost. "Ranchers don't ride like a wild teenager," she said. "I saw him and assumed it was a kid."

"If it was Freddy, then his pickup was somewhere down there, too," Gastner said. "He hauls that ATV around in the back of his truck, then bops out when he's got something to explore or terrorize."

"His dad says he wasn't home last night—at least he didn't answer his phone. He didn't call Casey, either. His truck wasn't in the driveway last night or this morning."

"Now the worried mom comes out," Gastner laughed.

She pulled the gear shift back into drive and swung the car around, leaving the restaurant to re-enter the street eastbound.

"So near and yet so far," Gastner said wistfully. "What now?"

Chapter Six

The Expedition used by Deputy Dennis Collins during the day shift still smelled new, everything meticulously in place, the four water jugs that were stored in the back full and sealed. Collins had even added a large cardboard box full of military MRE's to his stash. After her sedan, the big SUV felt like a behemoth.

They pulled out onto Bustos, and Estelle drove west. In less than two minutes, she turned onto Twelfth Street and then pulled in to the curb in front of her home. Two doors down, the Romero house was silent, the driveway empty.

"A moment," she said. "Need anything?"

"Not a thing," Gastner replied. "Give my greetings to your mother."

Inside the house, Estelle found the three volumes she sought in the bookcase by the living room fireplace. Her mother, comfortable in her rocker, was working through an enormous volume of Spanish history, perhaps motivated by Irma's interests. She tucked a crooked finger in her place as she watched her daughter.

"What's Reubén done now?" she asked, eyes twinkling. The old man, her uncle, had died eight years before, independent and feisty to the last.

"*Padrino* recalled that Reubén used to talk about seeing a jaguar, *mamá*. If he did, he would have mentioned it in his journal."

"Not the same one you were talking about yesterday. That's not possible."

"No. But *Padrino* was wondering about the date."

"Don't lose those. The first one is all before the war anyway. You don't need that one."

"Mother, please," Estelle laughed. "I won't lose them. And neither will *Padrino*." She kissed the old woman on the forehead.

"Irma is coming over for lunch," Teresa said. "What are we going to do without her?" She raised an admonishing finger. "But she needs to go, you know. She has her own life."

"That's right, *mamá*."

"But that doesn't mean I have to like it." Teresa Reyes smiled. "You be careful out there. That's not your car you're driving. What are you two up to?"

"I don't think we know. I'll stop by for lunch if I can."

"You do that. Bring *Padrino*."

Back out in the SUV, Estelle passed the three volumes to Gastner. Bound in red and black imitation leather with raised welts on the spines, the books were designed to look like old world masterworks. He opened the first volume.

"January 7, 1916 to…" and he gently fingered to the last page. "June 1, 1936." He glanced across at Estelle. "He moved here from Mexico in 1940, so that's in volume two." The second volume opened with an entry for June 11, 1936. "This is where to start, then." Estelle heard the excitement in Gastner's voice.

"He wrote each evening, I remember," Estelle said. "He always had to have just the right black pen." Gastner leafed through the pages, shaking his head slowly. The handwriting was angular, bold, easy to read, so uniform that it almost appeared to have been printed.

"You've read through these?"

"Skimmed," Estelle said. "That's a project I keep promising myself."

He chuckled. "No more promises for me. I'm going to indulge myself now."

As she drove south on Grande toward the intersection with State 56, she could see that Gastner was already hooked.

"I knew you had these, but I never looked at 'em," he murmured. "Not a single entry in English."

"Reubén used to say that English was not the proper language for written records. He used to talk about all the records that exist in Spain for the various voyages back in the sixteenth and seventeenth centuries, about how he would like to go to Spain and spend a year, just reading."

"Who wouldn't."

"I guess lots of people don't share an enthusiasm for the past."

"Unfathomable." He closed the volume and selected another. "Might as well start at the end and work backward. His last entry was September 12, 1996. It's hard to read."

"By then, he was so arthritic that he could hardly hold a pen." Estelle let the big SUV creep up to seventy on the state highway. She scanned the vast, tawny prairie, watching for the plume of dust that would mark passage of a truck or ATV.

"I knew Reubén as a stonemason," Gastner mused. "You need a fireplace, Reubén was the one to call. A fancy fence, facing on a house, whatever. I don't recall that he spent much time hiking and exploring. That about right?"

"He wasn't a hiker," Estelle said. "I lived with him for almost four years, and I don't remember anything beyond a walk to the shed or to the truck. He was fascinated by the night sky, and once in a while we'd go outside with binoculars and see how many constellations we could name. The nearest night light was miles away, and the sky could be so *black*. And meteor showers—when those happened, it turned him into a little child again."

"So…he didn't spend a lot of time hiking in the mountains."

"No. To him, the San Cristóbals were something to create the weather. He watched them, watched the clouds form, enjoyed the winds. A couple of times, Bobby tried to get him to go hunting with him. He'd just laugh."

"Then the odds that he saw the big cat over in the Cristóbals are pretty slim."

"I would think so."

"Huh."

Estelle glanced over at Gastner. He was frowning not at the diary on his lap, but into the distance, his heavy features set in that characteristic bull-dog expression that said he was shuffling puzzle pieces about, looking for a fit. After a moment, he returned his attention to the diaries, running a finger along each line of each entry, looking for the magic word that he would find floating in the sea of elegant Spanish.

Twenty minutes later, Estelle slowed and turned the SUV onto a rough two-track where Forest Service signs announced *Borracho Springs Canyon*. As soon as the truck hit the rough county road, Gastner closed the diary and put it on the floor with the other two volumes. The trail was a welter of tracks, including the periodic knobby prints of a four-wheeler.

In two miles, the road forked, joining Forest Road 122. Bullet-ripped signs announced both the Borracho Springs Campground and the hiking trail that wound up the mountain to join the ridge trail to Regál Pass…a twelve-mile hike through the most rugged country in Posadas County.

As they approached the fork, Estelle saw a flash of metal through the runty junipers and piñons. Just beyond the intersection, an older model Dodge pickup was parked off the two-track. Its tailgate was missing, but two oil-soaked planks with wooden traction cleats ramped into the bed. Tire prints ripped into the dry, dusty prairie behind the truck.

"Freddy's." Estelle felt a pang of apprehension. If the boy's truck had been here all night, something was very wrong. For a moment, both she and Gastner sat in the Expedition, surveying the site.

"He isn't going up there on an ATV." Gastner nodded at the vast slab of mountain rising ahead of them. "The road only goes as far as the campground. So why unload here?"

"I don't know." Estelle slid out of the SUV, careful where she put her feet. It didn't take an expert tracker to see where Freddy Romero had driven the ATV. He'd driven it out of the Dodge and then headed back toward the state highway. No tracks led back toward Borracho Springs.

The pickup was unlocked, not surprising since the right-hand wing window was held together by duct tape and didn't lend itself to security. The driver's door creaked on bent hinges as Estelle opened it. The cab smelled of motor oil, tobacco smoke, and beer. A small cooler rested on the floor on the passenger side, and Estelle reached across and tipped open the top, revealing a blue freezer pack and two cans of Corona. The cans and freezer pack were cool to the touch.

A cell phone in its nylon holster lay on the seat. Estelle slipped it out and touched the key pad. The small screen came alive promptly, then dissolved into a jumble.

"That's why didn't he take it along," she mused aloud. Gastner moseyed up beside her and leaned on the truck's door.

"So, where did he go? If that was Freddy that you saw yesterday…" He waved a hand off toward the north. "If that was him, he parked *here*, and then drove the ATV way the hell and gone over *there*. I gotta wonder why he did that." He pushed himself away from the truck and walked a few feet on Forest Road 122. "And sure as hell he didn't drive up this way."

"Let's hope his luck is better than his brother's." She knew there were dozens of ways to come to grief on an ATV—a moment's inattention, a simple misjudgment, or a mechanical break-down miles from the nearest highway or ranch. With his cell phone left behind, Freddy Romero's bad luck had only multiplied.

"Let's see what comes of all this." Back in the Expedition, she dialed dispatch and waited for half a dozen rings before Gayle Torrez answered.

"Posadas County Sheriff's Department, Torrez."

"Gayle, Bill Gastner and I are down at Borracho Springs. We've found Freddy Romero's truck parked down here. It appears he unloaded his four-wheeler and took off somewhere. I don't think he has his cell phone with him. Would you contact Mr. or Mrs. Romero up in Albuquerque and tell them we'll be in touch as soon as we have some answers?"

"No Freddy though?"

"No Freddy. At least not yet. He left a pretty clear set of tracks, so we're going to follow up on that. Has Bobby come in the office yet?"

"In and then out again. He's back in Cruces, but says he'll be home this afternoon."

"Okay." Estelle mentally riffled through the list of available staff. The county was still hers, and if there was a call in the village of Posadas, she was half an hour away.

"Jackie is having coffee with David Miller," Gayle said. Estelle had noticed with some amusement that of late Deputy Jackie Taber, denizen of the graveyard shift, often managed to find a moment to converse with the young state policeman when their paths crossed—perhaps one or both of them helped managed their activities so that paths *did* cross. Estelle heard a voice in the background. "She says she'll cover for you until you're clear," Gayle added.

"Good enough. And if Freddy has already contacted his parents, let me know." She switched off and glanced at Gastner. "You want a job?"

The former sheriff laughed. "Not even a *remote* chance, sweetheart. Thirty years is long enough. Now I'm embarking on an in-depth study of life on the sidelines." He shifted in his seat. "You'll remember that I came along merely on the promise of some breakfast...which we still have ignored."

"Have an MRE, sir."

"You know, the brownies in those things are really pretty good. And the crackers and cheese aren't bad. So don't tempt me."

They followed the ATV's tracks back to the highway, and then southwest along State 56. A mile beyond, the saloon's parking lot was heavily graveled, but the ATV's tracks marked the grass perimeter, then actually passing close to the east wall of the building. Behind the saloon and the owner's modest mobile home, behind a scattering of defunct cars and trucks some of which had slipped down into the arroyo, a two-track cut sharply down the bank. A brown pond of water marked one of the flats in the arroyo bottom, and tracks crisscrossed the gravel and sand.

"We can assume he went this way," Gastner said. "Maybe."

"I saw him turn into the saloon parking lot, and then disappear behind the building." She urged the Expedition into four-wheel drive and turned into the arroyo. The decent was so steep that the rear bumper gouged gravel at the bottom. A ledge of rock half-way up the other side bucked the Expedition, and it kicked sand and gravel, with nothing but a view of the sky as they reared up and out on the far side.

"I haven't been here in a long time." Gastner lowered his window. "It's going to get hot today." The two-track meandered across the prairie, already beginning to shimmer in the heat. The lane headed toward the low mesas to the north. For the first half mile, the going was reasonably smooth, the dried vegetation between the tracks raking the underside of the SUV, the fragrance powerful. Sand and prairie scrub gave way to a vast, gentle dome of gravel and rocks where the tracks of the ATV vanished.

"Stop a second," Gastner said at one point. He twisted in his seat and looked eastward, then reached across for the binoculars that rested in the center console. "It'd be a hell of a walk, no matter which way he went. Herb Torrance's place is way the hell off to the west, and Prescotts' is a *long* hike back to the east, off behind those little hills, there." He searched the prairie for a moment and then shrugged. "The only thing that makes sense to me is that Freddy was headed to where this trail crosses Bender's Canyon."

"Maybe so." She shut off the engine and they sat in silence, letting the breeze waft through the vehicle. In the distance, two ravens made sure everyone knew there were intruders.

"You don't have a whole lot of choices," Gastner said. "From here you can cut down this grade and end up T-boning into Bender's Canyon Trail. Then you hang a left, and head back toward the county road. Or you can go right along the trail and go northeast, around the backside of Herb Torrance's spread. You'll swing around to the county road again...eventually...or continue on north to the state highway." He patted the door sill as if marking time. "Or, we could get out and walk for a bit

and make like trackers, trying to pick up the ATV's footprint."
He squinted up at the blank blue of the sky.

Estelle popped her door, and Gastner grimaced. "That's what
I thought."

"If Freddy had come home last night, I wouldn't be concerned," the undersheriff said. "But I'd hate to think that he
might be lying out here somewhere with a broken leg...or worse.
That would have made for a long, long night."

Gastner touched his cap back and wiped his forehead. "No
danger of hypothermia, though. You ought to have Bergin up
flying if you want to search this country. You could hide a tank
out here, you know."

"That's next, *Padrino*."

For less than five minutes, the two searched the balding top of
the rise. The most logical route—straight ahead—turned results.
The ATV's knobbed tracks showed up on the north side of the
slope, cutting across the rough terrain to join the two-track that
came in from the west.

Estelle jogged back to the Expedition, and after thumping
and bumping down off the slope, the relative smooth going on
the two packed tracks of Bender's Canyon Trail felt like a paved
highway. The trail crossed the canyon bottom twice before set-
tling down on the north side of the arroyo. The tracks were easy
to follow where they cut into the softer ground. For another
mile, the two-track wound almost due east, then swung wide
around the buttress of a ragged mesa. Car-sized boulders had
peeled off the mesa rim above them, and at one point the trail
squeezed between a jumble of rocks that towered a dozen feet
above the SUV's roof.

"Herb always called this 'the window,'" Bill Gastner observed
as Estelle maneuvered the vehicle through, less than an inch
clearance beyond the side mirrors. "He's lost a lot of paint off
his trucks and livestock trailers in this particular spot."

The trail turned north, the country opening up to prairie that
rolled in gentle waves like a tan blanket snapped not quite flat.

They could see Bender's Canyon Trail winding ahead of them, up the rise of open country.

"Freddy probably puts more miles on that ATV of his than any other kid in the world," Estelle said.

"I admire him," Gastner said. "You know, most kids are content to rod it up and down the streets, or dust up vacant lots. This kids goes on *adventures*. I love it. If I wasn't so goddamn fat and old and creaky, I'd buy me one and chase after him."

"I'm starting to wish that *someone* had gone with him," Estelle added.

The two-track climbed the rise, and then bordered a stand of dense juniper and scrub as another deep arroyo closed in from the northeast. A small foundation, now nothing but a uniform line of limestone rocks emerging a few inches from the dirt, edged the runty junipers and creosote bush. An old corral, the posts gray and smooth, enclosed an area behind the foundation, and the remains of a fence meandered off into the distance. Various rusted machinery parts, a scattering of cans, and the tiny cab of an ancient truck marked a spot where someone, sometime, had felt that he'd found paradise.

"Morris Trujillo's grandfather," Gastner said, and Estelle looked at him with amusement. "Efugio. He came back from the Philippines in 1943, deaf in one ear and with a plate in his skull. He tried to live here for a couple years, couldn't make it work, and then moved into town."

Estelle surveyed what was left of the tiny homestead. "And left his truck behind."

"We could make up all kinds of interesting stories about why that happened," Gastner laughed. "It's a 1928 Ford."

"And you know that how?" The vehicle fragment included little besides the firewall and one fender.

"I found a number plate on the firewall."

"Are those your tracks?" She nodded at a set of vehicle tracks imprinted in the soft soil near the corral.

"Nope." The road narrowed even more, squeezing along the arroyo.

"Next century storm, the arroyo is going to chew a chunk out of the two-track," Gastner said. Just to the east, practically under his elbow, the arroyo yawned deep and wide, a great gouge across the prairie. "Herb was telling me that most of this was cut in one night, back in 1955." He glanced at Estelle. "Can you imagine a rain that hard? And that's something else that Reubén might talk about in his journal. He was here then."

"Only from time to time," Estelle said. "He built his cabin over off the county road in 1956."

"Have you considered translating these?"

"I do. I just haven't *done* it yet."

"Maybe Teresa would find it interesting."

"I don't think so. She can read them effortlessly enough as it is, but she doesn't spend a lot of time looking back at family history. History of the world, sure, but not family. I think it makes her a little sad."

"Remarkable woman. That's about all I do these days, is look back."

Estelle eased the truck onward, and they nosed up a sharp rise just north of the homestead. Just as they crested the knoll, she spiked the brakes and the SUV jarred to a halt. They faced a swale where the two-track swooped down through a graveled wash that joined the main arroyo. They could see tracks from the ATV, so close-set and characteristic, cross the wash and shoot straight up the other side. Estelle leaned forward, hands locked together on top of the steering wheel.

A second set of four-wheeler tracks were also visible just on the near side of the rise facing them, tracks that swerved erratically toward the crumbling arroyo edge.

Chapter Seven

Both the red ATV and its driver lay at the bottom of Bender's Canyon.

Estelle sprinted back to the Expedition, yanked open the door, and grabbed the mike off the bracket.

"PCS, three ten."

The five heartbeats before dispatch responded seemed an hour.

"Three ten, go ahead."

"PCS, ten fifty-five, one adult male." She looked across through the open passenger door at Bill Gastner, who was standing on the shoulder of the two-track, scanning the arroyo bank. "We're about four miles off County Road 14 on Bender's Canyon Trail. An ATV off the road." The ambulance was at least an hour away.

"Ten four."

"Ten twenty-one in about three minutes."

Directly in front of them, the arroyo bank was sheer, the edges crumbling. Gastner pointed to the south. A large juniper, the trunk thick and gnarled, leaned precariously from the bank, its roots fighting for a hold against the continuous undermining of erosion. "Maybe there," he said. "Maybe."

The last bout of erosion had been deflected by a root mass, gouging down through the bank to a large projection of rock. Estelle surveyed the bank for a moment, then scrambled down, using the roots as handholds. Hand over hand to the rock step was easy enough, leaving only an eight foot slide down the gravel and sand arroyo skirt to the bottom.

She slid in a shower of sand and gravel, keeping her balance on feet and rump. At the bottom, she stood quietly for a moment, surveying the scene ahead of her.

The motionless figure lay on his face, one leg oddly twisted, his right shoulder smashed against a bald slab of bedrock at the bottom of the arroyo. Estelle recognized the slender form immediately. If Freddy Romero had been wearing a helmet, it hadn't done much good. It now lay in the sand thirty feet away, the force of the crash fracturing the face shield.

Freddy's eyes were open, staring at the gravel. The undersheriff touched the side of his neck just forward of where the helmet strap would cut and felt nothing but cold, dry skin.

The ATV, fenders, handlebars and even fuel tank twisted and bent, lay inverted just beyond the body.

Estelle squatted on her haunches for a moment, one hand resting lightly on Freddy Romero's left shoulder. Then she pulled her cell phone out of its belt holster.

"Gayle," she said when the dispatcher answered, "We have a fatality here. It looks like Freddy Romero somersaulted his four-wheeler into an arroyo. I'll need Linda out here ASAP, and Dr. Perrone. And if you'll contact APD, they'll make contact with George and Tata for us."

"Oh, my," Gayle murmured.

"And you might tell the EMTs that they may have to come in from the north, from State 17, through Waddell's ranch. I'm not sure their unit will make it in here on the south fork of the trail."

"Matty Finnegan knows that country pretty well. I'll let her know. What's your exact twenty?"

"I would guess about four and a half miles in from County Road 14 on Bender's Canyon Trail. We're just a quarter mile or so beyond what they call 'the window,' and that's where the ambulance may have trouble."

"We'll find you. Freddy was alone?"

"It appears so."

"Oh, my," Gayle said again.

"'Oh my' is right," the undersheriff sighed, and switched off the phone. She turned to look back up at Gastner, who stood a step back from the arroyo edge, hands on his hips.

"He didn't move much," he said.

"No." She stepped carefully back, seeing the way Freddy's left hand had clawed briefly at the gravel, what looked like a single spasm. Slipping her fingers under the young man's wrist, she felt the characteristic resistance of rigor. "I would guess all night, and then some," she said. "He was out here yesterday afternoon, maybe. Could have been." *And nobody knew,* she thought. *We all thought mischief, and here you are, all by yourself.*

"I want to see if he hit anything," Gastner said. "I'll watch where I walk."

Estelle stepped back, trying to imagine the final cartwheel of the ATV, and the way its driver would have been flung away. The marks of the machine's first strike were on the arroyo bottom's bedrock, a black-tinged slash. She pivoted and looked at the arroyo bank. Where the ATV had swerved over the edge, the arroyo was a dozen feet deep, with a sheer, evenly under-cut bank. Airborne, the machine would have nosed over and down. If Freddy had managed to hang on, he would have been flung forward by the initial impact, then perhaps caught by the ATV on the bounce.

She got up and walked to the helmet. Its wild paint scheme was only moderately scratched, the face shield broken but still in place. Retracing her steps, she then crossed to the ATV and saw the mangled rack behind the driver's seat and the broken plywood carryall bolted to it. The butt of a .22 rifle, still tangled in its scabbard, projected out from under the vehicle.

One hard bounce, and then the ATV had taken Freddy from behind, smashing his head into the ground. If he'd been able to kick free during his high dive, like some of the wild riders he'd surely watched on television, he might have escaped with a broken leg...or neck.

"Left front?" Gastner called.

Estelle pushed herself to her feet and regarded the ATV more closely. Sure enough, the left front tire was flat, the only damaged tire of the four. A ragged cut tore the sidewall all the way to the inner rim. "Yes."

"Yeah, well," the former sheriff said with resignation. "He launched over this little rise and drifted a little bit to the left... just enough to collect a piece of sharp rock. That would have jerked him out of control. He was really whistling Dixie, though. There's a dozen feet of road here with no tracks, where he got that thing airborne over the crest of the hill."

"Freddy, Freddy," Estelle whispered to herself. Of course the boy would have been riding too fast. To an adventuresome kid, that's what powerful ATVs were for.

She stood quietly, sunshine warm on her shoulders, no breeze reaching the shelter of the arroyo bottom to sweep away the aromas of violent death.

"You want your camera?"

"Please. And the tarp from the back of the truck."

Estelle stepped close to the bank, caught the little digital camera and then the packaged blue tarp. She took a moment to thread the nylon camera case onto her belt, then trudged far down the arroyo to the far side, where she could look back at the entire scene.

"He swerved very hard," Estelle said. "The measurements are going to be interesting."

"How so?" Gastner squatted a yard back from the arroyo edge.

"How fast would he have to be going to go airborne over that rise, do you suppose?"

Gastner turned and regarded the trail. "Fairly fast, I would think. And then he hit that rock outcropping. Powee."

"And that turned him to the left."

"You bet. And over the edge he goes."

Estelle's cell phone chirped.

"Guzman."

"Hey," Sheriff Robert Torrez said. "What do you have?" The sheriff had been in court in Las Cruces, but Estelle could hear traffic in the background.

"We have Freddy Romero, Bobby. He put his four-wheeler into an arroyo off Bender's Canyon Trail sometime yesterday." The sheriff digested that in silence. "It looks like the machine crushed him on the bounce," Estelle added.

"He by himself?"

"Yes."

"Drinking?"

"I don't think so. It looks like he jumped a little rise in the trail, you know, like a moto-cross rider might. He managed to collect a rock somehow. The left front tire of the ATV is torn open, and *Padrino* found the initial strike mark on the rock."

She heard a long, slow exhalation of breath. "The folks are still up in Albuquerque with Butch," Torrez said.

"And that's not going really well. He'll lose the eye, and that's if he's lucky. And *por Dios,* now this. I asked Gayle to contact APD for an assist. They'll send over a chaplain."

"All right. Look, I'm on the interstate right now. I'll be out there in a bit. I got cut loose early from court."

"How did it go?"

"A waste of time," the sheriff replied, without amplification. "I'm just goin' up the hill out of Cruces now, so it'll be an hour. How far in are you?"

"We took the trail behind the bar," Estelle said. "We were following Freddy's tracks. He parked over on the Borracho Springs road, then drove the ATV over here. We're just a little bit east of the intersection on Bender's. Just beyond the window."

"Be there in a bit." He rang off without further comment. Estelle pocketed the phone and looked across at Gastner, who now stood with one hip propped against the Expedition's front fender as he surveyed the country through binoculars.

"There's a cattle trail on down about a hundred yards," he called, and lowered the binoculars to point. "You have plenty of cattle tracks in the bottom here, so we can guess there's another trail up and out somewhere."

"You don't have an extension ladder in your hip pocket, sir?"

Gastner laughed. "Wish I did. Look, I'm going to mosey on up here a ways and see what's to see."

Estelle continued her photographic survey until she was convinced that no secrets remained in the arroyo itself, then walked back to the ATV. She unpackaged the tarp and snapped it out, then covered Freddy Romero's body.

She turned her attention to the jumble of bent and twisted plastic and metal. The damage suggested that the four wheeler had burst over the rim of the arroyo and crashed nose-first to the bedrock of the arroyo bottom a dozen feet below. The left front suspension had taken most of the impact, crushed backward and upward so hard that the handlebars had been balled into junk, torn back on top of the rumpled gas tank.

The initial impact had somersaulted the rig, the rack behind the seat pounding into the arroyo bottom and the back of Freddy Romero's skull. The machine's final resting place was nine feet from the body, the ATV resting flat on its back, bent suspension turned to the sky like a dead beetle. A large patch of gasoline had leaked out to stain the rock and sand.

Estelle knelt and touched the left front wheel. It was jammed back against the frame and would not spin freely. The damage to the tire began an inch or so toward the rim from the tread. Had the tire struck the rock with its knobby tread, Freddy might have had a survivable wild ride with the bounce.

The undersheriff set the little camera on *macro* and took photographs of the tear, showing the rock particles imbedded in the rubber. The rock had opened the tire's sidewall like an enormous, rough can opener right to the rim, where the aluminum was dented and torn.

The force of the impact would have jolted the ATV savagely to one side, and there had been no time for Freddy to correct.

"A hundred yards that-a-way," Bill Gastner called from the rim. He pointed up the arroyo. "Cow trail makes it easy for you."

"What else did you find?"

"Well, trajectory, I guess. I'll show you when you come up."

"I'm on my way." Estelle trudged back up the arroyo, wanting to stop and turn around at each step. The last thing she wanted to do was leave Freddy Romero face down in the gravel, ruined and alone.

The cattle always found the easiest route, and over the decades, their hooves cut and packed long, diagonal trails that criss-crossed the arroyo banks, bringing them to shade, to protection from the elements, to the rare standing puddles that remained for a few hours after a cloudburst. Dodging the cow patties, Estelle climbed out of the arroyo. Bill Gastner met her by the two-track.

"You all right?"

"Sure, I'm fine." She *wasn't* fine, and that there was nothing she could do to make things right just added to it. She paused and took a deep breath, surveying the open country. "Freddy was ten when they moved into their house on Twelfth," she said. "Butch was six." She let it go at that, knowing that *Padrino* understood her anguish perfectly.

"Well, this is what he did," Gastner said. He turned and pointed back up the road, toward the rise that had catapulted the ATV to disaster. Just ahead of where they stood, a wide and deep quagmire, more than just a routine pothole, took up most of what had been the two-track. Fresh tracks had been cut on the side farthest from the arroyo edge. The sink collected runoff and became a rutted and slimy trap in the wet, and when dry, as it was now, presented a deep, jarring axle breaker.

Gastner turned and swept his arm in an arc. "He had a good run through here—flat and straight. He takes the route around it on the left going in, and retraces his route coming out. If he'd been going slower, he might have bounced right through the middle of it just for the hell of it, but not rippin' the way he was." Gastner walked across to the arroyo lip. "If he tries to skirt this sink on *this* side, he's running too damn close to the edge. Now..." and he interrupted himself and walked across the sink, standing perpendicular to the road and facing Estelle and the arroyo. He held up both arms, pointing in each direction. "Look how narrow that two-track is when it crests that rise, sweetheart. All the rocks and brush, there isn't much room. And there sure as hell isn't any room for error. Freddy comes through here, and he's intending to jump the hill. I mean, he came in that way, didn't he?" He swept his arms again in an arc. "He comes through here, but he doesn't want to end up in those rocks and trees there, on the uphill side of the trail, so after this pothole, he's got to swing back pretty hard."

"Show me the rock," Estelle said.

"Sure enough." She followed Gastner as he plodded up the slight grade. The ATV's tracks were clear. Both coming and going, Freddy Romero had chosen the same route over this particular rise. At the crest of the hill, there were no ATV tracks. He'd felt comfortable enough that he'd used the little hill as a ramp, both coming and going.

"I think that he just overcooked it," Gastner said. "He comes up here and ramps off, maybe a little crosswise after skidding around that sinkhole. If he does that, if he's not absolutely god-damn straight, then he's heading toward the left side of the trail. And pow. Right there."

Two dozen feet from the crest of the rise, just after the ATV had slammed down, a shower of gravel and broken rock marked the first contact. A sharp-edged limestone rock the size of a wide-screen television had been dislodged from the ridge. Gastner bent over and pointed at the bright aluminum traces, and the black scuff of rubber. "Pow," he said again. "My guess is that with this catching the left front tire, he just loses it." He straightened up. "I mean, what's he got here between the trail and the arroyo?"

"Maybe four feet."

"Exactly. And with an exploded tire, the rig doesn't turn like it should. He doesn't even have the time to grab the brakes."

"So tell me something," Estelle said. "Why was he over here? Why on Bender's Canyon Trail?"

"Because." Gastner shrugged.

"Just because?"

"That's what Freddy Romero does," he said. "Or did."

"Why park on the Borracho Springs road, and then ride all the way over here?"

"Couldn't tell you."

"He found the cat skeleton earlier this week, in a cave up in the mountains somewhere. I'd think he'd be attracted back there. Maybe that's what he planned originally when he parked where he did. For some reason, he changed his mind."

"That's not four-wheeler country," Gastner observed. "Not that I spend a lot of time trying to haul my fat carcass up that trail, but from what I remember, the only way you'd get a mountain bike up there, let alone a four-wheeler, would be to hang it from your shoulder while you hike."

"Bobby will be here before long," Estelle said. "It'll be interesting to hear his take on all this."

"Anyway, it was Freddy, remember," Gastner said. "He drives out somewhere and parks, off-loads the damn ATV, and goes raring and tearing around the countryside. Who knows where or why."

Estelle lifted the camera and peered through its tiny viewfinder at the trail that swept down off the little rise to cross the dry mud flat. "Nothing will show," she said to herself.

"What's to show?"

"Well, there isn't a lot of traffic on Bender's Canyon Trail. A rancher now and then."

"You'd be surprised. Herb Torrance gets this way regularly and Miles Waddell, off and on. Maybe Gus Prescott, although why I wouldn't know. His property is to the east of here. Then there's the hunters, the bird watchers, and people who just don't know where the hell they are…"

"Who turned around back at the homestead?"

"Can't tell you. And those turn-around tracks could be days old. Even weeks. We haven't had any rain now in at least that long."

"Which is longer?" she asked. "To turn around and go back out to 14 that way, or continue on the trail, loop around this mesa, and come out on the State 17 farther north?"

"Six of one. If I remember right, the north end of the trail, where it loops around the backside of the mesa behind Waddell's ranch, is actually in more open country. It'd be smoother, I'd think. Except in rainy weather, maybe."

"Huh." Estelle shook her head in frustration. "What puzzles me is why Freddy didn't just drive his pickup down the state highway for another two miles to the intersection with County 14, and park there to off-load his four-wheeler. If he'd done that, we probably would have run into each other. Park there, *then* go exploring. Why park at Borracho, two miles in from the highway, then have to drive the ATV along the highway to the saloon, then…on and on, *Padrino.* I just don't understand what he was doing."

"For one thing, he probably caught sight of the cop car, and figured he'd get a ticket for driving on the highway. So off he scoots, where you couldn't follow even if you wanted to. Other than that, I don't have any idea. When you crack the teenage mind, a Nobel is yours, sweetheart."

Chapter Eight

"He never moved," Dr. Alan Perrone said. The medical examiner had taken his time at the site, as if he had nowhere else to be than this desolate arroyo bottom, now starting to shimmer in the harsh sun. He glanced up at Linda Real. Her cameras had been busy. "You have what you need so far?"

"Sure do."

"Let's roll him over then." He looked up at Estelle, at the same time pointing at Freddy Romero's neck just under the ear. "If he was wearing the helmet, it wasn't buckled on," he said. He made a flipping motion with his hand, and Estelle helped him turn the body over. "I don't think we're going to have any surprises, but you never know." Understanding the need for comprehensive documentation, Perrone worked patiently with Linda at each stage of the process, as if he were *her* assistant, never rushing, never demanding.

The ATV framework had smashed into the back of Freddy's head. Had he been wearing the helmet, the wreckage would have caught him below its margin with the full weight of the four-wheeler behind the blow. Fancy paint job or not, the helmet would have done Freddy little good.

"My guess is that it crushed the cervical vertebrae and the occipital both," Perrone said. "He never knew what hit him." The victim's expression was almost serene, as if he'd been enjoying the flight until the switch had been turned off.

Perrone commented on the shattered right shoulder, the broken left ankle, and finally the obvious lividity. After being smashed into the arroyo bottom, the victim hadn't moved a centimeter. Blood had settled, the stagnant puddling in the lower tissues blotching the torso. "We'll see more of that during the post," Perrone said, and sat back on his haunches. "Sad business, as always. Your neighbor, am I right?"

"Yes," Estelle replied. "Butch's older brother."

"Christ," he said. "Francis was telling me about the fang in the eye. This family is having all their bad luck in one day." He twisted and regarded the crumpled ATV. Even damaged, it was obvious that the machine was a veteran of many rough miles, the paint faded, the tires worn and irregular, the engine encrusted with oil varnish. "He wasn't a newcomer to this."

"No. I think he'd rather be out exploring than just about anything else. He should have been in school yesterday. Instead..." She let the thought go unfinished.

"Well," Perrone said, pushing himself to his feet, "I'm finished here." He looked up at the arroyo rim where Bill Gastner kept the two paramedics company. "No alcohol at the scene, apparently?"

"None that we've seen so far. There were two unopened cans of beer in the truck. None opened."

Perrone nodded absently. "We'll see. Right now, it looks like he made a simple mistake and overcooked it." He reached out with his foot and gently nudged the exploded front tire with his boot. "Everything is going just hunky-dory, and then events conspire."

They heard another vehicle, and a second white Expedition eased into view.

"That would be himself," Perrone said. "Let me get out of here before the circus blocks me in." He reached out a hand and touched Estelle on the arm. "I'll let you know ASAP. But don't expect any surprises."

"Thanks, Alan."

She saw the sheriff's vehicle backing up, away from the paramedics' unit. In a moment, Robert Torrez appeared in the arroyo bottom and trudged with no particular urgency down the center of the arroyo, where cattle tracks chewed the gravel. Fifty yards away he slowed to an amble, looking at this and that as he approached. At one point he stopped and turned to face down the arroyo toward the southwest. He scanned the edge of the cut, taking in the rise of ground where Bender's Canyon trail skirted the edge, the sudden swell on top of which Estelle's vehicle was parked corking the road.

He turned without approaching any closer and regarded the wreckage of the ATV and Freddy Romero.

"He was comin' this way?" His voice barely audible.

"It appears so, yes. They didn't keep you long today," Estelle remarked.

Torrez grimaced. "Wasted trip. The DA knew that they were going to plea yesterday. He could have said something then." He shrugged and crossed over to where Estelle was standing, towering over her by a foot. His dark features were impassive, but the eyes constantly surveyed the area, inventorying who was present, noting what might be out of place. His standard uniform of blue jeans and casual western style shirt hadn't been modified even for a court date.

"The ATV caught him on the back of the neck," Estelle said. "The accident is straight forward, I think. I just don't know why he was over here."

"There ain't a postage stamp of ground where this kid hasn't been," the sheriff said with a touch of admiration. "You said his truck is over at the springs?"

"Yes. Right at the fork where 122 joins the county track. Ramps are down from the tailgate. He left his phone in the truck, along with a small cooler. Two cans of beer. None open."

"Huh," Torrez grunted. "So what's with that, I wonder. He coulda just parked out on 14 and been half way here."

"I just don't know, Bobby. Our next step is to follow his tracks farther on up the trail. I'd like to know where he went… where he turned around. Whatever he was doing, or scouting, or hunting, it appears that he was on his way back. Maybe."

"His folks know?"

"Not yet. APD is working on that."

"What a day for them."

"Did you read the article in the paper about the cat skull?"

Torrez nodded but offered no comment on the story.

"That's an interesting coincidence, I think," Estelle added. "Freddy told the newspaper that he found the skull way up above Borracho Springs, up in a cave just below the top ridge. That's a long way in, up above the springs. That was earlier in the week. Now, I can see why he would want to return to that area…maybe find something else. Maybe he wants some claws or something."

"But he didn't do that," Torrez said. "You can't get a four-wheeler up in that country anyway."

"No, and this time, he didn't hike in. In fact, it doesn't look like he went up into the mountains at all. He parked his truck below the campground, but the four-wheeler tracks say that he drove directly over here."

"I don't go along with the cave bit, anyway," the sheriff said. "I've been up above Borracho all kinds of times. I don't know of any caves up on the ridge, like the kid was claiming. Maybe some rock shelves or undercuts. Maybe that's what he meant." Torrez stepped over to the rig and knelt down. "And no place to drive this rig, either. You know this kid better than I do. Was he a hiker?"

"I don't know. I see him working with all the machinery—the bikes, ATVs, the boat, even that dreadful motorized skateboard that my two urchins think is the greatest invention on the planet. I know Freddy liked to play golf with his dad. The whole family liked outings at the Butte for fishing and water skiing." She sighed. "They've been neighbors for eight years, and I've never been in their house." She slid her hands past one another, two ships passing.

Estelle knelt and examined the victim's well worn, even tattered, trainers. They weren't the sort of footwear that would stand up to much hiking through rugged country.

"Well, he did what he did," she said, and Torrez shrugged again.

"It probably don't matter," he said. "What happened *here* looks pretty obvious. Are you ready for transport?"

"Yes." The sheriff glanced once more at the mangled ATV, then walked back up the arroyo far enough that he could make himself heard by the two EMTs up on the trail without raising his voice. They disappeared behind the ambulance and shortly reappeared with one of the light gurneys. They climbed down into the arroyo using the same trail taken by the sheriff.

"You sure find some spots," Matty Finnegan said. She pivoted at the waist, taking in the desolate country, then glanced at Estelle. "Or maybe I should say *he* found the spot, huh. Who called this in? Some rancher drive by?"

"Luck on our part," Estelle replied. "We followed his tracks." She didn't explain why.

"Yesterday his brother? Now Freddy." Matty grimaced. "What did they do to deserve this run of luck."

Torrez interrupted her musings. "When you're done, I need a hand with the ATV."

"That's us, the wrecking crew," Mattie muttered good-naturedly.

"Ten seconds," the sheriff said. "That's all it'll take."

The abrupt noise of the body bag zipper prompted a flinch. *A life finished,* Estelle thought. Just like that. A life reduced to memories and the sound of one long zipper. She glanced at her watch, wondering if the Albuquerque Police Department had had time to make contact with George and Tata Romero.

"Hey," the sheriff prompted quietly. Estelle turned to see him standing by the ATV, the two EMTs ready. "Give us a hand now?" He made a flipping motion with his hand. "Over that way. Everybody make sure they got hold of something that ain't sharp." The five of them managed the wreckage more easily than Estelle had imagined. It thumped back on its wheels, the one mangled and bent, both handlebars and luggage rack twisted.

"God, we're good," Linda Real said.

"And we're out of here," Mattie called. The EMTs set off down the arroyo with their burden, and Estelle watched their

progress. The bagged figure on the gurney looked too small to
be Freddy Romero.

"Stubby's going to be able to get his rig in here somehow?"
Linda referred to the driver of the county's contract wrecker.
The question jarred Estelle back to the task at hand. The sheriff
pointed at the arroyo bank.

"Winch it right up there," he said. "No problem." Linda
stepped back and took a series of photos of the wrecked machine.
In the sunshine, the oil and gasoline were still fragrant. Torrez
pulled the short .22 rifle out of the nylon boot. He popped the
magazine out, and Estelle could see the bright noses of the cartridges. The sheriff jacked the bolt, but the chamber had been
empty. He pushed the cartridges in the magazine, so there was
no play to allow more to be added, and shook his head. "No luck
huntin'. All ten still there." He slid the rifle back into the boot,
but kept the magazine, bouncing it thoughtfully in his hand.

Estelle's attention was drawn to the plywood box that was
bolted to the rear rack, its lid held in place with two stout bungee
cords. The box had taken the brunt of one of the flips, but the
three-quarter inch plywood out of which it was constructed
had suffered only digs and gouges. The latch was secured with
a twist of wire.

The sheriff loosened the wire and swung the lid back. A package of Oreo cookies had been reduced to crumbs and chunks
that cascaded down into the box. Below the cookies, three bottles
of water had nestled, two of them apparently exploded with the
force of the crash.

"Cookies and water," Estelle remarked. "The outdoorsman's
diet."

"Works." Torrez reached past Estelle. "Stop a minute."

She had already seen what had prompted his interest. "Linda,
please?"

As Linda Real stepped close, Estelle added, "Get a good close
up of this *in situ* for me."

"The oily rag?" Linda asked.

"Yep," Torrez said. He stepped aside slightly, allowing the sunshine to fall fully into the battered carrier. The photographer's camera snicked a series as she moved in and out, her last three photos taken so close that only the cloth would be in the frame.

"Got it," she said.

Estelle gently pulled the wrapped object out of the carrier, holding it in the palm of her right hand. Through the cloth, she could feel the familiar hard steel. The cloth had once been a T-shirt, and she unwound it as if about to reveal a treasured diamond. The handgun was encrusted with a uniform coating of dust and dirt, including a liberal assortment of what looked like animal droppings adhered to the smooth metal.

"Here," Torrez said. "Hold it still." He slid a pencil into the bore, marked where it stopped with his thumb, and withdrew it, laying it along the pistol's slide. "Still got one in the chamber."

"This isn't something Freddy was just carrying," Estelle said. "It's been in the elements for a *long* time."

Torrez bent down a little and scrutinized the handgun. "Smith and Wesson. Not a bad piece. Be interesting to know if that bad boy's been fired."

"And at what."

"Hunters, maybe. Remember the revolver that power walker found along the roadside over east of town? We had all kinds of theories about how that ended up there until we found out it belonged to some kid who'd been shooting from the roadside. He laid the gun on his jeep, and then got preoccupied with something else. Drove off and sure enough, the gun bounced off. That's most likely with this. Some hunter got careless. If it wasn't stainless steel, it'd be just a hunk of junk right now."

"It wasn't Mr. Romero's," Estelle said.

"Not likely. He was nervous enough about his son drivin' around with *that*." He touched his toe to the .22 carbine in the nylon boot. "He called me to find out how many laws Freddy was breakin' by carrying that on his ATV. Made him kinda nervous that the kid was doin' that."

"You need anything?" Bill Gastner's voice interrupted them.

"If you'd find me an evidence bag for this." Estelle held out her hand so Gastner could see the gun. "In my briefcase."

"You got it."

While she waited, she carefully wrapped the gun in the cloth, mindful of where the charged weapon's barrel pointed.

"Let me take that and have Mears get started on it," Torrez said. He strolled with no urgency to the arroyo bank and reached up to catch the plastic bag that Bill Gastner dropped to him. "How are you doin'?" he asked the older man.

Gastner knelt with one knee in the dirt, surveying the scene below him. "I'm okay," he said. "What's with the gun?"

"Don't know yet," Torrez replied. "We're *gonna* know. That's for sure. She got any masking tape in that briefcase? That and a marker."

Gastner returned with the two items, and Torrez peeled off a long strip, wound it across the outside of the evidence bag and wrote LOADED in large, block letters.

Chapter Nine

The four-wheeler tracks crisscrossed the two-track here and there, and it soon became apparent, as they reached low spots where the sand was a perfect matrix for tracks, that more than one round trip on Bender's Canyon Trail had been made. At one such location, Estelle stopped the Expedition and she and Bill Gastner got out.

"At least three," Gastner said. "Now, that's interesting." He bent his head back, gazing at the sky. "Look, we haven't had a drop of moisture in three weeks. If we hadn't found the kid and his wrecked machine in the arroyo, there'd be no way we could tell if these tracks were made this morning, yesterday, last week, or three weeks ago."

"There's a time puzzle here," the undersheriff agreed. "For one thing, it's likely that Freddy rode in here maybe yesterday some time. Fair enough. Then," and she stepped across a hummock of grass, looking down at a particularly clear, deep impression left by the knobby tires, "did he ride back and forth? In and out? And this?" She paused, a toe almost touching another track.

"Not an ATV," Gastner said. "Truck, car, jeep, something. Ground's too gravelly to give us an impression."

"But it's on top, isn't it."

Gastner knelt down with a loud popping of knees, one hand on the ground to keep his balance. "Sure enough. But look, like I said, out in the boonies as this might be, there's still a fair amount of traffic on this two-track, sweetheart."

"Interesting," Estelle muttered.

"What is?"

"All of it. Freddy didn't say what day he found the jaguar skull, but the school records show that he was in school all week—except yesterday. Now, if you were a teenager getting his kicks out of exploring caves, and if you found something as neat as that skull, what would you be likely to do?"

"Oh, I'd be back there," Gastner said without hesitation. "Damn right."

"So would I. Why would I be over here, across the valley, out on the prairie counting cow pies? And where did I find the handgun? That's quite a discovery all by itself."

"That could have been anywhere, even along the highway," Gastner offered. "Things bounce out of trucks all the time. You've seen that collection that they have over at the state highway barns. People drop the damnedest things. Gloves, chains, jacks, hubcaps, coolers, *shoes.* Have you ever lost a *shoe* along the highway?"

"Ah, no."

"How do they do it? Always amazed me. I once found a loaded shotgun up on Regál Pass. Turns out that a guy had it in the back of his Jeep, and somehow it bounced out when he turned onto the highway from the ridge trail. People are just plain *numb,* sweetheart." A sudden recollection lighted his heavy features. "My all-time favorite was finding a set of dentures up on Cat Mesa. A perfect set of choppers, lying on an old, moldy mattress. Now you could have a grand time making up a scenario to fit *that.* No matter how hot the moment of passion was, how could someone forget his *teeth?*"

He grunted to his feet and shook his head. "But a fair enough question. Regardless of where he picked up the handgun—*if* he picked it up somewhere and didn't just buy it from somebody—then what was he scouting over here?" He held out a hand as if to add, "after you." Estelle snapped a series of photographs of the tracks, knowing that they showed little.

For another mile, the two-track skirted the base of a mesa whose top looked as if it had been laser leveled. The rim itself was a vertical jumble for the last fifty feet, but despite the formidable barrier was still scarred by cattle trails. Rounding the mesa, the path headed due north past a dilapidated windmill missing most of its blades. The water tank, one side caved in, was peppered with bullet holes. The barbed-wire fence around the well head had fallen in a tangle, the posts weathered to steel gray.

The ATV tracks led past the attraction, keeping to the two-track. In another hundred yards, the road forked, the tracks leading northwest. They jolted to a stop facing a small arroyo too shallow to hide a car. The ATV apparently hadn't hesitated.

"You'll make it," Gastner encouraged.

"When was the last time you were out here?" Estelle asked, and Gastner laughed.

"Mid-afternoon of June 21st, nine years ago. Good God, come on, sweetheart. I have no idea when it was."

"But you've been here, in this very spot."

"Yes. Absolutely. I have no recollection of why or when. I know that this two-track here winds around about a million acres of worthless prairie, and in about two miles we'll run into one of Herb Torrance's gates, and if you go that way, you'll end up right in his back yard. Otherwise, we're going to go around that big mesa behind Herb's and come out to a fork in the road. One path goes on through Miles Waddell's place, back out to the county road. The other choice heads north, out to the old state highway." He sat up a little straighter, peering over the hood. "Just where Freddy Romero *didn't* go."

They had just bumped into the shade of a scrub oak grove, the dry leaves scraping along the Expedition's flanks, when Estelle's cell phone buzzed. She stopped the vehicle. For a moment, the connection produced nothing. Finally, a voice that clearly was struggling with emotion said, "Estelle?" The connection wasn't particularly good, with plenty of background noise.

"This is Estelle."

"George Romero," the caller said, and Estelle found it impossible to imagine the stocky, gruff auto mechanic trying to choke the words out. "Look," he said, and stopped, then tried again. "Look, is all this true?"

Trusting the distant police department, but knowing how messages can sometimes become entangled, the undersheriff delayed the moment. "What did the officers tell you, sir?"

"Two cops and a chaplain came to the hospital. They said Freddie had an accident on his four-wheeler." George's voice cracked, and Estelle could hear him taking deep breaths.

"He did, sir. I'm sorry."

"He's dead?"

"Yes, sir."

"Jesus, how…"

"He flipped the unit into an arroyo off Bender's Canyon Trail, sir."

"Oh, my God. Wait…" Thumpings and voices were loud in the background, and at one point Estelle could hear an electronic voice, and a series of chimes that sounded like an elevator signal. "The cops didn't know when," Romero said. "When it happened."

"We're not sure, sir."

"What do you think?"

"I don't want to guess, sir."

"Look," Romero said, and his voice trailed off. "He was lying out there all night? Is that what they're saying?"

"It appears right now that the accident happened sometime yesterday, sir."

"So he was out there all night?"

"Yes, sir."

"Oh, Jesus. You mean he could have…" Romero's voice trailed off, and then Estelle heard him try to speak to someone else, perhaps Tata. "When did you find him?" he managed finally.

"We found him about three hours ago, sir."

"Oh, my God. Who? Who found him?"

"Bill Gastner and I, sir."

"You were looking for him? How…"

"Yes, sir. We were following the tracks of his ATV. He parked his truck over by Borracho Springs. Then he drove over to

Bender's Canyon from there. I can't be sure, but I think I caught sight of him yesterday around two o'clock. Driving along State 56, sir. He turned off at the saloon, and took the back trail over to Bender's Canyon."

"You didn't talk to him?"

"No, sir. I didn't have the chance."

"He ain't supposed to be driving along the highway, is he?"

"No, sir, he's not. But he was on the shoulder, and just for a mile or so. By the time I passed by, he was off in the distance, off-road. I couldn't have followed him if I had wanted to. And at the time, I didn't know it was him."

"I don't know why he'd be over there," Romero said. His voice was husky, right on the edge of a sob.

"Nor I, sir. Is there anything I can do for you or Tata?"

"Christ, I don't know. I don't know what to think right now. Butch is going to be all right, I guess. I mean, he's going to be blind in that eye, but everything else is under control. But now this…"

"I'm sorry, sir."

"I just don't know what to think. We're in the ER right now. They had to give Tata a sedative." Romero heaved a great, shuddering sigh. "Where is he now?"

"At the hospital, sir." Estelle avoided the blunt, awful word *morgue* that would have been more specific. "Dr. Perrone is with him."

"Okay. I guess that's all…all I needed to know. But I want to see where it happened."

"I can understand that, sir. Whenever it's convenient for you. In the meantime, if there's anything I can do, please don't hesitate."

"Well, right now, I guess we're driving back down there. Tata wanted to stay here, but…"

"I understand, sir."

"My sister lives here in the city. I'm thinking that we'll ask her to come stay with Butch so we can break away for a little. God, I don't know." He sighed again. "We'll be there in five hours, Estelle."

She looked at her watch. Five hours would put the Romeros on the highway well after dark. "Sir, is there any way I can convince you to drive down tomorrow?"

"I can't wait until tomorrow."

"Then travel safe, sir. And again, I'm so sorry."

"Yeah, well. We all…we all are, I guess."

She rang off and took a deep breath, letting it out slowly as she slipped the little phone back in its holster. "What a thing," she said to Bill Gastner. "A day starts out one way, and changes so fast there's just no keeping up."

"We've seen it too many times," Gastner grumbled. "When it hits close to home, it kind of jerks our chains. They're driving back tonight?"

"Yes."

"And that's not good, either."

Chapter Ten

She pulled the SUV into gear and let it idle along the rough two-track. In a few moments, they reached a fork, and just beyond on the left, a closed gate.

"Herb's back forty," Gastner said. "Freddy didn't go through there." Sure enough, the four-wheeler tracks, here and there clear, but most of the time just a vague scuff on the hard ground, veered to the right, where the two-track dropped down into a shallow arroyo and then around the buttress of the mesa. "If we continue out this way, we'll be on Miles Waddell's property in about two miles, and then back to the county road," he said. "So where the hell was he going?" Almost immediately, he sat up straighter, just as they reached another grove of piñon and oak scrub. Estelle slowed.

"Right there," he said. The ATV tracks, now little more than a swath of bent and crushed dried grass and range weeds, swept to the left, off the trail. Estelle stopped the truck, staying in the two narrow ruts of the two-track. They both got out and circled around in front of the SUV.

"Now, the question is…" Gastner started to say, then shrugged. "Who knows what the goddamn question is." He walked a few paces to the southwest, then turned and knelt down. "Joe Tracker here says that there have been enough people through this spot in the past week or so to fill a parking lot." He pointed, sweeping his arm back and forth. "Get the light just right, and you can see that."

Estelle walked ahead, staying on the raw dirt of the trail's ruts. "He—or somebody—went on, that's for sure." She waited for Gastner to catch up. In a section no more than six feet across, merely a wash of sandy trash between two smooth, flat rocks whose crowns were now part of the trail's paving, they could see a clear impression of the knobby tires from what looked like the big, soft tires of an ATV. And other tracks as well…truck, car, even motorcycle, perhaps a mountain bike or two.

A portion of the ATV's prints were obscured by other tracks, too indistinct to signal anything other than that they were there.

"Useless," Gastner said. "Nothing we can tell for sure."

"But let's suppose that Freddy went through here, along with everyone else. Hunters, ranchers, BLM, tourists, lost illegal immigrants, kids out partying."

"And so? Let's suppose that. So what? That's what it *all* is, sweetheart. Supposition. We just don't know, and we may *never* know. And even *after* the kid crashed, it'd be easy enough to miss him." He shrugged. "Herb Torrance could have come out his gate and gone down this way. Could have gone the *other* way, too. Ditto anybody else you care to mention."

Estelle sighed and rubbed her head. "I just want to know, *Padrino*. That's all. I just want to know. I want to know why Freddy rode out this way, I want to know where he went."

"Of course you do. But." Gastner strolled down the two-track, hands in his pockets. "Oh, you got more tracks up here," he said, stopping at the edge of another sandy wash where run-off down the flank of the mesa had carved a shallow crossing. "Several, as a matter of fact. See? That's what I mean."

"It won't hurt to follow the two track out a bit farther," Estelle said.

"You aren't going to see anything," Gastner offered. "I mean, so what? So he rode out this way? You know, the ride he took yesterday, when you saw him, wasn't necessarily the only recon he's taken in this area." He surveyed the countryside, hands on his hips. "Probably pretty good hunting out this way. He's got the rifle, so he's making life miserable for the coyotes and bunnies. You know what I'll bet?" He waited until Estelle raised an eyebrow in question. "I'll wager lunch, which by the way we haven't enjoyed yet, that if we walk out into the prairie here a hundred paces, we'll cross at least one set of vehicle tracks."

"I don't doubt it, sir."

"Rats. I wanted lunch."

"We will, eventually."

"You could fly over this country from the air, and it'd be a lattice-work of tracks, vehicle, cattle, and otherwise."

"Rough going, all of it."

"Not for a kid on a hot machine, it's not," Gastner said. "Bouncing and jouncing is half the fun, anyway."

They returned to the truck and meandered along the two-track, eventually running into another barbed-wire fence. Ahead they could see a power pole, concrete well house, and just ahead down a slight slope, a large galvanized stock tank—this one full with fresh water not yet scummed over with algae.

"This is the back way into Miles Waddell's property," Gastner said, "and that's his well house. And I can see tracks from here, every which way. You want me to open the gate?"

"No. There's no point."

"Waddell built this a few years ago, thinking that there would be money to be made when the BLM develops the cave property across the county road. Maybe a good guess, maybe a waste of money. He runs livestock here, and I know he leases some of it to Herb."

Estelle pointed to the right, away from the gate, across the prairie where the main Bender's Canyon Trail headed off to the north.

"Two more choices," Gastner said. "If you stay on this road, it's the easy way out to old State 17. Before you get there, there's another really rough son-of-a-bitch that runs east through all those foothills, and eventually runs right down to Gus Prescott's ranch. Right through his back yard."

"I've never driven that."

"Rough, washed out in spots, a kidney crusher."

"How many miles to Prescott's? About fifteen or so?"

"I would guess about that."

"Freddy could have gone that way. He could have ridden over to see Casey."

"He *could* have." Gastner flashed an amused grin. "Or he could have taken the paved highway to Moore, and a mile and a half would have taken him in to the fair Casey's front door."

Estelle regarded the route ahead thoughtfully.

"Please tell me you're not going to crash and bang along that trail in this crate," Gastner pleaded.

"You don't want to do that?"

"No, I don't want to do that. I want to eat *lunch,* sweetheart. Anyway, that route isn't going to offer up any easy answers. If I thought it would, I'd say go for it. Jounce and bounce until we both piss blood."

"The Romeros are going to *want* to know, sir. They're going to want to know what Freddy was doing when he was killed."

"I understand that. And the answer is simple. He was careening down Bender's Canyon Trail far faster than he should have been. He got careless. He got killed." Gastner made a face that mirrored Estelle's frustration. "You'll find a more tactful way to explain it to them, I'm sure. But that's the nut of it all."

"The handgun in his kit says that's not all of it," Estelle said quietly.

"Ah...the gun." He ducked his head in acquiescence. "Now you're right about that." He glanced at his watch. "And if I'm not mistaken, you may have some answers about that when Mears is finished processing the damn thing. *That* I'd like to hear."

Chapter Eleven

"Some clear prints." Sheriff Robert Torrez passed to the under-sheriff first a card bearing Freddy Romero's finger prints lifted by Perrone at the morgue, and then a latent print collection. "Freddy didn't make any effort to keep his prints off the gun."

"I can't imagine why he would," Estelle replied. She studied the card, blinking to clear tired eyes. The clock on the office wall read nearly nine thirty, and she had already fielded a second call from George Romero a couple hours earlier. She'd managed to convince Romero that a visit to the crash site would serve them both far better in the fresh light of morning. He and Tata had settled instead for a visit to the morgue, a brief moment that would keep them sleepless for the rest of the night. Perrone had been there, had been gentle and thoughtful, allowing them only to see their son's face.

Tata Romero had been unable to ask questions other than *why*, a word she repeated a dozen times. Estelle had no answer. George Romero's face was set in grim lines, and at one point, as they left the hospital, had asked, "What do you know?"

Estelle had been almost honest in her answer, erring only in being deliberately incomplete. She hadn't mentioned the handgun found on the ATV.

"Kind of interesting," Torrez continued. "The gun had a round chambered, but wasn't decocked." He slid the heavy automatic across to Estelle. Sgt. Tom Mears had spent considerable time with the gun, retrieving whatever evidence he could. The sum total was several smudgy prints, all belonging to Freddy Romero.

"Freddy wrapped the gun in that cloth, with one round in the chamber, hammer cocked, ready to go," Estelle said. "He didn't try to unload it, and I doubt that he fired it."

"Looks like." The sheriff hefted a sealed plastic envelope and displayed a handful of stubby .40 S&W cartridges. "The gun has a ten round magazine. You could add one in the chamber, and that would make eleven. We recovered nine. One was in the chamber, eight in the magazine. All Speer Gold Dot. Mears is processing a couple of prints that might work for us."

"So it could have been fired once, or maybe twice, depending on how it was loaded." Estelle took a moment to mull the sheriff's shorthand explanation.

"Could have been fired a thousand times, far as that goes," Torrez said. "But that's what was *in* the gun when we found it in Freddy's carry-all…cocked, with one in the pipe, eight more in the magazine."

Estelle gazed at the stubby, heavy automatic, then picked it up and thumbed the decocker lever. The cocked hammer snapped down, but the large, rotating bar of the decocker mechanism prevented the hammer from striking the firing pin. The gun then could be carried safely with a chambered round, hammer down. Then snap the decocker up, leaving the gun in double-action mode, and all the shooter had to do was pull the trigger. When the gun fired, the hammer was cocked by the slide slamming backward, and would remain that way, cocked and ready to fire, unless the decocker was activated.

"I can think of a hundred ways Freddy could have come to grief with this," she said. "Not the least of which is having it bounce around in the carrier of that ATV, charged and ready to go."

"Odds are slim that it would go off by itself," Torrez said. "Slim and none. But then he gets home with it…"

"*That* thought gives me the willies. I didn't mention it to George Romero yet. I wanted to know more before I did that."

The sheriff nodded. "So instead the kid does something *really* dangerous. He drives into an arroyo," Torrez said, almost philosophically. "Anyway, Mears said the gun looked like it had been locked away in somebody's attic for a few years. We can comb through any unresolved break-ins or thefts, but I don't remember anything."

"No. Plus I never got the impression that was Freddy's style. I don't think he would have taken the gun in a burglary. It almost looks as if it's been outside. It's stainless, so it didn't rust, but look at the rest of the condition. If that gun was in somebody's closet, they sure were the world's worst housekeepers."

The sheriff turned as another figure appeared in the doorway. "What do you want," he said in mock truculence, and Doug Posey flashed him a smile. The New Mexico Game and Fish officer was in his late thirties, but still managed to look sixteen.

"I'm working my ass off, sheriff," Posey said. "If you don't think talking to a class of second graders is scary, you can take the next round. That's what *I* did this afternoon, for starters."

"Ain't gonna happen," Torrez said.

Posey's expression turned serious. "I heard about what happened to the Romero kid. Shit, his fifteen minutes of fame didn't last long."

"Bender's Canyon arroyo," the sheriff said.

"Son of a gun, that's too bad. I liked him. Real wild hares, those two boys. How's Butch coming along, anyway?"

"He lost the eye, but will recover otherwise. Probably," Estelle said. "He's up in Albuquerque."

Posey grimaced. "What's with the Smith?" He leaned over Estelle's desk and peered at the gun without touching it.

"This was wrapped in a cloth inside the carrier of Freddy Romero's ATV," Estelle replied.

"No kiddin'. May I?" Estelle nodded, and Posey hefted the gun, racked the slide back and inspected the empty chamber and magazine. "Never used one of these. What's the deal?" He looked across at the sheriff.

"Don't know," Torrez said. "We'll talk with George tomorrow, maybe. See what he knows."

"It's been cleaned up some," Estelle said. "When we found it, it was loaded and cocked, and looked like it had been out in the weather. Or a loft up in someone's barn or garage some-where. Covered with all kinds of nasties." She opened a folder and pulled out an eight by ten print of the gun as it had first appeared, cradled in the oily cloth. Posey looked at it, turning it this way and that.

"Huh." He turned it again, then pointed at one spot on the forward portion of the gun's slide. "What's that, bat guano?"

"Guano of some sort."

"Huh." He handed the photo back and leaned on the desk, staring at the automatic. "Prints?"

"Only Freddy's."

"Gun like that shouldn't be hard to track down," Posey said. He straightened up, not taking his eyes from the Smith and Wesson. "You guys got a minute?"

"Of course."

"I'll be right back. Let me go out to the truck and get some-thing." In no more than two minutes, he returned and handed Torrez a small plastic evidence bag. "Coincidences make me *really* uncomfortable," he said, and waited while Torrez read the tag and then handed the bag to Estelle.

The single bullet was discolored and hugely mushroomed, its brass jacket peeled back around the lead core so that the resulting projectile was nearly twice its original size.

"From?" Torrez asked.

"I picked it out of the cat skull. I talked to Underwood over at the high school this afternoon, when I finished up with the little ankle biters." He put a finger to his own skull. "There was that hole right behind the right orbit? This was wedged into the bone low on the other side."

"Bill Gastner was talking about that," Estelle said. "The bullet hole, I mean."

"He mentioned that. I was on the phone with him for about an hour this evening. He wanted to know what sort of records we had concerning jaguar reports." Posey grinned. "That part was easy. We don't have squat. Nobody's seen one in these parts, or any parts north of the border, for that matter. Not in years and years." He looked at Estelle. "He's going through some old Spanish records from your uncle?"

"Great uncle. He might have seen one, and if he did, he'd mention it in his journals."

"Well, neat-o. The US Fish and Wildlife Service is interested in spades, I can tell you that," Posey said. "We'll be cooperating with them. They'll give the school a permit to keep the skull in the school's permanent collection, but they want to know more about this. But..."

He dropped the evidence bag containing the single bullet down beside the automatic. "This is way, way bizarre. I'm willing to bet that this is either a forty, a ten mil, or a forty-one mag."

Torrez reached across and retrieved the bag again. "Too short to be a forty-one mag," he said. "You were talkin' about coincidence?" He held up the bag of ammo recovered from the automatic.

"Freddy finds a skull," Estelle offered, "and it looks like Freddy maybe found a gun, too. There's a hole in the skull with the slug still rattling around inside." She reached out and touched the evidence bag. "And it could be the same caliber as the gun Freddy had in his possession."

"Could be," Posey said. "Wild." He pulled out a pen and used it to point carefully to the undistorted rear portion of the fired bullet. "Not going to take much to come up with a comparison."

"Mears can do a preliminary comparison for us first thing in the morning," the sheriff said. "No point in waiting on the state." He frowned. "Ancient history, though. You got a cat that's been dead for what, five years? Ten? Fifteen? There's nothing left but some bones and bits of hide." He shrugged. "It's no big deal now." He looked across at Posey. "It'd be like finding the remains of a bald eagle somehow. They get themselves killed all the time—sometimes by ranchers, or whatever."

"And if the Fish and Wildlife Service can dig up enough evidence to bring charges, it will."

"Don't doubt it," Torrez replied.

"We have three events going on here," Estelle offered. She leaned back in her chair and rubbed her forehead wearily. "The skull with a bullet recovered from inside it. That's one. A few days later, the guy who *found* the skull crashes his ATV into an arroyo and breaks his neck. That's two. In his ATV, we find a loaded handgun that all bets say wasn't his. We'll find out more about that tomorrow when we can think straight. But that's three. Now, if that handgun," and she reached across and tapped the relic through the bag, "happens to be the one that fired the bullet that killed the cat..."

"Fish and Wildlife is going to want to know," Posey said. "A jaguar skull is kind of a big deal, you know. If it's legit, then it's an important find. The feds are going to send one of their field biologists down to take a look probably by the first of the week. They're real interested in dating it, if they can." He shook his head in frustration. "They sure would have liked to talk with Freddy."

"Wouldn't we all," Estelle said.

Chapter Twelve

By Saturday morning, Estelle was reasonably sure that the entire community had heard of Freddy Romero's death. The timing of events had shut out coverage by Frank Dayan's *Posadas Register*, of course, but other newspapers would report the incident with a paragraph or two. The Romeros themselves would have spoken to friends of the family, and from there, like a wildfire roaring across the prairie, the news would sweep through the community.

That grapevine could be a powerful tool, Estelle knew. If there was a relationship between the discovery of the handgun and the bullet hole in the cat's skull, someone besides Freddy Romero knew about it. It made sense to her that Freddy had found the handgun only recently. Otherwise, he likely would have let someone in on his secret—Freddy actually turning the gun in to authorities was too much to expect—and he likely would have cleaned it up…at least wiped off the grime and guano.

Early Saturday morning, Linda Real and Sgt. Tom Mears had taken the Smith and Wesson for a comprehensive series of macro-photos, documenting the condition of the gun before it was cleaned and prepared for a comparison firing. Even scrapings of the dust and droppings had been sampled and preserved for analysis should that become necessary.

Estelle had agreed to meet with George Romero at nine, and ten minutes before that time, she looked out from her office and saw her neighbor standing at the dispatcher's island talking with Sheriff Robert Torrez. George looked as if he had tried for sleep while crumpled in a hard plastic waiting room chair. Dense stubble darkened his face, and his eyes were sunken with fatigue. When he saw the undersheriff, he slumped a bit more, as if hit with the awful news for a second time. He shook Torrez's hand and approached Estelle, surprising her with a powerful hug.

"Hey, neighbor," he murmured. After a long moment, he pushed back a bit, one beefy hand on each of the undersheriff's shoulders. It appeared as if he wanted to say something further, but couldn't.

"Can you take George out to the site?" Torrez asked, and the man nodded at him thankfully. He'd been unable to find words for that simple question.

"Of course," Estelle replied. "Give me a moment to collect a few things."

Back in her office, she selected a series of photographs and placed them in a folder, tucking that into her briefcase. "Tata's with you?" she asked when she returned to dispatch.

Romero shook his head. "She wanted to stay at the house. It ain't been a good night, I can tell you that. She told me to go ahead and go, if that's what I wanted to do. She was tending to the neighbors that came over. It's just something, you know? Something that I got to see. Couldn't tell you why."

They left the building, and Romero turned toward his own Suburban.

"Let's take mine," Estelle said. "I need to have my office with me."

He settled in the passenger seat of the county SUV, stiff and uncomfortable, obviously feeling out of place. He watched her go through the routine with the log and dispatch.

"Makes it a little easier having something to do, don't it."

"I think it does," she said.

"You said Bill was with you? I mean when you found the boy."

"Yes, sir. He was."

"Well, that's good, at least. He still getting out quite a bit?"

"You bet."

His right fist pounded a slow, thoughtful tattoo on the door's arm rest as they pulled out onto Grande and headed southwest.

"Yesterday sometime," Romero said.

"Thursday, sir. That's what it appears."

"And we drove off up north without even knowing he was lying out there."

"There was no way you could." Estelle knew full well that the assuaging comment wasn't even close to the truth. When he should have been in school, Freddy Romero had loaded his ATV into the back of his aging pickup truck and set off for the boonies. Tata Romero was home all day, every day. For her not to have seen the boy making preparations for his escapade was unlikely. But Freddy was an independent, feisty eighteen-year-old. Estelle knew that it would be easy to let him go his own way, unquestioned.

"I'll show you what we did yesterday," Estelle said. "If you know anything about what Freddy might have been doing, I'd appreciate hearing it."

Romero nodded, but said nothing, and they rode in silence until Estelle turned onto the Borracho Springs access road. The tracks of Stub Moore's vehicle hauler were obvious. "We found his pickup truck parked here," she explained. "Stub took it down to the county impound until we're done with it." Romero would have known exactly how the procedure worked, but the small talk might help cut through his fatigue.

"He unloaded his four-wheeler and rode it out to the highway. No tracks back up toward the campground or the springs." She maneuvered the SUV around and they returned to the highway. "He drove along the shoulder to the saloon. I was parked down the highway a little, on the shoulder just beyond the County Road 14 cattleguard. I saw him ride down here, right along the highway. He skirted the saloon and took the backcountry trail out to Bender's Canyon."

"I don't understand what he was doing," Romero said. "You talked to Casey?"

"Not since earlier yesterday."

"She lives out this way, you know."

This way was fifteen miles as the crow flew, and on that Thursday, Freddy Romero would have know that Casey was in school—where he should have been. Because the girl of his dreams obviously wasn't home, there would have been no reason to stop by the ranch.

"Tata was going to call her," George added. "That Casey... just a real swell girl, you know? The boy and her were pretty tight. This...this is going to be tough for her." He shook his head. "Tough for all of us."

Estelle slowed and turned into the Broken Spur's parking lot and skirted the building. As they nosed down into the arroyo, her passenger reared backward, one hand flying to the dash.

"Jesus, you're really going down in..." he let the rest trail off as they did just that, the SUV jouncing and spitting gravel. As they crested the north rim and trundled along the rough two-track, Romero relaxed back. "I rode out here with him once. Must have been a year ago now."

"On one machine, or two?"

"Me and Butch on one, Freddy on the other. We were going to see if we could find that big prairie dog town that Herb Torrance said was over here...all the way over on the back of his place. He said it was easy to find, but we sure as hell never did. Just some scattered colonies."

"Freddy had his .22 rifle with him. Would he have gone prairie dog hunting, do you suppose?"

"Maybe. He's done that a time or two, but not with a .22. Never reach out with that."

"Freddy's had that rifle for a while?"

"That little Ruger? I bought that for his sixteenth birthday," Romero said. "Made him take hunter safety...all that. Told him I didn't want him carrying that rifle loaded on the ATV."

"Well, the rifle isn't the issue," Estelle said gently. "It was in the boot with the magazine in place but nothing in the chamber. As nearly as we can tell, sir, your son was riding a little fast, cleared a sharp little rise, went airborne, and hit a rock coming down. The trail is narrow there, and he didn't have time to control it before he went over the edge."

"He wasn't drinking," Romero said, a flat statement rather than a question. "He wasn't twenty-one."

"Mr. Romero, kids take liberties all the time. As a matter of fact, there *were* two cans of beer in his cooler, but he left them in the truck. The cab smelled of beer, but that could be from any time."

Romero fell silent, watching the prairie pass by.

"Your son explored a lot on his own, sir?"

He nodded. "I had words with him now and then, but what can you do, you know? Look, I knew that he skipped school. I knew that. Tata and I argued about that, too. But his grades were all right. He went to school when he had to. That's the way I look at it." Romero wiped his eyes. "Freddy wasn't all too concerned with planning ahead," he said, and then, as if that topic held memories too painful, asked, "So you and Bill followed his tracks all the way out here? Is that what you're telling me?"

"Yes, sir."

"I got to thank you for that. For worrying about him, I mean. He could have been lyin' out here for days even…" He choked the thought off. "This isn't easy for you. I mean, you got the two little ones yourself." He reached out a hand to brace himself as the Expedition lumbered over an outcropping. He fell silent again as they crested the rise above Bender's Canyon Trail, joining the wider two-track that ran east-west.

"You have no idea why he would have taken this particular route?" Estelle asked. "Other than that you had been out hunting before in this general area?"

"No idea. Except there's a trail here that he could follow. I told him that private property was just that—private. He wasn't to go riding around on somebody's ranch just because there wasn't no fence to keep him out. Folks don't want to see those tracks all over everywhere. And if he was going to shoot dogs, then he needed to ask the rancher first."

"He generally did that, then?"

"Sure, he did that. Freddy has an independent streak a mile wide, but he's a good kid. You know that."

They reached Trujillo's homestead, and once more Estelle looked at the faint traces of a vehicle's turning around in the brush and grass beside the two-track, and the short section of clearer tracks in the sand beside the corral. Linda had photographed those every way possible, but they showed next to nothing—not clear enough to show tread, not even defined enough for an accurate measurement center to center, no way to tell when they'd been made. Estelle found herself curious about them only because they were *there,* in this particular, isolated place, so near to the scene of the tragic accident.

Cresting the small hill, a welter of tracks marked the two-track and the area around it. The big duals of Stub Moore's tow truck crisscrossed the trail where he had maneuvered to bring the hoist into line with the crushed ATV. The edge of the arroyo had crumbled back another foot or so, a cascade of fresh dirt collapsing down to the bottom of the cut. She stopped the truck and saw that the tracks and the disruption of the arroyo edge were not lost on George Romero.

"Oh, God," he whispered.

"It appears that he came over this little rise ahead of us way too fast, sir. His left front tire clipped the rocks, and he lost it."

Romero didn't reply, but slipped out of the Expedition, hanging onto the door as if his knees had turned to jelly. Only scuffs in the gravel arroyo bottom remained to tell the story, but Estelle could see the ATV and the quiet form of Freddy Romero, his helmet thrown to the other side of the arroyo, as clearly as if they were still lying there. Perhaps mercifully, George Romero saw only the arroyo gravel. He wiped his eyes on first one sleeve and then the other.

"He was out here all night," he managed to say after a moment, and he beat his fist gently against the Expedition's fender. He stared down into the arroyo. There was something about the site of a personal tragedy that drew people like magnets—they erected markers along the highway, laid wreaths on sidewalks, anything to help them remember that this was the spot where a loved one breathed his last. Estelle stood quietly, leaning against the open door on the driver's side, allowing George Romero time to come to terms with his ghosts.

"Maybe he didn't suffer," he said at last. *Maybe, maybe not,* Estelle thought. Her husband had said that in most cases, *killed instantly* was a nicety invented for grieving relatives. She gave Romero another full minute with his own thoughts.

"I'm still wondering why Freddy parked his truck over by Borracho," she said when it looked as if George was going to turn away from the arroyo. "If he was going to ride over here, it would make more sense to park down at the intersection of this canyon road with 14."

"I have no idea," Romero said. "No idea whatsoever."

"There's really nowhere to ride the ATV over at the Springs, unless he was going to take the old county road to the east… up on Salinas mesa."

"He'd been up there a time or two," Romero said. "He's been all over."

"I would suppose so. Sir, let me show you something." She reached in the window of the SUV and picked up the folder of photographs. Selecting a view of the handgun as it lay on the oily cloth used to wrap it, Estelle handed the photograph to Romero.

"Now what's this?" He frowned at the photo.

"That was tucked in the carrier of your son's four-wheeler, sir." She handed him a second photo taken of the wrapped gun *in situ,* its blocky shape easily discernable through the cloth.

"He doesn't own anything like this," he said, and Estelle almost smiled. But George Romero's surprise was genuine, and that surprise quickly turned to apprehension and concern. "You mean to tell me that he had that gun with him on the four-wheeler?"

"Yes, sir. The only fingerprints on it are his."

"Nobody's been shooting that thing." He brought the photo close and his eyes narrowed with concentration. "Looks like it was dug out of the bottom of a chicken coop. Where…"

"We don't know, sir."

"Why do you think *he* had anything to do with it?"

The question was so obvious as to be nearly rhetorical, but Estelle said patiently, "It was in the carrier on his machine. It has his fingerprints on it."

"Well, he found it somewhere. That's what I say."

"I agree with you." She left the obvious question hanging.

For a long moment, George Romero stood with his shoulders slumped, hands clasped together at his belly as if waiting for the knots in his gut to untangle, gazing out over the peaceful arroyo. His head started to shake, a slow, agonized oscillation. "What are we going to do without Freddy," he whispered.

He turned his back to the arroyo, facing Estelle. "Tell me what you're doing with all this." He wiped his eyes and started to climb back into the SUV.

"What are you asking, sir?"

He nodded at the folder of photos on the seat. Estelle got in the driver's side and waited while he settled himself. "I got a right to know about what's going on with Freddy," he continued. "Look, I've been to my share of wrecks and such. You know that. I even drove a wrecker for a while. I know there's always questions nagging. You got that," and he nodded at the folder again. "That says to me that you got questions about how all this happened. Tata and me got a right to know."

The undersheriff hesitated. The Romero family had suffered an unimaginable upset in the past two days, and still more lay ahead for them. There was no point in digging at open, painful wounds, but she didn't wish to dissemble with George Romero by offering mindless platitudes.

"We have two questions lingering, sir. One may be more important than the other. Number one," and she tapped the steering wheel with her right index finger. "I'm curious why Freddy parked his truck over at Borracho, then rode his ATV all the way over here. There's probably a simple explanation, but I'd like to know what it is. There's nothing illegal about what he did, there's nothing illegal about parking over there, and then riding over here, as long as he stays off the highway. The beer is a violation, but I don't care about that right now." She looked across at George Romero, and her dark, aquiline features softened. "Why he did what he did just seems an oddity to me, and I'd like to know."

"So would we," George Romero murmured.

"And second, I'd like to know where Freddy found the handgun. That's all. I think he *did* find it, sir. I have no reason to believe that he stole it, or bought it illegally, or anything like that. We know folks who have found all kinds of crazy things out in the boonies, and the most simple, innocent explanation is that the junk bounces out of trucks or Jeeps or whatnot. I just want to know, that's all."

"Sure don't look like something he'd buy from somebody," Romero said, nodding. "And no gun shop is going to sell something like that to an underage kid. Least I *hope* they wouldn't. Maybe a friend? I don't know."

"As new information comes to light, I'll be in touch," Estelle said. "I'll keep you and Tata informed."

Romero nodded again as if that satisfied him. Estelle did not add that finding a bullet lodged inside the jaguar skull also fascinated her, or that there was a coincidental possibility that the bullet had come from the very Smith and Wesson that Freddy Romero had found...somewhere.

Chapter Thirteen

By the time Estelle and George Romero returned to the Public Safety Building, the day blistered as any breath of wind died, clouds melted away, and the sun baked Posadas County. After a choked thanks and a self-conscious handshake from the stricken father, Estelle watched Romero trudge across the parking lot, shoulders slumped, head down.

School might not be in session, but Estelle knew exactly where she could find Nathan Underwood. She drove the few blocks down Grande and took the dirt road that led behind the administration building toward the gymnasium and the athletic field.

A swarm of padded players were already on the field, and Estelle saw Underwood standing with two students who were not in uniform. While he talked, a whistle on a heavy lanyard snapped in circles around the coach's right hand, first one way and then the other. Estelle saw that one of the students was working a digital camera, apparently trying for just the right coach portrait. Another whistle shrilled, and Underwood grinned at something one of the boys said, turning toward the field.

"Sir?" Estelle called, and Underwood stopped, looking at her questioningly.

"Sheriff," he said pleasantly, but glanced toward the field where his services were obviously expected. "What can I do for you?" He waved a hand in gentle dismissal at the two student reporters who appeared eager to remain with him. "Let me catch you guys later." He held out a hand and shook Estelle's. "What's up?" He had the habit of leaning close to his target when he spoke, as if huddling with a player who might not be trusted to listen carefully.

"I have a couple of follow-up questions, Mr. Underwood. You spoke earlier with Officer Posey, I understand."

"Sure did. We in trouble again?" His smile was easy and wide.

"Again?"

"Posey told us that we needed to get a permit from the feds. We'll do that, but it'll be next week. I appreciated that the officer didn't confiscate the skull right away. Many of the students haven't had a chance to see it yet."

"That's good, sir." She reached out and touched his elbow, steering him toward the end of the bench, well out of earshot of the students. "No, actually, I was wondering what day Freddy Romero brought that in to you."

He puffed out his cheeks and looked up at the blank sky. "Would have been Monday. First thing in the morning. He told me that he didn't want to leave it in his locker."

"Did he want to take it back home with him after you'd had a chance to see it?"

"Originally, yes he did. But I told him that there was a possibility that the Fish and Wildlife Service wouldn't allow it. Like eagle feathers, you know. And in fact, that turns out to be the case. They told us that we had two choices after everyone was finished looking at it. We could either give it to the feds, or get a permit for it and keep it here in the school's collection." He grinned again. "Well, in the maybe someday-to-be collection." He held up four fingers. "We have a coyote, a raven, one broken prairie dog skull, and now this cat. That's not really a rival for the Smithsonian." The whistle shrilled again and Underwood looked toward the field. "What else can I do for you?"

"Freddy was in your biology class?"

"Was. When he was a sophomore. Great kid. I tried to talk him into taking chemistry and physics, but..." He shrugged. "Not his bag. He's enjoying the vocational programs right now. Does well. Great kid."

"He found the skull on Sunday, perhaps? Did he say?"

Underwood bit his lip thoughtfully and regarded the sod as he dug in a cleat. "I wouldn't be surprised. You know, I didn't actually ask him *when* he found it. You've talked to him, I assume." He didn't wait for an answer, but swung the whistle again and then caught it deftly. "What's the department's interest in all this, anyway?"

"May I see the skull, sir? I know that now isn't the best time, but I'd appreciate it."

"Well, sure. I guess so. But you're right. Now isn't the best time." He nodded at the field.

"You're the defensive coordinator?"

"That's me."

"Can you find someone to sub for you for ten minutes?"

He sighed. "Sure. I guess." Turning, he surveyed the field, then bellowed, "Coach!" Out on the field, head coach Art Lucero turned and Underwood pointed first at Estelle, then flashed ten fingers. Lucero nodded and waved a dismissive hand. "Let's do it, Sheriff."

She followed him up the sidewalk to the rear of the gym, and they walked straight through the yawning cavern and out the front door, along the breezeway to the main high school building.

"Officer Posey said that the cat was shot." Underwood selected a key from the enormous jumble latched to his belt with a retractable chain, then held open a hall doorway for the undersheriff. "Did he pass that on to you?"

"He did. We have the slug."

"Interesting stuff," Underwood said, and jangled the keys to select the correct one for Room 128. He let it close behind them. "I've got it over in this cabinet," he said, and selected another key. "We need to build some sort of secure glass display cabinet for it. Maybe Freddy can find the time to do that in shop."

Estelle frowned. The gossip vine hadn't reached out its tendrils to Coach Underwood yet. Obviously Freddy, the solitary explorer of the Posadas desert and prairie, wasn't a team player.

The skull was large and blunt, the size of an average cantaloupe. Underwood picked it up carefully, slipping his hand under the loose lower mandibles. "We're lucky we got the whole thing," he said. "Freddy said the jaw bones were scattered away a bit. Kind of expect that sort of thing with rodents doing their work." He reached across and touched the skull fracture as Estelle turned the skull. "That's the bullet hole that Officer Posey was talking about. He found the slug wedged into the heavy bone right here," and he touched the skull just behind and below the left eye socket. "A lucky shot. Jackass who did that was lucky he wasn't mauled to death."

"An old cat." Estelle touched a worn and broken canine tooth.

"That's my guess. I told Freddy that it'd be amazing to have the whole skeleton. Rearticulate it and get it mounted properly. Wouldn't that be something?"

"Yes, it would."

"You've talked to him? To Freddy?"

Estelle handed the skull back to Underwood. "Freddy Romero was killed on Thursday, sir."

The teacher started backward as if Estelle had slapped him, and for a second she thought the skull might crash to the floor. But Underwood took his time putting the skull back in the cabinet, closed and locked the door, and then stepped to one side, leaning his weight against a heavy lab table.

"How?"

"He was killed in an accident with his four-wheeler, sir."

"Oh, you've got to be kidding," he whispered. "Where was this?"

"Out in the ranch country southwest of here. Near the Torrance ranch."

"Good God. Thursday, you say?"

"We think so. An associate and I found him yesterday morning."

"Jesus."

"Mr. Underwood, when Freddy brought this skull in to show you, where did he say that he found it?"

Underwood frowned. "That wasn't altogether clear, Sheriff. But he said that it was a cave up above Borracho Springs. He didn't say exactly where."

"He said 'cave' specifically?"

Underwood nodded. "Although I didn't think the rock formations up in those hills lent themselves to serious cave formations. Maybe just an overhang, you know. I was going to talk to Freddy about that." His distress was obvious. "I was going to."

"I'd like our department photographer to take a series of the skull," Estelle said. "Sooner rather than later. If she comes over this morning, will you break away from practice for a few minutes? It's important."

"Of course, Sheriff. Sure. Anything you need. Anything at all." He looked askance at Estelle. "Is this somehow going further than just a relic picked up in the boonies by a curious kid?"

"We don't know yet, sir. We just don't know."

"Freddy was…we all liked him."

"I understand that. He was my neighbor, Mr. Underwood. I've known him and Butch since they were little tykes."

He shook his head sadly. "He was back up at the cave? Is that what he was doing?"

"It appears not."

"Huh. And Butch? Now I heard from some of the kids that Butch got hurt, too. They got things mixed up, then? They meant Freddy?"

"No. Butch was playing with a rattlesnake. He and my oldest son. He got a piece of fang stabbed in his eye."

"Oh, shit. How…"

"An electric string trimmer." She spun one finger in the air. "An envenomed fragment pegged him in the eye."

Underwood cringed. "Jesus, how do kids do it," he said. "And this all happened before the accident with his brother?"

"Yes."

"My God. Freddy wasn't with him, then?"

"It appears that Freddy was out on his four-wheeler at the time." *Lying dead at the bottom of an arroyo,* Estelle amended to herself. She straightened up and extended her hand. "Thanks for taking the time. Linda Real will be by in a few minutes. I know it's an awkward time for you, but it needs to be done."

"You got it. I mean, anything at all that I can do to help. The parents know?"

"Oh, yes."

Underwood hesitated. "Did someone talk with Casey Prescott?"

"I'm not sure if Mr. or Mrs. Romero called her or not. I'm headed out that way right now."

"They were close, you know."

"That's what I understand."

"Cute couple. You've talked with the boss? He's working this morning."

"My next stop," the undersheriff said. "Coach, thanks. Linda will be by in a few minutes." On the way out of the building, she called dispatch to request Linda Real's expertise at the school, then stopped by Superintendent Glenn Archer's office. She could see him through the open door of his inner office, leaning back in his massive swivel chair, Hush Puppies up on the corner of his desk.

"Well, now," he called with pleasure, and waved her inside. "What brings you here, stranger?"

The superintendent's benign, pleasant visage turned sober as she related a condensed version of the events on Friday, leaving out any mention of the discovery of the handgun. "That's the story I heard," he said. Archer turned to his computer monitor and rapped the keys for a moment, then gazed sadly at what appeared on the screen. With only 260 students K-12, Archer took pride in knowing every youngster in his school's charge. Pulling Freddy Romero's class schedule served as a reminder, apparently.

"Mrs. Bates informed me about Butch's escapades with the snake," he said. "And one of the students told me late yesterday afternoon that Freddy had been killed." He turned and regarded Estelle. "How are Tata and George?"

"Well…" and she let it go at that.

"Of course. I'll make sure I swing by there today." He gazed at the computer for another moment. "I talked to Freddy earlier in the week about that jaguar skull he found. He was as excited as I've ever seen him. You know," and he leaned back in his chair, "he was one of those youngsters who spent a lot of time and energy convincing us that he wasn't interested in much that we had to offer." He flashed a rueful smile. "But he liked Nate Underwood, and he's done wonderful work in advanced shop. Have you seen that table he built?" Estelle shook her head. "Then you should go over and look at it. He'll have it in the fall student arts and crafts show in November." He realized what he'd said, and looked pained. "Well, it *would* have been in the show."

"He said that he found the skull up above Borracho Springs."

"That's my understanding. That's what he told me."

"Did he say specifically where, sir?"

"Ah, no. I *do* know that's a hell of a climb up there, and it sort of surprised me. That four-wheeler of his was like an extension of that young man, you know. I can't imagine him parking that thing and then hiking for hours up in those rocks."

"Puzzling." Estelle stood and extended her hand to Archer. She held his firm, warm grip as he rose. "Butch is still in Albuquerque at University Hospital, sir. All this catches the folks in a real nightmare. They need to attend to Freddy, but they'll want to return to the city as soon as they can for Butch's sake."

"He's in a bad way, then."

"Very serious, Dr. Archer. Very. He's lost the sight in his right eye, and last I talked with the physicians, they weren't sure of possible brain damage."

"My God."

"If there's anything you can arrange for them, it would be appreciated. Even someone to drive them…they're distraught and exhausted. I hate to think of them on the interstate."

"Let me get right on that. Oh…and by the way, while I have you here. David Veltri emailed me a while ago, asking if it was all right to use my name as a reference for your department. He's applying, I suppose you already know that."

"Yes, sir. I was working on his application yesterday."

"He'd be a good one. I'm behind him a hundred and ten percent."

"He has strong references, that's for sure." She accepted another handshake from Archer as he escorted her to the door.

"I'll see what I can do for the Romeros. Maybe Jim Bergin can fly them up. The service clubs are usually more than eager to help with something like that."

Estelle nodded. "Anything at all. They need a hand right now." Archer walked her to the foyer, and Estelle saw Linda Real's red Honda pull to the curb in the bus zone.

"You can run, but you can't hide," Archer quipped.

"She's going to do a profile of the skull," Estelle replied. "I need to go out and tell Mr. Underwood that she's here."

"Oh, you don't need to drag him away from practice," the superintendent said, and hauled out his own impressive, clanking ring of keys. "He's out on the field. Let me get you all started."

Lugging a large camera bag, Linda greeted them with her usual sunny smile. "Superintendent Archer," she said. "Estelle, Sergeant Mears wanted you to give him a call when you're clear. What do you have for me here?"

"Mr. Archer is going to take you down to Nate Underwood's room so you can do a profile of the jaguar skull," Estelle said.

"Cool beans. Everything?"

"Absolutely. Over, under, around, and through. Three-sixty." She tapped her own right orbit with an index finger. "And special attention to any damage or signs of injury."

"Ten four." Linda flashed Dr. Archer a brilliant smile. "I'm with ya, sir."

Estelle waited until she was in her vehicle before dialing Sgt. Tom Mears' cell. He picked up on the fifth ring.

"Did I catch you in the middle of something?" she asked.

"Hey," Mears replied. "No, I'm just cleaning up my mess here. Look, Bobby and I ran a preliminary, and we're both completely certain that the Smith and Wesson 4026 that Romero had in his possession fired the bullet into the cat's brain."

"*Ay.*"

"Interesting stuff. I'm packaging things to send off to the FBI, but right now, that's the way it looks. Absolutely characteristic. Be nice if we had the fired shell casing to do a primer indent and breech-face match, but even without it, I'm sure of a match. So is Bobby. You'll want to take a look at what we have when you get back."

"That may be an hour or two. I have another stop I need to make this afternoon."

"It'll be interesting to know if Freddy found anything else out there," Mears said.

"First we need to know where the 'out there' is."

Chapter Fourteen

Just beyond Moore, Estelle turned onto the Prescott ranch road, a two-track deeply cut in spots with a steep plunge across Salinas Arroyo. Once up and out of the arroyo, the road wound across a mile of open prairie dotted with complacent cattle who stood in ragged groups, waiting for a pickup truck to arrive with feed supplements. Two windmills each pumped a trickle of water into battered stock tanks.

The undersheriff drove slowly, letting the bouquet of the prairie waft through the truck. As the fat tires disturbed the stands of bunch grass, grasshoppers clattered off, some flying only far enough to thump onto the hood or windshield.

The road to Gus Prescott's ranch passed through country that was hardly conducive to an active social life. The ranch wasn't the sort of place where people casually stopped by for a chat. Perhaps, Estelle thought, that was the sort of solitude that Gus Prescott didn't handle so well. She knew that he spent long hours at the Broken Spur Saloon eighteen miles down the highway.

Casey Prescott, the youngest daughter, drove herself to school each day in an older model Volkswagen rather than parking out by the state highway bus stop.

Estelle wasn't sure what Casey Prescott could tell her about the events of the past week, but she was certain that the two teenagers had talked on a daily basis—that's what kids with cell phones and text messaging and Twitter and *stuff* just did, whether or not they had anything to say. And she couldn't imagine Freddy being so tight lipped that he wouldn't brag about his discoveries to his *amor.*

As the Expedition juddered across a cattleguard a quarter mile from the Prescotts' double-wide mobile home, three dogs bounded out from under the front porch, taking the shortest beeline through the bunch grass and cacti to intercept the visitor. When they reached her vehicle, one that might be a yellow lab cross jogged point, staying just ahead of the front bumper. A large mostly shepherd loped beside the driver's door while the third, a wild-eyed heeler pup, tried to spin in ecstatic circles while she dodged through the vegetation along the lane.

Casey's older model Volkswagen was parked in the shade of one of the elms, beside a battered SUV. Once through the gate, all three dogs sprinted ahead, tails thrashing, ready to play should the new arrival be willing.

Jewel Prescott opened the screen door and stepped out onto the small front porch. A heavy woman, she moved as if her legs were turning to wood. She whistled once, a shrill, commanding note that stopped two of the dogs in their tracks. The youngest continued to dance, but an additional command brought her into line with the others. They waited near the front step with tongues lolling.

"They won't bother you," Jewell called as Estelle got out of the county car.

"They're eager to play," Estelle replied, and the dogs all quivered, feet jittering. As she passed them, the oldest dog stretched his nose out, catching scent. Apparently satisfied, he turned and trotted off toward an aluminum water dish by the corner of the porch, followed by the other two.

Estelle extended her hand. The woman's grip was firm and moist. "It's good to see you again, Mrs. Prescott," the undersheriff said. "I'd like to speak with Casey if she's home."

"Oh, my," Jewell Prescott whispered. "Isn't this just an awful thing, though? That Freddy…" Her broad face crinkled into a painful grimace that nearly buried her eyes. As if the wooden legs were giving out, she reached for the back of an aluminum lawn chair for support. "Casey-girl took one of the horses out," she said. "That's what she does when she wants to be alone. Would you like something to drink?"

"Thanks, but no…not just now." Behind Mrs. Prescott, from the depths of the house, the sound of a television set was insistent. "Will she be gone long?"

"You know, I didn't ask. I could see that she just wanted to be alone." The lawn chair creaked under her weight. "This is an awful thing, just awful. I mean, what do we tell a child when something like this happens? Just senseless." She waved a hand in frustration. "Of course, she'll be back by dark, you know. She won't ride with failing light. She knows better than that." Jewell thumped the back of the chair. "Christine's coming home this weekend. Those two will talk the whole night long, and a good thing, too." Casey's older sister, Christine, had finally broken from her long-time job as bartender at the Broken Spur to attend the state university.

Estelle looked off toward the scattering of sheds and the single large, dilapidated shop building with the corral and livestock shelters behind it. Behind those, a dozen or more abandoned vehicles were arranged in a row, some hoods up, some missing entirely, a door here or a set of wheels there scavenged.

"Does she have a favorite place to go, Mrs. Prescott?"

"It's a big country," the woman replied. "But you know, if I had to bet, I'd say over by Lewis Wells. He lived here before we did, you know, Bertrand Lewis did. That's what we've always called the mill over east of here, over by that old grove of dead elms. That's where the spring used to be. That was the first windmill he put in."

Jewell's comment reminded Estelle of Bill Gastner's passion for such connecting links with other times and places. Every spot had a history, she thought. Every patch of ground, every two-track, every foundation and windmill…places of solace when life turned ugly.

"That's one of Casey-girl's favorite places," Mrs. Prescott continued. "Now you're welcome to drive out that way. Just take the trail right behind the corral, and head east. You'll see the little stand of dead elms once you cap the rise. If she's not there, well…like I say, it's a big country." She leaned more heavily on the chair. "We're awfully proud of that girl, sheriff."

"I can understand why."

"Now don't take this wrong, but I wasn't all that thrilled with her carrying on with the Romero boy, I'll be honest with you. And I know that Gus just hates the idea. But my daughter's like this," and she thrust the flat of her hand out, cleaving the air like the bow of a boat cleaving water. "She knows where she's going and what she wants. Freddy…well, he's a wild hare, Estelle. Those big brown eyes of his melt your heart, but he's what my granny used to call 'just plain dizzy.' I'd never wish him ill. Just senseless, is what all this is. Just senseless."

"Do you recall when she was with Freddy last?"

Jewell twined two fingers together. "Like this," she said. "*All* the time. And you can imagine what a parent thinks about *that*. I keep thinking, all the time I keep thinking. If Casey-girl can just get through the next two years. She'll have scholarships, you know. One of the counselors at school predicts a full ride, they call it? To Texas A & M for engineering. Now isn't that something?"

"You must be very proud."

"Oh, more than proud. But the way she carries on with Freddy Romero…well. Like I say, you know how a parent thinks." She heaved a mighty sigh. "She's turned sixteen now, so I try to keep my mouth shut. But when I see the two of them take off on that four-wheeler of his, my heart just sinks." She managed a pained smile. "Sometimes I think that convents are wonderful inventions. But as I said, she's sixteen now, and it has to be her choice, doesn't it."

"She'll do fine," Estelle said. "I think I will drive over that way." She extended a business card to Mrs. Prescott. "If I don't cross paths with her this afternoon, will you have her call me? Right away?"

"May I tell her what this is all about?"

"I need to know when she was with Freddy last. When she was actually with him."

"At school, I would think. But who can keep track of these kids." She leaned forward a bit and the chair creaked dangerously. "What happened, actually? Will we ever know?"

"It appears that Freddy lost control of his four-wheeler and went into the arroyo off Bender's Canyon," Estelle said. "That's all we know at the moment." She could see the muscles in Jewell Prescott's jaw set.

"You know what I'm thinking, so I won't say it," Jewell said, and pushed herself erect. "You know, I don't mind Casey girl riding off by *herself.* Some would. I don't. She's got sense." And she paused for a second before saying what she had promised not to. "She could have been with Freddy in that crash, sheriff. I've told her a hundred times that she wasn't to go careening off with that boy on that machine, but I might as well be talking to thin air. But she has sense, that girl."

Keep hoping that, Estelle thought. "If you'd pass on the message for me?"

"Of course. And please, you stop by on your way out for something to drink."

The trio of dogs escorted Estelle to her vehicle, then turned back to the house. She watched them slump in the shade as she started the truck. Casey Prescott hadn't even wanted their good-natured, nonjudgmental company.

The undersheriff had driven no more than a quarter mile, the Prescott homestead still clear in the rearview mirror, when her phone chirped. For a series of rings, she considered ignoring it, but then grudgingly pulled it from her belt.

"Guzman."

"Where you at?" Sheriff Torrez asked with his usual lack of preliminaries.

"I'm looking for Casey Prescott. Her mother thinks that she rode out to Lewis Wells. I just left their place. What's up?"

"Look, I got something you need to look at when you're finished out there. We're over at the barn," Torrez said, referring to the secure Quonset hut at the county boneyard where the Sheriff's Department kept impounded vehicles.

"Is there something I should know before I talk with Casey?"

Torrez hesitated. "I'm not sure what we're lookin' at here, but for one thing, Mears found a little chunk of metal on the inside of the kid's front tire."

"Metal?"

"Brass. Sure as hell looks like it, anyway. A little fragment of brass. We'll put it under a microscope here in a few minutes. I think we still got some diggin' to do. In the meantime I'm sending Pasquale out to sit the Bender Canyon site."

For a moment, Estelle didn't respond, instead letting the front wheels jar this way and that, twisting the steering wheel under her light grip as the Expedition idled along the rough two-track.

"What are you after?" Torrez prompted.

"I want to know if Casey was with Freddy when he found the skull."

"You think she might have been?"

"I don't know. But you know how kids work. What are the odds they *weren't* together on Sunday? It was a beautiful day, perfect for exploration. Or anything else."

"Someone sayin' that's when he found it? On Sunday?"

"No. Freddy apparently didn't tell anybody exactly where… or when. He took it to Underwood on Monday. So it makes sense. Saturday or Sunday."

"Huh. Well, look…we'll be back at the office when you're done out there. Swing by."

"You got it." She switched off and dropped the phone in the well of the center console. A mile later, reaching the pinnacle of one of the prairie's undulations, she stopped the Expedition and slipped her binoculars out of the case. The late afternoon shadows shimmered as she scanned the distance. Eventually she found the windmill, its blades idle and facing west. The metal framework, with a ladder running up one side, presented a composition of geometric, harsh lines in an otherwise tawny world.

A saddled horse grazed near the water tank, cropping patches of green that were nourished by tank seepage. Estelle could make out that the animal was saddled but riderless.

The two-track meandered around rises and through swales, and each time the windmill came back into view, Estelle checked to make sure the horse hadn't wandered. At last the path turned into an expanse of laser-flat prairie, the windmill a hundred yards ahead. The horse swung its head to watch her approach, and Estelle could now see the reins leading into the shadows of the water tank.

Casey Prescott sat with her back against the tank's water-cooled galvanized steel.

Chapter Fifteen

The teenager didn't rise as the sheriff's department vehicle approached, but the horse sidestepped nervously. Estelle stopped twenty yards from the tank and palmed the mike.

"PCS, three ten."

"Three ten, go ahead."

"Three ten will be ten-six at Lewis Wells."

Dispatcher Ernie Wheeler managed to sound completely disinterested. "Ten four, three ten."

Estelle shut off the engine. Casey might have been watching her, but the wide-brimmed straw hat shaded her face. The horse shifted again, uttering one of those heavy, deep-in-the-throat *huh, huh, huh* mutters that said she was thinking hard but hadn't reached any decisions.

As the undersheriff swung out of the SUV, Casey pushed herself upright. With her lithe figure in boots, blue jeans, and a flowery blouse and her strawberry blonde hair braided into a long pony-tail flowing from under her white straw hat, the teenager looked ready for an appearance as a rodeo queen. But her face belied any festive mood. Her flawless complexion was puffy from crying, her green eyes bloodshot, her nose reddened.

"Hi." She let it go at that. Almost absent-mindedly, she reached out and stroked the mare's broad, flat forehead.

"I'm sorry to intrude," Estelle said quietly.

"That's okay. Am I in trouble?" A logical question, Estelle thought. Cops didn't drive out across miles of prairie simply to offer condolences.

"Hardly. Your mom said you might be out this way." The girl nodded but said nothing. "Casey, I am so sorry about all of this. I wish there was something I could say that would make it easier for you." The girl shrugged helplessly and turned toward the horse, butting her head gently against the horse's neck in agonized frustration. "Will you try and answer some questions for me?" Casey managed a small nod. "Did Freddy tell you what he was looking for out in the canyon?"

Casey turned away from the mare and slumped against the tank, her elbow resting on the rim. The horse's ears twitched at the sudden motion. She thought about the question for a long time before answering. "He wanted to find the rest of the skeleton. The jaguar skeleton." Her voice was small and distant.

"In the canyon?" Estelle asked.

Casey nodded.

"He told Mr. Underwood that he found the skull above Borracho Springs," the undersheriff added. "Up on the mountain. That's what the newspaper article quoted him as saying. That's not what happened?"

Casey brought both hands up and squeezed her cheeks, digging the tips of her fingers into her eyelids. "He didn't want them to know," she said. "He didn't want anyone to know."

"Know what?" Estelle asked gently.

"He said that there was more stuff in the cave. But he needed…he needed to move a couple of rocks. It was going to take a little time." The girl took a deep breath. "I *told* him that he shouldn't. Like, for one thing, it isn't on *his* property. But Freddy didn't really understand the concept of trespass." She ground a palm into her right eye.

"You two were out there on Sunday?"

Casey dug out a handkerchief and blew her nose loudly. "Yes." The tears wouldn't stop, and she gave up trying. "Yes. I wouldn't go in the cave with him." She managed a ghost of a smile. "Caves are gross."

"But *Freddy* had no problems with the spelunking?" Estelle asked. That news about her neighbor didn't surprise Estelle.

"Oh, no, he sure didn't. Once he found the cat's skull...or maybe there's more skeleton there too...he was so excited. He thought it had to be a mountain lion, and then Mr. Underwood said for sure it was a jaguar. That's really something, I guess. Everyone got even *more* excited."

"And Freddy wanted to go back."

"I'm sure he *did* go back, Sheriff."

"Did anyone see you two out there on Sunday?"

Casey nodded. "Herb came by. Mr. Torrance? Freddy was up in the rocks on the mesa, and I was waiting for him down by the four-wheeler. Mr. Torrance has a little herd out that way, and he said he'd just dropped off a couple nutrient blocks."

"That's all he said?"

"That I should be careful of snakes. Like, I needed to hear *that*. But Freddy wasn't the least bit afraid."

"Did he know that Freddy was with you? Did he see him?"

Casey hesitated. "Well, no...I guess not. I mean, *I* couldn't see him from where I was standing by the four-wheeler, so Mr. T couldn't either, I guess."

"Did you mention to him that Freddy was up in the rocks? That you'd found a cave?"

Casey shook her head. "He probably knows about it, though."

"Maybe he does. Herb didn't see the skull?"

"No. He was kinda in a hurry. He had some problem with a calf and he was going out to get some medication. He asked how my mom and dad were doing, and then he left." Tears seeped from her eyes again, and she turned to the mare, wrapping an arm over the animal's neck and burying her face in the brown pillow.

Had the horse not been there, Estelle would have enveloped the girl in a long hug, but the mare served the purpose. "Did Freddy show you anything else that he found in the cave?"

"No. I don't know what else he found, if anything. Or what else he *thought* was there. He didn't tell me. Maybe it was nothing. But he was excited about the skull. He wanted to make sure that he carried it back without breaking it up any more than it already was."

"Did he actually say that he wanted to return to the site?"

"No. He didn't say. But I figured out that he would. I mean, why else would he make up that story about Borracho Springs? That's what I decided. There was something there, and he didn't want anyone else knowing."

"Not even you."

That brought a grimace and more tears, and Casey Prescott shrugged helplessly.

"Would you have gone back out there with him?"

Casey shook her head. She patted the mare's neck. "He skips school. I won't. And I didn't want to ride on the four-wheeler any more. Not double, anyway. And that's what Freddy was always pestering me to do." The tears flooded out despite her best efforts. "I mean, I drive one all the time around here when we're working, but I don't like 'em much. And riding double is *really* uncomfortable. Freddy, I mean...he won't..." Her face crumpled up again, and she fought for composure. "Always so fast. I mean, that's fun sometimes, but not hanging on to the back." She looked at Estelle. "I wanted Freddy to ride horseback with me, but he's afraid of horses...can you believe that?"

"Hard to imagine."

"Well, it's true. Go figure." Casey blew her nose on a bright blue handkerchief.

"Freddy liked horsepower, but more than one, maybe," Estelle said. "My two little boys worshiped him. There were plenty of opportunities for Carlos or Francisco to ride double with him or his little brother on all manner of crazy machines, but their mean old mom wouldn't let them."

Casey bit her lip and wadded her handkerchief against her eyes. "Will Butch be all right?" Her lips quivered. "Mr. Romero said Butch was in a bad way, but he couldn't talk about it on the phone."

"It is bad. He'll lose the eye, maybe with other complications. It's a bad time for them."

"I like Tata."

"She's a good person."

"She doesn't deserve any of this."

"We don't always get what we deserve." She reached out and stroked the mare's velvety nose. "Will you show me the cave, Casey?"

"If I have to."

"I'm not asking you to go *into* it," Estelle said. "Just where it is." She glanced at her watch. "Would you take me there now?"

"We won't see where Freddy… "

"No. We won't go that way."

"Did Freddy do something wrong? I mean when he took the skull?"

"It just doesn't matter, Casey. Technically, it's like taking an eagle carcass that you might find, maybe so you could use the feathers. Or even picking up an elk skull with rack. But his retrieving the skull is not the issue."

With the handkerchief crumpled into a ball and held over her nose, Casey regarded the undersheriff. "What *is* the issue? Did Freddy do something else?"

"Whenever there's an accident, we try to find out all the answers," Estelle said, and she could see that Casey caught the evasion. "Can I meet you back at the house, then?"

Casey nodded. "Flory doesn't want to go up into all those rocks, do you, lady." The horse muttered another *huh, huh, huh.* "She was bitten by a snake last year right here on her pastern." She bent and stroked a hand down the mare's left leg, stopping near a bald spot on the hide above the hoof. "She gets skittish sometimes."

Estelle stepped back as the girl swung effortlessly into the saddle. "I take short cuts." Casey managed a full smile. "I'll let mom know." With no apparent movement of the reins, the horse wheeled and charged off past the Expedition, following the two-track for only fifty yards or so before veering off through the scrub.

Back at the truck, Estelle thumbed the cell phone, and it rang half a dozen times before Sheriff Robert Torrez picked up.

"Bobby, I'm out here with Casey Prescott. It looks as if Freddy Romero made up the story about the cat's skull. He didn't find it above Borracho Springs at all."

"Imagine that," Torrez muttered. "I said there weren't no caves up there."

"Casey is taking me to the spot, but it's over near the canyon, not far from where he crashed."

"Pasquale's out there now," the sheriff said. "Does she know why Freddy lied?"

"No, she said she doesn't, and I believe her. Other than that maybe there's something more to the cave. That's the logical assumption. She did say that Freddy was excited about bringing out the entire skeleton. He didn't want anyone else to find his stash. That would be enough for him to play it clever."

"You ask her about the gun?"

"No. I wanted to wait a bit on that. Until we found out a little more about what she knows."

"Just as well. We're still over at the garage. Got interesting stuff going on. Mears is dead-on sure that we have a bullet fragment."

"A fragment..."

"In the tire. Left front. And there's a little scuff on the fender panel. Looks like it lines up."

"*Ay,*" Estelle breathed. "The fragment was enough to make the tire go flat right away?"

"No way of tellin'."

"So it might have been from some other time. Something that didn't cause a flat, at least not right away. Maybe Freddy got careless with his own rifle."

"Nope. Twenty-two slugs are lead. This is brass. Mears is goin' over the tire inch by inch. We'll see."

So many possibilities, Estelle thought. A well-placed shot and a suddenly exploded tire, sending the four-wheeler into the rocks. A sudden startle by the rider, maybe when he saw someone or something in the two-track just as he crested the hill, sending the ATV slightly off course to graze the rocks. The way Freddy rode, pell-mell and airborne half the time, any slight distraction could lead to a disaster. And just as easily, the fragment might have been picked up by the tire in normal running—a scrap of something in the roadway, then carried for miles before the tire went flat.

"You be careful out there." Torrez didn't need to remind her that some possibilities were uglier than others.

Chapter Sixteen

Rather than driving from the Prescott's back out to the state highway and then heading south to the Broken Spur and that access to the back country, Estelle took a rough two-track north from the ranch, intersecting the oldest patch of pavement in the county, State 17. Ten miles west, across a dilapidated cattle guard, they turned onto the northernmost terminus of Bender's Canyon Trail, and for at least two miles, the two-track was relatively smooth, cutting through a few hundred thousand acres of state-owned prairie. They reached the intersection that took them to Miles Waddell's gate north of the mesa and turned east.

More than once, Estelle saw Casey Prescott lean forward in her seat. They plunged into deep shade on the east side of the mesa's flank.

"Just up there." The girl gestured and Estelle slowed the SUV. "We parked right under that big old juniper there." Estelle recognized the spot where she and Bill Gastner had paused earlier.

"This is where we were on Sunday," Casey said. "We hiked up the mesa a ways."

"Tell me something." Estelle opened the door. "What was the attraction here in the first place?"

Casey bit her lower lip. "Freddy was talking to a friend at school about the canyon? That there were a lot of fossils in that area just south of the window where the bottom of the arroyo is washed clean down to bedrock?" She nodded at the memory. "He'd been pestering me to go with him, so," and she shrugged. "I did. We took a picnic lunch and made a day of it." She blushed. "I know…my mother told me that I wasn't to ride with Freddy on the four-wheeler. But she and my dad went into town, and the weather was perfect and I thought…"

"What did you think?" Estelle prompted gently.

"Freddy was talking about not bothering to finish the year, you know. At school? He'd had a job offer down in Deming and was thinking of just getting it on. Soooooo stupid, Sheriff. I mean, just one year to graduation, and he's going to drop out? That made me so mad."

"So you hoped to talk some sense into him?"

"Yes."

"Freddy drove out to the ranch to pick you up?"

"Yes. In that awful old truck of his. The oil fumes make me sick."

"And you parked it where?"

"Over on the trail just off the county road. We drove into Bender's just a little ways and unloaded so we could ride up the canyon road." Her expression ran the gamut from vexation to sadness. "Way too fast. We rode up to the spot where the fossils were supposed to be, and poked around for a while. Freddy got impatient, which doesn't take much."

"So you left that spot and rode here. What prompted stopping and then climbing up the mesa?"

Casey hesitated, the memory obviously painful. Her hands wadded the handkerchief, and she showed no inclination to open the door. "I got mad at him." She shook her head. "You know, it *could* be really nice out here, just putting along and enjoying the ride. But Freddy always has to career along like he's trying to win a race."

"So you yelled at him to stop."

"Sort of. He ran through a bunch of ruts, and I cracked my elbow on that stupid plywood tool box he has strapped to the back of the ATV. He laughed, and I punched him and told him to stop." She pointed at the juniper. "We pulled up under the tree there."

Estelle stepped out into the center of the two-track and looked up the steep slope of the mesa. The approach to the rim was a rugged jumble, with no single attractive feature that called out, "Climb me."

"Where did he go, exactly?" Estelle asked.

"The first thing he wanted to do was run all the way up to the top," Casey said. "I told him he was crazy…it'd be after dark by the time we got back down. And we had all this food and stuff that he bought at the Handi-way. We're like really going to lug all that up the mesa? I don't think so. So he charges up saying that if we climb up just a little ways, we could see the ranch."

"The ranch," Estelle said. "Yours, you mean?"

"Sure. And I'm really excited about that," Casey said dryly. "I mean, duh? I *live* there. I don't need to see it from half way up this mesa." The mesa's shade was now comfortable, and Estelle beckoned.

"Show me where he went. Will you do that?"

Casey pointed off to the left, where a rim boulder had tumbled for a few feet and then perched, overhanging the slope like a two-story house that had slid off its foundation. "He wanted to see if he could climb that. Maybe up the back."

"¡*Caramba!*" Estelle breathed. "Interesting," she said. "Boys seem to need to *climb* things. That's where he found the skull?"

"If you want to climb up there, I'll show you." It didn't look particularly far, perhaps a hundred yards. But by the time Estelle placed the flat of her hand on the wall of the boulder, feeling its rough warmth, she was breathing hard. "This is where I stopped." Casey was not the least bit winded. She took another couple of steps and pointed behind the boulder. "Right there. Freddy went around the back there, and he hollered at me that he could feel this gush of cold air coming out of the rocks."

Estelle followed the girl with caution, seeing altogether too many convenient flat surfaces for reptiles to coil, enjoying the residual warmth from the rocks.

The house-sized boulder could have tumbled from higher on the rim anytime in the past millennium. Stunted trees tried for purchase here and there on the slope behind the wall of rock, shaded both morning and afternoon. Estelle could see the scuff of tracks, and saw the way several rock outcroppings formed a mild overhang. The floor under the overhang was mounded with debris, the efforts of a diligent packrat.

"That's where the skull was. See, right there?" Casey knelt and pointed up under the overhang. Estelle crouched beside her. From where she crouched to the back of the overhang was perhaps six feet, and the packrat had made the most of it. The undersheriff saw bones here and there, but nothing that she would immediately have identified as a cat. She shifted a bit, edging closer to the packrat's nest, wary about dark corners.

By the time she'd moved so that her head was just under the upper portion of the overhang, she could feel the flow of cool air from her left. Bending still further, letting the air flow touch her face, she turned and saw the black slit of an opening, a roughly elliptical mouth no more than eighteen inches high at its extreme, tapering at the corners. Rocks had been tumbled to one side, perhaps by Freddy as he explored.

"You're kidding." Estelle spoke more to herself than to Casey.

"Oh, he had to explore *that*. He was all excited about the air coming out. I told him that he was crazy."

"He couldn't possibly see a thing."

"Well, he kept chucking little rocks into it, figuring if there was a snake there, it'd rattle."

"By then he'd already recovered the skull, though?"

"Yes. It was lying toward the back of the packrat's nest."

"You'd have to squirm in on your stomach to explore that hole," Estelle said.

"Not me."

"But Freddy did?"

"Of course. 'Cause he's Freddy." Casey leaned against the house-rock, eyes closed, tears brimming again.

"How could he see?"

"He had his lighter. He turned it up like a torch. I told him that if he got caught in there somehow, *I* wasn't going to be the one to pull him out. He'd just have to stay stuck until I could find help. But he didn't go very far. He moved a couple of rocks, and then said something about needing a pry bar."

"Delightful. Is that when you went back to the ATV?"

"No. Freddy crawled in a little ways on his tummy. Not very far. I was kneeling right about where you are now, and I could hear him breathing. Then he said, 'Whoa!' real excited. And I said, 'what?' and he said there were *bats* roosting in there. He could see 'em up on the ceiling."

"Bats," Estelle grimaced. "Well, why not."

"And I could imagine him crawling through all kinds of guano, and coming down with hantavirus or whatever. I mean, just the sort of place I'd want to be. I told him that the skull was really neat, and that we needed to take care of it. That's when he backed out of the cave and ran back down to the four-wheeler to get one of the old towels that he had folded up in the tool box." She wiped her eyes again. "I mean, it's an amazing skull. You've seen it?"

"I saw it when I talked to Mr. Underwood earlier today. It's impressive."

"He told Freddy that it was illegal to keep it—even for the *school* to keep it without getting a permit for it."

"All true. So you two had the skull, wrapped in an old towel."

"Freddy wanted to go home and get one of his dad's big shop lights—he said it's one of those big battery-powered floods on one of those little tripods?"

"A simple flashlight wouldn't do?"

"Well, that's Freddy," and she flinched as if the name was a knife twisting in her heart.

"But he didn't come back right away, then?"

"No. He packed the skull as carefully as he could, and he kept talking about the rest of the skeleton. I told him that he should take the skull in to show Mr. Underwood... I mean, he's really up on things like that. And then there might be a proper way to collect the rest of the skeleton, instead of just jumbling it all in a big mess. You know, like an archeological dig, or something? Freddy didn't want to take time to do all that, but I told him that it was too important to ruin." She shrugged. "I don't know why. I mean right then we both thought it was just a mountain lion. But even a mounted *lion* skeleton would be a fun project, don't you think? I mean, there are lots of those old musty stuffed lions around, but not an articulated skeleton. That's what Mr. Underwood talked about."

"It would be neat. So Freddy agreed to that?"

"Sort of. He didn't want to, but I can be fairly persuasive." Her pained smile came at considerable price, Estelle guessed. "When I told him there was probably even a right way and a wrong way to clean the skull so it wasn't ruined, he understood that. So that's what we did. We packed it up as best we could, we had our lunch back down in the shade in Bender's Canyon where the fossils were supposed to be, and then…just kinda hung out."

"But Freddy *did* come back out by himself. And he brought a flashlight with him." Estelle pointed at the opening. "Rocks have been moved recently. Freddy might have done that?"

"I don't know. If he did, he didn't tell me. I know he talked to Mr. Underwood a *lot* on Tuesday morning. And then we went to the bio room during lunch, even, and Mr. Underwood showed us what he'd found out…that it was for sure a jaguar, not a mountain lion. There was still a little cape of fur left on the back of the skull, right where it would join the neck?"

"Had he called the Fish and Wildlife Service at that time?"

"No. He was going to, that afternoon. He wanted to know if Freddy would agree to talk with the newspaper, and Freddy thought that was sort of neat. They did that after school on Tuesday. Mr. Dayan came over."

"You're sure all of this was on Tuesday?"

"Yes. And this past week, I was buried in work, so I got Freddy to agree to come back here on the weekend…I mean, like *now?* I said I'd go with him and help…whatever he needed."

"And he agreed to that."

Casey nodded. "So much for promises."

"As far as you know, he didn't tell anyone else about this location? He stuck with the Borracho Canyon story?"

"Yes. I told him that I thought that was silly. I mean, who's going to find this spot, anyway? But he said just to let it be. He knew what he was doing. Oh, sure."

"You were both in school Tuesday and Wednesday, but you didn't see him on Thursday?"

"No. I don't know where he was…I mean," and she gulped, "I *didn't* know. His stupid phone was broken, so I didn't reach him. And then I tried to call his house Thursday night, and nobody answered. I didn't know about the deal with Butchie until yesterday in school. So I thought that Freddy probably was with his family up in Albuquerque." She thumped the boulder with her fist. "And all that time, he was out here somewhere, so hurt…"

Estelle squeezed Casey's shoulder. She thought about her conversation with Bobby Torrez. If something, or someone, had been responsible for Freddy's losing control of the ATV, then just as surely there *was* someone who had looked down into that arroyo after the crash…perhaps had even clambered down to the arroyo bed and approached close enough to see the aftermath of the wreck, to witness Freddy's final struggle.

Casey Prescott didn't need to be haunted by that possibility.

"I need to go back to the truck for just a moment," Estelle said. "I'll be right back. Would you like a bottle of water?"

"No, thanks. I don't think so."

Estelle nodded and hugged her again, just a one-armed caress that also said, "stay here," and then she made her way back down the slope to the truck where she threaded the case for her small digital camera onto her belt, and pulled the big Kel-lite from its boot on the far side of the center console. "I just love this," she said aloud, mocking her own impatience. But she knew exactly what Sheriff Robert Torrez's first question would be when she reported finding the little cave.

Chapter Seventeen

Walking back up the side of the mesa, Estelle came to the conclusion that she knew exactly the emotion that had driven Freddy Romero's return trip to the cave after finding the skull. Sure, there were proper ways to do this…especially for the undersheriff of Posadas County, who had access to all manner of resources, equipment, and personnel. All of that took time. And Estelle could not bring herself to wait. Just a quick look—that would be enough to satisfy her.

Casey Prescott looked at the flashlight, and wilted. "You're kidding."

"I have to see a little more than a cigarette lighter will show," Estelle said. "Trust me. I don't like caves any more than you do." She took a deep breath and dropped to her knees, regarding the narrow slit. The even flow of cool air said that this was more than a tiny irregularity, a small pocket. On the far western side of the mesa, the network of caves had attracted considerable interest, even talk of another national monument or park…at the very least, a site of spectacular interest, perhaps on a par with Lechuguilla, the huge cave system in the southeastern part of the state that rivaled some of Carlsbad's branches. It was conceivable that this could be more of the same. That would be enough to take anyone's breath away.

What had caused the overhang that now housed the happy packrat was anyone's guess. Perhaps decades ago, someone had dug a small exploratory pit, then given up. When the house-sized boulder had crashed down from above, loose rocks could have skidded away, causing the overhang.

"When Freddy crawled in here, how far did he go?"

"Oh, not far. Just his shoulders. I had one hand on his left foot the whole time," Casey said, and Estelle laughed.

"I won't go even that far." She adjusted the hardware on her belt around to the small of her back, and then handed first her jacket and then the small two-way radio to Casey. "Maybe you'd hold this so it doesn't get all grunged up." A broken juniper limb, with a wand of dried needles on the end, made a fair probe, and Estelle carefully swept the cave entrance, not hard enough to disturb the dust, but enough to annoy any critters into announcing themselves. Loose rocks, most the size of a basketball, plugged the cave opening—perhaps Freddy's work. It wasn't the neat work of a stonemason, just a quick effort at camouflage. One at a time, Estelle moved the jumble, at the same time watching fragments that hung down from the ceiling. Finally satisfied, she grasped the light and found that in the widest portion of the slit, she could work her way forward on her elbows and toes.

The light revealed a fairly smooth ceiling, dotted here and there with tiny brown bodies. One of the bats yawned, showing needle teeth. "Yes, there are bats," she said.

"Oh, boy."

"Okay," she said, and inched forward a bit, cranking the light around to illuminate the jumble of rocks that arched around her. The silence and cool air could have been refreshing under other circumstances, like when strolling through Carlsbad Caverns on a nice walkway with a printed tour booklet in hand.

By shifting a football-sized rock, she could inch forward a bit more. By the time her belly rested in the cave's entrance, she could see that the ceiling was studded with a vast puzzle of interlocking rocks, some poised for the slightest jar or tremor or bump of a shoulder. Several that had fallen littered the floor of the cave.

Estelle wiggled another foot forward and stopped. The beam of the flashlight was harsh, and several of the little brown bats were fretful, one of them fluttering to a new perch.

Off to the left, a fragment of metal winked, and Estelle juggled the light to free one hand. Slipping her ball-point pen from her breast pocket, she deftly hooked the artifact, a heavy brass buckle with the remnants of a leather belt still attached.

"Hello," she said.

"That's probably far enough," Casey responded.

"Did Freddy ever mention anything other than the cat's skeleton?" Estelle's voice sounded amplified by the chamber, small as it was. "Anything at all?"

"No. He wanted the rest of the skeleton."

"But that's out with the main packrat's nest," the undersheriff said. *And cats don't wear belts.* Loath to move the buckle, she shifted the light and saw that the brown patch of rotting hide was in fact dust-covered black. Ever so gently, she slipped the pen under one edge and lifted. She had no trouble recognizing the object, especially since there was one almost identical to it strapped to her own waist.

For a long moment she held the pen so that the holster was elevated. It was no longer attached to the belt. Although the rats and mice and who knew what other sets of teeth had chewed the leather to bits, enough was left to judge shape and size. It was a perfect fit for a heavy-framed automatic.

Chapter Eighteen

Estelle squirmed backward from the cave. Her tan trousers and white blouse shed billows of dust and debris as she brushed herself off. She took the jacket from Casey and spread it on a nearby rock, along with the radio.

"This is where we have to change strategies a little bit," she said, and watched the puzzled expression on Casey's face. "Freddy never said anything about any artifact *other* than the cat skeleton. Is that right?"

"Not to me. I don't know what he told Mr. Underwood."

"There was no mention in the newspaper article, either." Estelle stepped closer to the girl, locking eyes. "Freddy had a handgun with him when we found him," she said. "Its condition leads me to believe that he might have found it in this cave. He had it wrapped carefully in a cloth in his carrier. It wasn't packed as if it was just something he habitually carried with him."

"I…I don't know about that. He had that little rifle, that's all I know."

"You didn't see him bring it out of the cave on Sunday… along with the skull?"

"No. Nothing like that."

"And later in the week sometime…he didn't mention the handgun to you? Or that he'd found one?"

"No, ma'am. He didn't. Who would it belong to?"

"That's a question, isn't it." Estelle looked first at her watch, and then the sky. Going on three o'clock, the sun was well past the edge of the mesa, and the shade around them was cool. "I need to get you home, Casey, but it's going to take a few minutes."

"Oh, there's no hurry."

"That's good. First, I need you to call your mom and dad and let them know that you're still with me, and that it'll be at least an hour or two. I don't want them to worry. As soon as I can round up a deputy to sit this site, I'll drive you home. But we can't leave it unprotected." Casey didn't question that, and they made their way down to the SUV, where Estelle waited while Casey called her mother. The conversation didn't last long, and after a quiet conversation and then three or four "yes, ma'ams," Casey closed the telephone.

"My sister Christine just got home from Cruces," she said. "She hopes you'll have time to stop by."

"I look forward to seeing her," Estelle said. She thumbed several digits into her own phone and Deputy Tom Pasquale answered promptly.

"*Tomás,* where are you now?"

"Workin' my way up the canyon road. Sheriff told me to park it by the old homestead, and I think I'm just about there."

"Stay on the west side of that," she said. "There are tracks near the cabin foundation that I don't want disturbed."

"Ten four. I'm there now and there's nothin' going on. Well wait, I got one coyote across the arroyo, about six hundred yards out. And he doesn't look too interested."

Estelle laughed. "I need you right where you are. I don't want anybody disturbing that scene. Not the canyon road or the arroyo. And there's some evidence down this way that needs to be protected until morning." Her curiosity about the cave was a powerful attraction, and the dark depths of that formation were independent of the day and night above ground. A generator and lights would be necessary in the cave, but whatever was there to be discovered had been lying there in the dust and bat guano for years—it could all wait until morning, when logistics became exponentially easier.

"Tony's lookin' for something to do. He was at the office earlier," Pasquale said.

"I'll tell him you suggested it." As Estelle redialed the phone, she watched Casey Prescott. The young woman paced head down in front of the Expedition, hands in the back pockets of her jeans, idly kicking a pebble out of the ruts. Circuits clicked and then Dispatcher Ernie Wheeler responded. Estelle requested a deputy at the cave location, and suggested Tony Abeyta.

"He's workin' graveyard tonight, remember," Wheeler said. Estelle could hear a voice in the background. "Jackie has the night off, but she says she can work if there's a problem."

"*Ay,*" the undersheriff said, trying to visualize the personnel assignment board that hung on the wall behind the dispatch island. "Well, Tony gets to work graveyard out here in the middle of peace and quiet," she said. "Check with him and find out for me. I need to know his ETA this location."

In less than a minute, the dispatcher came back on line. "He's on the way. He said he wants to stop by the house and change clothes. Just a few minutes."

"Ten four. Thanks, Ernie. I'll be coming in as soon as he arrives."

She folded the phone thoughtfully as she approached Casey Prescott. So much time, Estelle thought. From the moments on Monday when Freddy had showed the skull to the teacher until his death sometime on Thursday, the young man had had ample time to return to the cave. Perhaps more than one trip. There was no reason to take the four-wheeler each time, except that the machine was obviously fast and fun to ride—and much cheaper to operate than the old, jouncing pickup truck.

Estelle looked down the empty, silent two-track. At what point had Freddy Romero decided that there was enough interest in the cave to try to protect it with the cover story about Borracho Springs? Had he actually seen the handgun on his first visit, he would have recovered it. There was no way he'd leave it behind. Unless he was concerned that Casey would object, complicating his life with suggestions about what to do with the find.

"And no one else came by while you two were here, other than Herb Torrance's brief stop earlier?"

"No, ma'am."

Estelle shook her head slowly. "When you had the skull all wrapped and stashed on the ATV, did Freddy say that he was planning to come back? That he was planning to make another trip?"

"No. Earlier, he had mentioned getting some of his dad's shop lights. Or even just a decent flashlight. But no, he didn't mention it again." She gazed back up the slope. So rocky and boulder-strewn was the mesa flank that their passing had left no tracks, nothing to indicate the cave's location. And because of the lip of rock that overhung the work of the packrats, only the exhaling of cool air from the bowels of the earth would hint at the cave's location.

Such odd circumstances had tangled in this lonely place, Estelle thought—and long before Freddy Romero first felt that gush of subterranean air.

Chapter Nineteen

The tire was clamped in the spreader, the sidewalls sprung wide to expose the inner surface. Sergeant Tom Mears had chalked the tiny imperfection five centimeters above the sidewall bead. As Estelle watched, he inserted a smooth wire probe.

"The exit hole, if there is one, could have been obliterated by the impact with the rock," he said. Small-framed and fastidious, Tom Mears was one of those people for whom time stood still when he worked. When presented with a problem, he began by looking at the smallest parts, rather than the whole picture. He pushed a section of sidewall on the opposite side of the tire outward. It appeared that the rock had sliced into the sidewall just above the bead, ripping a large flap. "It's just impossible to tell."

Estelle looked again at the clear plastic evidence bag that Mears had handed her earlier. The fragment of brass was about the size of a snapped-off pencil tip—no more than half a centimeter long, and irregular in shape. Eyes concerned with seeing only a flat tire would have missed it.

"If this is from a rifle bullet…" She looked across at Sheriff Robert Torrez.

"It *is* a rifle bullet," the sheriff said as if she were somehow contradicting him. "Nothing else it could be. There's no brass in the wheel assembly or anywhere else on that ATV."

"From earlier?"

"Now, we can't be certain *yet,* but I don't think so," Mears offered. "That's not much of a hole, but it *is* a hole. It's nothing compared to what colliding with the rock did, but that's enough of a hole to let air out over time."

She turned to the ATV, now sitting on the concrete floor with a triangular jack supporting the left front suspension.

"Right here," Torrez said. He knelt and took a mechanical pencil out of his pocket, pointing at a gouge in the soft plastic margin that formed the very front of the machine's bodywork. The gouge in the colored plastic was just a touch, a faint scar that could have been caused by any number of things—a breaking tree limb, the pickup truck's tailgate, a dropped tool. Mears maneuvered the shop light closer so Estelle could look through the five inch magnifier.

"It's fresh," she said. The film of grit and grime on the rest of the fender had not been disturbed by whatever had made the mark.

"And then here." Torrez hefted the wheel. A small gouge marked the margin of the rim.

"You got the folder?" Torrez asked Mears, and the sergeant nodded. He retrieved a manila folder from the bench and handed it to Estelle. The digital photos were wonderfully clear. In the first, the wheel and damaged tire had not yet been removed from the ATV. The gouge in the plastic fender, where the fender swept over to join the bodywork, was aligned with the wheel and tire. A metal pointer aligned the scuff in the fender with the gouge in the rim and the tiny rent in the sidewall.

"How definite is this?" Estelle asked. So many things could have caused the ding in the plastic skirt. It didn't appear difficult to rotate the damaged tire until the spot on the rim and in the sidewall were approximately opposite the mark on the fender, no matter what had caused either.

"Not one hundred percent," Mears said. "Maybe a *long* way from one hundred percent. But it's possible. I don't see how the bullet could even strike the inside wall of the tire except from the front."

"Would the one shot cause an explosive flat?"

"I would guess not." Mears scratched his shoulder. "Those ATV tires aren't inflated real hard." He reached across and pushed his fist against the tread of the other front tire. Estelle could see it flex slightly. "They're stout enough that they'd actually run flat for quite a ways. What you've got going into the tire are fragments."

"If you're talkin' about an explosive blowout that would cause a swerve into the rocks, the odds are slim and none," Torrez said.

"So, then." Estelle leafed through the portfolio of photographs. She paused at a macro enlargement, shot through the stereo microscope in the downstairs darkroom in the Public Safety Building. Torrez reached past her arm with the pencil and indicated a portion of the photograph.

"That's a rifling groove," he said. "Part of one, anyway. There's no doubt in my mind about that. That's a bullet fragment. We're lookin' at part of the brass jacket."

"That won't tell us much, except that if it *is* a bullet, it's a small caliber, high-velocity job. The sort of thing that just explodes when it hits something hard."

"You got that right," Torrez said. "Something big and lumbering like a pistol bullet would just stay in one piece, more or less. And if it was a big bore, high velocity rifle, the damage would be significant to the wheel rim and the tire both."

"Could it have happened before Freddy rode out from the truck, then?"

"No." Mears looked at Torrez for affirmation.

"Nope," the sheriff said. "Unless he's so numb that he rides several miles and doesn't notice he's got a flat tire. Ain't going to happen."

"Then somebody took a shot at him," Estelle said. "By accident or intent."

"Maybe," Torrez said. "It'd be a hell of a shot to pot a tire intentionally when the target is movin' at thirty miles an hour, up, down, sideways. Just not likely. More likely the shooter was tryin' for something else."

"To hit Freddy, you mean?"

"Maybe. Could have been shooting at something else entirely."

Estelle envisioned Freddy Romero's ATV blasting along the two-track, the snarl of its marginally muffled engine carrying for a mile or more. A hunter would have heard him coming. So would a coyote. That a hunter was poised to take a shot at a varmint, and shot in such a way that suddenly the four wheeler leaped into the bullet's trajectory...

She shook her head. The country around Bender's Canyon didn't lend itself to long shots—too many scrubby trees, undulating hills, the buttress of the mesa itself. The odds were good that if someone had struck the four wheeler with a bullet, he'd meant to do it.

"Linda's going to have a long day." She rapped the folder of digital prints. "When we go out to take another look at the cave, I want her to take photos before anyone crawls in there."

"That's a trick," Torrez said.

"I know that *Freddy* crawled in at least part way, and probably more than once. There'll be marks from that. I think he found the pistol in there, maybe on a second trip. The first time, Casey held his ankle." Estelle smiled sympathetically. "She didn't want him going in at all. I don't think he could have seen much with just the flame from a cigarette lighter. That's all he had with him."

"The first time," Torrez amended.

"Exactly. When I slid in there, I had to scoot over a bit before I saw the holster and belt fragment. Freddy would have seen that too, *if* the pistol was in the holster. But I don't think it was."

"Wouldn't have been all covered with shit if it was," the sheriff added. "You didn't go farther than that?"

"No, I didn't. And I lifted the holster just far enough to identify what it was. It's still in place, and I want photos. Once we crawl in there and disturb the cave, that's it. Whatever evidence there might be will be ruined. So we need to take our time and do this right."

"Posey wants to be in on it," Torrez said. "It's their cat, after all."

"I don't blame him. We're going to need all kinds of people that we don't have. But right now, I don't care about a dead cat. I care about finding out what happened to my neighbor."

Chapter Twenty

By the time Estelle Reyes-Guzman was satisfied that she'd seen all there was to see with the four-wheeler, and then surveyed the photo array of the cat skull, finally finishing up by willing herself to review for things missed, it was nearly nine o'clock that Saturday evening. Before heading home, she phoned Bill Gastner. For a moment, she thought he might have gone out on another of his night-time recons, but on the eighth ring, he answered the phone.

"Damn, you're patient."

"Yes, sir."

"Have you gone home yet?"

"No. I'm about to." She quickly filled him in on what they had discovered. "I wanted to know if you'd found a date for the cat in my great-uncle's journals *Padrino*."

"No. But I'm gradually going blind trying," he laughed. "I've gone back to 1967 so far. Nothing yet. No *gato*, no *jaguar*."

"Interesting. We're going spelunking in the morning, if you'd care to join us."

"That's the darkness and bat-shit thing, isn't it."

"Oh, *sí*."

"You're going to actually need my help?"

"I think so."

"Well, all right then. How about you pick me up?"

"Done."

"Who buys breakfast?"

"The county will, sir."

"Fat chance. I know how this is going to go—about twelve hours out there in the sun without food. I'll buy."

By the time she reached home that night, Irma Sedillos had gone home, Teresa and the two boys were in bed, and her husband was engrossed in his office, the light from the computer screen casting weird shadows down the hallway.

She settled in the large leather chair, and waited until the physician had finished whatever thoughts were driving his fingers as they flashed over the keyboard.

"How's it coming?" she asked as he swiveled his chair around.

"Like crazy," Francis said. "You look absolutely beat."

"I am." She leaned forward with her elbows on her knees, then reached out and circled his legs with one arm as he walked around her chair, bending down to sink powerful fingers into the muscles of her neck and shoulders.

"You're one big bunch of knots," he whispered, working down the kinks. "I stopped by to talk with George and Tata for a few minutes. They've got a flood of relatives and friends at the house."

"I saw the traffic when I drove up." She sat bolt upright, eyes closed, as his fingers drove down her flanks, following the tension down to her beltline. "I spent the evening with Casey Prescott, out at the cave where they found the cat."

"How's she taking all this?"

"Well, she's struggling with it."

Her husband shifted both hands and worked on her right side, and she leaned against him. "Why did you need to do that?" he asked.

"The cave? It turns out," and she shifted her weight as he did, "that Freddy lied about where he found the cat skeleton."

"You're kidding."

"No. It's actually a spot over behind Herb Torrance's place, at the north end of the canyon. When we found Freddy, there was a handgun in the carrier of his four-wheeler. There's every reason to think it came from the cave as well."

Francis paused, and his hands moved up and encircled Estelle's skull. "Now that's bizarre."

"It is. And I have a feeling that things are going to get *más bizarro* before we're through with all this. There's evidence that someone took a shot at Freddy shortly before his crash." His hands hesitated at that, and then she groaned as he worked his thumbs in unison up the sides of her neck and over the dome of her skull. His silence was question enough. "We're not sure how that might have happened."

"I talked with Alan," he said. "He has the autopsy scheduled for tomorrow. He didn't seem to think there would be any surprises. But you said someone shot *at* him. They didn't hit their mark."

"*Nos vemos.*"

"The shot caused the crash, you think?"

"I just don't know. I can't imagine any other way." She reached up and took one of his hands in hers. "But I can't imagine *that,* either." It seemed an enormous effort to pry herself out of the chair. "Let me shed some hardware."

She unclipped the holstered pistol from her belt, along with the two-way radio, cuffs, and the leather badge holder and stashed them on an upper shelf beside the door. "What's the update on Butch? Do they know anything yet?"

"I talked with Dr. Berryman on the phone at some length this afternoon. The boy is responding to treatment as best as can be expected. They're in uncharted waters with this, I think." He hunched his shoulders, a habitual expression of *I don't know* that Estelle often saw mirrored by their oldest son, Francisco.

"Your mother asked me tonight if you'd made up your mind about Leister," he added.

"*Ay,*" she moaned. One of the brochures about Leister Musical Conservatory had been near at hand for a week now. She'd probed the school's background and reputation, talked with professors, students, and graduates…a check as thorough as if national security was involved.

The campus in Philadelphia was picturesque, the stone, ivied buildings surrounding a verdant quadrangle crisscrossed with cobblestone walkways, a scene that could have been shot at any number of eastern campuses. Her son had surprised her by discovering Leister on the internet after a recommendation from the itinerant elementary school music teacher—a woman Francisco didn't particularly like, but to whom he'd apparently listened with at least half an ear. The little boy had presented Estelle with the notion of attending Leister two weeks before, when the brochures he'd ordered arrived in the mail.

The resident school offered an interesting curriculum—a music-driven program that presented the full spectrum of traditional middle and high school courses wrapped around a core of intensive music theory, application, and performance.

Acceptance at Leister was determined by audition, and Estelle was surprised to see the claim that a full sixty percent of the 230 students were on full-ride scholarships. Apparently, the bulk of the school's funding came from massive endowments.

"I talked with Maestro Miles Cornay a day or two ago."

"You're kidding. How did you manage that?"

She wagged an eyebrow at him. "We have ways." She smiled. "No, I was going to talk to you about it, but Butch and then Irma…I got distracted. Anyway, Dr. Cornay gave Leister a shining endorsement. He said the place changed his life."

"How so?"

"That's where he discovered conducting, apparently. They encouraged him in that direction."

"And now he's principal conductor in New York," Francis said. "Not bad."

"He suggested we do nothing until we have the chance to visit. In fact, that's what all the references told me. Unequivocal recommendation, but you have to go there and look for yourself."

"Then we need to schedule that, if Francisco is serious."

"I *think* he is."

"He's been quiet about it."

"That's what makes me think he's serious," Estelle said. "I get the feeling that he's afraid we'll say no if he pesters."

"Then we need to visit for everyone's sake," her husband said. "We can't just say no…just because. And we need to do it sooner rather than later." He wrapped Estelle in his arms. "Right now, he's trying to make sense of everything that's happened yesterday. We talked for a while before he went to bed, and he told me that Carlos came out with a zinger. Carlos asked him how long Freddy had to be dead."

"*Ay,* how long," Estelle groaned. "A long, long time." She thumped her forehead against his chest. "Things can change so fast. You know, when I was holding Butch, waiting on the EMTs, his brother was already lying dead out in Bender's Canyon."

"There's nothing you could do about that," Francis said.

"I think that someone watched Freddy die, *oso*. It doesn't look as if they even went down into the arroyo to check on him. They just left him there."

"But you're not sure of that."

"No. I'm not sure. As *Padrino* is fond of observing, I have this cloud of tiny puzzle pieces swirling around my head. None of them make sense. None of them fits. All I know is that the roof has fallen in on my neighbors and there was nothing I could do about it."

Francis enveloped her in his arms again. "We can't imagine how things might have gone for Butch if you hadn't responded so quickly," he said, and Estelle patted his arm impatiently.

"Sometimes it's better to be lucky than good," she said. "I... he...was lucky despite being so *unlucky.*" She patted his arm again. "Freddy didn't even enjoy the tiniest snitch of luck." She drew away. "You ready for some sleep?"

"I'm ready to try," she replied. "Let me look in on *los hijos* first."

The boys' bedroom door was ajar, and Estelle toed it open just far enough to slip through. The two heavy bunk beds, site of such joyful carnage, pillow fights, and tent castles most of the time, were stone quiet. Carlos, who enjoyed the top bunk since his sleep patterns mimicked a hibernating bear, was a small lump under a light blanket. He didn't stir at his mother's presence, and Estelle saw that his hands were tightly clasped under his chin.

Francisco, on the other hand, was a prowler at night. He might rise half a dozen times, his mind a whirl. His soundless practice keyboard rested on the window ledge within easy reach, and Estelle knew that it wasn't unusual for the little boy to rise, pad out to the living room swathed in his favorite corduroy robe, and sit at the grand piano, fingers roaming the keys with a touch so light that the action didn't twitch.

The nine year-old didn't fight his nocturnal restlessness, and Dr. Guzman's theory was that the "wolf gene," as he called it, was inherited from the boy's late paternal grandmother, an architect who had done as much work during the night as she had the day.

Estelle knelt down beside the lower bunk.

"When is Butch coming home?" Francisco whispered.

"Soon, *hijo. Papá* says that he's going to be all right."

"Does he know about Freddy?"

"I suppose so, *hijo.* His parents would tell him." She touched his forehead, smoothing back the lock of black hair that always threatened his eyes.

He let out a long sigh. "I don't think I want to go."

"To Leister, you mean?"

He nodded.

"I think we should visit, *hijo.* So does *papá.* People can put anything they want in a brochure. You need to see it. You need to talk with people about it."

"Do you think I should go?"

She stroked his cheek. "I think we have to work hard to find just the right school, *hijo.* This is an important decision for you. For *us.*"

"Butch and Freddy were best friends," Francisco said.

"Yes, they were. And Butch is going to be grateful that you and he are friends, *hijo.* He's not going to feel very good for a long, long time."

"We can't be friends if I'm at Leister."

"Ah." The little boy's logic tugged at her heart. Time would heal, she knew, and they would be able to visit the musical academy and make a decision. But the immediate hurt needed to stop first, and she felt as if a huge scimitar was poised over their heads, waiting for an unguarded moment.

Chapter Twenty-one

The remains of a leather belt passed through the holster. In the glare of the lights, Estelle Reyes-Guzman could see that rodents, or skunks, or bored coyotes had chewed the leather, and insects had then enjoyed the moist remains. Perhaps the taste of gun oil had been a deterrent, since the holster was nearly untouched.

"Oh, joy," Linda Real whispered.

"How are you going to do this?" Estelle answered. They were huddled close together in the confines of the overhang, the flow of cool air coming from deep within the mesa through the small slit in the rocks. A few more rocks had been removed, marginally enlarging access.

"I'll try everything," the photographer said. "This might be time for the old tissue trick." The camera's flash, even set on the manufacturer's optimistic "auto" setting, was simply too powerful for the tight spaces. The bolt of light washed out the image's detail. To block it, Linda doubled a small square of clean tissue and held it over the flash, experimenting with several efforts until she had defused and muted the light to her satisfaction. She fired off a dozen photos, and each time Estelle looked away, taking the milliseconds of opportunity to survey the rest of the cave as it was illuminated by the muted flash.

In places, a coyote could walk upright once he'd squeezed through the entrance. The floor of the passage was studded with rocks, and more hung precariously from the ceiling. Great fissures extended off in all directions, but there appeared to be a central crack, a central vent, from which the air flowed.

"Okay. This is interesting." Linda reached back and moved one of the spot lights that was supported by a squat tripod no more than ten inches high. "Here I was worried about H1N1. Now I can set my sights on something more interesting, like hantavirus or rabies. Maybe a touch of distemper." She adjusted her cotton face mask and then pulled down her baseball cap a little tighter.

"Hold still a minute," Estelle said, and she could feel Linda's body tense as if she'd announced a spider or worse. The under-sheriff reached out with a pencil and touched a portion of the belt. "What's that?"

"Oh, gross," Linda replied cheerfully. "That, my friend, is a belt loop from a pair of pants. Or what's left of it. And this…" She reached out and pointed, the tip of her finger within a millimeter of a scrap of something… "looks like fabric, like some more of the trousers."

The camera blasted several more times. "You up for this?" Linda asked.

"Sure. Why not." Estelle could think of a hundred reasons why not. Her breath in the face mask kicked back hot and moist, fogging her safety glasses. Most of the bats had left in protest, but they hadn't found any other creatures who objected to their presence other than a spider or two and one energetic stink beetle. What lay deeper in the crevices, watching their progress, was anyone's guess.

"Oh, double gross," Linda said. "You see that?"

"Yes." The remains of the belt terminated in a buckle, a large brass utility buckle. Estelle could see where the end of the belt with the adjustment holes passed through the buckle, still securely attached. She touched a dust-covered hump, flicking a bit of bat or lizard guano to one side. "That would be a vertebrae."

"Oh, joy."

"Bobby?" Estelle called.

"Yep." The sheriff had settled down directly in front of the packrat's nest, and he reached out and tapped the bottom of Estelle's boot.

"I need a soft brush. There's one in my briefcase out by the entrance."

"Ten four." In a moment she felt the tap again and she reached back and secured the soft-bristled artist's brush.

"*Deep in the Egyptian tomb,*" Linda said, her voice a bass imitation of the voice-overs for movie previews, "*lay a secret covered by the dust of the ages.*" She then provided a couple bars of appropriate theme music.

With deft strokes, Estelle gently ushered layers of dust off the belt and the bones it encircled. Just beyond her hand, the floor of the crevice fell away, with stones blocking her view. "I can't really see what's what," she said, loud enough for Torrez to hear. "We have bones. The belt is still around a portion of vertebrae, but I don't know about the rest. There are some rocks in the way. If I can move a couple of them…"

"Negative that," Torrez snapped. "I'm not diggin' *you* out after everything collapses."

"It's not about to," Estelle replied, and she heard Linda whisper something to herself. "Push the light so it shines over this way a bit," she added, and the photographer did so. "I think this is as far as Freddy managed. I don't see any fresh scuffing where he would have had to have crawled. But this…" and she thumped a rock the size of a microwave oven with the heel of her hand. "Is right in the way, unless I pretend I'm a coyote."

"That rock hasn't been there for eons," Linda observed, and any tone of levity had disappeared. "Look up."

And sure enough, a football-sized rock hung above them, prevented from falling by a couple of tiny projections that had jammed against neighbors. The microwave oven had lost its grip, but the space where it had been suspended until some time recently…by geologic standards anyway…shown pale.

"Let me try something," Linda said. "Back up a little."

"You can't slide in there." The photographer was young and agile, but far from sylph-like.

"No way, *José,*" she replied cheerfully. "But the camera certainly can." She slipped back into her promo voice. "*Releasing an unspeakable evil trapped for centuries within the very bowels of the earth."*

As Estelle waited for Linda to maneuver her arms forward, she looked back toward the comfortable wash of sunlight where a fair collection of people now waited. More than once, she'd heard Game and Fish officer Doug Posey's characteristic bellow of laughter, and Bill Gastner's quiet, quirky narrative, but another voice or two she couldn't place.

"We're going to need a tarp," Estelle called. "When Linda's done, I'll pass out one item at a time, but it's going to be a while. Once we move things, that's it. The site is worthless after that."

"Roger that. We got all day," Torrez said.

Padrino called it just right, Estelle thought.

"Yowser," Linda said. "Kinda interesting."

"What's the preview show?" Estelle asked.

"Just a sec." Linda squirmed forward and Estelle reached out and slipped her fingers under the photographer's belt. She tugged just enough to let the girl know she was there.

"That's far enough."

"Well, almost, it is." Holding the bulky camera in one hand, Linda worked the spotlight and tripod a little farther, shrinking back as the heat of the bulb passed uncomfortably close to her face. For a long moment she lay quietly. Estelle could hear her measured breathing. Behind them, out in the morning sunshine, a voice rose a little and said, "Well, *damn,*" followed by a string of hushed conversation she couldn't understand.

"The air is coming from a hole that's kinda down from me? This little cave kinda ends, except for that one hole. It's about the size of a five-gallon bucket. The hole, I mean. Kinda like a chimney, so to speak. Cool beans. Wouldn't I like to be a little lizard." She laughed and added, "Not so much."

"Can you see the floor of this chamber?"

"I can't. It dives down a little, just enough to put it out of sight. If the camera's auto focus works, *it* can see. Lemme show you what I got after I try something here." The *something here* included another series of flashes, some cautious maneuvering, and a grunt or two. Estelle kept her hand locked around Linda's belt.

"Okay. Let's look." She shrank back, and the two of them pushed away from the opening. Huddled in the shade of the rocks outside the entrance, Linda fussed with the camera's controls. The Nikon's preview screen was bright and clear. The spectrum of color ranged from light to dark grays, with a twinkle here and there from minerals imbedded in the rock. Linda had managed the muted flash just right.

"Time for big screen, huh," Linda said as Estelle brought the camera closer to her face, straining to see details of the image. "Let's chip it to your laptop."

"Oh, *sí*." She turned the camera toward Linda so the photographer could see her own handiwork and pointed at the lower left area of the preview screen. "Can you shoot over here a bit more?"

"What's the caucus?" The intrusion of Bobby Torrez's voice was startling. "What do you have?"

"We have remains," Estelle said. "It appears to be a partial skeleton. But it's really hard to tell."

"You going to need Perrone?"

Linda laughed loudly. "I pronounce this guy dead, dead, dead, Bobby. And if he isn't, then we're in deep, deep *caca*."

"Someone needs to alert him that remains are coming," Estelle said. "The sooner we start the I.D. process, the better."

"You're talkin' recent?"

"I would guess any time within the last...who knows how long."

"I need to take a look."

Linda laughed again. "Mr. Cork," she whispered to Estelle.

"I ain't no bigger than the both of you," the sheriff said. "Back out of there."

"In a bit," Estelle said. "Let us take one more series." She touched the screen again. "Right over here. If you can hold the camera right up against the ceiling, looking down."

"I can do that," Linda said cheerfully. After a dozen photos, she asked for the power pack and cord, and with that supply of juice, she continued one photo after another. At eighty-seven, Linda finally sighed with satisfaction.

"I don't think there's a grain of dust that isn't recorded," she said. "And you're going to be interested in what's over to the left, way behind the rocks." She squirmed backward and presented the camera so that Estelle could see the preview screen. "Scroll backward. About number fifty or so, you'll see it."

Looking at negatives morphing out of the old-fashioned developing solution in the dark room trays was spooky enough, but for the most part that era was past. This time, the little screen's effect was disturbing enough in the dark, musty confines of the cave. The round object that the camera had recorded could be nothing else. The skull rested in a crevice, eye sockets staring down at the dust.

For a few seconds, Estelle froze, and then let out a long, slow breath. "There he is...or *she* is." The skull lay in no particular relationship to anything else in the cave. Some creature had found a bonanza here. The skeleton was scattered and pillaged, the remaining bones nothing more than little lumps of indistinct gray.

Estelle scrolled through all of the photos once more, and finished the series satisfied that Linda had documented every square centimeter of this dismal little grotto. "Freddy, what did you find," she whispered.

Chapter Twenty-two

For long enough to frustrate Sheriff Robert Torrez, Estelle studied the screen of her laptop, examining the photos downloaded from Linda Real's camera. The sheriff's *"just do it"* approach was sometimes the best strategy, but in this case, Estelle was loath to disturb the cave until everything that could be documented had been…and until she had a clear notion of how she wanted to go about the recovery process.

Little things might come back to haunt, she knew…coming back with new questions that could not be answered once the scene had been not only disturbed but eliminated.

"For one thing, the gun was *out* of the holster," she said, and Torrez made a little growling sound of impatience.

"That's quite a photo," Bill Gastner interjected. He reached out and touched part of the photo that was displayed in all its digital clarity on the laptop computer's screen. "Dust and debris on the *inside* surface of the leather, at least right there at the mouth of the rig. Even I can see that. And the gun that Freddy had wrapped up in that damn cloth was completely covered with all kinds of shit. Had it been in the holster all these years, it would have been at least a little bit protected. I can think up all kinds of theories…the guy went in to retrieve his jaguar specimen, gun in hand. Then *blam*. Either the cat swatted him silly, or he had a heart attack, or…" Gastner waved a hand. "Any number of things."

"Cat with a bullet through the brain ain't going to swat anybody," Torrez said. "So where was the gun, then? Estelle says there wasn't any disturbance of the cave farther on in. If that's true, then it don't look like Freddy crawled any farther back in than you guys just did. He found the gun, and then what? Ran out of light? He just had that one flashlight. That's all we found on his four-wheeler." He smiled at Gastner. "You think somebody havin' a heart attack would squirm *into* that cave, rather than *out?*"

"I've given up thinking," Gastner replied. "I'm just rubbernecking."

"Who was where," Estelle said. "That's the whole issue. Freddy rooted around in there a bit, and now we'll never know exactly where the gun was when he found it. We don't know the relationship of the gun to the skeleton—if there is one. That's a part of the puzzle that's been obliterated."

"I'm takin' a look," Torrez said. He thumped his heavy flashlight against his thigh, regarding the depression, the over-hang, and the jumble of rocks warily. Not only a big man, standing more than six feet four inches and weighing a solid 230, the forty-two-year-old sheriff had suffered enough misadventures to stiffen his joints.

"You want a grid?" Linda asked quickly as Estelle turned to follow Torrez.

"Yes, everything that comes out of that cave," the undersheriff replied. She reached for the laptop that Linda offered. "Numbered and recorded." She scrolled quickly through the photos, selecting an overview that had been taken with the camera held high, up against the ceiling rocks. "Grid that one."

Torrez slipped carefully into the initial crevice, taking his time as he examined the carcass of the jaguar. "Surprised there's anything left," he said to Estelle, who crouched behind him. "Weather's going to get in here some, wind, critters."

Torrez had spent more than thirty years hunting every game animal in the southwest, tramping the most remote corners of Posadas and surrounding counties. He'd even hunted desolate stretches of Mexico, and more than once, Estelle knew, had risked his own safety by doing so without permit or permission.

"You want to make a guess on how long this has been here?" she asked.

"Nope." Torrez reached out and ran his fingers down the length of one dusty leg bone, a touch of almost tender affection. "Damn shame." He turned and regarded the opening to the small cave.

"If you slide up there to your left, you'll be able to see over that hump of rock," Estelle said. She could smell the musty odor, now enhanced by the heat of the bright spotlight. Hitching hardware out of the way, Torrez slid forward on his belly. Despite his apparent impatience, Torrez moved with care, hiking himself forward on elbows and toes, his flashlight probing the harsh shadows left by the spotlight.

"Huh," he muttered, and lifted himself as high as he could, his cap and shoulders touching the ceiling. Estelle gauged the width of his shoulders against the opening. He could slide farther in, if the urge was irresistible. Whether they'd be able to pull him out was debatable.

"Let's get movin' on this," he said, and pulled back. Estelle climbed out past the packrat's nest where Linda waited, turning the laptop's screen for Estelle to see. The fine white lines overlaid the image, labeled in bright orange A through K down the left side, 1 through 10 across the top.

"*Perfecto*," Estelle said.

"Now the fun begins," Gastner quipped. "I thought maybe you were going to stuff Bobby in there and leave him."

"Not a chance," Torrez growled as he straightened up. Linda offered the computer to him, and he glanced at it without much interest.

In a moment, a blue tarp had been spread out on one of the few level spots of ground behind the huge boulder. With a roll of masking tape, Linda and Tony Abeyta made short work of the grids, zipping down strips of tape until the tarp was divided into the same one hundred squares represented in the photograph.

"You be careful in there." Torrez watched Estelle snap on a fresh pair of latex gloves. The respirator she hooked around her neck was many clicks improved over the small cloth masks that she and Linda had used earlier. The two valves stuck out on either side of her face like parts of some strange insect.

"There's a good spot for this so that I can see it," Estelle said, taking the laptop from Linda. "I'll hand whatever I find to the sheriff, and assign a number for each piece. For now, let's keep it simple. Each piece is numbered by its grid location, and then one through how many ever we end up with. As each item comes out, I want it placed on the corresponding grid on the tarp. Tony, the sheriff will hand the items to you. Just pass 'em out so Bill can bag everything with a number and grid tag. So you'll have something like A-6, number 1. And so forth."

"Got it."

"You're trusting me to count?" Gastner asked.

"You're probably the only one here who can," Torrez said.

"Linda, I want digital for *every* piece," Estelle continued. "As soon as *Padrino* places it on the tarp. *Every* piece. Every single one. Okay?"

"Absolutely."

"What we're going to end up with is a copy of what's in that cave, spread out on this tarp." She squinted up at the blank blue of the sky. "A perfect day for it. We go slow and sure. We miss nothing."

"Did you call Miles Waddell yet?" Bill Gastner asked.

"I did. Early this morning."

"Did he have any ideas?"

"None whatsoever, but he was annoyed that I wouldn't discuss this with him. He was definite about one thing, though...he wanted to make sure we had a warrant to be on his property."

"And here he is," Deputy Abeyta observed. Estelle turned and looked to the northwest. The vapor trail of dust rose behind a fancy red pickup.

"Asking for a warrant is fair enough," Gastner said. "Kinda wonder why he'd worry about it, though."

Chapter Twenty-three

The rancher was dressed for town—clean, pressed blue jeans, a white western-cut shirt with embroidered pockets flaps, and a purple scarf knotted around his neck like a 50s country western singer. He picked his way carefully up the slope, not looking up at the officers until he reached the flat by the guardian boulder.

"Morning, all," he greeted. "Sorry I'm late for the meeting." He stopped when he saw the gridded trap. "Well, how about that." He shook hands with each member of the party like a politician, adding a gallant little bow and a two handed grip for Estelle. "Is somebody going to tell me what's going on here?" His pleasant smile faded immediately and he lowered his voice as if the rocks might harbor eavesdroppers.

"Herb Torrance called to tell me about the Romero boy." He frowned. "I can't recall his first name."

"Freddy," Estelle said.

"That's the one. Gosh, just too damn bad that things like this have to happen. You know, I've seen him out and around now and then, flying low on that four-wheeler of his. Jesus, I'm surprised something hasn't happened before this." He turned and looked at Bob Torrez, eyebrows arched. "But that was down there in the canyon, wasn't it?"

"Yup."

"So what's the deal here?"

"You read the papers?" Torrez asked.

"Once in a while, I do."

"You read about the kid finding the jaguar?"

"Well, I did. Wasn't that just the damnedest thing, though. But that was over at Borracho, I thought."

"That's what we thought, too. Turns out it was right here." Torrez pointed at the rock overhang behind him with his upper lip, like a Navajo.

"Is that right?" Waddell stepped closer and peered at the packrat nest, then squatted down. "You got some lights in there," he announced. He ducked his head even more, trying to peer into the rocks. "Goes on a ways? I can feel the air."

"You ever crawled back in there?"

Waddell scoffed and stood up. "Not this son-of-a-bitch, no sir. Gives me the heebie-jeebies to be underground. I'm no spelunker." He stretched out each syllable as if knowing the word impressed him. "So tell me something. You got one, two, three, four people here, and I saw Doug Posey down on the two-track a ways back. What's the deal? All this just to recover some more bones, or what?"

"That's just about exactly the size of it," the sheriff said.

"Your tax dollars at work, Miles," Gastner quipped.

"Did you know this was here, sir?" Estelle asked.

Waddell shook his head. "You know, I got a bad knee. I'm not much for hikin' around in the boonies. I like to keep level ground under my boots. But that's interesting, you have a pretty good air flow coming out here, too. Most of this mesa is one big jumble of caves, seems like. *Somebody's* going to have a ball exploring them. You know, when we were grading that two-track up the side of the mesa, I bet we found five or six spots where air was leaking up to the surface. Kinda makes you wonder, doesn't it?"

"Indeed it does," Gastner said, but he didn't pursue the thought. "You ready?" he said to Torrez.

"'Bout an hour ago," the sheriff replied.

"You know, I was kidding about a warrant this morning," Waddell said to Estelle. "You guys want to *spelunk* all day, have at it." He hadn't sounded so cooperative on the phone, but then again, it had been early on a Sunday morning. Perhaps he hadn't had his coffee and Sunday paper yet.

"We appreciate that, sir," Estelle said. Waddell glanced in puzzlement at the laptop computer that she carried.

"Hi-tech stuff," he said.

"We're nothing if not hi-tech," she said by way of explanation.

"I'll just stay on out of the way," the rancher said. As he backed up, he almost stepped on the gridded tarp. "Now what's this for?"

"Like she said, we're hi-tech," Gastner said, a pleasant non-answer that seemed to satisfy the rancher.

"Hey, what do you think about the new digital ear tags? What, GPS located and all that?"

"It's coming, Miles. It's coming."

"What the hell are we going to do about that? All this is just getting out of hand, Bill."

As Estelle ducked into the crevice, careful not to whack the laptop on the surrounding rocks, she only half-heard Gastner's reply. Moving carefully to disturb the dust as little as possible, she slid forward, staying far to the right. She repositioned the spotlight to her left so that she could use the flat spot for the computer. In the odd light, a combination of soft darkness and harsh spotlight, the screen was bright, almost garish.

She touched the respirator to make sure it was secure, took a deep breath, and reached out for the holster—the first artifact. Removing only enough dust to see where the belt fragments might be attached, she saw that a three-inch portion was caught in the buckle, the rest gnawed off. Two trouser loops remained, one dangling by a thread. The piece of trouser fabric was crumpled, no larger than a small napkin.

"We have a couple of vertebrae caught in the belt, but nothing else," Estelle said. She could hear Torrez's breathing behind her, but he said nothing. "I don't see any sign of the pelvic bones yet." Taking a moment to orient herself to the computer, she then typed in a number. The bright yellow digits *H-3,4* appeared on the screen.

The holster and belt slipped off the vertebrae as Estelle eased them out of their place on the cave floor. They felt wispy light, all of the life long dried out of them. She repeated the numbers to Torrez, who simply held out both hands, palms up. "The three vertebrae will be the same numbers," she said.

Piece by piece, she worked her way into the cave. Bits of bone were mingled with scraps of clothing and desiccated carcass. With each discovery, she reached back and touched in the data. The grid on the computer screen became an explosion of yellow numbers, a random scatter that didn't coalesce into any recognizable pattern. After an hour, her neck and shoulders aching, she paused and gazed at the computer screen. "There's no way to tell how the body lay in here originally. We can't tell if he was curled up, flat on his belly, or what."

"He?" Torrez asked.

"That's a fifty-fifty guess," Estelle said. "Someone wearing a gun like the one Freddy found? I don't see many Annie Oakleys around Posadas County." She picked up an artifact that was easily recognizable, despite years of critter chewing. "Or that wear size twelves," she added, and passed the pathetic remains of the boot and its contents out to the sheriff. He took it without comment.

"You see the skull yet?" he asked.

"It's in the very back. I'm working that way."

"That's where the answers are."

"*Sin duda.*" Reaching the back of the chamber, even though it was only five feet across at the broadest point, was a chore for a gymnast. Unyielding geology dug into her hips and bumped her head and shoulders as she maneuvered, trying to disturb the gray dust as little as possible. Each time she moved, another small piece was revealed and she forced herself to remain patient and methodical as she worked her way in.

Finally, the gray mound that she recognized as the skull was within reach. Whether the skull had rolled thanks to gravity, or whether a resourceful coyote had played soccer with it, was impossible to tell. It had come to rest with its face against the back wall of the little cave, just inches from the air vent. A little more coyote play, and it might have tumbled into the bowels of the earth, gone forever.

None of the neck tissue remained, and as she brushed off dust, the harsh light revealed gnaw marks on the occipital mounds. Mixed now with dust and other detritus, a thin wisp of hair the size of a dime remained on a patch of skull above where the left ear had once been.

"A-nine." But she paused before passing the skull to the sheriff, considering how she might hand it backward without yielding her progress into the chamber. A large rock jutted out of the ceiling, forcing her head low.

"You got claustrophobia yet?"

"I'm close," Estelle said.

"Can't put a name with the face," Torrez said drolly as he watched her rotate the artifact. She stopped when she saw the ragged hole low on the left frontal bone, immediately over the orbit. The skull was badly fractured around the quarter-sized hole, and a half turn revealed the smaller entry fracture on the posterior surface of the parietal.

"Okay," she whispered to herself.

"This guy didn't crawl in here to die of old age," Torrez said.

"A-nine," she repeated, and managed an awkward under-handed pass to the sheriff, running her hand down along her leg.

Other voices outside the cave were muted, but the arrival of the skull prompted a rush of conversation, most of it Miles Waddell's articulate tenor.

Estelle kept her voice down. "Waddell shouldn't be here. Not now."

"Bill's keepin' him back. There ain't anything *outside* the cave anyways."

"*Nos vemos.* I'd like to see Alan out here now, though."

"You got it."

She waited for a moment, letting her pulse back off from its pounding, spiked by bad air, the dust, the confines of the rock sarcophagus, the adrenalin rush of the discovery. How much had Freddy seen?

For another hour, she combed the cave floor, sending fragments back to the sheriff. Some, like the left side of the lower jaw, were sizeable, even though the right half was missing, a treasure that some creature had grabbed as a trophy. She could imagine the coyote or skunk scuttling away with his find, maybe attracted by the wink of a gold tooth filling.

By lying flat, she could worm her way toward the rush of cool, musty air that forced its way up the chimney. A flashlight revealed only fissures where the limestone had fractured and slumped, streaks where moisture had followed those fissures, and dust—always the fine gray powder that covered every surface.

"What are you doin'?" Torrez asked. He tapped the sole of her boot.

"Thinking."

"There's more comfortable places to do it."

"*Sin duda.*" She turned her flashlight in an arc, probing the small corners where the glare of the spotlight didn't reach. She moved several rocks that lay loose, finding nothing. "I need a sifter. We need to sift whatever we can scrape up from the floor in here, and then we need to go through the packrat's nest back behind you."

That brought a moment of silence from the sheriff.

"C-six, three," she said. That fragment, probably bone, had been roughly the size of a dime, and perhaps an eighth of an inch thick—a tiny piece that her fingers, clad in the thin surgeon's gloves, had found almost by accident as her hand relaxed for a moment. "And if that's a piece of the skull, that means he was *in* this cave when he was shot."

"Or shot himself," Torrez amended.

"I would bet against that."

"Not to mention one little thing…it's hard as hell to shoot yourself in the *back* of the head. I mean, you can *do* it, but not too many folks try." He coughed gently. "Maybe it's the idea of seein' their own face explode out right in front of their eyes."

Estelle shifted and examined the ceiling with care…dust, loose rocks, stains here and there that were most likely bat guano. An earth tremor of insignificant magnitude could rearrange this place in an instant—and probably had over the years.

"It would be no small trick to push a body up in here. Close to impossible. But if the victim *willingly* crawled in, and then *pop.* Right in the head."

"Could."

"I need a sifter screen," she repeated.

"Lemme see," Torrez said. "You going to stay there, or are you comin' out?"

"I'll stay put."

Five minutes later, she glanced back over her shoulder to see the sheriff working his way back in, mask hanging down under his chin.

"Doug Posey's going to run over to Torrance's and see what he can find."

"He's going to go back past Waddell's well and take the county road?"

"I'll tell him to."

"I don't want any more traffic down through the canyon. Not until we have the chance to take a careful sweep through there."

"He knows that," Torrez said. "You need to back out of there for a while."

He tapped the sole of her right boot again.

The sun felt unusually hot and welcome as Estelle emerged out from under the overhang. Head clear of the overhanging rocks, she turned and saw Linda Real with camera poised, a wide grin on her face. Always the shutter-bug opportunist, Linda rapped off four or five exposure before Estelle could raise a hand in self-defense.

"The earth insect look," Linda said. "I love it."

Estelle removed the respirator, aware for the first time of how hard the rubber seal had been digging into her face. Her cheeks ached, but fresh, unfiltered air tasted wonderful.

Bill Gastner stood at the far end of the blue tarp, hands on his hips. He held out both hands toward the bones, as if they might suddenly reassemble themselves. "Let the fun begin, Madame Undersheriff."

Chapter Twenty-four

The packrat had been busy. His collection formed a veritable rodent mansion, a vast mess six feet across and eighteen inches high, filling a shelf under the ragged overhang of limestone, dried roots, and a scattering of plants tough enough to survive.

Tony Abeyta used a small army shovel to transfer the rodent's hard work a bit at a time into the screen shaker. Herb Torrance had found a piece of galvanized screening that had once formed the bottom of a rabbit hutch, and it had taken him no more than five minutes to build a two foot wide, four foot long frame from cast-off lumber, creating a rough version of the archeologist's site sifter.

Unable to resist the pull of curiosity, Torrance had arrived at the site a few minutes after Abeyta. He and Miles Waddell stood down in the parking lot that the wide spot in the two-track had become, smoking and talking with Bill Gastner. The retiring livestock inspector had assigned himself the task of keeping civilians out of the crime scene, and he'd retreated to the vehicles with Waddell and Torrance. The ranchers provided an interesting comparison, and Estelle saw Linda Real zoom her lens to take their portraits—Waddell slender, elegant, almost effeminate in his precise movements, while Herb Torrance looked elderly and battered, a stoop now in his bony shoulders, a bad knee that gave him a hitch, and a face lined and blotched from too much sun.

The two men watched the operation up slope with interest and a continuous cloud of cigarette smoke.

The quarter inch squares of the sifter were coarse enough that most of the rodent's collection was caught for examination. The little creature showed an affinity for strips of inner bark from juniper, no doubt a fragrant, soft lining for his bed chamber. The small, stunted acorns from scrub oak, several steel staples that had drifted loose from a barbed-wire fence post somewhere, bits of this and that—the collection was vast and aromatic, at least aromatic from the rodent's point of view.

On the eighth shovelful shook out on the sifter, Tony Abeyta said sharply, "Hold it a minute." Doug Posey and Bob Torrez had been manning the crude device, and they waited patiently while Abeyta flicked bits and pieces to one side. The metallic wink that had attracted the deputy turned out to be an irregular bit just large enough that it had jammed in the screen rather than passing through. "Linda?"

Linda Real leaned forward, focused quickly as Abeyta pointed with a pencil.

"Okay."

The deputy flicked the fragment loose.

"Part of a molar," Estelle said. She nudged the fragment into a small plastic evidence bag. "A gold cap." She glanced at the sheriff, whose face remained expressionless. Holding it up, she rotated the bag this way and that. The flavorful root of the tooth had been gnawed down, leaving the glob of gold and traces of adhesive.

The eight shovelfuls of detritus had barely dented the voluminous nest, and Abeyta resumed his excavations energetically, digging deep into the rodent's favorite stashes. Another tooth followed shortly, this one still embedded in a fragment of jawbone.

Concentrating on the screen's surface so hard that her eyes started to water, Estelle straightened at the sound of a vehicle, expecting to see Dr. Alan Perrone's BMW. Instead, two state police cruisers lurched along the two-track, the first a large SUV, followed by one of the ubiquitous black and white Crown Victorias.

"A convention," Torrez muttered.

"More help with the sifter," Estelle said cheerfully. The two vehicles parked behind Waddell's truck. In a few moments, after

a short chat with Bill Gastner and the two ranchers, State Police
Lieutenant Mark Adams reached the boulder, accompanied by
a young officer whom Estelle didn't recognize.

"Whoa," Abeyta said, and the shaker stopped. Linda's digital
camera snicked another series, and Estelle bent close, slipping
her pen into the mouth of the single shell casing. She tipped the
case upward to read the head-stamp markings.

"Forty Smith and Wesson," she said.

"So there we go." The sheriff watched her tip the casing into
another evidence bag. "Just about impossible to thumb cartridges
into a magazine without leaving a print. There are some clear
ones on the cartridges in the pistol's magazine, and they ain't
Freddy's. I'll bet on that. 'Course, with this one, by the time
the skin oils dry out, the case gets rolled and licked and kissed
by the rat and all his buddies, I wouldn't like to bet on prints."

"I'll take what we get," Estelle said. "At the moment, the
rat's our ally here." She saw Torrez smile a greeting at someone
behind her, and the undersheriff turned to see Mark Adams as he
stepped carefully around the tarp. The lieutenant said something
to his companion, who remained by the corner of the boulder.

"Sir, how's it going?" she asked.

"What in the *hell* do you guys have going on here?" Adams
said. "Hey, Linda. How's my favorite shutterbug?"

"She's fine," Linda replied. "Welcome to the party."

"This is Charlie Esquibel," the lieutenant said. "New to the
district." He half turned and made quick introductions, then
lowered his voice as his gaze swept over the scatter on the tarp.
"So. Do we know who?"

"Nope," Torrez said. "But we're *gonna* know."

"I have no doubt of that." Adams knelt on the limestone projection just to the right of the entrance. "Interesting coincidence."

"Which one?" Estelle asked.

"Fatality in the canyon sometime yesterday, and now this,
right in the same neighborhood." The state policeman looked
around at the blue tarp, where Deputy Tom Pasquale, earlier
relieved at the homestead site by Jackie Taber, had extended his

shift to help instead of going home to bed, where he belonged. "The newspaper said that the jaguar was found over by Borracho. That's not the case?"

"It was found right here." Torrez pointed at the tarp. "Those bones above the tape are all the cat."

Adams regarded the bones with a frown. "So why did the kid lie?"

"Because he found them *here*," Estelle said, "among other things. And right now, it's the other things that we're concerned with."

"Found like what?"

"We found a Smith and Wesson semi-automatic pistol in the carry-all of the boy's ATV. I'm ninety-nine percent sure it came from here."

Adams stepped closer to the tarp and leaned over, examining the dusty holster. "In that?"

"No, sir. Not when he found it. Nothing's been in that holster for a very long time. At one time, it's likely that the gun was. That's what makes sense to me."

He stood up and walked around the tarp, punching Tom Pasquale lightly on the shoulder as he stepped around him. "You stayin' out of trouble?"

"You bet, sir."

Adams knelt and gazed at the skull, tipping his head this way and that, his fingers laced together as if to prevent the impulse to reach out and touch. "Somebody put one right through his brain."

"It appears that way."

The lieutenant looked up quickly and grinned at Estelle's reticence. "Perrone's on his way. We passed him on the way out." He stood up and brushed off the knee of his black trousers. "What can I do? What do you need?"

"I think we're set, unless someone hits the bank while we're all playin' around out here," Torrez said.

Adams chuckled. "Mighty impressive 'playing,' folks. What tipped you off to this location?" He glanced down the hill toward the two ranchers.

"Freddy was here," Estelle said. "We wanted to know why."

"Ah. There's that." Adams nodded. "Tell you what, we'll keep a car central until you tell us otherwise," he said. "Is there anything from the mobile lab that you need?"

"Don't know yet, but thanks." The sheriff nodded toward the angular-featured Esquibel, who had yet to speak a single word. Fresh out of the academy, the young state policeman hadn't yet acquired the easy self-confidence enjoyed by his lieutenant.

"Not much in the way of clothing left," Adams mused. "Some little bits of shirt, maybe. Khaki trousers. Turn up a wallet?"

"Not yet," Estelle replied. "No wallet, no rings, no pocket change, no pocket knife or utility tool. One boot."

"One boot? You're shitting me. Really? This is a hell of a country to be hikin' around barefoot."

"Coyote dragged one off, more than likely," Torrez said.

The lieutenant looked down the hill at the two ranchers, both of whom had now settled on the tailgate of Herb Torrance's pickup, enjoying their conversation with Bill Gastner. "What do the neighbors have to say?"

"That's still to come," Estelle said.

"This is Waddell's land now, am I right?"

"Yes."

"Huh." Adams pointed off into the distance. A small, dark shape meandered along the two-track, driving slowly enough that it raised little dust. "Here comes the good doctor," he said. "Be interesting to hear what he has to say."

Chapter Twenty-five

Making his only concession to the remote location, Dr. Alan Perrone loosened the top button of his white shirt, pulling his tie down a bit. He talked briefly with Bill Gastner before heading up the hill, and Estelle noticed that he didn't bother with a medical bag.

He stopped halfway up to chat with Mark Adams as the two state police officers made their way back down. When he reached the little plateau behind the boulder, he stopped and held up both hands in mock impatience. "You couldn't have found a spot a little farther out from anywhere? Here I was complaining yesterday about the canyon."

"We try, sir," Estelle said. "We try."

"Well, this guy sure as hell is dead." The medical examiner thrust his hands in his pockets, his gaze flicking from one end of the tarp to another. "And that's the extent of my expertise." He knelt and reached out with his right index finger, stopping just short of one of the long bones. "Critters have been helpful." He looked up, toward the crevice in the rocks. "How deep?" He pushed himself to his feet, and as he approached the disturbed nest, the sheriff and deputy Abeyta shifted to make room. He held up a hand. "I'm not going in." He knelt again, peering into the depths of the overhang, then looked toward the cave entrance.

"I'll turn the spotlight on for you," Abeyta said, but Perrone held up his hand again.

"Nothing in there that I need to see." He twisted around and looked at Torrez. "Someone shot him and then stuffed the body in here? That's what you're saying?"

"Don't know what happened. What we're thinkin' now is that he crawled in here somehow, and *then* got himself shot." He pointed at the remains of the packrat palace. "Found a shell casing in here."

"Just one? Casing, I mean?"

"Yup."

"But the rat could have found it just about anywhere within an acre. Recover a bullet yet?"

"Not yet."

"Suicide is possible, you know," Perrone said, pushing himself to his feet. "I mean, it's unlikely, but it's *possible*." He reached around with his right hand, easily putting his index finger against the back of his own skull, and letting his thumb mimic the hammer fall.

"It's possible," Torrez agreed. "But it ain't likely."

"Well," Perrone added, "I agree with that. It ain't likely." Torrez ignored the little jab at his grammar.

"Can you estimate TOD for us?" he asked, and Perrone laughed.

"Ah, no. A *long* time ago, Bobby. That's my best take. You're not talking weeks or months with this. You're talking *years.* And in part, it's going to be deceptive, since the critters have been so active. Every beetle and his cousin has been and gone, and then the guys who like to chew just to pass the time? Well, they've had a field day, too. When we get all this packed up, I'll be in touch with Leslie Toler, up at the university. She works with the state lab, and she's the best osteologist we've got. There's so little here…it's going to be a real puzzle." He waggled his eyebrows. "You've got one advantage. Inside that boot? Some of the remaining bones? You're going to have a *lot* of available DNA. And you've got dental evidence, no doubt."

"Got to be since 1989 or '90," the sheriff said, more to himself than anyone else. Perrone frowned at him.

"Because?"

"That's when the forty Smith was developed." Torrez shrugged, looking a little uncomfortable at having to sound as if he knew something the others didn't.

"Well, that's interesting, and I wouldn't be surprised." The physician took a deep breath, stretching tall, looking out across the prairie. "Folks find such interesting spots, don't they." He turned back and looked first at Torrez and then at Estelle. "And let me know where you find the other boot," he said. "That's interesting. No coat, either? No gloves." He stepped back to the tarp and considered the scattering. After a bit, he bent down and with the eraser of his pencil lifted a small patch of fabric away from one of the vertebrae. "Shirt fabric, no undershirt. At least nothing that looks like the remains of one."

"The cotton would rot quickly," Estelle offered.

"Maybe so. Just damn odd. Between a good source of DNA and dental records, I don't think finding out who this guy is will be a big deal. Our list of missing persons is pretty short."

"Like none," Torrez said.

"Exactly." Perrone nodded at the holster. "No weapon found?"

"That's what Freddy Romero had with him on his ATV."

"*Reeeeeally.*" The physician twisted around to look back at the cave. "So that's why he was in such a fatal hurry."

"We think so. An excited kid."

"Well, then. No problem. With any luck at all, the gun will take you there. Where do you suppose he found the gun? The holster doesn't look disturbed."

"We have no idea," Estelle said, and a sweep of the hand included the entire hillside.

"Fractured femur and radius, and two crushed cervical vertebrae, by the way," Perrone said. "That's what the preliminary on the Romero boy shows. Toxicology won't be back for a while, but there's no reason to believe anything will turn up. Some cuts and bruises, but no other significant injuries—certainly nothing that I wouldn't expect from a twelve foot free-flight into the arroyo."

He nodded once more at the artifacts spread on the tarp. "You guys be careful in there. Is that one of the fire department's respirators?"

Estelle touched the device, still hanging around her neck, and nodded.

"Well, make sure you use it," Perrone said. He nodded at everyone once more and set off down the hill.

For another hour, they scoured and sifted the shelf under the overhang, and by the time they finished, the packrat had lost every scrap of his home and collection. But they had found nothing more of particular interest.

"I want to sift what's left in the cave," Estelle said, and she knew exactly why that prompted a frown of distaste from the sheriff.

"You can't do that in there," he said.

"No, but I can bring it *out*," she said. "We have a generator, and we have a shop vac."

"Take a couple hours to bring it all out here," Torrez said, but he beckoned Tony Abeyta and recited the list to him.

"Add a piece of fine screen to that," Estelle said. "Like black nylon window screen. We'll want to sift the vacuum contents when we're finished. While we're waiting, we need to figure out how we want all this collection marked and stored."

That in itself turned out to be a significant challenge, but eventually, every scrap of recovered material from the cave and the packrat's nest was carefully labeled, referenced to the photographs and the grid, and stored in a large cooler.

Torrez looked at his watch, grimaced, and then dispatched Tom Pasquale and Linda Real to raid Victor Sanchez's Broken Spur Saloon for food. "And ask Bill what he wants," he added. "He's part of this gang. If Victor won't take your county card, tell him I'll be down after a bit to settle up with him. Go out the canyon road and take care of Taber at the same time."

When the deputies had left on their various errands, Torrez found the semblance of a soft spot and relaxed back. He regarded Estelle with amusement.

"You look a wreck," he said.

"Neat and tidy, that's us," Estelle replied.

"You're lookin' for the bullet?"

"Yes. I'm not going to sweep up the dust and small stuff in there. In two minutes, we wouldn't be able to see a thing. I think the vacuum will work."

"And you think the bullet's there?"

"It *might* be. If our guy was shot when he was *in* the cave, or when he was about to crawl in, and if the path of the bullet entered right rear and exited out left front, then it could be in there."

"Rat might have got it."

"Maybe…but it wasn't in the nest."

"Go through his skull, then ricochet around in there? That's just about impossible to figure out."

"But," Estelle said, and she leaned her back against the boulder, stretching her spine. "That's a relatively low velocity bullet, no? The forty?"

"Thousand feet per second or so. For a handgun, it's hot enough."

"But after blowing through the full volume of a human's skull?"

"Once it busts out through the bone in front, it wouldn't have much poop left. I see what you're sayin'." He fell silent, his heavy black eyebrows raised in consideration. "We got the one from the cat."

"That's right. If we can find the one that killed the man, that's a link we have to have."

He nodded and raised an index finger to point down hill. Estelle pushed away from the rock to see Bill Gastner taking his time on the rocky slope. Herb Torrance had climbed back in his truck, but Miles Waddell appeared content to continue residence on the tailgate of his truck.

"Thanks for sending the troops for food," Gastner said when he was within easy earshot. "I was about to give up hope and hit up your MREs."

"Glad to do it."

"What's next? Tony said he was headed after a vacuum?"

"We need the bullet, sir. That's the only way I can think to do a thorough search. I hope you've been thinking hard."

Gastner looked surprised. "Who, me? You're kidding."

She toed the large cooler. "We need to know who this is, sir."

"I've been working on that. It's kind of tricky to do with an audience, though. Old Herb, he gets wound up, and he's hard to turn him off. I've spent the last two hours listening to a litany of every rancher's woe from both him and Miles. But I've got some ideas."

"I was hoping that you would, sir."

"Well, don't hold your breath, sweetheart. I have ideas, all right. Now the trick is to remember what the hell they were." He stood with his hands on his hips. "The first thing I'm thinking, and I don't like it one bit, is that this is empty country. A guy could kill a friend out here, and the odds of there being any witnesses are slim and none, other than the ravens and such, and they're not talking. Accidental discovery is the rule, not the exception. Someone got clever with all this, and it worked out just fine until Freddy Romero stuck his nose in this cave. I just hate to think who that someone might be. There aren't that many choices out here, and most of 'em are good friends of mine. Old friends."

Gastner gazed down the hill, and Estelle let him think without interruption. "This is Waddell's land," he said finally. "That's the obvious place to start." He flashed a quick smile at first Estelle and then Bobby Torrez. "But you guys have figured that out already."

Chapter Twenty-six

The food—enormous, sloppy burgers, heaps of French fries, six-packs of soda, all carefully packed in an ice chest—arrived and was consumed long before Deputy Tony Abeyta returned with the vacuum. It didn't take Estelle long to make a mental note to include a letter of commendation in Abeyta's personnel folder. The lawn-mower chatter of the small generator was one thing, but the howl of the rotund shop vacuum in the close confines of the cave was mindnumbing. The young deputy had thought the whole process through and brought a hose extension, along with all the various brushes and wands. He'd cleaned the vacuum itself so that it looked brand new and put in a fresh filter. He'd remembered two white, light-weight hard hats.

But most important were the comfortable electronic ear phones he'd borrowed from the range cabinet in Sheriff Robert Torrez's office.

Abeyta had eagerly volunteered for the final vacuum job in the cave, but the logic of Estelle's argument was unassailable. She was the smallest person on the site, with the most room to maneuver.

For a half hour, she worked the vacuum, edging farther and farther into the narrow confines, using first the tapered wand and then the brush, covering every surface. She twisted on her side and gently brushed the ceiling, always working to one side of her position in case even the brush's light touch dislodge rocks.

Fragments rattled down the hose and fine detritus whooshed through into the vacuum's collection chamber.

Eventually she waved a hand and the sound of the vacuum died.

"The bats now have the absolutely cleanest quarters in the entire southwest," she said.

"You think they'll appreciate it?" Linda's voice sounded oddly metallic through the earphone's electronic boosters.

"I doubt it. It's just not as homey as it was." Estelle lay quietly for a moment, letting the ache subside in her shoulders. "Would you ask Bobby for his Kel-lite? I want to check one more thing." In a moment the large, black flashlight tapped her leg lightly. With the light, and moving with exquisite care, she wormed her way forward.

"How far are you going to go?" A note of worry crept into Linda's voice. She rested a hand on the back of Estelle's right boot.

"Just a bit." Her target was the vent, the chimney, toward the back of the little cave. The opening was a body-length from the rise where she had earlier balanced the laptop and the spotlight. To reach the vent and be able to peer into it, to face the rush of air from somewhere deep in the earth, meant she would have to squirm all the way in, heading slightly downward. And there was no room to turn around, even if she rolled onto her side and hunched herself into the smallest ball possible. She would have to edge in on her elbows and toes, and back out the same way.

"This is not a good idea," Linda whispered, and Estelle laughed in spite of her absurd position. Linda was right, of course. But short of systematically dismantling the mesa ton by ton, she could think of no other way to convince herself that she'd probed whatever secrets this little spot guarded.

"What a calendar shot, eh, *hermana?*" Estelle said.

"Oh, you betcha," the photographer said. Her calendars had become treasured possessions each year, with one of the department staff featured each month. The portraits were always wonderfully comical or a pull on the heartstrings, taken during the year when opportunity presented itself.

"Just give me some warning when you're going to pop that thing. I don't want to crack my head against mother rock." As Estelle crawled forward, her breath coming loudly in the respirator, she discovered that the downslope was uncomfortably angled. What had first appeared as an insignificant grade now registered on the muscles of her forearms. The slope wasn't enough for her to slide forward, but it was going to be a difficult squirm to climb back out. She paused, her belly resting on the entry hump of rock.

"You know, if a body was lying here," she said, "it wouldn't be real hard to push it the rest of the way in."

"I'll take your word for it," Linda replied.

"That's about as far as you need to go," Bob Torrez said, his voice boosted by her electronic headphones.

"Almost." By the time her thighs rested on the entry, she could almost touch the rim of the vent with her fingers. The flow of air was a constant wash, cool enough that it felt wonderful against her sweat-tickled forehead. She edged the flashlight forward and switched it on, amplifying the unfocused illumination from the spotlight. The vent, really little more than a yawning crack in the limestone, narrowed quickly to just inches, a little passageway of sharp edges not much wider than a the wingspread of a small bat.

The top of her hardhat touched the rocks, and she flattened a bit more, spreading the bipod of her arms, wincing as the rocks dug into her elbows and forearms. The sheriff mumbled something, but Estelle ignored him. In another eighteen inches, she'd squirmed in as far as she could, the roof sloping down to block her passage. Her face was within a foot of the vent, and she reminded herself that any bats snoozing in that protected spot might burst out past her in an explosion of little leathery wings. She had no room to startle without cracking into the rock.

The flashlight beam showed nothing except limestone, the minerals in the rock twinkling through eons of dust. The vent angled down out of sight.

"Turn on the vacuum," she said, and in a moment Linda did so, the hose jerking with the suction. Estelle worked it forward, shoving the nozzle as far into the vent as she could, feeling for the trickle of particles as they shot down the hose.

She moved slightly, repositioning the hose. Covering the stone surface a centimeter at a time, she toured with the flashlight beam, looking into each small cranny. It was the wink of bright brass that attracted her attention. Wedged into a tiny crevice to the left of the vent, its position hidden by a projection of rock but announced by a tiny swatch of gray splashed on the limestone, the mangled piece of metal had come to rest.

Pulse now pounding, she signaled that the vaccum be switched off.

"Go ahead and pull out the hose," she said, and as it snaked past, she forced herself to breathe slowly, methodically. "Linda, you there?"

"Sure."

"I need your camera."

"If you come out, I can get in there."

"No need. Just set it on auto and macro. And I'll need the tissue for the flash."

"You got it. Hang on just a second." Linda's hand didn't leave her boot. "You all right?"

"*Perfecto,*" Estelle said.

"What did you find?"

"The puzzle piece," the undersheriff said.

Chapter Twenty-seven

Sheriff Robert Torrez held the plastic evidence bag so that full sun caught it, his eyebrows knit with concentration as he turned the bag this way and that.

"We don't know if this is the bullet that passed through the victim's skull," he said.

"No, we don't." Estelle hunched her shoulders. "But it's *consistent*." To even consider that it might *not* be the projectile in question was unthinkable, but she forced herself to remain patient and explore doubts.

"We need more'n that," Torrez said.

"Yes, we do. But it's a start."

"Let's assume it is the one," Bill Gastner agreed. He took the bag handed to him by the sheriff and then knelt beside the tarp. He held the little bag close to the frontal bone of the skull. "It had just enough energy to do that, because that exit hole isn't very big."

"You're right about that," Torrez said. "It ain't like a magnum shockwave blew off his face. The exit is about the size of a nickel."

Gastner held the bag up for the gathered officers to see. "The hollow point is mushroomed pretty thoroughly, but it isn't broken up."

"So it wasn't movin' too fast by the time it busted out of his head."

"So…that's *consistent*." Torrez observed. "And for it to end up where it did, he would have had to be in the process of entering that little cave. At least lying on the slope of rock so he could see in."

"Why would he have been doing that?" Torrez asked. "What's he lookin' at? The dyin' cat?"

"I don't know. That, or curiosity at the air flow, maybe."

"If the same gun killed both the cat and this guy," Bill Gastner mused, "that's an interesting scenario. Really interesting."

"Damn confusing, is what it is," the sheriff muttered. "Cat ended up over by the packrat nest, not in that cave."

"That's where it *ended up*," Estelle offered. "But it could have crawled into the deepest corner of the cave and died. Our victim went in after it, maybe. When he was convinced that it was dead, he hauled it out. Or somebody did."

"Would you do that, Madame Spelunker?" Gastner asked. "Intrepid explorer of the earth's bowels?"

"No, *I* wouldn't. But a hunter would, right?" She looked at Torrez.

"Sure," he said. "No big deal. Jaguar's a hell of a trophy. He sure as hell wouldn't just leave it."

"But he'd sure have to be convinced that it was dead, dead, dead," Gastner said. "Imagine being trapped in that tiny space with 180 pounds of wounded cat?"

"Freddy would have done it if he'd thought that the cat was dead."

"Sure."

"Except when that cat died, Freddy Romero was about ten years old," Gastner laughed.

"Someone *like* Freddy, I mean," Estelle added. "An intrepid explorer, an avid hunter. Lots of folks would." She reached out for the evidence bag. "We need a ballistics match. And if there's some DNA to be had from this, we need that, too. Brain or bone tissue. Something. With the bullet wedged up into the rocks, it's unlikely that the rodents got to it."

Torrez stood up, took a deep breath, and hitched up his belt. "All right, listen. We got a whole shitload of stuff that needs to be packed up and taken to the state lab." He pointed at Tony Abeyta. "You head that up, all right? You're due a little vacation time."

Abeyta nodded with resignation, perhaps not seeing fourteen hours on the highway as his vacation of choice.

"While we're packing that up," Estelle said, holding up the bagged bullet that Torrez handed to her, "I want Mears to do a comparison with the other slug. That won't disturb any residue that might be on it. We might get lucky."

"That's right. Look," Torrez said, "there's sure as hell enough dental work here that we might get a match. There's for sure enough DNA. But match to *who*? That's where we're stuck." He twisted at the waist, slowly and with care, as if something might snap. He looked down the mesa slope at Miles Waddell. "It's his property. That's where we start."

"He wants to know as badly as we do," Gastner said. "He hasn't budged from there all day. And his cell phone batteries must be busted flat by now."

Miles Waddell's body language gave no clue as to what he wanted. Estelle saw that the rancher still sat on the tailgate, boots swinging inches off the ground, bracing himself with his hands locked on the edge of the tailgate, arms stiff and shoulders hunched, studying the sparse grass and dirt below his feet.

"Let me talk with him," the undersheriff said. "Join me, sir?" Bill Gastner nodded and drained the last bit of coffee from his Styrofoam cup.

"Sure, why not. I've had about all the fun I can stand."

Waddell turned his head without changing position on the tailgate, watching them approach. His eyes narrowed as if his patience was running thin.

"Yup," he said.

Estelle looked at him quizzically, but Gastner beat her to the question.

"'Yup' what?" the older man asked.

"This sure as hell isn't how I'd planned to spend *my* day," Waddell said, "I was going to go out and pop some prairie dogs, but I got distracted by this convention." Estelle leaned against the truck, arms resting on the edge of the bed liner. She looked at the older model rifle in the rear window rifle rack, a light caliber gun with powerful scope. It had ridden in pickup trucks for so many years that she could see the wear polished into the wooden fore-end and butt stock.

"That's how it happens," Gastner said. "We get distracted."

"You guys about to wrap things up?"

"A long, long way from it," Gastner said. "And that's how *that* goes, too."

"Sir," Estelle said, "when did you actually acquire this property?"

"Up there on the mesa side, you mean? Hell, it's been… what, Bill? Five years or so? Maybe six." He looked down at the ground. "I bought it from Herb, you know. *He* got it from George Payton…well, George's estate, anyway. You remember how that mess went."

"Did you know about that little cave?"

"Nope. Like I told you earlier, I don't go hikin' much. If I do much of that, somebody's going to find *my* carcass out in the boonies. If I can't *drive* there, I don't *go* there. That's about as simple as I can make it. And no, young lady…number one, if I'd known there was a cave up there, and number two, if I'd known there was a corpse, I would have called you folks myself. Trust me on that."

"Are you going to be able to help us with this?" Gastner asked.

"What's that mean, Bill?"

"Well," the livestock inspector shrugged. "We find a pile of bones, we're kinda curious about who they belong to."

"I can make a pretty good guess about who they belong to," Waddell said, and if his response surprised Bill Gastner, the older man's face didn't show it. Estelle had the thought that *Padrino* had been careful to keep his own counsel while the site recovery was in progress, since he had voiced no theories, offered no creative opinions.

"And who might that be?" Gastner asked.

"Look," and Waddell eased himself down off the tailgate and wiped off the seat of his jeans. "The minute I saw that belt and holster…" He picked up the cell phone that had been lying on the tailgate. "Is this going to get me in Dutch?"

"Couldn't tell you," Gastner said easily, nodding at the phone. "If you want to call a lawyer, that's your right. It might not be a bad idea. This is your property, and right now, it's your corpse." He smiled engagingly.

"Sir, if you have information that is important to this investigation, we need to know it," Estelle said.

Waddell ducked his head and held up both hands in resignation. "You remember Eddie Johns?"

Again, Bill Gastner's poker face didn't register any surprise. "Sure enough," he said. The revelation meant considerably less to Estelle, who vaguely remembered a short, powerfully built man, a former cop, real estate entrepreneur of questionable talent, and a one-time associate of the rancher who now sat on the tailgate, looking uncomfortable.

"Bet you dollars to donuts that's who you got up there," Waddell said.

"Well, now. I haven't seen him around in a long time," Gastner said, and Waddell barked a short laugh.

"Maybe now you know why."

Chapter Twenty-eight

"What leads you to believe that the bones are those of Eddie Johns?" Estelle asked as she leafed through her small notebook to a clean page, jotting down the date, the time, and the name.

"I remember that holster, for one thing," the rancher said. "I saw that, and right away…" He took a deep breath. "Johns wore that 24/7, I think. Always wore that damn gun, everywhere he went. Always." He looked at Gastner. "You probably remember that."

"I do, as a matter of fact."

Estelle reached to the back of her belt and slipped the small hand-held radio free, keying the transmit pad. "Sheriff, can you come down here for a minute?" She watched as Torrez straightened up from what he was doing and looked down the mesa side at her. "We have some information, sir."

Torrez waved a hand, tapped the transmit pad once so his radio squelched a burst of static, and headed down the hill.

Bill Gastner's left arm was cradled across his belly, giving support for his right. He rested his chin on the knuckles of his right hand, regarding Miles Waddell like an old Bassett hound waiting for the chase. The rancher started to say something, but Gastner held up his hand, then with a wonderful economy of motion, bent his right index finger to point toward the approaching sheriff.

"Sir," Estelle said as Torrez drew within easy earshot, "Mr. Waddell tells us that the skeleton may be the remains of Eddie Johns. He has reason to believe it might be."

"No shit," Torrez said. Estelle kept her smile to herself. The sheriff *was* surprised by the announcement, since he took a few seconds to kick the toe of one well-worn Wellington boot against the sidewall of Miles Waddell's back tire, dislodging some non-existent dirt from the waffle sole. "How do you know that?"

"For one thing, the holster rig," Waddell said. "Like I was telling the young lady here, I've seen that often enough. Johns always had that damn gun on, all the time. Never saw him go anywhere without it. Even when we'd drop into the saloon for a beer, you know. He had it. Not supposed to carry in a place like that, I don't think."

"Nope. But lots of folks do. You know what kind of gun he carried?"

"I'm not much for handguns, sheriff. But I know it was bright steel, with rubber grips."

"Stainless steel, or nickel? Something like that?"

"I couldn't tell one from the other. I remember a time or two seeing him fussing with it. Adjusting it in the holster…that sort of thing. A big, awkward looking cannon. I remember that. Seems like more of a nuisance than anything else." He chuckled. "Last time I remember any kind of fight in the Broken Spur, it was Victor using a cast iron frying pan."

"And that's it? You think the *holster* was like the one that Johns wore?" Torrez didn't bother to disguise the skepticism in his tone.

"You recognize the boot, too?"

"Ah, no. I'm not sure *anyone* is going to recognize what's left of that. But Johns *did* wear boots. Always."

"When did you see him last?" the sheriff asked. "You were partnered up with him now and then."

Waddell leaned back against the tailgate, face pursed, and looked up at the blank blue sky. "I gotta think about this, now." The thinking went on long enough that the sheriff let out a sigh of impatience.

"It's been a while," Waddell said. "Four, five years, maybe. At least that."

The rancher's eyes narrowed a little, and he selected his words carefully. "Look, we didn't see eye to eye on a lot of things. When he got involved with other deals—down in El Paso, I think, well…it didn't just break my heart."

Estelle had been watching Waddell's face, and then glanced at Gastner, who raised a skeptical eyebrow. "Sir, you're telling us that you haven't seen Eddie Johns for five years?"

Waddell nodded. "And he was a whole lot more alive when I last saw him."

"What were the circumstances of your last meeting with him, sir?"

"Well, we weren't seeing eye to eye on some things. Let me put it that way."

"You argued with him, you mean?"

"We had our disagreements. Ask Herb. He knows."

"Mr. Torrance was present the last time you saw Johns?"

"Herb? Hell, I don't remember. He might have been."

"And then after that, you never saw Johns again. Is that what you're sayin'?" Torrez looked sideways at the rancher.

"Never saw him again."

"And how would that happen?"

"Well," and Waddell seemed to stumble on the memory. "I just didn't, that's all. I mean, I didn't see him again. Simple as that. Time went by, and I kinda wondered, you know. I was thinking of giving him a call, but…" He let the thought go unfinished.

"But, sir?" Estelle prompted.

"But I didn't." He smiled self-consciously at an answer so obviously evasive. "Not seeing Eddie Johns again wasn't the worst thing in the world, in my book."

"You didn't think it odd when he just dropped from the picture? When he never called you, or visited again? No email, no notes, no nothing?"

"Well…sure, I wondered. A little bit."

"You know, my memory is not worth a damn, but the last time I can remember seeing you and Eddie Johns together was that day out at Herb's place," Gastner mused. "That day we were talking to Herb about his boy—when he borrowed your cattle. That's been what, five or six years, at least?"

"*Borrowed,* hell," Waddell guffawed. "When the little shit *stole* a trailer full of them, you mean. You recall that Johns was with me that day? I couldn't swear to it. But sure. Except that's longer ago than what we're talking about."

"So you saw him after that, obviously."

"I couldn't say, but sure. Probably I did. Eddie and I were working on several projects after that. I guess when I get home, I could check my old day planners. I keep them—whatever for I don't know. I'll see what I can dig up."

"Interesting that someone could just go missing like that, and no one would report it." Gastner looked first at Estelle, and then at Waddell. "No one cared enough to inquire? You didn't wonder where Eddie Johns went?"

Waddell ducked his head in embarrassment. "Look," he said. "This is complicated in some ways. I don't want to speak ill of the dead, you know. What was his business, was…his business. He and I didn't see eye to eye on a lot of things, and some of our last meetings were pretty hot—well, from my perspective, they were. Eddie…well, listening to other people and understanding their point of view wasn't one of his strong points."

Estelle tapped the cover of her notebook impatiently. "Sir, we're going to have to hear about some of those things—your disagreements with him. What you understood he was doing. But not out here. You'll come by the office later this afternoon? Say at six?"

Waddell laughed weakly. "I have a choice?"

"I can come out to the ranch, sir. Either way. We'd appreciate your cooperation, sir."

"Miles, there's no point in skating in circles around this," Gastner said. "The sooner this is cleared up, the better for everybody."

"I don't know who killed Eddie Johns," Waddell said. "That's as simple as I can say it."

"We appreciate your cooperation," Estelle said. "We have a few things to close out here, and then we'll be back in town. If you'd stop by, that would be good."

"I'll do it," the rancher said. "You know, you might want to talk with Herb. He might have seen Eddie sometime recently."

"Not too recently," Gastner quipped.

"Well, you know what I mean." Waddell nodded at the procession of people now starting down the hill, laden with equipment. "I'll get out of your way. Canyon road still closed?"

"Yes, sir."

"Then I'll head north. You have my cell. If there's a problem, or you guys get hung up with something so you can't meet, let me know before I drive all the way into town."

"We certainly will, sir."

They stepped back as the rancher climbed into his truck. He swung the vehicle around in a wide circle, and waved a salute as he rumbled off.

"Bobby, what's the rifle in the back of his truck?" Estelle asked.

"An old 250 Savage," the sheriff said.

"Drives a really light bullet really fast?"

"Yup. Depending what he's loading it with, it's probably a light twenty-five caliber bullet, pushed out there pretty quick for its day. That ain't the gun used on Freddy's four-wheeler, though, if that's what you're thinkin'."

"And we know that because…"

"That big scope? That's for shootin' at four hundred yards, maybe more. It's a prairie dog gun. You try findin' a target at twenty-five or thirty yards, all you're going to get is a blur."

"The scope can't be focused for short distances?" Estelle was intrigued with how instantly Robert Torrez reached his decisions—especially those involving firearms.

"Could, maybe." He held up both hands, forming a circle the size of a basketball. "With that much magnification, something movin' real fast and up close is going to be just a big blur. I don't care how careful he's got it prefocused. It ain't the gun."

"The bullet hit the fender, then the rim and tire. Whoever pulled the trigger didn't hit Freddy…if Freddy was the target."

"I don't think he was." Torrez said. "If he really wanted to, he would have tried more than once."

"Except he didn't *need* to try more than once. The arroyo finished the job for him."

"Yup." He nodded down the two-track toward the southwest. "We need to spend some time down in the canyon. You got time for that?"

"Of course." They both looked at Bill Gastner.

"Hey, I've been fed," he said, holding up both hands. "I'm ready for anything. Jackie is going to be wondering if she's been abandoned."

"She won't have wasted the time," Estelle said.

Chapter Twenty-nine

Providing security for a crime scene—simply *being* there to prevent disturbance—could be deadly boring. It was certainly expensive. Estelle was reminded of that expense when she crested the little hill beyond where Freddy had launched his final flight and saw that, across the next swale, the county manager had arrived, looking voluminous even in her khaki trousers, khaki shirt, and bright yellow baseball cap. Stopped in the middle of the two-track, the manager had parked nose to tailgate with Jackie Taber's older Bronco, the last vehicle of its type in the sheriff's department fleet. Behind Leona Spears' county vehicle was a blue Toyota sedan. The spirits living in the old homestead were enjoying lots of company, but Estelle reminded herself not to say something like that to Leona—the county manager would take her seriously.

Estelle parked squarely in the middle of the road at the crest of an undulation, the homestead a hundred yards ahead of her, the site of the ATV crash behind her. But the sheriff, following a hundred yards or more behind her, didn't follow suit. Instead, he parked far behind her, within a dozen feet of the rock that had torn the front tire of Freddy Romero's four-wheeler.

"Now I know why Bobby let you go first," Bill Gastner laughed. "Brunhilde is waiting for you. And Frank. What a pair."

"Ah," Estelle sighed. "Nothing is ever simple." She glanced across at her passenger.

"You want me to run interference? Make myself useful?"

"I don't think that's necessary. Leona is going to see all the overtime requests anyway. She'll be curious for some answers. And Frank...you know what day of the week it is." Sure enough, Frank Dayan had often chided the local law enforcement agencies—only half kidding—that they conspired to break major cases just *after* his weekly edition of the *Posadas Register* had hit the streets. That gave the big metro papers, television, and radio a week's edge on the little local paper.

Listed as *publisher* on the masthead of the paper, Frank Dayan was no number cruncher who refused to jump into the trenches. He waged his scoop war with ferocious dedication, still finding the time to solicit a hefty advertising schedule. His editor, Pam Gardiner, rarely left the office herself, choosing to remain at her desk for long hours, making sense of the news and photos that Frank produced. A part-time reporter covered sports, but little else.

County Manager Leona Spears had cornered Deputy Jackie Taber, and the two of them had a map spread on the hood of the deputy's Bronco. Frank leaned on the fender, both hands cradling his little digital camera with which he managed somehow to take amazingly fuzzy pictures.

Estelle waited beside her own vehicle for a moment while Bobby Torrez took his time. For a time he stood beside his truck, surveying the prairie with binoculars. Eventually, as Linda's little Honda, and then Tom Pasquale and Doug Posey lined up behind him to turn the prairie into a parking lot, the sheriff waved at them to park behind his unit, and then ambled forward.

"He had to shoot from either here, or way up ahead, up the slope behind the homestead," the sheriff announced as he reached Estelle and Bill Gastner. He made a rolling, wave motion with his hand. "Hills get in the line of sight otherwise."

Still out of earshot of the county manager and the newspaper publisher, Torrez stepped off the two-track and looked down at the tracks and gouges in the arroyo bottom's gravel.

"How much do you want Dayan to know?" he asked. His tone didn't carry the usual dismissive note that he was fond of using when referring to the media, whether it be Frank Dayan's modest little weekly paper or the largest metro television station or daily. He was perfectly content to leave the media with the undersheriff.

"If Miles Waddell is right—if that skeleton is the remains of Eddie Johns—then we need to know who saw Johns last. This trail is years old, Bobby. Some newspaper coverage might be useful."

"I'm thinkin' we don't need to let all of it out yet."

"I agree a hundred percent. Maybe someone fired at least one shot at Freddy—whether by accident or design, we don't know, but I wasn't going to discuss any of that with Frank."

"Leona either."

Estelle nodded, but didn't chide the sheriff that his circumspection regarding the county manager was unwarranted. Despite her ebullient nature, Leona Spears could be the soul of discretion when the occasion warranted.

"Good morning!" the county manager warbled when they walked to within earshot. She beamed at Estelle, and then offered her hand to Torrez with a mock frown. "And how are you, sir?" Leona swung on Bill Gastner and embraced him in a hug before he had a chance to flee. "You're looking fit."

"You may be the first person ever to tell me that," Gastner laughed. He nodded at Frank Dayan. "How's Frank?"

"I'm having a good time trying to figure out what's going on out here," the newspaperman said. "What a shame about the Romero boy."

"It is that," Gastner agreed. As he spoke, Torrez beckoned at Jackie, walking away from all the civilian ears. In the meantime, Linda Real and the two other deputies had strolled across the swale, and while Linda's bright smile and bubbly personality engaged the county manager, Jackie led them around to the rear of her Bronco.

The deputy's voice was a husky whisper, and Estelle had to lean close to hear her. Jackie pointed up the flank of the mesa. "Absolutely nothing, sir," the deputy said. "I combed every conceivable spot where someone could engage that area of the two-track where Freddy went off." She shook her head. "Nothing. No shell casings, no cigarette butts, no fresh tracks. A big zero."

"Well, we're going to comb it some more," Torrez said. "That busted up bullet recovered from the tire didn't leave us with shit. We gotta come up with *something*." He sighed and surveyed the mesa flank. "If it ain't here, it ain't here. That's just the way it is. But I want to be sure. How far up did you go?"

"All the way to where the rim rock pallisades meet the vegetation," the deputy said. "I couldn't imagine why anyone would need to climb higher. Or even *that* high." She pointed toward the ruins of the homestead foundation. "If he parked there for whatever reason…"

"To wait for Freddy," the sheriff interrupted.

"Well, maybe. But if he did that, then he wouldn't have to walk very far up the slope to find a vantage point."

"If we line up the nick in the front brush guard with the cut in the wheel rim, that doesn't give us much of an angle," Estelle said.

"I don't see why the shooter didn't just stroll down the two-track to meet Freddy," Jackie said. "Why bother with all the ambush stuff?"

"Some folks find face to face hard to manage," Estelle said.

"He wanted it to look like an accident, that's for sure," the deputy said.

"Impossible," Gastner said. "There's no way you could lie in wait up in the trees, fire a shot or two, and assume that it's going to startle the kid enough to lose control of his rig. For one thing, with the noise of that four-wheeler, he wouldn't even *hear* the gun go off. Even if he wasn't wearing his helmet."

"And what would make him swerve?" Estelle asked.

"*Seeing* someone with a rifle, pointing his way. That might startle him a little."

"That means the shooter wasn't very far upslope," Torrez added.

"And one other thing," Jackie said. "And you might want Linda to work some magic with it…where someone backed up alongside the foundation over there? His truck had an oil seep."

"Seep?"

"Just a drop or two. Maybe power steering fluid, maybe from the oil pan drain plug. But it's from up front if he backed in."

"That narrows it down to about every truck in the world," Torrez grumbled. "If he wasn't parked there long, it's a hell of a lot more than a *seep*. Look, we got," and he turned, counting heads, "we got seven people. I want us to sweep from just back beyond the homestead all the way east to where Freddy cleared the top of the rise. Just to be sure. Bill and I are going to take either side of the two-track. Everybody take a lane and take your time."

Another hour of looking so hard that it made the eyes water produced nothing of immediate interest. Tom Pasquale found a well-tarnished 1961 quarter. Leona Spears picked up an unfired twelve gauge shotgun shell that had nestled in bunch grass for so long that the red hull had faded to dull pink. Adding to the haul were bits of glass, scraps of discarded cardboard, and an oil filter now full of blow sand. Further up the hill, Jackie Taber discovered a nest of nine .22 caliber rimfire shell casings and the bottom cushion of an easy chair. But no one discovered anything that might suggest an event as recent as Freddy Romero's crash.

Through the entire process, Frank Dayan waited patiently, occasionally snapping a digital photo of them at work or drawn into discussion.

"You're a patient man, sir," Estelle said as she strolled back to the vehicles.

"I figure that if I block the road long enough, someone is going to give me the interview of a lifetime," he laughed. "You ready to do that?"

"I wish I had more to tell you." She pulled out her notebook. "The body of a man was discovered in a small cave up on the flank of the mesa," she said, and watched Dayan's eyebrows shoot up.

"*In* a cave?"

"That's correct. It would appear that the body has been there for a number of years. It's now skeletal remains, widely scattered by the critters." She watched Dayan fiddle with his pocket micro-recorder, and when he was satisfied that it was working, he rested it on the hood of Jackie Taber's Bronco. "The obvious question is *who,* of course, and we're not ready to talk about that. When we have a positive I.D., I'll let you know."

"Illegal?"

"His death? Almost certainly," Estelle smiled, knowing full well what the newspaper man had meant. "We don't have an I.D., Frank. Until we do, we won't know if this is an illegal immigrant who got caught up somehow, or something else."

"So you have an unidentified body. Who made the discovery? I mean, who the heck is out *here* to do that. Lost tourists?"

"We found him, sir."

"*We?* The S.O., you mean?"

"Yes."

Dayan frowned, and Estelle could almost see antenna twitching. "Jackie tells me that this is where the Romero boy went into the arroyo."

"That's correct, sir. He went off right back there." She pointed toward the rise.

"How far from here to the cave where the body was found?"

"One point three miles."

"The two incidents are related somehow?"

"I'd be interested to hear how that might be possible, sir."

"Well, it's just odd, that's all. There isn't much out here other than barbed wire, cows, and an occasional rancher and his pickup truck. What was the Romero boy doing over here, anyway?"

"Riding his four-wheeler, sir. Probably a little faster than he should have been."

"That was quite a find he made over by Borracho Canyon. Lots of folks are excited about that. Nobody that I've talked to can remember when the last time a jaguar was seen in this country."

Estelle nodded silently, looking down at the little recorder, gauging her response, considering carefully what she wanted to tell Frank Dayan—what she wanted to feed to the *Register*. Although the newspaper's next edition wouldn't appear until the following Wednesday with counter sales, and then in the mail on Thursday, Frank would no doubt mention any juicy tidbit to someone. And then word would spread like wildfire.

"We were presented with new evidence about the cat that led us over here, Frank. It appears that Freddy Romero didn't find the jaguar over at Borracho at all. The cat's skeleton was in the cave just down this road. That's where he found it."

"I don't understand."

"Apparently, Freddy was interested in recovering the rest of the carcass. He didn't want anyone else disturbing the site. So he made up the story about Borracho."

"But it was over here all along? Is that what you're saying?"

"Yes, sir."

"And in the process of following down that lead, you discovered the other skeleton."

"That's essentially correct."

Dayan looked confused. "How did you know where the cat skeleton actually was? Did you talk to Freddy before his crash?"

"No, we didn't. But certain information came to our attention."

"Ah. *Certain information.* That's intriguing, Estelle. So that leads us to all kinds of questions, doesn't it. Perrone was out here, wasn't he?" He nodded toward Jackie. "I heard some radio traffic. Is he going to be able to determine cause of death, you think?"

"It appears that the victim was shot, sir."

"You have that already?"

"Well, there's what appears to be a bullet hole through the skull, Frank. At the moment that's pretty much the sum and substance of what we have."

"That's what Nate Underwood told me. A hole through the cat's skull. Isn't *that* something." He smiled with anticipation at the story, and then his face sagged. "How much of this are you going to be able to sit on until next Friday?"

"I'll do my best," Estelle replied.

"The cave's on Herb's property?"

"No. Actually it's on the Waddell ranch."

"You've talked to him?"

"Yes."

Dayan grinned at the finality of her response. "Charges pending?" He held up a hand quickly. "No, let me. *Investigation is continuing.*"

"Exactly." She reached out and took Frank by the arm, shaking it gently. "We can really use your cooperation in this, Frank. 'Investigation continues into the ATV crash that claimed the life of Freddy Romero.'"

"That's what you want me to write? Pam's not going to like that."

Then she ought to be here, Estelle thought. Editor Pam Gardiner had her own slate of problems and issues, but hotly pursuing news outside of the office wasn't one of them. "Investigation also continues into the discovery of a human skeleton in a cave southwest of Posadas."

"On the Waddell ranch. You're not willing to speculate on whether the two incidents are related, then."

"No. We're not. And I hope you won't either."

"News, not speculation and rumor. If something breaks, will you let me know?"

"Absolutely."

"First?"

Estelle smiled, reached out and shook Frank's arm gently. "We'll try, Frank."

He held up his camera. "I'd like to take a photo of the cave, maybe with you and one of the deputies? Will you do that for me?"

Estelle shook her head. "Not yet, sir. Right now, we need to be a little discreet about this whole thing."

"Ah, one of those deals. But you'll let me know? I mean, sooner rather than later?" He glanced at his watch. "I really need to get back to town."

She nodded. "Thanks for coming out on a Sunday, Frank." She watched him maneuver his car on the narrow two-track, and as he drove off, she mused at how irritated the newspaper publisher would be when he found out that he'd missed the big headline—that Freddy Romero's plunge into the arroyo had likely been prompted by an errant rifle bullet.

Chapter Thirty

The rancher looked as if he'd taken the time to drive home to Newton, shave, spit-polish his Tony Lamas, and don fresh western-cut trousers and a white shirt with mother-of-pearl buttons. His silver belt buckle was tarnished and worn just enough to announce that he was no newbie. The purple neckerchief still protected the tender skin at the base of his throat.

He took off his tan Stetson, revealing a thick head of wavy hair held glossily in place. The hat band left a faint dent in the skin of his forehead, and it appeared that over the years Miles Waddell had worked hard to avoid the two-tone tan line that resulted from a life under the sun and under the Stetson.

Estelle motioned to a chair, and the rancher sat down, his movements quick and graceful. The undersheriff closed the door.

"May we get you something, sir? Coffee? Soft drink?"

He waved off the offer. "Not now, thanks. This whole thing has my gut a little upset." He rested a hand on his trim belly. Estelle caught the faint aroma of his cologne, a fragrance that reminded her of kelp beds along the seashore rather than the high prairie.

She slid a recorder across her desk, stationing it directly in front of Waddell. "Sir, your deposition is important to us. If you don't mind, I'll record our conversation, and then when it's transcribed, you'll have a chance to read it for accuracy before signing."

"Fine with me. You got to do these things. I know how the drill goes. Are you going to be reading my rights next?" His crows feet deepened.

"Do I need to, sir?"

"Nope. It's my land out there, but I sure as hell didn't put that corpse in that cave." His grin was tight, his eyes watchful.

"We appreciate your cooperation, sir. I'd like to start with your comments earlier about the identity of the skeleton found in the small cave on your property."

"Eddie Johns? I think it's him. I think that's who it is." He nodded vigorously.

"And your reasons for believing that?"

Waddell held up a finger. "Number one, like I told you. The holster rig. I've seen that often enough. Wish you had the gun. *That* I could positively identify."

Estelle rose and walked to a locked file cabinet. From the top drawer she pulled a large clear plastic evidence bag that contained the semi-automatic Smith and Wesson recovered from Freddy Romero's four-wheeler. She handed it to the rancher, whose eyebrows shot up in surprise. "We believe that this automatic was recovered from the same area." She did not add by whom.

"Well, damn. You *did* find it." He laid the gun on his lap, smoothing the plastic. "That's it. Well, now…" and he tipped his head. "I might not be able to *swear* that this belonged to Eddie Johns, but it sure as hell *looks* like the one he had. Carried it all the time. Probably slept with it. These grips look like the ones, the way the rosewood is inlaid into the black rubber like that." He leaned back away from the gun, as if wanting no further part of it, then held it out to Estelle.

"Other than the pistol and the holster, is there anything else that leads you to believe that the remains are those of Eddie Johns?"

"Not enough left…other than the boot, maybe. That could be his." He shifted uncomfortably on the wooden chair, taking his weight on his forearms as if he had hemorrhoids. "Isn't there DNA or something that can tell you?"

"We have to have someone to *match* with the DNA, sir."

"Ah." He nodded. "So you got to find DNA that you know is his, and go from there. Match that with whatever you found in the cave."

"Yes, sir."

"Look, here's what bothers me." He leaned forward and lightly chopped his hand down on the edge of the desk. "Like I told you out at the site, I haven't seen Eddie Johns for the better part of five years. You know, you asked me earlier about that, and I *did* check my planners. I don't keep a diary or anything like that, but I jot stuff down. You never know." He shifted again, and pulled a scrap of paper out of his left breast pocket. He extended the moment of silence by fishing a pair of narrow reading glasses out of a pocket case. "May 28th, 2006. Eddie and me were walkin' the mesa top. You heard of StarGaze?"

"The astronomy proposal?"

"That's the one. See, they're an Aussie company that puts in these tourist-based observatories. I think they have maybe six of 'em so far around the world, different spots. That's what they call it. *Tourist based.* They put in an observatory, facilities, the whole nine yards. And folks supposedly come to star gaze. The developers are looking for spots where there's no light pollution. That's what they call it now, around cities, interstate interchanges, things like that. *Light pollution.*"

"Posadas County would be a good choice for that."

"Damn right. And some other things, too. We're convenient for transportation. Well, sort of convenient. We have a flow of snowbirds comin' through that probably haven't even *seen* a real night sky. Easterners, star buffs. Folks like that. Even from down south of the border. There's lots of tourist money there. We've had a few preliminary talks with the Aussies, but nothing definite. For one thing, I was thinking that I don't really *need* to partner up with some big firm, 'specially foreigners. I mean, hell, all it takes is money, right?" He shrugged. "I can see a facility right on top of that mesa. Observatory, gift shop, maybe even a restaurant. A star gazers' recreation area. Maybe even a camp ground. Hell, maybe even one of those little excursion trains." Waddell leaned back in the chair, spreading his arms wide. "And you got a view of the whole damn universe up there. Every star there is." He laughed dryly. "We were even talking about

a lights-out policy at nine o'clock in the evening…no parking
lot vapor lights, no outside lights on the buildings. Something
really special. The Aussies have some good ideas, so it might be
best after all to go with them."

"And this is what you and Eddie Johns were talking about
the last time you saw him?"

"Yep. And you know, I never should have mentioned the idea
to him. Don't know why I did, except I was so damned excited
about the whole notion. But I did, and that's that. He takes the
idea and runs with it. That's what old Eddie does, you know. He
hears an idea he likes, and away we go. Trouble is, I don't always
think much of the direction he takes 'em." He stroked the top
of his hat thoughtfully. "First thing *he* starts to do is talk money,
and all these ideas he has about where to get it. See, *he* wasn't
thrilled with workin' with the Aussies. I don't know why." Waddell
shot a glance of contrition at Estelle. "That's where I should have
stopped it, sheriff. I should have just told Eddie to go to hell. I
mean, I didn't *ask* him to come in on the deal. He just elbows
his way around, you know. Kind of a bully in ways like that."

"And why didn't you refuse his offer, sir?"

"Don't know. For one thing, it wasn't an *offer.* And you know,
sheriff, sometimes he can be an engaging son-of-a-bitch. I don't
like to admit it, but…" Estelle waited patiently. "I'm not too
easy with that guy, you know what I mean? Sometimes he's okay,
Eddie is. Sometimes he's a royal pain the ass. Rubs me the wrong
way sometimes. Makes me nervous."

"There's reason to be a little afraid of him?"

Waddell frowned. "Don't know as I'd go that far, but maybe.
Anyway, I tried to head him off a little. I told him that the first
thing we…*I*…needed to do was create some access, you know.
If you can't get up on top of that mesa, then the whole thing
is a pipe dream. So I started with the idea of gradin' that new
road up the side of the mesa. There was an old washed out cattle
trail there already, but not enough to be practical. More like a
deer or cattle run. Half the time, you couldn't get up there with
the best Jeep."

"But you and Johns managed on that day? The day five years ago when you and he were on top, talking about the project?"

"Drove some, walked too much. But yeah…we got up there. Eddie drove his big old four-by-four, and it did pretty good." He frowned. "The trouble was that Eddie had all these ideas where we were going to get funding." Waddell looked up at Estelle. "And see, that's what I mean about him. He just *assumed* that he was partnering with me on this. I know, I know. We done a land deal or two together in the past. But he didn't ask or anything. Just bulldozed in, you know. That kind of got my goat. Eddie was pushy. I mean, sometimes, he was just a nice guy, kinda fun to be with. But when he got ideas, he got pushy. You didn't agree with him, he got belligerent. He said he could get funding, no problem. But see, I knew what he meant, and didn't want any part of it."

"Part of what, sir? What did he mean?"

"Eddie…he had connections, at least he claimed he did. Down south."

"In Mexico?"

Waddell nodded. "There were some guys that he saw, down south of Juarez." He held up both hands defensively. "Don't know 'em, don't *want* to know 'em. But Eddie was always talkin' about his big contacts. That's why he moved to El Paso, you know. '*That's where it's all happening,*' he liked to say. Now look, *I* know that things didn't go all that good for him over in Grant County when he worked law over there. I got the impression that he liked seeing that place in his rear view mirror."

"Do you have a contact in El Paso for him?"

"I had his cell phone around somewhere. Got his email, too. Don't know what for. I don't have a computer."

"We'd like to have that, sir."

"I'll find it. I should have thought to bring it with me this time. Don't have his snail mail address, though. El Paso, is all I know. Or it could be Sunland Park. Somewhere over there."

"We'll track that down. Did the two of you discuss how much investment was going to be needed?"

"That irritated the hell out of me. *'Don't worry about that,'* Eddie liked to say. *'This is going to be BIG.'* That was his favorite line. Gonna be big. Gotta be big. Think big. You know," and Waddell stroked the brim of his hat again. "I don't think Eddie spent much time thinking about a little item or two…like, the property on that mesa top is *mine,* not his. He don't have a share in it. He just *assumed,* you know. Assumed we were going to buddy up."

"Did he say how he was going to come up with the money?"

"Nothing specific, sheriff. Just his grand, wild schemes. But I can guess where the money would come from, if he managed it." He rapped the edge of his hat brim against the desk. "And I can guess why they'd want a toehold in the United States."

"They?"

"You know who I mean. Those Mexican cartels." He spat out the words as if they were sour, and then ducked his head in apology. "I mean, I have nothing against the Mexicans, most of 'em."

"You believe that Eddie Johns was involved with the cartels? Or had contacts with them?"

"Wouldn't be surprised. Seems like that's the latest fad, right?" Waddell raised a hand in self-defense. "I'm not saying he was. I don't know for sure. But I can guess. You know, he used to joke about how easy it was to come across the border with just about anything a body could want. *'You just got to do it right,'* he'd say." Waddell shrugged. "I wasn't interested in that kind of thing, so I tuned him out, mostly. It wasn't always easy to tell when Eddie was just bullshitting. He did a lot of that, too."

"But you *are* interested in the observatory idea," Estelle said.

"Sure. You know, that mesa top isn't worth a tinker's damn for ranching. I bought it thinking that someday, the feds were going to do something about the cave complex that's under there. They have land on the other side of the road, but nothing on my side. You know the air you said was coming out of that little hole in the cave? Well, that's just one more sign that I'm right. You know how when you drive to the caverns over in Carlsbad, you have to drive *up* on the mesa top? Then you look out on all that country down below? Well, hell, the way I see it, that low country that you're looking at is on the same level as the bottom floor of the caverns. This mesa is the same thing. I haven't had it surveyed or anything by geologists, but I figure the mesa top is just the roof of the caverns down underneath. Think about that, sheriff. I haven't walked every square inch of that mesa, but I'll bet over the past few years, I've found half a dozen vents like that, all spewing out cool air. *Subterranean* air. That's the sign."

"Did you ever check that cave yourself? Where we were this morning?"

"Nope. Like I told you earlier, I didn't know that one was there."

"But you had someone working from time to time on that little access road to the top."

Waddell nodded. "Just enough to be able to drive up on top without wrecking the truck. I'm not going to pay for more than that until something firms up. I'll tell you one thing…this is *slow* business. You think we're *mañana*-land, you ought to work with the feds and the Aussies."

"Who did the road work for you?"

"Gus Prescott, most of it. He's got that old grader of his. For a few days there when he could keep it running, he gouged out that two-track for me. Enough to reach the top, but I'm going to have to have someone come in with some serious equipment to do it right. Put in culverts and the like."

"That's tough country."

"You bet."

"And a lot of money."

Waddell huffed agreement. "You're telling me. I paid Gus a fair lick, but I figure it's going to cost me fifty grand just to make a quarter mile of safe gravel two-track, and that's *after* what he did. Maybe more. Sometimes I think that Eddie had the right idea. Capital's capital. Maybe it doesn't matter where it comes from."

"But some years have gone by now," Estelle pointed out. "You hadn't heard from Eddie Johns in what, four or five years?"

"At least that. And I haven't heard much from the Aussies. I don't know if they lost interest, or what. Maybe Eddie scared 'em off. What I'm figuring to do is talk to the Park Service. I think we could work a partnership. That'd be the way to go." He put on his hat, and leaned forward. "But now we have this mess to worry about. If it isn't one thing, it's another." He thumped the arm of the chair. "I'll get that cell phone number and email for you. Sorry I don't have his address."

"We'll find it, sir." She reached across and turned the tape recorder slightly, as if Miles Waddell needed to be reminded of its presence. "How is it that you didn't inquire about Mr. Johns when he didn't turn up again? You've known him for how long?"

"Off and on for maybe twenty years. Knew him when he was a detective over in Grant County...even before that." Waddell shrugged. "I don't know, sheriff."

"You didn't try to call him? You didn't wonder when he never showed his face around the ranch? Never saw him at the Broken Spur?"

Waddell studied his fingernails. "Time slips by, I guess." That sounded lame, and Waddell obviously knew it. "Look... you ever had an acquaintance that you'd just as soon see vanish off the face of the earth one day? Me and Herb Torrance used to joke about Eddie now and then. 'Surprised nobody's shot that son-of-a-bitch,' Herb used to say. If this was the 1880s, Eddie Johns would be the sort of bully who'd end up face down in some muddy street." He shrugged again. "So maybe I didn't care that he went missing. Didn't think about it too much. Hate to say it, but that's the way it is."

"What was Eddie driving the last time you saw him, sir?"

The question caught Waddell by surprise, and his face went blank. "Driving?" He frowned and stared at the floor. "A nice rig, that's what he always drove." He looked up quickly. "Ford three-quarter ton. Diesel. I remember that, for sure. He'd never shut the damn thing off. Seemed to think that was the thing with diesels. Have to let 'em run. I could never figure that one out. A black Ford."

"That's what he took to the mesa top?"

Waddell nodded. "Without a scratch. He was a hell of a driver, I'll give him that. I'd ride with him anywhere."

"Regular cab?"

"Crew cab. Big as a ship."

"Camper shell or anything like that?"

"Nope."

"Texas plates the last time you saw him?"

Waddell smiled. "Maybe so. Maybe not. I couldn't swear to it. Never paid attention." He heaved a sigh. "You know what I figured all along? God's honest truth? I figured Eddie got crosswise with some of those folks south of the border. I figured his bones were bleaching out in the Mexican desert somewhere. And you know, that's probably where his truck ended up, too."

"He certainly got crosswise with someone, sir," Estelle said.

Chapter Thirty-one

The undersheriff could hear Miles Waddell's boots rapping on the polished tile as he walked out past the dispatch island, and then he paused. A warbling voice greeted him, but the conversation didn't last long.

A moment later, County Manager Leona Speers appeared in Estelle's office doorway. She had changed her clothes too, favoring this time an enormous, shapeless, violet muumuu that featured an endless world of grape vines twining here and there, full of creatures and fruit. The muumuu meant that even though she might be in the building that Sunday afternoon, she was off the county's clock.

"My dear," she said dramatically, "have you *by any chance* noticed the time in the past few moments? Or even the day of the week?"

Estelle smiled and did so, startled to see 6:39. "¡*Ay, caramba!* she groaned. She pushed back from the desk. "You look ready to do the town, Leona."

"Oh…rest assured, I am, I am." She put one hand behind her head and the other on her hip, pivoting a quarter turn. "What if I take you out to dinner?"

"I'd love that, but…"

"Oh, but, but." Leona swished into the office, bringing with her a small cloud of hibiscus perfume. She stopped in front of the calendar by the filing cabinet, looking not at the dates but at the photograph of Sergeant Tom Mears, Mr. September. He was sitting on the huge back tire of his Sportsman race car, helmet resting on his thigh. So relaxed did he appear in the glare of the night lights that it was only on second glance that the viewer would notice his car lying upside down, battered chassis to the stars.

The county manager tapped the page that featured Linda Real's candid portrait of Mears. "I watched Miss Linda working out there today. She's amazing."

"Yes, she is."

"She and Deputy Pasquale make a lovely couple. Makes me wistful. And you know, Miles Waddell appeared relieved not to be wearing handcuffs. Perhaps I should see if *he's* free for dinner."

"That might work, Leona."

"I become impatient with these confirmed bachelors," Leona sighed. "Do you think he had a hand in any of this?" Leona let the *this* remain self-explanatory.

"I don't think so. It's possible, but I don't think so."

"Mr. Smooth."

"He is that."

"What now? May I ask? I mean other than a shower and nice dinner and some entertainment from your two darling little boys and that gorgeous husband of yours?"

Estelle looked down at her tan pants suit and the coating of dust and grime from the prairie and the cave. Her hair felt heavy, as if dust had seeped under her cap and hardhat. If she patted the top of her skull, she was sure a cloud of powdered cave would billow upward.

"That's first," she laughed. "We have inquiries going out in about a dozen directions. By morning, we'll have something to put together."

"You have someone working tonight?"

"Sure. Our part-timer is staying central. Everyone else is on call."

"That would be Kenderman?"

"Yes. He needs the experience."

"Who's dispatching with him?"

"Wheeler." Estelle glanced at Leona, puzzled at the question. The county manager was usually most careful about treading on turf where her authority didn't extend. As an elected official, Sheriff Robert Torrez didn't answer to the county manager—and the sheriff's deputies and staff were under his charge, not the manager's.

"Will that young man move into one of the vacancies?" Leona frowned. "And that's assuming I'm successful in twisting money from the commissioners." The department budget was also Torrez's province...once the county commission approved it. Without the county manager's support, the sheriff faced tough times.

"I don't think so, Leona."

"May I ask why, even though it is *absolutely* none of my business?"

Estelle took a moment to frame her thoughts. "I use Deputy Kenderman as support and back-up, and occasionally under circumstances like tonight, when we just don't have the staff. We'll have state police in the area as well, so he's not working alone. Beyond that, I don't think so."

"He has an attitude, I've noticed."

"On occasion, yes, he does."

"And on occasion, he seems to favor inventing the law himself."

"You've had dealings with him personally, Leona?"

"Others have whose opinions I trust, my dear."

"Then if they have complaints, they should come to either the sheriff or to me, Leona. I hope you tell them that."

"I'm meddling, aren't I?" The county manager bent and circled an arm around Estelle's shoulders and gave her a quick squeeze. "Well, I do suggest that they refer their complaints to you, but you know how gutless some people are. On a happier note, you know the budget workshops loom next week. Will you let me know when we can meet for a few moments?" She drew back, regarding Estelle critically. "About a week of sleep would do wonders for you, but that's not going to happen, is it."

"Things will work out." Estelle did not believe that platitude for an instant. She saw the expression that flitted across Leona's broad face, and knew the county manager didn't either.

"We don't know yet how young Freddy's death is related to the skeleton, do we?" Leona paused in the office doorway.

"Not yet."

"But you will, my dear."

Estelle smiled. "I appreciate the vote of confidence."

"One has to wonder." Leona wiggled five fingers as a farewell, leaving behind only the scent of hibiscus.

After another five minutes of fussing, Estelle finally shut down her computer and locked the files. Out in dispatch, Ernie Wheeler's tall, angular figure was bent over a cabinet drawer, a sheaf of papers on one hand, fingers of the other puzzling through file headings.

"You out of here?" he asked as Estelle appeared.

"I am. I'll be home."

"Jackie's comin' back on at midnight." He glanced at the assignment board. "I guess Kenderman can keep himself out of trouble until then."

"Let us hope so, Ernie. Do your best."

The village was quiet as she pulled the Crown Victoria out of the parking lot. She looked down Grande Avenue in time to see Sheriff Robert Torrez's battered Chevy pickup truck, its wrought iron bed and roof rack distinctive, pull out of McArthur and head south. If she had interrupted his solitude to ask, she could predict what he would reply. "Just some thinkin'," he would say, and let it go at that.

Turning onto Twelfth Street, she saw that solitude wasn't in the cards for her. She breathed a sigh of relief. Her tired brain had reached a stage of repetitive and unproductive thought, and she welcomed the mob scene that the parking lot in front of her house promised. Irma Sedillos' Datsun was snuggled into the curb with Bill Gastner's SUV just behind. Her husband's new BMW sedan left just enough room in the driveway for her county car.

After backing into her slot, she let the car idle for a moment as she sorted through her mobile office, then reached for the radio as she jotted down a final entry in her log.

"PCS, three ten is ten-forty-two."

"Ten four, three ten," Wheeler acknowledged.

Officer at home. That had a far warmer ring than the sterile ten code, Estelle thought. With briefcase in hand, she slid out of the car, and then stopped, one hand on the door frame. Down the street, George Romero's Suburban was parked, but Tata's sedan was gone. The front yard was clear of other machines—not the usual squadron of motorcycles, scooters, powered skateboards, ATVs, or dual-spring, chromed pogo sticks. Estelle gently pushed the cruiser's door closed. The street was so quiet that the metallic *chunk* of the door seemed an intrusion.

The front door of her own home opened.

"Hey, there," her husband called. "You okay?"

"Sure. I'm fine. Just slow." Francis met her at the bottom step, and by the time she reached him, she could smell the aroma wafting from the house.

"You look like you've been playing in Carlos' dirt pit," the physician said. He engulfed her in a fierce hug. "That's nice."

"What's nice?" she murmured, face buried in his soft polo shirt.

"*Eau de packrat,*" he laughed, and reached up to ruffle her hair. "Alan told me what you guys were doing."

"You should probably turn me upside down and shake me." She pushed him away as he stooped to do that very thing. He ushered her inside, and Carlos appeared from the kitchen holding a colander, several other ingredients of the evening meal smeared on his face.

"Better hurry up, *mamá,*" he called. "We gots it almost all done."

"You gots it, all right, *hijo,*" she replied. In the living room, Bill Gastner sat on the end of the sofa nearest the fireplace and the rocking chair, where Estelle's mother sat wrapped in a white Afghan.

"You go clean yourself up," Teresa said as Estelle started to cross the living room. Her voice was as tiny as she was, raspy and cracked, but her black eyes sparkled. She had drawn the Afghan up around her face as if the gentle gas fire beyond her chair produced no heat at all on this mild late summer evening. "*Por Dios*," she groused as Estelle bent to kiss her cheek. "Where have you been, *hija?*" Her aquiline nose wrinkled and she waved an arthritis-clawed hand.

"Doing a little spelunking," Estelle laughed, and she glanced at Gastner.

"Yeah, I told her some of it." He raised the can of dark ale to salute her. "I hope you didn't forget that you invited me for dinner, sweetheart."

"I had ulterior motives, *Padrino*. But let me get cleaned up a little."

"*Por favor,*" Teresa snipped. Nevertheless, her face, as wrinkled as the surface of a walnut, lit with a proud smile.

In the kitchen, Irma and Francisco were working together at the window counter, the pan of lasagna bubbling as it rested on hot pads between them. Now tall enough that he didn't have to reach up to the counter surface, Francisco was sculpting green chiles on a wooden board. As the boy deftly fashioned each piece of chile, he scooted it toward Irma, who slipped a fork under it and transferred it to the top of the lasagna.

"You have fifteen minutes," Irma said when she saw Estelle. "Or so," she amended.

"You're staying to enjoy all this, aren't you?"

"If I may. Gary has a game in Artesia today. I'm a football widow."

"Ah. Well, that's good for us." She leaned over her son, resting a hand lightly on his bony shoulder. With the razor sharp knife, he was cutting the slabs of skinned and seeded chile into small rosettes, little green bursts of flavor and aroma that Irma then arranged on top of the lasagna. To her left was a second pan, already decorated.

"This is an experiment," Francisco explained. "Ten minutes should be just enough to make them curl and crisp just right." His brown was furrowed with concentration.

"If it doesn't work, I brought over some hot dogs," Gastner called from the living room. Francisco ducked his head with pleasure. Estelle squeezed his shoulder.

"You've made enough for an army," she said.

"That one's for Mr. and Mrs. Romero," Francisco said without pausing in his work.

"Oh," she sighed, "They'll appreciate that, *querido*." She gave him another quick hug and then turned toward the sink where Carlos, just tall enough to see over the rim, was attacking carrots with the peeler, sculpting the roots into fantastic shapes that only he recognized.

"Will you take us to see the cave sometime?" he asked, pausing in his work.

"I'll have to think about that," Estelle replied. "It's just a dusty hole in the ground, *hijo*." That was hardly a deterrent, she knew, since excavating holes in the ground was the little boy's passion.

She felt grubby and out of place in this center of industrious creation, but five minutes later the blast of hot water from the shower began to pound away the grime and fatigue. For a long moment, she let the stream beat on her forehead and shampooed hair. She was standing thus when she heard the first shout.

Chapter Thirty-two

Francis Guzman slipped through the bathroom door just as Estelle punched off the water. When the roar ceased, she could hear the loud, incoherent shouting from the front of the house.

"George Romero is out on the front lawn trying to raise the dead," her husband said. "He's drunk as a skunk. Bill's talking with him."

"My radio's on the kitchen counter. Make sure Bill has it."

"He took it out with him."

"I'll be a just a minute, then, *Oso*. Keep him out of the house."

"That already happened. *Padrino* intercepted him on the front step."

Estelle toweled herself off quickly, her clothing soaking up the wet spots as she did a fireman's dress. As she came out of the bathroom, she saw Carlos standing in the dining room, looking toward the front door, his hands curled under his chin in that characteristic pose of delight or concern, depending. Irma had her hand on Francisco's shoulder, and Estelle motioned for them to relax and stay where they were.

When he'd gone outside, Doctor Guzman had closed the front door behind him, but even so Estelle could hear George Romero's alcohol-fueled harangue. She paused, hand on the knob, and listened. Bill Gastner's gruff voice offered up an assuaging stream of mellow commiseration, but George Romero was accepting none of it. His incoherence was fueled by alcohol, but she could hear the full measure of grief that had finally broken loose. Her name was thrown into the mix, but Estelle could not follow the context. If she appeared in the doorway, her very presence could fuel further eruption. But as Romero's voice choked in a tone that grew wilder, she saw no choice.

A second consideration presented itself, and she turned, heading for the back door. "Stay put," she said to the trio now gathered in the dining room. She tucked her Tazer into her belt and then slipped out the back door. With the massive open pit mine that Carlos was excavating, the swing set, the garden shed, the bicycles and trikes, the backyard was a burglar trap. She negotiated around them carefully in the dark, finding her way to the side gate.

The passage between the house and the side fence was five feet wide, illuminated by the street light in front of the neighbors. She could hear Romero clearly now.

"Look, I *talked* to her, see?" the man bleated, his voice high-pitched and cracking with emotion. "I talked to Carla and she oughta know. She saw the whole thing. She *told* me she saw the whole thing."

"That's a long way across that field, George," Gastner said, his tone gentle and conversational. "I'm not saying…"

"She wrestled the boy down, Bill. That's what Carla saw her do. When she shoulda been taking care of him, she *tackles* him. I mean, Jesus, what for? Couldn't Estelle see that my boy was hurting? Carla said…"

"Now look," Gastner said, "what she said she saw, and what really happened? You know, those can be two different things, George. She's what, two hundred yards away? Lookin' into the sun? And hell, she's an old lady. Probably got vision about like mine. Couldn't see a house at that distance."

"She coulda took him to the emergency room straight off. She coulda. But no, she wrestles with him, and makes him wait forever until the ambulance gets there." He blubbered something that Estelle couldn't understand. "And now he's blind." Romero balled his fists and took two steps away, head tilted back. "You tell her," he shouted, turning on Gastner, "that I want some answers, by God." By now he was openly crying. "I want some answers, by God."

Gastner reached out a hand as if to touch the man on the shoulder, but Romero apparently misinterpreted the motion. He swung a lumbering, clumsy blow at the older man, more of a fend-off than a punch, a swing that Gastner had no trouble in ducking.

"It's her fault." Romero staggered backward a step. Gastner saw Estelle advancing across the lawn, and held up a hand. "If she'd just taken care of the boy…I got to talk to her. Got to find out why…" He lunged as if to pass Gastner, and Francis Guzman stepped forward, blocking the sidewalk. But Gastner was faster. He reached out a hand, triggering another wild swing from Romero. So fast that even Estelle didn't see it coming, Gastner clamped Romero's right wrist, twisted, and spun the man around, his left hand hard on Romero's left shoulder, the man's right arm behind his back.

"You need to go home, George," he said. "It's a bad time, and you're drunk and upset. You don't know what you're saying. Keep this up and it's only going to cause you more grief."

Romero blubbered something incoherent, and twisted wildly in Gastner's grip. "My boys!" he wailed.

"Yeah, I know," Gastner said. "Let me walk you home, Georgie. Is your wife home?"

"No," Romero whimpered. "She's up in the city. She doesn't know…"

"Doesn't know what?"

"Carla said she saw the whole thing," Romero cried. "She saw it." He struggled and Estelle could see that this confrontation wasn't going anywhere constructive. And as soon as George Romero turned and saw her, he would erupt again. Coming to the same conclusion, Gastner's foot shot out and deftly jerked the man's legs out from under him, and in a moment Romero was flat on his face in the grass. With a smooth transfer of his grip, Gastner held the man down while his right hand swept his sweater to one side, darting to the handcuffs that draped over his belt.

"You can't..." Romero cried.

"I can until you behave yourself," Gastner said conversationally. He put a hand through Romero's right elbow and helped him up. The man swayed uncertainly. "Now, you can see how this is going to go," the former sheriff continued. "You're going to calm down, or are you going to have to spend the night in jail?"

"No," Romero moaned. "You can't. My wife is going to call me."

"And you want to be home and sober for that, my friend."

"She's with Butch. She was going to call..."

"Well, you can't talk to her like this," Gastner said. "Look, let me take you home."

"You got me all handcuffed," Romero said. "You aren't even sheriff any more."

"That's true, thank God," Gastner chuckled. "Look, here's what we're going to do. Estelle and I are going to walk you home, all right?" Romero turned enough and finally saw that Estelle Guzman was standing a couple paces away. "And if you want to talk with her, maybe when you're sober, we can arrange that. But right now you're stinking fall-down drunk, and that doesn't do anyone any good."

"You..." Romero said to Estelle, and then seemed to loose track of his jumbled thoughts. He swayed, eyes closed. "I can't sleep. I just lie there..."

"Maybe the doc can give you something," Gastner suggested, and Francis looked briefly heavenward.

"Not with what he's got in his system," he said. "He just needs to lie down for a bit and let the alcohol work."

"You hear that, Georgie?" Gastner said. "Just lie down for a little while. If Tata calls, I'll let you know. And then in the morning, we'll sort all this out." It didn't matter what he said, what promises he made. Estelle knew that George Romero wouldn't remember a bit of the conversation in the morning. "Come on," Gastner urged. "Let me walk you home."

Still mumbling, George Romero allowed himself to be led across the lawn, Bill Gastner's path a straight one, Romero's a meander. As they reached the sidewalk, a state police cruiser swung into Twelfth Street, its tires chirping on the pavement. It slid to an abrupt halt by the curb, and Officer Rick Black stepped out of the car, hesitating by the front fender.

"We're okay, Rick," Gastner said. "George here is just walking home to sleep it off." Black saw the handcuffs and then looked at Estelle questioningly.

"They'll be all right," she said.

"You want him charged? Public intox, anything like that?"

"No, no, no charges. That's the last thing he needs just now," Estelle said. "You might give Bill a hand getting Mr. Romero back inside." She pointed at the Romero residence. "Just over there."

The state trooper stepped to the sidewalk and slipped a hand through Romero's left elbow. "You going to be okay with us now, sir?" he said, voice kindly and helpful. "Too nice an evening for a ruckus, don't you think?"

Romero managed a string of unconnected syllables, and his knees wobbled.

"Just hang in there, sir," Black coaxed as he and Gastner weaved Romero down the sidewalk to his own front door.

"Keep my lasagna warm," Gastner said over his shoulder. "I'll be back just as soon as Georgie passes out."

Francis and Estelle stood on the grass, watching the odd trio—the uniformed Rick Black, nearly six feet-three and as slender as a track star, Bill Gastner a head shorter, burly, plodding, big buzz-cut head leaning close to George Romero's right ear, whispering encouraging instructions, and George Romero in the middle, now not much more than a sack of inebriation.

"Well, *that* was entertaining," Francis observed. "*Padrino* has done that sort of thing a time or two."

"Half a million or so," Estelle replied. "The world is full of drunks." She shook her head. "*Oso,* it's so sad, what's happened to that family." The physician put his arm around her shoulders, at the same time bending forward and looking at the Tazer in her belt.

"You were going to zap him?"

"If I had to. There's always room for a lot of talk first. *Padrino* knows that. But just in case."

"Who called the trooper?"

"I don't know. *Padrino* maybe. He has my handheld. He's very careful about not being a heroic victim himself."

"I don't have a clue what George was trying to say."

"Maybe when he's sober. Right now, in his alcoholic fog, nothing makes sense to him. He seems to think that I was wrestling his son just for the fun of it, when I should have been transporting." She shook her head wearily. "If I was in his shoes, and I thought that...I don't know what I'd do. Poor guy." She slipped her arm through her husband's. Down the street, lights came on in the Romero home, and a door slammed. "I'm glad the lasagna wasn't finished a half hour earlier," she added. "I can't imagine Francisco walking over to deliver it and stepping into the middle of *that*."

Back inside, Teresa stood in the foyer, braced upright with her aluminum walker.

"That's a sad, sad man," she said.

"Yes, he is, *mamá*. Maybe he'll have a long night's sleep. That's what he needs."

"He doesn't need to add to it by being stupid."

"I'm sure that deep in his heart he knows that," Estelle said.

"*Se me encogió el corazón,* what that family's been through," Teresa said.

Estelle escorted her mother to the dining room. "Maybe things will get back to normal now," she said. Both little boys watched her, their eyes big.

"I can take the lasagna over," Francisco said.

"Not tonight, *hijo*. Maybe tomorrow. Or maybe we'll freeze it and take it some other time. When Butchie comes home from the hospital, maybe."

"His dad was *ticked*."

Estelle laughed. "He was that, *hijo*."

"He thinks you hurt Butch?"

Ah, the ears of the young, Estelle thought. "I hope he doesn't think that, *querido.* We both would have liked to have seen help get there about ten minutes earlier, though."

"He wasn't *hurt* ten minutes earlier," the boy said.

"Exactly, *hijo.*" She hugged him, and directed him to his chair at the table. "And you did everything that you could for him. And I did what *I could.* So that's what we all have to live with…Mr. Romero included."

"Is *Padrino* coming back?"

"Yes. Just as soon as he's sure Mr. Romero is going to be all right."

"Are you going over, too?"

"Not just now, *hijo.* Mr. Romero and I will come to terms with all this when he's sober."

"Can we wait for *Padrino,* then?" Francisco asked.

"Yes. He won't be long."

"I want him to see what the top looks like before it gets all messed up," the boy said. They didn't have long to wait. In ten minutes, the state police cruiser pulled away from the curb, and Bill Gastner returned, frowning so hard his bushy eyebrows almost touched in the middle.

"Do you hoodlums have *any* idea," he said, glaring at first Francisco and then his little brother, "how good this all smells comin' in from outside? You guys split one between you, and I'll eat the other one."

"That's for our neighbors!" Francisco screeched in delight, fending the old man away from the lasagna. Gastner spun the boy around and gave him a knuckle sandpaper on the top of his skull before letting him go.

"He'll be all right," Gastner said to Estelle. "Out like a light. I corked up the booze and put it away. Rick's going to pass the word to Kenderman, and they'll do a close patrol for the rest of the night." He set the radio on the counter and grinned at Estelle. "That thing still fits the hand pretty good."

Chapter Thirty-three

Two elderly women had asked her to move suitcases down from the attic, a cramped dust-laden cavern with impossibly low, rough ceilings. She ended up dragging the suitcases out by crawling backward on her stomach, the wood splinters from the floor tearing her uniform blouse. The two suitcases became entangled in an impossibly long garden hose, unyielding after the freezing temperatures. She jerked awake. The three inch numerals on the clock said 2:13 a.m. She lay quietly for a moment, staring at the ceiling, wondering what had been in the dream suitcases.

And how does a murder happen in a cave? That was a heavy suitcase of puzzle pieces.

To her surprise, Bill Gastner hadn't been much help, other than to categorically deny that Mexican cartels had anything to do with the killing of Eddie Johns.

"That's not their way," he said when the two little boys were occupied helping Irma between main course and dessert. "They're KISS operators if there ever was. 'Keep it simple, *señor.*' If they had wanted Johns dead, they would have popped him down in Juarez, or in a quiet alley in El Paso, right then and there. They wouldn't travel all the way up to Posadas County so that they could crawl after him into a cave."

"Inspecting their real estate?" Estelle had posed.

"Nah." Gastner waved a hand in dismissal. "What for? There's no point. Eddie Johns had nothing to sell but an idea.

The land wasn't his. The cave wasn't his. And it wasn't even *his* idea, for God's sakes. Maybe he had some contacts for weapons or crack dealing, but I doubt it. Eddie Johns was more talk than anything else."

He leaned back in his chair, patting his rotund gut and looking wistfully toward the kitchen. "Somebody in the neighborhood took a shot at Freddy Romero," he said, voice a whisper. "Bender's Canyon isn't the sort of place that attracts casual tourists, sweetheart, but it's amazing how many human beings there actually *are* in a couple square miles. Jumpy hunters, ranchers, bird watchers, BLM, the list goes on and on. Maybe somebody lay in wait, maybe. And maybe boom! Bobby says it's a bullet fragment, and he's never wrong about things like that. But unfortunately," and he folded his hands in front of him, "you don't have squat for evidence. What little you have says that's what happened. And if that shooting is related to the body in the cave, then we're looking for someone local, sweetheart. Bet on it. Someone's got himself a secret. Or *had* one. He got edgy when Freddy's story hit the newspaper, and more so when he saw him snooping around."

The boys reappeared with the cherry cobbler and toppings, just seconds after Teresa Reyes had said, with considerable acid, that more of that dark topic didn't belong at the dinner table.

Someone local. Estelle listened as that thought rolled around in her head for the rest of the evening. It stayed there through dessert, through Francisco's concert, through small talk and late evening coffee. It stayed there long after Bill Gastner and Irma Sedillos had left, and the house fell quiet.

Local. If taken literally to mean local *residents,* then the list was short. Herb Torrance owned the pasturage southwest of the mesa, all the way out to Bender's Canyon Trail. Freddy Romero had died on Herb's property at the bottom of the arroyo. Miles Waddell owned the northeast side of the mesa, including the cave where Freddy's apparent efforts at spelunking had taken place— and in all likely hood where Eddie Johns had met his end. Both men knew Eddie Johns—and both men knew Freddy Romero.

"That's a short list," Estelle whispered to the darkness. Her husband twitched and stuffed his face even farther into the pillow, but two fingers found her shoulder and tapped gently. "I'm just mulling, *querido*," she whispered. "Don't mind me." The two fingers tapped once more and curled away. In a moment, his breathing grew deep and regular.

Who else could be considered local? A few Bureau of Land Management employees who roamed the area on a regular basis from their field office in Deming. Members of her own department on occasion, especially the sheriff himself, who could give Bill Gastner a run for his money as a walking, talking gazetteer of Posadas County. A few patrons of Victor Sanchez' Broken Spur Saloon, who might wander up the canyon once in a while.

Spread the net a little wider and it would catch high school kids who sought secluded spots for partying. Gus Prescott, who sometimes paid attention to his failed ranch and sometimes didn't. He'd driven his old road grader over to Waddell's and bladed a ragged scar up the side of the mesa. Maybe he'd known Eddie Johns, maybe not. His daughter had been dating Freddy Romero—Casey Prescott, as delightful as any child who walked the planet.

Estelle turned over with a quick toss, enough motion that her husband's breathing snorted out of rhythm and then settled again.

Unless he was both supremely confident and a supremely good actor, Miles Waddell was telling the truth. He hadn't dirtied his trim hands with the murder of Eddie Johns. Bill Gastner had suggested starting the suspect list with Waddell, but it wasn't promising.

Herb Torrance had the volatile temper, no doubt the opportunity, the savvy. But why would he bother? The fantasy of a mesa-top observatory certainly wasn't *his* dream. He would gain nothing from the project except the possible nuisance of more traffic, more folks with cameras, more voices drifting down from the mesa top on the still night air.

Freddy Romero. Estelle closed her eyes against the glare of the clock, trying to recall the last time she had talked with the teenager. Perhaps a month or more, but she couldn't remember the circumstances. A hand raised in recognition on the street when they passed, or from the field in the dust of a four-wheeler. She remembered one instance, driving by on Twelfth, when she had seen the Romero brothers, along with their father, with truck parts spread on a tarp on the driveway apron.

If Freddy had talked with someone that fateful Thursday, it could have been when he first parked his truck—no four-wheeler tracks led up to the Borracho Springs campground. Or, it could have been on the two-track below the cave. Or...

Estelle rubbed her forehead with frustration. Backtracking the boy's movements from that awful moment when he'd hurled into the arroyo was going to be a hit-or-miss undertaking. Her hand froze, the light in the room just enough for her to see the shadow of her fingers. She replayed the memory of seeing the boy on his four-wheeler, raising dust along the highway, and knew exactly where to start.

Chapter Thirty-four

An hour at the Sheriff's Office in the quiet of early Monday morning was more than adequate to review the depressingly short list of evidence. The bullet fragment in the front tire of the four-wheeler was brass, which meant a jacketed projectile, rather than the pure lead of a .22 rimfire. The Smith and Wesson that Freddy had recovered offered two clear fingerprints that belonged to the young man, along with some smudgy, useless prints, but nothing more. Fingerprints on the magazine and a thumbprint on each cartridge belonged to the gun's owner, Eddie Johns, matched to a set faxed to their department by Grant County. No longer did they have to depend on Miles Waddell's opinion for the corpse's identity. Where Johns had purchased the weapon was still open to question, but Estelle expected no great revelations there.

Sgt. Tom Mears had found an address in Las Cruces that appeared to be the most recent residence for Johns, and had set out for the city before dawn to start the process toward obtaining a warrant. The man's landlord—if there was one—might have interesting things to say, as might a mortgage holder. That no one had reported Johns missing in the first place didn't surprise Estelle. Johns wasn't the sort who would be missed—or at least whose absence would be regretted, except by those to whom he owed money.

The puzzle remained about one boot—the remains found in the cave included remnants of shirt, trousers, and underwear and a sock. Coyotes could account for that, tugging the boots away as playthings, the leather soles offering a pleasant chew.

The single pistol bullet recovered from the cave ceiling was a tentative match with the slug found in the cat's skull, and the loaded rounds remaining in the Smith and Wesson. The single .40 shell casing, the packrat's prize, was a certain match with the handgun.

Tires had bent grass near the homestead but little else—enough only for a rough measurement that would fit the track of any modern, full-sized pickup, or even some sedans. Nothing linked those tracks to either the evidence in the cave, or for that matter, to Freddy's fatal dive. The oil seep that Jackie Taber had found was just that, indicating only that someone had recently parked beside the old homestead. *Recently,* so that the oil hadn't soaked away. But that was no certain clock.

Shortly before eight that Monday morning, Estelle left the office and drove south on State 56, mulling the added puzzle of the five years that had passed between the deaths of Eddie Johns and Freddy Romero. Freddy's lie about the cave location was simple enough—he'd found something intriguing, and with a teenager's confidence that his actions would prompt no consequences, had kept the cave's location a secret so he could explore further. He'd then found the pistol, and bolted, speeding back toward town. To inform authorities? Probably not. To return better equipped for exploration and recovery? Probably. Had someone chased him off the site? Had someone chased him *toward* another party, lying in wait with a rifle?

The tires of her Crown Victoria thumped across the expansion joints of the Rio Guijarro bridge, and Estelle realized that so preoccupied was she that she had no recollection of the twenty-six miles that had passed. As she braked to turn off the highway, she keyed the mike and checked in with dispatch, but the rest of the county was thankfully quiet.

No patrons were parked in front of the Broken Spur Saloon, but the establishment's hours were flexible—the bar was open whenever owner Victor Sanchez decided to turn the key—sometimes by seven in the morning to catch the traveling breakfast flock, sometimes by ten. The sign on the front door claimed 8:00 a.m. to midnight daily except a sleep-in until 1:00 p.m. on Sunday. Victor managed his somewhat casual version of that 107 hour workweek with assistance from his son, Victor Junior, and the mother-daughter team of Mary and Macie Trujillo, who commuted over the pass from Regál each day.

The Trujillos had worked at Victor's for less than a year, hired after Gus Prescott's eldest daughter Christine had resigned from bartending to attend college in Las Cruces.

As Estelle pulled into the Broken Spur's parking lot, she saw the Trujillos' Jeep nosed in along the east side of the adobe building. Just visible behind the squat saloon was Victor Junior's aging Dodge Ram Charger. Estelle drove around the rear of the saloon, and saw that Victor's semi-vintage Cadillac was missing from its usual spot beside the mobile home that teed into the saloon itself.

She parked beside the Jeep. The dash clock read 8:12 a.m., and Estelle made the notation in her log before climbing out of the car. She stood in the blast of morning sunshine for a moment, looking down the highway. The sun would have been at her back on Thursday, when she'd seen the ATV roaring down the highway shoulder. She hadn't paid any attention at the time. There had been no other traffic that she could remember. If someone had been pursuing Freddy, he wouldn't have seen the boy turn off the highway, swerving down behind the saloon.

But someone at the saloon *could* have. She turned and surveyed the building. Only the small, frosted restroom window faced east, but someone standing in either the saloon's front door or the kitchen entrance would have an unobstructed view. The undersheriff closed her eyes, forcing her memory to concentrate, but there had been no reason to pay attention at the time. She'd been preoccupied with paperwork, remembered catching a glimpse of an ATV, and that had been it.

She could *imagine* the agile little machine cutting across the saloon's parking lot, but she had no clear recollection of it. The

ATV *had* to have done that—or disappear into thin air. The ATV and rider would have been momentarily obscured by patrons' vehicles…a handful of pickups and SUVs, perhaps?

She shook her head with impatience and walked toward the back door. The kitchen door was open, and she rapped on the screen's frame.

"Hey, in here," a husky woman's voice called, and Estelle tipped the door open and stepped inside. Mary Trujillo was standing on a short, three-step ladder, hard at work on the stainless stove hood with bucket and sponge. "Well, how about that," she said with a broad smile. She stepped down carefully and set the bucket on the floor. "You come for some coffee? Just made a pot."

"No thanks. How are you doing, Mary?"

"Well, when it comes down to it, I'm just fine. Victor had to go to Cruces, if it's him you're looking for."

"Probably not," Estelle replied. Victor Sanchez had not built his moderately successful business with pleasant personality. In fact, his foul temper was legendary. Bill Gastner could usually goad the saloonkeeper to civility, and Bobby Torrez could but didn't bother. Estelle had noticed that on the rare occasions when she'd been in the Broken Spur, Victor had simply ignored her. He had no love of law enforcement, and Estelle respected his reasons.

Mary Trujillo, on the other hand, was a plump, bustling ray of sunshine who managed to avoid Victor's personal cloud of gloom and grump.

"So, what are you all about this lovely morning?" she asked, and snapped off her rubber gloves. She fetched a coffee mug and held it toward Estelle. "Sure?"

"Really, no thanks. I'm looking for a little information, Mary. I was wondering if you worked last Thursday?"

"Thursday?" The woman regarded the ceiling for just a moment. "Sure I worked Thursday."

"Both you and Macie?"

"You get one, you get the other," Mary quipped. She pulled a hand towel off the rack beside the sink and wiped her face and neck, patting at the various rings of fat under her chin. "I *hate* that cleaning fluid," she said, nodding at the bucket. "Victor says it's the best, but the fumes are positively *hell* on my skin."

She snapped the towel out, folded it neatly, and hung it up. "So…"

"Do you remember somebody on an ATV riding in the area?"

The woman closed her eyes and drew in a breath through open mouth. She held that thoughtful pose for a moment, and then said, "Oh, *him*." She didn't open her eyes. "You know, was *that* the youngster that they say ran into the canyon? What, later on Thursday?" She opened her eyes and stared at Estelle, her hands entwining in her apron. "One of the guys said that's who it was."

"You saw him?"

"I did. Heard first. That thing he was on was *loud*, you know. Don't they make mufflers for those things?"

Estelle smiled. "It's supposed to sound powerful and aggressive, Mary."

"Well, it did that. Junior and I were standing by the back door, taking a smoke break. Down the road comes this kid, and when he cut across the parking lot, I was sure that he was going to slide right into the side of the building."

"He saw you?"

"Oh, I'm sure he did. He looked right at us. And that's who that was? The Romero boy?"

"We think so."

"Well, I'm sorry it happened, but I'm not the least bit surprised. He was riding like a maniac. But that's what those kids do when they're on those things, isn't it." She sipped her coffee while the other hand groped in her apron for a pack of cigarettes. "Right out here," she said. Estelle followed her back outside.

"What a view, you know?" She gazed off across the prairie toward the east, the hand that held the cigarette shielding her eyes from the sun. "Anyway, we were right here. He cut down off the highway, and right through here." The sweep of her arm included the parking lot and then the country to the north. "In fact, you can still see his tracks, over there where the dirt's kind of soft."

"Victor Junior was with you?"

"Yep."

"Is he here today?"

"He will be. He took the truck and went to town for a bit. But he was right here with me. That's the truth."

"And anyone else?"

"Just him and me, sheriff. That's all. I mean, it's no big thing, right? The kid rode by, and off he went." She drew deeply on the cigarette and then ground it out as she exhaled. "Shame what happened. These boys...they think they're indestructible, don't they."

"Mary, can you tell me who else was in the saloon at the time? Who else *might* have seen the youngster ride by? From the front door, from even—I don't know—the bathroom window? Someone who had just arrived and was still outside?"

Mary patted her apron as if to double check the cigarette pack, but she resisted the temptation. "We weren't terribly busy. That's all I remember. Just some of the guys...I think. Now, Macie was inside, so she might remember. But you know, you can't see the parking lot from the bar. These guys like the deep dark cave thing, you know."

Estelle laughed, and Mary looked at her quizzically. "But so what, I mean. I saw him, Victor saw him. I mean, everybody knows he went by here."

"Just a question of loose ends," Estelle said. "Do you think Macie has a minute?"

"Oh, I'm sure," Mary said. "She was going to go with Junior, but I said no. I mean, I don't have any intention of running the place all by myself while those two are off mooning together." Apparently romance could conquer even the cloying aroma of onions, green chile, and perspiration, Estelle thought. Mary pushed the door to the barroom open. "Macie! The sheriff wants to talk with you."

Macie Trujillo, dressed in a fluffy white blouse with Mexican lace and a flowing scarlet skirt that would have been perfect for a twirling dancer, was frowning at glassware behind the bar. Short and stocky like her mother, Macie wore enough jewelry that it clinked and winked from her wrists, fingers, and ears as she worked. An enormous necklace of turquoise and silver—worth a fortune if the stones and metal were real, and expensive even if they weren't—rested on the broad, voluptuous curves of her chest above the deep dish of her blouse.

"Thanks, Mary." Estelle let the door swing shut behind her.

Macie favored the undersheriff with a radiant smile, generous mouth armored with straight, large teeth whose brilliant white was set off by wide swaths of crimson lipstick. "Hi!" she greeted, and there was nothing reserved or cautious in her manner.

"Good morning, Macie." Estelle slid onto one of the tall stools, elbows on the polished wood of the bar, and she held up a hand as Macie started the bartender's coordinated shuffle sideways, looking at Estelle with raised eyebrow while her left hand reached for the coffee pot. "No thanks. I just wanted to ask you a couple things about last week."

"Oh," Macie said, and both hands dropped to the bar's surface. Ten fingers, eight rings. Only the middle finger of each hand was unadorned. "I *heard.*" Her face wrinkled up in sympathy. "That boy who got killed, right?"

"Yes." Estelle waited to see what Macie might add without prompts.

"Mom probably told you that he rode right by here that day? When was it, Wednesday or Thursday? *I* could hear him from in here."

"You didn't see him?"

"No, but at least one of the guys did."

"One of the guys?"

"You know, the patrons."

"Would you tell me exactly what happened that day?"

"Well, nothing happened in here, you know." Macie reached in her apron pocket and found a piece of peppermint candy. She unwrapped it thoughtfully, and then popped it in her mouth. "We heard his four-wheeler come *roaring* through the parking lot…crazy kids, you know. I remember that Miles Waddell came out of the restroom, this big grin on his face, shaking his head."

"Mr. Waddell was here, then."

"Oh, yeah. He said he glanced out the window and thought that the kid was going to crash right into the side of the building."

"Kids ride around here a lot, I imagine?"

"Well, not a *lot*." She sucked on the peppermint and crunched a small piece. "There aren't so many kids around these days, you know? Herb Torrance's boys are all grown. But I felt real bad. Freddy had stopped in a time or two." She smiled, but the smile faded to regret. "He was kinda cute, you know? He was goin' with Casey Prescott. You know her, I bet?"

"Sure."

"I guess that might be why he was way down here, huh."

"That could be, Macie. You'd seen them together before?"

The girl frowned. "No, but my sis...she's a senior this year... she told me about it all." She finished with a shrug. "Freddy was a wild one." A note of admiration crept into her tone.

"Do you remember who else was here at the time?"

"Oh, God..." Macie frowned and looked toward the door as if the ghosts of customers past might be parading through. "No, wait...there was that big family that stopped in. From Mexico? They were sitting at those two tables over there, by the window. They were afraid something was going wrong with their Excursion."

"You could see the vehicle?"

"No. They were talking about it, and that's what Mr. Waddell said they had. Him and Mr. Prescott were joking about it, wondering how they could afford such a fancy rig." Macie wrinkled her nose with some displeasure. "*I'd* hate to be stranded in a foreign country like that, but the ranchers thought it was funny."

Of course, Estelle thought. *All Mexicans are poor, and all their problems are funny.* She found herself liking Miles Waddell even less. "The folks were southbound?"

Macie shook her head. "They wanted to get to Albuquerque. They talked to Victor some. He gave them a gallon of antifreeze and some water to get them to the garage in Posadas."

"Ah. Well, that was nice of him."

"Victor can be a good guy when he wants to be." Macie glanced toward the kitchen. "Nine kids. That's what they had with them. The Mexican family, I mean. *Nine.* Can you imagine? *Madre, padre, dos tías, y un* poodle." She splayed out fingers. "Thirteen people and a dog in the same truck."

"Do you remember if Mr. Waddell left right after he saw the four-wheeler ride by?"

"Well…I don't know. Let's see…some guys from the gas company stopped by, and Mr. Waddell was talking with them. And then Herb Torrance stopped by—he was on his way somewhere and wanted to pick up a Thermos of coffee. I remember that. He didn't stay long, though. Him and Gus left together, but then two more gas company guys came in, and I lost track." She shrugged. "Lots of people, you know? What was it exactly that you're trying to find out?"

Estelle laughed gently. "Just loose ends, Macie. And I appreciate your good memory."

Chapter Thirty-five

Her cell phone saved any further explanation, and she pushed off the stool to answer it.

"Guzman."

"Hey, Estelle," Tom Mears said. "Catch you at a bad time?"

"No...let me get outside." She turned to the girl. "Macie, thanks. I appreciate your help."

After the dark of the saloon, the sunshine was bright enough to make her flinch, and she turned her back against it. "What do you have, Tom?"

"For one thing, some people with *long* memories," the sergeant said. "I'm standing in front of the last known address for Eddie Johns. It's a little two-bedroom furnished rental over on East Pellor Street. The folks who live here now say they've been in the house for four years. The landlord says that Johns lived in the place for almost two years before that, and was a good tenant. Even painted the place and put in new kitchen tile."

"And then?"

"And then he skipped. Just walked away from it."

"Moved out?"

"Nope. Just walked. Went out the door one day, and didn't come back. The landlord doesn't know what happened."

"What about all his personal effects?"

"According to the landlord, there wasn't much. A nice stereo, flat-screen TV, some simple furniture. The usual kitchen stuff, some clothes. He waited to hear for two months, then cleaned everything out and put it all in one of those little storage units? Another month went by, and he rented the place out again. At the end of the year, he gave all the stuff to a hospital auxiliary thrift shop. He kept the stereo and flat screen as payment."

"Thoughtful. Did he try to track Johns down?"

"Nope. 'I ain't no private detective,' he told me. Said it wasn't any of his business what happened. He said Johns paid his rent in cash all the time, which the landlord appreciated."

"Plus I'm sure he's enjoying the TV and the stereo," Estelle observed. "Any luck with his vehicle? Waddell says that the last one he remembers was a Ford truck."

"Last known registration expired October, 2007. The Pellor address was the only one the MVD showed. The registration should appear on a 2004 Ford three-quarter ton crew cab, color black. License Adam Charlie Baker niner seven one. You want the VIN?"

"Sure." She jotted the lengthy string of digits and letters in her notebook as the sergeant recited them.

"It's south of the border somewhere by now, enjoying a new life on those beautiful dirt roads, no doubt."

"I wouldn't be surprised."

"Look, I'm going to nose around a few other places and talk to some folks. I found out who his insurance agent is, and I'm going to visit with her here in about an hour. Maybe she can give me a line on where Johns was doing his banking. On a truck like that, I'd expect that maybe he was making payments. The bank might be interested in what happened."

"But if it was free and clear, that would explain why no one from the bank ever nosed around, looking for their truck," Estelle added.

"Yep. This guy's a ghost. That's the impression I'm getting."

"He is now, anyway. In a way, it's sort of sad, Tom. No one seems to have cared about him enough to miss him when he took a dive. You'll be back this afternoon sometime?"

"I'll work at it. I'd really like to find his dentist, Estelle. We have Waddell's word that these remains might belong to Eddie

Johns, and now we have a couple of fingerprints from the ammo. None of that is one hundred percent, though."

"That would be a priority, Tom. The Cruces PD is cooperating?"

"You bet."

"By the way, it turns out that Miles Waddell was at the Broken Spur when Freddy Romero rode by on his ATV. Mary and her daughter saw the boy, and she says that Waddell did too. He happened to look out the bathroom window when he heard the four-wheeler."

The phone remained silent as Tom Mears digested that. "He was able to positively ID the rider as Freddy?"

"I haven't talked to him yet about that. But Mary did. She had a clear, close-up view. Freddy waved at her."

"Odd that Waddell didn't bother to mention that little fact when we talked to him out at the cave."

"Slipped his mind," Estelle said dryly.

"Yeah. Sure enough. You gotta wonder how many other things have slipped his mind. But that's something, then. I filled in the sheriff, by the way. He's pulling in some resources from the state police and the federales. He wants to know what Eddie Johns was up to down south, especially after what Waddell said about Mexican money being interested in the astronomy project."

"Seems a likely connection, doesn't it. And on the other hand, probably not."

"You don't think so?"

"No, I don't. I agree with Bill Gastner. No Mexican hit man is going to pop Johns up here in a small cave, and then try to conceal the job. A dark alley in El Paso or Juarez works much better. Far more efficient."

"You're going to corner Waddell again this morning?"

"We'll see. I have some other contacts that I want to check out first."

"And that be..." Estelle could hear the amusement in his voice.

"Macie Trujillo says that Gus Prescott was in the saloon on the afternoon when Freddy Romero rode by. Both he and Waddell... *and* Herb Torrance. And some folks from the gas company. *And* a big extended Mexican family worried about car problems. And, and, and. That's a large pool of potential witnesses. And it turns out there *I* was, a quarter of a mile down the highway."

Mears sighed wearily. "And so it goes. Do you have the old man working with you this morning?"

"I haven't seen Bill since last night, but I was thinking about waking him up to go with me out to the Prescotts. I want to hear Gus' take on all this, and *Padrino* knows him better than I do."

She knew that there was no worry about waking up Bill Gastner. He might take a quick nap after a heavy breakfast, perhaps, but nothing more than that. The undersheriff started the car, checked in briefly with dispatch, and then pushed the auto dial for *Padrino's* cell phone. Ten rings later, she switched it off and pulled out onto the highway behind a northbound white van with Mexican plates. She had seen the same vehicle on other occasions, and this time counted ten heads inside. The men were headed for the auto auctions in Denver as drivers, and in a day or so, their tandem rigs would be daisy-chained on the interstate, one older model car or truck pulling a second, headed to markets in Mexico.

The van stayed a bit below the speed limit, and Estelle watched it take the various humps and bumps in the pavement. The left rear tire mushroomed out, too soft for the load.

"PCS, three-ten will be stopping Chihuahua tag Victor Echo Charlie seven, mile marker eight on State 56, Borracho Springs. Safety check, no violation."

"Ten four, three ten. It's going to be a while for the Mexican license check."

"Negative on that. I know the vehicle." She waited a moment until the driver had an obvious choice for a safe spot to pull over, then reached down and flipped the switch for the grill lights. The van wobbled slightly as the red light display behind him startled the driver. Just ahead of them, at the Borracho Springs turn-out, Estelle saw a late model pick-up truck parked, a fair collection of radio and computer antennae sprouting from the roof, and the shield of the livestock inspector on the door. The van driver may well have thought he was the target of a squeeze play between officers, but he stopped the van carefully, four-way flashers blinking.

As Estelle approached on the right side of the vehicle, she saw a head or two straighten up inside. Half the passengers had been dozing, and they now turned to watch her approach. The passenger window wound down, the young man's hands in view.

"Good morning, sir," Estelle said in Spanish. She stepped just far enough forward to see the driver, a middle-aged man with a thin mustache and bright smile who kept both hands on the steering wheel. "Sir, I stopped you because it looks like your left rear tire is going flat."

The driver looked heavenward, and tapped the gear lever with his hand as if making sure it was in Park. "May I get out, sheriff?" he asked in flawless English.

"Of course, sir."

He turned and looked back at his passengers. "Stay in the van," he ordered in Spanish, and then climbed out. Walking back to the rear of the vehicle, he knelt beside the offending tire, now so soft that the sidewall was buckled.

"*Ay,*" he said, and reached out to touch the tire as if it were somehow suffering. "I was hoping it would last until Posadas, but I don't think so."

"You have a spare, señor?"

"But of course."

"It would be best if you used it. You're running heavy, señor."

"And that's if…" he said with a wry nod. He pushed himself upright and walked to the back doors. The spare was covered with a well-worn boot, and he thumped it tentatively. "Not good," he said. "So…the tire is flat, the spare is flat, and here we are."

"I have a can of Fix-Flat," Estelle said. "Let's see if that's enough to get you into town."

As she walked back toward her vehicle, she saw that Bill Gastner had gotten out of his truck and was ambling down the shoulder of the highway toward them, hands in his pockets, enjoying the sunshine. He reached out to shake hands with the van driver, and they waited together until Estelle returned with the aerosol can of tire magic. She shook it briefly and handed it to the Mexican.

"Ah," he said. "This would be good. We *hope* it will be good."

Estelle glanced inside the van and saw that nine sets of eyes were regarding her with varying degrees of interest. The Fix-Flat hissed, and the tire slowly inflated a bit. The Mexican adjusted the nozzle and spritzed some more. "I think that's the best we can expect," he said, and disconnected the can.

"Keep it," Estelle said as he started to hand it to her. "You have twenty-two miles to go."

He waggled his eyebrows and grimaced in consternation. "Then I should not waste time," he said.

"Good luck, Bernardo," Gastner said.

The Mexican looked at Estelle. "We are free to go, *agente?*"

"Of course, sir. You folks have a good day."

"Many, many thanks. You've been very kind." He patted the flank of the van as he made his way back to the driver's door. Bill Gastner settled comfortably against the fender of Estelle's Crown Victoria as they watched the Mexican van accelerate away. He folded his arms across his considerable paunch and regarded Estelle with amusement.

"You've been in the lion's den," he said. "I saw your car at the saloon when I drove by. Did you find out anything I should know?"

"First of all, Victor is in Las Cruces and Junior went to Posadas, so I was able to talk with the two girls. Interesting."

Gastner waited while Estelle joined him in leaning against the fender. An enormous RV rumbled down the highway southbound, and the driver lifted two fingers from the wheel in salute. Gastner returned the salute. "And how interesting was it?"

"Well," Estelle said, "for one thing, Macie said that Miles Waddell watched Freddy Romero zoom by the Broken Spur on his four-wheeler—at the same time that *I* was just down the road and caught a glimpse of the ATV. They said that Freddy rode along the highway shoulder, then swerved across the saloon's parking lot. Mary was standing outside by the back door, taking a cigarette break when she saw him. And when Waddell came out of the restroom, he joked that the boy looked as if he was going to skid right into the side of the building."

"Huh."

"Gus Prescott was in the saloon at the time, along with Herb Torrance. They both left shortly after the boy rode by."

"And you're assuming… "

"I'm trying not to assume anything, *Padrino*. But I have this allergy to coincidence."

Gastner uncrossed his arms and drummed his fingers on the sedan's fender. "Either the shooter was out near the cave when Freddy arrived, or he followed the kid out there. If he followed him out there, he had to see him go by at one time or another."

"That's what I'm thinking, sir."

"You're assuming that no one saw him over at Borracho."

"They could have. I don't know. But I don't have any indication that someone did, *Padrino*."

"Huh." His heavy eyebrows furrowed and he rapped the fender again. "The girl knew, right?"

"Casey? I'm sure she did. She was with him the first time, and they had an argument about both his driving and his spelunking. She helped him pack the skull so it wouldn't be damaged. She had to know that Freddy wouldn't be able to resist more exploration."

"Odd that she didn't want to go with him."

"His driving, for one thing, *Padrino*. On a four-wheeler, he's close to being a lunatic…well, sadly, *was* close to it. She didn't share his enthusiasm for going airborne."

"Casey reminds me of her older sister in that respect. Christine is about as levelheaded and mature as it's possible to get."

Estelle nodded. "Both of them are. Freddy was a polar opposite, which was part of the attraction, I suppose."

"You gotta wonder…"

"Sir?"

"Now I'm a parent, and so are you. I can't imagine Gus being too thrilled about young Freddy squiring his daughter around."

"No, sir. That would be an understatement…and for several reasons."

Gastner grinned. "You want to go up there now? He might be home on a Monday morning."

"I would."

"He'll be delighted to see you, I'm sure." Gastner's light sarcasm wasn't lost on her.

"Well, it's hard to live in New Mexico, right up against the border of Mexico, and not run into us Mexicans," she laughed. "But we get along all right. You might think of something to ask that I miss."

"Oh, sure." Gastner laughed and nodded toward his state truck. "I'll follow you in."

Chapter Thirty-six

Just south of Moore, a well-used two-track turned off to the north, crossing the Rio Salinas at a spot where the bedrock had been scrubbed bare by periodic gushers. On the arroyo's bank, as if the land owner knew that the deep arroyo crossing would intimidate visitors, a neat sign encouraged them: *Prescott Ranch, 1.5 mi.*

Estelle glanced in the rear-view mirror to see Gastner, always the gentleman, pause at the south arroyo edge as she guided the Crown Vic down the steep slope and up the other side. When she was safely across, he followed, the stiffly sprung, high-clearance rig making short work of the crossing.

The 1.5 mi. promised by the sign took them in a circuitous route around a low mesa and across another much smaller arroyo which, with one more frog strangler, might pose some interesting challenges. From a small rise, Estelle could see the double-wide mobile home, framed on one side by a windmill that was missing half of its blades and off to the left, the scattering of outbuildings, a fair museum of old machinery and vehicles, and at least two corrals.

A plume of dust arose as a front-loader swung in a tight circle, its mammoth bucket loaded. From a quarter mile away, Estelle couldn't tell what the activity was, but as she drew closer, she saw that the front-loader was stacking junk on the back of a long flatbed trailer. With finesse, the operator set the pancaked car body on top of the load, deftly nudging it into a secure position before backing away.

As she and Gastner approached, she could see the front-loader operator pause. He was working down the line of junked vehicles that Gus Prescott had accumulated over the years, but he stopped the machine, its bucket resting on the roof of an ancient International pickup that appeared to have sunk into the prairie sand over the years.

The operator shut down the diesel and swung down.

"Ah," Estelle whispered, and glanced behind her again. Gastner was in no rush, several hundred yards behind her, arm out the window, hand draped over the wing mirror. Stub Moore, the front-loader operator and a county employee, was no doubt embarrassed at their arrival. The round insignia on the loader's door announced the Posadas County Highway Department. Neither Stub nor the loader belonged on Gus Prescott's ranch doing private work. At the same time, Estelle knew this was not the least bit unusual—a culvert installed here, a ditch there, a surplus load of crusher fines spread on a driveway.

As she slowed the car and swung in behind the truck, Stub pulled off his gloves, dusting his jeans with ineffectual slaps. As the undersheriff shut off the car, she heard a door slam, and saw the lanky figure of Gus Prescott angling out of the house.

"Mornin', sheriff," Stub said. He found a handy spot along the flat-bed trailer to lean, and groped a cigarette from his shirt pocket…his county shirt, complete with *Posadas County Highway Department* embroidered over the right breast pocket flap, and *Stub Moore* over the left. He watched Bill Gastner park behind Estelle's county car.

"You folks are hard at it this morning," Estelle said, keeping any note of reproof or curiosity out of her voice.

"Cleaning up," Stub replied.

"What a day, eh?" Bill Gastner greeted as he sauntered up. He extended a hand to Stub, then turned just in time to do the same to Gus Prescott. The rancher looked awful, Estelle thought…the gray, sunken skin of either a cancer patient or someone running near the edge of exhaustion. His cheek bones stood out in sharp relief, his eyes sunken. A nasty sore marked the corner of his lower lip. The constant string of cigarettes didn't help. Gus and Stub matched puff for puff, and Bill Gastner, a recovering nicotine addict himself, shuffled to one side so that he was standing upwind of the effluvia.

"I just decided it's time," Prescott said, anticipating the question. "You know, this string of junk's been collecting since 1951, when old Lewis bought this place. I inherited most of it, but," and he shrugged, "been addin' to it some over the years." Eyeing the trailer load growing behind him, he stepped closer and tapped end of a bumper with all but a postage stamp of chrome missing. What was crushed on top of the bumper was unrecognizable. "This here was a 1946 Chevy pickup. Probably coulda found some son-of-a-bitch who would buy it for restoration, but there wasn't enough left. Got caught up in that flood on the Salinas." He looked at Gastner. "You remember that. The one in '55?"

"Nope, I don't. I was in Germany in 1955, Gus. Freezing my tail off. How'd you happen on it, anyway?"

"Thought maybe I could use some parts off it. Bought it for twenty-five bucks from old man Clark." He sucked on the cigarette thoughtfully, and glanced at Estelle. "And there she sat all this time. Never used no parts, just took up space." He heaved a deep sigh, exhaling smoke. "So what the hell. Got bills to pay. Some of this steel is worth a little something now, don't you know."

"Worth a bunch, I would think," Gastner agreed. "A hell of a lot more than what you paid for it. And now's as good a time as any. Most folks never get around to sorting it all out."

"So there you go," Prescott said. "Got Stub here to crush up a load." He looked across toward the remaining relics. One semi load certainly made a dent in the collection, but there would be a second load left behind. "Haul it all out of here, and maybe turn some things around." He ground out the cigarette and found another one. "You guys ready for a beer?"

"No thanks," Gastner laughed. "I like beer, but it sure as hell doesn't like me."

"Sir, I stopped by just to chat a little about a couple of things," Estelle said.

Stub Moore, who had remained silent, glanced at his watch. "We're puttin' in a couple culverts over off 42 this afternoon, and I just swung by here for a few minutes on the way."

"You do what you have to do," Estelle said easily. "Don't let me interrupt you." She surveyed the flatbed trailer, its small front steel support wheels digging into the oak pads as the weight was piled on.

"Trailer belongs to Florek," Stub offered. Cameron Florek, the owner of the huge auto salvage business just north of the interstate, had pulled hundreds of vehicles out of ditches, ravines, canyons, and roadside wreck sites for the Sheriff's Department. Crushed a dozen or more per load, the carcasses of past tragedies went to an auto recycling center in Las Cruces where they were further reduced to little, dense cubes. Florek would have happily crushed all of Prescott's collection, but he would have charged for the service—Stub Moore was handy that way.

"Could we talk for a few minutes?" Estelle asked Prescott.

"I'll get back at it," Stub said. "Get this one load done, then I got to skiddaddle."

"Come on over to the house," the rancher said. "The wife's got coffee on."

"Thanks, but no. How about just over by the barns, there? Away from the noise of the loader?"

"Suit yourself." He looked at Gastner. "How about you? Never knew you to turn down a cup of coffee."

"Well, hell," Gastner said, as if the decision was a monumental one. "The way your good woman makes it, how can I refuse? I have one of those nifty travel cups in the truck. Let me get it."

The last thing Estelle wanted to do was talk with Gus Prescott with an audience of spouse or children, so she ambled toward the barns. As Prescott started toward the house, a gimp breaking his gait, Gastner caught up with him, cup in hand. Prescott took it, and Estelle heard him say, "So now what? I hear you're givin' it up?"

Gastner shrugged dismissively. "I'm going to write my memoirs," he said with a laugh. "Reveal all this county's nasty little secrets."

"That'll keep you up nights," Prescott nodded. "Black, as I remember?"

"You got it. Thanks."

Prescott went into the house, and Gastner strolled across the yard, head turned as he watched Stub Moore's progress with the loader. Estelle saw him stop, hands in his pockets, as Moore placed the huge bucket just right on the flat roof of the old truck, then hit the hydraulics. The loader reared like a dinosaur, its five-foot tall front wheels rising off the ground. At the same time, the old truck's roof caved in, the door posts buckled. Working methodically along the truck's length, he smashed it down until the entire vehicle was a uniform eighteen inches thick, a pancake easily stacked on the trailer.

Gastner took his time, walking the length of the trailer that now carried half a dozen vehicles or pieces of abandoned farm machinery. Apparently the man had never traded in a vehicle or piece of farm equipment, driving it until it dropped, and then pushing it into line to fade in the blistering New Mexico sun.

When Prescott reappeared carrying two cups, Gastner pulled himself away from the crush and bash spectacle and met the rancher halfway across the yard.

"So, it's been a time, ain't it," Prescott observed. Estelle leaned against the warm, round contour of a 250 gallon diesel fuel storage tank. Its sweet aroma was almost pleasant, and it made a good table for her notebook.

"It's been that," Gastner agreed. He sipped the coffee contentedly.

"Sir, when was the last time you saw Freddy Romero?" Estelle asked.

"Who, now?" Prescott had shown no signs that he was hard of hearing, and he would certainly have heard of the boy's accident. His lean face looked the part of a seriously ill, trail-hardened cowpuncher, his hands large and rough, showing the results of too much sun for too many years. But his eyes weren't the tough, icy blue that would place him nicely in a cigarette ad. Rather, they were a soft, haunted brown, constantly in motion. *Looking for the bottle,* Estelle thought. She could smell the alcohol on him even at this early hour, and wouldn't be surprised to discover that his stash was right in the cab of his pickup truck.

"Freddy Romero. Casey's boyfriend."

"Oh, Christ, that little punk. Don't wish anybody harm, but Jesus H. Christ, that little Mexican…" He bit off the sentence, eyes shifting to Gastner, who remained as placid as ever.

"When was the last time you saw him, sir?" Estelle repeated.

"Don't keep track of that kid," Prescott snapped, but immediately looked as if he regretted the sharpness of his tone. "Look, I heard what happened to him. Damn fool thing to do, riding like that. Bet you dollars to donuts that he didn't have no helmet, right?" He didn't wait for an answer. "He took Casey for a ride a time or two, and I told *her* that was the end of that. I don't want to see her hangin' on the back of that thing. Well, see what happened? Maybe that shook some sense into her." He pulled on his cigarette and talked through the exhale of smoke. "Don't know what she sees in that little shit."

"When was that, sir?"

"When was what?"

"When you saw him on the four-wheeler. Or when he and Casey were together?"

"Hell, they're spendin' way too much time together. *Way* too much. You know as well as I do what's going to happen." His mouth worked as if it wasn't sure what expression its owner wanted. "Don't need a flock of little half-Mexican kids runnin' around the place."

Estelle didn't rise to the bait. "You were in the Broken Spur when Freddy rode by on his four wheeler on Thursday, sir?"

"Where do you get that idea, *señora*?" He made the single Spanish word sound like an insult, and Estelle saw Bill Gastner's grizzled eyebrows twitch.

"I'm asking you, sir."

"I don't keep no diary of what I do."

"Do you remember talking to Miles Waddell that afternoon? At the Spur?"

"So what? I talk to Waddell all the time."

Bill Gastner set his cup on top of the oil tank with exaggerated care. "Gus," he said, "we've known you for a long time." He rubbed his hands together thoughtfully. "Now, you know how these things work. We have an accident, and we check things out. That's all there is to it. A little cooperation here would be helpful. That's all we're asking."

"I know that."

The undersheriff kept her tone gentle and respectful. "Did you happen to notice if Freddy was by himself that afternoon, sir? We need to know that."

"He better have been, I'll tell you that. I find out that Casey was ridin' around with him again…"

Except the boy's dead now. "Was he by himself, sir? Did you see him?"

"No, I didn't see him. I *heard* it was him ridin' by. Waddell said it was. Took his word for it. Said he was alone. Took his word for that, too."

"Do you recall what time that might have been?"

"Might a been… hell, I don't know when it *might* a been."

"You left the saloon shortly after that?"

"I come and go when I please."

"Kinda ouchy today, Gus." Bill Gastner made the observation couched in amusement, but it caught the rancher's attention.

"Well, I…" but Gastner interrupted him.

"Kinda wonder why."

"Now, look. I don't mean to be givin' you a hard time, Bill."

"It's not about me, Gus."

"Well, it's just that, well, you know."

"I *don't* know."

Prescott looked as if he wanted to say something else, but bit it off, taking the opportunity to jam another cigarette between chapped lips. He snapped the lighter so hard he almost dropped it. His gaze roamed the ground in front of him, as if the answers lay there. Estelle watched the performance with fascination. It was hard to imagine someone loathing Freddy Romero, but Gus Prescott clearly did. "He rode by the Spur," he said. "Waddell says it was him." He shrugged. "That's what I know."

"Did you leave the Spur shortly after that, sir?"

"Yeah, well I got work to do, you know."

"I understand that, sir. You and Herb both left shortly after?"

He settled for a nod, perhaps realizing now that others could easily confirm what he had or hadn't done.

"Bender's Canyon—that's sort of the back road into your ranch, isn't it?"

Prescott coughed out a laugh. "Hell of a back road. But yeah, it is."

"You went home that way?"

"Hell no, I didn't go that way. Hell, it's eight miles longer, and a rough ride. What's the point?"

"So you didn't know where Freddy was headed."

"I don't keep track of no freakin' kid. As long as he don't cut fences, who cares?"

"Was he out here a week ago Sunday, sir?"

"Heard that he was. I was in town. The wife told me, and Casey and me, we had some words about that." He hawked and spat off to one side. "I don't care where that kid rides, as long as he stays away from Casey."

Well, he will now, Estelle thought. "How long has it been since you've talked with Eddie Johns, sir?" The change of subject caught Prescott by surprise, and his eyes did a veritable dance.

"Hell, Johns? I ain't see *him* in years."

"You haven't talked with Waddell or Herb Torrance since yesterday?"

"Nope. Well…that ain't true. Waddell called me last night."

"Then he probably told you."

"About Johns? Yeah, he told me. You guys think you've found him over there on Waddell's place. That's a hell of a note." The rancher's eyes became watchful as he waited for Estelle's response.

"Can you tell me when *you* saw Mr. Johns for the last time?"

"Nope. All I recall is that it's been years. *Years.* He used to hang around with Waddell all the time there for a while. They was up to some kind of development up there on the mesa behind Herb's place."

"You had the chance to talk with him?"

"Didn't look for it." Four words, and then his mouth clamped shut, a hard line.

"You and Eddie didn't get on too well?" Gastner asked. Prescott just shrugged. "I mean, you didn't exactly see eye to eye?"

"Man chooses his own."

Estelle cocked her head, regarding Prescott with interest. "Mr. Waddell said that you had done some of the grading on that road cut up the mesa."

Prescott took his time lighting another cigarette. "Yeah, I done that."

"Is that your machine over beyond the corral?"

He pivoted and looked across the paddock. The yellow road grader, still bearing the round scar on the door where the county emblem had been stripped before the machine was auctioned as surplus, was parked beside a forlorn box trailer. "Got a bad cylinder. I think it ate a valve or something like that. And I can tell you right now, *that's* going to cost a fortune to fix." He turned back to Estelle. "I'll get to it. Ain't needed it, so I ain't fixed it yet. Get some of this junk sold off, and maybe."

For a moment they watched the front loader pummel another hulk, this one not much more than a chassis with fire-wall still attached.

"He's going to finish up here in a few minutes," Prescott said.

"And then Cam Florek will have work to do," Gastner said with satisfaction.

"You bet. Look," and Prescott spread his hands in apology. "I'm sorry I ain't been much help, but that's the way it is. I ain't seen Eddie Johns for years, and I don't know what the Romero kid was up to...except what I read in the papers, and what my neighbors tell me, and what little I can dig out of Casey. And there ain't no guarantee *they* got it right. So things will just sort of sift out."

"They will indeed," Gastner agreed emphatically.

"Interesting about that damn cat, though. I woulda liked to have seen that. Gonna have to stop by the school sometime. That's where it ended up?"

"Yes, sir," Estelle said. "At least that's where it probably *will* end up." She didn't add that the skull had been transferred to the Posadas County Sheriff's Department evidence locker. "The last time you saw Mr. Johns, did you have any occasion to argue with him about anything? Did he seem upset or preoccupied? Like something might be on his mind?"

Prescott laughed softly. "If you'd wanted to know that, you shoulda been around years ago, when I mighta remembered."

"But *you* had no cause to argue with him?"

"Don't guess I did. He liked dealin' with the Mexicans, and I guess that's his privilege."

Estelle nodded, thumbing through her notes, and then looked at Bill Gastner. "Sir, did you have any questions?" Gastner shook his head, still obviously intrigued with the junk loading process. "Then we'll be on our way."

"Hey, you," a melodious voice said, and they turned to see Christine Prescott walking toward them from the house. Dressed in a simple white western style shirt and tight blue jeans and trainers, she beamed at Bill Gastner, heading directly to him first. As she passed her father, one hand reached out and touched his elbow, a small intimate gesture of affection before she held out both arms and engulfed the former sheriff in a hug.

"How's my favorite lawman?" Christine asked. It occurred to Estelle that, until this moment, she had only seen Christine Prescott behind the bar in the Broken Spur. The girl's strawberry-blonde hair, now free of her bartender's ponytail, was striking in the sunshine. The resemblance to her younger sister was strong.

"Well," Gastner said, "for an old fat man, I'm doing okay. How's college?"

"Bizarre," Christine laughed. "Ma'am, it's good to see you again." She held out a hand and shook Estelle's, her grip strong and lingering. Her expression became serious. "This is all so sad, this whole thing," she said. "Casey's a wreck over Freddy." Her father grunted something, but Christine ignored him. "Do you need to talk to her again?"

"No, I don't think so," Estelle responded. "Maybe later."

"She told me about Butchie," Christine said. Her amber-green eyes flooded with sympathy. "How *horrible*. Your son was with him?"

"Yes."

"But he's okay?"

"Francisco is fine. Shaken, but fine."

Christine blinked hard. "I can't even imagine what it's like for George and Tata right now."

"A hard time," Estelle said.

"You let 'em run wild, that's what you get," Prescott said ungraciously, and Christine shot him a withering glance.

"I came out to tell you that Cam Florek wants you to call him," Christine said to her father.

"Now I'm crushed," Gastner quipped. "I thought you came out to deliver a much needed hug."

"Oh, I did, I did," Christine laughed, and she slid her arm through Gastner's, ready to promenade.

"I got to make that call," Prescott said, obviously thankful for a handy excuse. "You need anything else from me?"

"Thank you for taking the time, sir." Estelle watched the rancher stalk off and then turned to Gastner and Christine. "Christine, do you recall a fellow named Eddie Johns?"

"Dad and mom were talking about that earlier," Christine replied incredulously. "They were saying that somebody's skeleton was found over on the neighbor's, and that it might be Eddie Johns?"

"That's correct."

"My God. Is that…Freddy's accident, I mean…are they…"

"We're not sure," Estelle said.

"My God."

"You remember Johns, then?"

"Who doesn't," Christine said. "I didn't like him, and I *know* daddy didn't."

"You remember why not?"

"Well, sure. I mean, I know why *I* didn't like him much. Johns was a bully. You know the type. Pushy, loud, my way or the highway." She glanced at the house as if she didn't want her father to overhear. "You know what I think? I used to watch Johns, you know. In the saloon. You do that with someone who's going to cause trouble. And that's the deal with Eddie Johns. *Every* time he came into the saloon, I was always half expecting him to get in a tangle with somebody, just because he couldn't keep his fat mouth shut. He couldn't just take a beer and drink it and leave. He liked to scare people. He got a kick out of that."

"He carried a gun from time to time," Gastner offered.

"Oh, yeah, he carried a gun. I once told Victor that I was going to call the cops, but he always waved it off. It would have been one thing if Johns kept it concealed, but it always seemed important to him that other people *know* he was armed. *Packing,* he called it. What a jerk. I mean, I suppose I shouldn't talk ill of the dead, but that's what he was…a jerk."

"Did he ever argue with your father, Christine?" Estelle asked.

"He argued with *everybody,* sheriff. My dad didn't like him, and tried his best to ignore him. Johns liked to pick at him, you know. See if he could get a rise out of him."

"With any success?" Gastner asked.

"My dad's patient most of the time," Christine replied grimly. "He drinks too much, but he has a lot on his mind. He just did his best to ignore Mr. Johns. I did too, but sometimes a bartender has to be more of an actress than anything else."

"To put up with the jerks?"

"That's exactly it, Bill. Victor doesn't like to see the paying customers driven away. So we have to pretend sometimes."

"And you had to do that with Eddie Johns?" Estelle asked.

"Too much," Christine replied. "Mr. Johns assumed that women were naturally attracted to him. Dream on. He needed to look in the mirror more often and spend some time considering his 'yuck' factor. I know that when he was flirting with me, my dad was on a low boil. But he didn't say anything. He knows I can take care of myself."

"He just worried a lot," Gastner added.

"That's what dads do, right? Now he's worried about Casey. He didn't like Freddy Romero very much, but I know he's sorry Casey has to go through all this." She smiled faintly. "That's why I showed up on the doorstep, I guess. I'm sort of the *de facto* family mediator, and it's hard to meddle from Las Cruces."

"I'm sure no one considers it meddling, Christine," Gastner said. "Damn hard times for everybody involved."

"It is." She turned as her father reappeared from the house, then looked back at Estelle. "Any notions about Johns? Who he tangled with?"

"Not yet," Estelle replied.

"He talked about his connections south of the border."

"So I understand. We're looking at that, but it's a slim trail."

"He was shot?"

"It appears so."

Christine shook her head slowly. "Makes you wonder. Shows that I wasn't alone. I wasn't the only one who didn't inquire about Eddie Johns going missing. Doesn't look like anyone missed him enough to look into it."

"We're getting a late start," Gastner said. "Like five or six *years* too late."

"You think it happened that long ago?"

"It could have," Estelle said. "You were full time at the saloon around then?"

"I was. I just quit last year, you know. And here I am, twenty-seven years old, and only a sophomore in college." She chuckled. "Slow starter, that's me."

"What do you think of this college kid?" Gus Prescott said as he approached. Christine reached out and hooked his arm once more, a protective gesture as if she were the parent and he the child. Estelle slipped her notebook into her hip pocket.

"You must be proud, sir. I may need to talk with you again."
When Prescott nodded, he was looking at Gastner, not her.
"Christine, how long will you be home?"

"Just this week, probably. I really need to get back to class.
I'm not one of those fireballs who can miss half the lectures and
still sail through. I want to be able to go to Freddy's funeral with
Casey. I think it's on Thursday."

"Well, we're gonna talk about that," Prescott muttered, but
Christine ignored him.

As they walked back to their respective vehicles, Estelle
noticed that Gastner's gait was even more leisurely than before,
but his face wasn't its usual cheerful self, despite a warm final
hug from Christine Prescott. His brow was furrowed in thought
and she recognized the vexed set of his mouth and heavy chin.
He walked with head down, not soaking in the pleasures of a
sunny day on the prairie.

"Check with you in about a mile," he said cryptically, and
headed for his truck. Behind them, Stub Moore was putting the
finishing touches on the top of the load, adding the remains of a
Chevy Suburban to even the pack. "Oh," and he stopped short.
"You got your camera?"

"Of course, *Padrino.*"

"Do me a favor and take a good picture of that load before
Florek gets here with the tractor," he said. He pointed his index
finger pistol-fashion at the trailer.

"Easily done."

"I'll meet you in Moore."

Estelle watched him settle into the truck, and saw him glare
at the steering wheel for a moment, then shake his head in dis-
gust. Bill Gastner's usual unflappable humor had been flapped
by something. She unzipped her digital camera and walked off
to one side, framing the loaded trailer neatly from margin to
margin using the zoom. Both Stub Moore and Gus Prescott
watched her, but didn't intrude. She took a series of a dozen
shots, and by the time she closed up the camera, the dust from
Bill Gastner's pickup had dissipated across the prairie.

Chapter Thirty-seven

"You know," Bill Gastner said, "there's a lot to be said for being wrong." He leaned hard against Estelle's county car, both hands flat on the roof above the window. "I hope to hell that I am." He nodded toward her camera, still sitting in its boot on the center console. "Lemme have a look at what you took."

The camera's preview window was tiny, and when she found the first of the series taken of Florek's trailer, she held it out toward him, earning a disgusted grimace.

"God damn it, how am I supposed to see that," he said. "Do some magic or something."

The "magic" was a simple connection to her lap top computer. Gastner drummed his fingers impatiently on the sedan's roof. Eventually, the photo popped up in brilliant color. Gastner reached in with his hand and gestured for her to advance the image. Two of the photos included both Stub and Prescott, both staring directly at the camera. Gastner peered at them, frowning. "Back," he said, and she scrolled the photos back to the first.

"Can you make it bigger?" he asked. "Take my advice, and don't ever get old." He touched the screen, indicating the front half of the trailer. "I want to see that." The image expanded, cropping the edges away. "More. More. And down a little bit." For a long time, Gastner rested on the window sill as Estelle held the computer balanced on the steering wheel.

"See," he said, and touched the screen. "This first vehicle. The very bottom one."

"Not a lot to see," Estelle said.

"Exactly. Can you tell what it is?"

"No. It appears to be burned, though. Burned and rusted. They're all rusted. If I had to guess, I'd say that it was a pickup. That's what Gus Prescott seems to prefer."

"Don't think he ever sold one in his life," Gastner said. "They crap out, and he parks the damn things. 'Oh, I'll fix it someday.' And the someday never comes."

"The country is littered with them, *Padrino*. You know, when Francis and I were up in Minnesota, I thought at first that they didn't collect junk. Everything so clean and green. And then one day I had the opportunity to hike a long, wooded hedgerow between a couple of fields? From a distance, so picturesque. And sure enough...the hedgerow was full of junk."

"Down south, that's what the damn kudzu is good for," Gastner said. "And that's the whole point. There's people who trade in their vehicles when they get a new one, and there's people who don't. People like Gus Prescott just park the dead stuff. And you know what? They *never* get rid of it." He thumped the door sill. "That's my theory. Even a row of junk is part of their wealth...their accumulated wealth. And then they die before they ever have the chance to clean up their mess. They leave hedgerows of junk behind."

Estelle looked up at him, and saw that he was staring off across the prairie, jaw set.

"I'm not seeing what has you so upset, *Padrino*."

"Well, hell. Look at what we got here. Maybe you can't see it in the picture so well, but I took a good long look. Damned odd that Gus chooses to take this day to get rid of old junk, don't you think?"

"He wants the money, maybe to fix his grader."

"Hell, that grader's been out of commission for a couple of years. He's no more going to do a deep overhaul on a big diesel engine than I am." He reached across and tapped a finger on the screen, none too gently. "That's a crew cab," he said, and slapped the door frame with his other hand. "A God damn crew cab. And right there," and he touched the image again, "you can see the end of the tailpipe."

"The tailpipe?"

"See it? Crunched up right into the fender?"

"All right."

"Diesel," Gastner said. "Turbo diesel with a tail pipe as big as a sewer line. They didn't do that on older trucks."

"What are you saying, sir?" Estelle asked, even though she knew exactly what had turned his mood upside down. "That this is Eddie Johns' s truck?"

He slapped the roof. "I hope to hell not, but…" He turned as the sound of a large truck floated toward them, and in a moment an aging semi without a trailer slowed and pulled off the paved road. In the cab, they could see the heavy, mountain-man image of Cameron Florek. He raised a hand in salute as he drove by, massive tires kicking up a cloud of dust.

"He's going to be able to cross the arroyo?" Estelle asked.

"He got in with the trailer, so he can get out," Gastner said. "It's wide enough that he won't scrape much." He patted the door again. "Look, I may well be wrong as hell, but it's something that needs scrutiny, sweetheart. What color was Johns' truck?"

"Black."

"You want to bet me that if we look hard enough, we'll find a splash of black paint that survived the fire? And a VIN number would be helpful as hell, but I'll bet *that's* gone."

Estelle looked off across the prairie, watching the big tractor negotiate the twists and turns until it disappeared around the mesa. "Not good," she said finally.

"I tell ya, sweetheart, this is one of those times when I'd much rather be wrong than right." He pushed himself back. "But I've been stewing about this." He held out a stubby index finger. "Somebody plugged Johns in the back of the head. Okay, that means he was either riding *with* Johns in the pickup, or driving himself. What's that leave, when all is said and done?"

"If he's riding with Johns, he takes the victim's truck when it's over. If he was driving himself, then he would take off, leaving Johns' truck behind."

"And what happened to it, then?"

"He came back and got it later, maybe."

"No hurry about that, lonesome as that country is. That's one possibility, and I'm sure there's a whole platterful of others." He looked at Estelle again. "So what do you think?"

Estelle took her time folding the computer and storing it in its boot. "I think," she said, "that we take a very, *very* close look, *Padrino.*"

It took an hour for Cameron Florek to secure his towering load, and then to hook up the tractor, and finally, to maneuver along the narrow two-track to the Rio Salinas, where Estelle, Bill Gastner, and Deputy Tony Abeyta watched the mammoth beast discharge billows of black exhaust from dual stacks as it lurched up the steep grade out of the dry crossing. During that hour, a warrant from Judge Lester Hobart had been secured and delivered by the deputy.

As he handed the warrant to Estelle, Abeyta nodded at Bill Gastner. "Judge Hobart said just because it's you, sir."

"Glad I still have some clout," Gastner replied. "And it's me who's going to be God damn embarrassed here in a bit, probably…embarrassed and relieved as hell."

"We'll want to stop him right here," Estelle said, nodding at the remains of the Moore Mercantile building. "Nice and level, and well clear of the highway."

The deputy moved his Expedition so that it blocked the dirt road, putting it headlight to headlight with the approaching semi. He lit the roof-rack when Florek's rig was a hundred yards away, and they immediately heard the diesel choke as the driver slowed. Estelle could see Florek leaning forward, hard against the steering wheel.

He let the rig idle to a stop, and Estelle stepped closer, looking up into the tall cab.

"I sure as hell wasn't speeding," Florek said, "and I ain't got no livestock. What are you guys up to this morning, anyways?"

"Sir, would you climb down?"

"Sure enough." Florek emerged from the cab and lowered himself to the ground, a great bear of a man in full beard and denim bib coveralls. "Bill, you old bandit, how's life treatin' you?"

"I've been better," Gastner said.

"So what's this about?"

Estelle held out the warrant. Florek glanced at it, then ignored the document, looking to the undersheriff for answers. "We'd like to examine your load, sir."

"I know I ain't overweight," he replied. "And she's all tied down good. Just goin' to the yard, anyways."

"Yes, sir," Estelle said. "Would you mind staying with the deputy for a few moments, sir?" Deputy Abeyta and Florek remained by the front of the truck while Estelle and Gastner walked back to the trailer. Now eighteen inches thick, the pancaked wad of metal and plastic on the bottom tier showed the clear patina of age and burned metal.

"Doors are gone," Gastner observed, "but this sure as hell is the center post between front and back." He tapped the crumpled tail pipe. "This is what I was talking about. That's diesel hardware. And right here?" He moved along the wreck and touched a spot of metal. "That's where the fender insignia would be. Probably said something like XLT Powerstroke Diesel or some such. Something like that anyway, depending on the year."

"If we're going to look for much more, we're going to have to unload it and take it apart." Estelle leaned inward, between the semi's cab and trailer. "An engine, you suppose?"

"I would bet against it," Gastner said. "*That's* worth a lot of money."

She lowered her voice. "If this truck belonged to Johns…"

"Then we have a few choices," Gastner added.

"*Ay,*" Estelle whispered. "We need to know."

Chapter Thirty-eight

By the time they reached Florek's wrecking yard, Sheriff Robert Torrez was there to meet them, along with Deputy Tom Pasquale.

"Got a really good buy on this stuff," Gastner quipped. Torrez shot him an amused look, and offered a salute to Florek, who stood on the running board of the tractor, waiting instructions.

"Mears has found the dentist," the sheriff said to Estelle. "Nothing yet, but maybe. It's a step. So tell me what you got here."

"I have reason to believe that this baby down here—" Gastner stepped forward and pointed at the wreck—"this vehicle right here is a late model Ford crew cab, Robert. It's a diesel. It's been burned enough that the paint is gone, but not so much that we couldn't find a trace somewhere in a protected area."

"Johns?"

"Could be. We need to know the *year*. That's critical."

Torrez turned and looked at Estelle. "You talked to Gus about this?"

"No. Not yet. I want an identification first."

The sheriff pursed his lips and frowned. "You had to pick the one on the bottom, didn't you," he said to Gastner, and followed that with a tight smile. He stepped closer. "You trust Florek with all this?"

"Yes," Gastner said without hesitation, then shrugged. "And no. As much as I trust anyone. Up to an hour ago, I trusted Gus, too."

"Okay." The sheriff ambled up along the truck and looked up at Cameron Florek. "How long will it take you to unload?"

"Well, see, I was going to run this load right on down to the plant in Cruces."

"Nope. Not yet, anyway."

"Look," Florek said as he swung down. He stood eye to eye with Torrez. "You want to tell me what's going on here? What's the interest in the wreck?"

"Cam," Gastner said, "you're the expert to ask. If I wanted to know the year of this one," and he reached out and touched the diesel tailpipe, "how would I do it?"

"Door plate would tell ya, but the door's gone, so that's out," Florek said. He examined the wreck. "VIN is…well, hell, you know where the VIN is as well as me."

"And if the vehicle identification number plate is missing?"

Florek shrugged. "It's a later model. That's for sure. Burned some."

"What year?"

The salvage yard owner scratched his hairy forearm. He strolled along the trailer to the rear of the wreck, his mobile face active as he worked his tongue around the inside of his mouth. Hands jammed in his pockets, he turned his head this way and that.

"That'll tell ya," he said, and reached up to pull at the remains of a tail light lens. There was no way to judge how large the lens might have been, since it was broken, partially melted, and jammed into the crumpled steel that had formed the housing around the unit. "Lemme get a bar." He turned and strode over to his small office by the gate, and returned in a moment with a short wrecking bar.

Torrez held up a hand to stop him as Estelle worked the camera. She took a series of half a dozen photos of the tail-light area from various angles, then nodded.

With a few deft probes, Florek loosened the remains of the lens. It hung from the carcass by several wires, themselves melted to the copper. "Now see, it's got three sets of wires that would attach with quarter turn sockets. Still got one left." He popped the light out of its socket, and the plastic lens fragment, about the size of a tea cup saucer, came loose in his hand. "Socket up here, broke off. Socket right here. And between 'em…" He held the fragment so Estelle could see it.

"ASY four-el-three four dash six nine…and then it's broken off. Below that, *hecho en Mexico.*"

"That's the part number," Florek said. "And if I remember right, the number after the first letters is the year. So *four*, is two thousand four."

"Not ninety-four?"

"Nope. They used a different series back then. And before that, I don't know if they used a separate number or not."

"So two thousand four. You're sure of that."

"Yep." He turned back to the wreck. "You know, unless someone replaced the lamp with another one of a different year. That's unlikely. And if you look down in there, you'll see some overspray that the fire didn't touch. Just a second." He walked up to the cab of the truck, rummaged in the door pocket, and returned with a flashlight. "Look here." Estelle stepped close and looked inside the bent and folded carcass.

"Black."

"That's right."

"What we have here is a black, 2004 Ford crew cab, with a diesel engine."

"At one time," Florek said. "At one time, that's probably what she was."

"Shit," Bill Gastner said quietly.

Estelle turned to him and lowered her voice. "We can't be sure it was his, *Padrino.*"

"How big a coincidence are you looking for?" He waved a hand. "Yeah, yeah. I know. Evidence. Thank God for evidence, right?"

"Look, we need that unit," Torrez said to Florek. "If you'd unload the others, I'll get the county to pick this one up. Hour or so, maybe."

Florek sighed hugely. "You're the boss, sheriff." He backed up a few steps so he could see around the rig's cab. "I'll pull up right there, in that open spot past the fence. I think we'll only need to take off the front six, unless they're all tangled." He looked at first the sheriff, then Estelle, and finally at Bill Gastner. "You folks ready to tell me what's going on?"

"Nope," Torrez replied, and Florek laughed.

"How'd Gus happen by this carcass?"

"Good question," the sheriff said, and his glare was impressively black. "And by the way…if he happens to call you, or you him, you didn't see any of this. You're headin' down to Cruces just like always."

Chapter Thirty-nine

All that they knew for sure, Estelle thought ruefully, was that the crushed truck had come from Gus Prescott's collection. That was all. The questionable recollection of another rancher had offered that Eddie Johns had driven a black, three-quarter ton Ford diesel crew cab. She could imagine the bemused expression of District Attorney Dan Schroeder.

The undersheriff was tempted simply to confront Gus Prescott with the question, but knew the risks of that. Tipping one's hand prematurely was a dangerous poker move…and even more so here.

She forced herself to remain patient as Cameron Florek took his time with his mammoth fork lift, shifting the carcasses of the crushed vehicles from trailer to ground. An hour later, the burned pancake of a late-model pickup was transferred to Florek's smaller flatbed car carrier and delivered to the Quonset hut behind the barbed wire fence in the county boneyard.

Then, using wrecking bars, an assist from the fire department's Jaws of Life, and considerable sweat and cursing, the officers unfolded the truck's corpse one bend at a time.

Sheriff Robert Torrez glared at the heap that leaked driblets of oil and other bodily fluids on the floor of the impound building. "No engine. No tranny. No wheels, no brake rotors or calipers. Hell, this thing's been stripped like a derelict in downtown Juarez."

"You know what puzzles me?" Bill Gastner said. "This crate was burned, but only sort of, you know what I mean? Look here." He rested his hands gingerly on one crushed front fender, and pointed at the firewall. "Windshield is gone, of course, and that's where the VIN impression used to be. That's all ripped to hell and gone. But all this shit?" He leaned farther in and pointed at some of the firewall connections. "The fire didn't reach there. In fact, just not much at all in here." He straightened and backed a step or two away. "In fact, it's sort of a *surface* burn…a scorch."

"Somebody got there quick with an extinguisher," Tom Pasquale offered.

"Yes, but. Look at it…the whole thing is nicely toasted, know what I mean? On the *outside*."

"Front seats are gone, so they didn't melt. But they left the back bench in."

"And that's an odd combination to me," Gastner said. He turned and looked at Estelle, who, along with Linda Real, was saving images with a variety of cameras. "This was burned long enough ago that the sheet metal has had time to patina pretty nicely. It's hard as hell to tell what color the thing was, at least from a distance. You dig around inside, and you can see that it was black, but it takes some work."

The sheriff had been kneeling at the back of the wreck, and he stood slowly, beckoning Tom Pasquale. "Need to unfold that," he said cryptically. The *that* was the tailgate of the truck, now crushed forward into the bed, the side bed panels folded inward to lock it in place. The tailgate itself had folded in a ragged line, collapsing in on itself. The sheriff beckoned to Estelle. "See in there?" He held his flashlight for her. By looking into the tunnel formed by the folded tailgate, she could see the remains of an emblem.

"Part of it left, anyways," Torrez said. "Be careful with that," he added as Tom Pasquale brought the jaws close. "If that's a dealer emblem, I don't want it wrecked."

For nearly half an hour, they worked, the metal screeching and groaning as it was peeled back layer by layer. With a come-along looped to a building support at one end and hooked to the fender with the other, they spread the crushed bed apart, freeing the tailgate a bit at a time.

"Sure as hell be easier if they'd left the license plate on it," Torrez grunted at one point. "But this is gonna be almost as good."

As the envelope of crushed tailgate was pried open, they could see a fragment of burned pot metal lying askew. The adhesive that had affixed the name plate to the tailgate's surface had been tough enough that the plate had broken in two places.

Torrez waited patiently as Linda Real moved in close with her macro lens, and when she finished, pushed the two pieces of name plate together. "Borderland Fo," he recited. "Paso, Texas."

He looked up at Estelle. "We need to get Mears over there ASAP. Borderland Ford will have records. Then there's no question. He..." The sheriff was interrupted by the jarring buzz of the building alarm, and then a tentative rap on the metal door.

Abeyta shot the bolt and opened the door a couple inches. "Good morning sir," he said, and turned to the others. "Herb Torrance?"

"Ah," Estelle said. "I asked him if he'd stop by. Bill and I will be right out."

"*Bill* and I?" Gastner grunted. "I'm getting too damn deep in this."

"Your impressions are always welcome," Estelle said. "After all, you're the reason we're here at the moment."

Herb Torrance, owner of the H-Bar-T ranch, had retreated away from the door, and now leaned his forearms on the hood of his truck, hands clasped together as he watched the performance on the other side of the boneyard as two county employees worked with a hoist to sling a repaired back tire onto a county road grader.

"Hey," he said as Estelle and Gastner appeared from the Quonset. At a distance he could be confused with someone from one of the utility companies, dressed entirely in a brown double pocket work shirt and brown trousers. A grubby baseball cap with the bill folded just so rested on the back of his head.

"I saw this comin'," he said. "I figured you were going to show up on my doorstep sooner or later." He shook hands with both of them, then relaxed back against his truck again.

"I appreciate your stopping by," Estelle said.

"Well," Torrance said with a resigned smile, "you said you wanted to see me, so here I am. We got a mess, don't we? Pretty quiet neighborhood I live in most of the time."

"Sir, tell me about Eddie Johns."

Torrance's leathery face remained impassive, and he pointed at Bill Gastner with his chin. "Hell, you know that son-of-a-bitch as well as me." He looked back at Estelle. "Waddell tells me that you found Johns up on the mesa."

"We think so, sir."

"Been there a while? That's what Miles said."

"It appears so."

"Well, *that* don't surprise me. I was gonna call you, but then figured what the hell…if you wanted my two cents, you'd call."

"Why doesn't it surprise you, sir?"

Torrance laughed. "I never could see why Miles encouraged that guy. I mean, what's to come of it?" He shrugged. "Never cared for him much. You know, one time he tried to buy a piece of property from me. Wasn't interested. Johns didn't seem ready to understand that. He got real pugnacious. That don't work so good with me."

"I really have two things to ask you, sir," Estelle said. "First of all, were you in the Broken Spur last week—it would be Thursday, we think. Freddy Romero rode through the saloon parking lot on his four-wheeler. Do you recall that?"

"Sure." He shook his head slowly, ice blue eyes never leaving Estelle's face. "Sure sorry *that* had to happen. That trail's a dangerous place."

"You saw him that day?"

"Nope. Miles said he did. Now, I sure as hell *heard* him. That's the noisiest God damn thing, that little buggy."

"Gus Prescott was at the Spur as well?"

"Well, yeah. He was."

"Did you leave the Spur shortly after that, sir?"

Torrance frowned. "You're askin' me to remember something longer ago than breakfast, young lady. But sure enough. I had things to do. I only stopped by to see if Gus was going to have his road grader fixed by this time next week. He ain't, so there we are. But hell," and he smiled, "it's only been two years."

"You and Gus talked about that?"

Torrance laughed hoarsely. "About fifteen seconds. From what I can gather, his grader's gone south for want of parts that he can't afford to buy. But you'll talk to him about that."

"And then you left the saloon?"

"I did, and then just about the time I was pullin' out of the parkin' lot, Gus left the saloon, too. Don't know about Miles."

"You drove home?"

"Guess I did."

"And Gus?"

"And Gus what?"

"Did you happen to notice which way he went? Toward Regál, or back north to Moore?"

"Neither one, I don't guess. He went up through the canyon."

"The back trail?"

"That's what him and me were talkin' about. There's a section in there that just tears my truck all to hell. I've been tryin' to get him to grade that—there ain't no one else with a machine, except for the county, and *they* won't do it. Got about a hundred yards that's more like a quarry than a two-track."

"Ah," Estelle nodded.

"If he'd turned east at Bender's, he'd likely have seen the kid on the four-wheeler, but I guess he woulda turned west on the canyon road. Just too bad, the whole thing."

"Sir, do you know what kind of vehicle Eddie Johns drove?"

"Well…" Torrance looked up at the blank sky, eyes narrowed to slits. "Been a while. Big old pickup, as I recall."

"An older model?"

"Well, no, I don't guess so. He's in real estate now, you know. Got to look good."

"Real estate, *then*," Gastner corrected.

"Yup. Guess so. Pretty damn strange."

"Sir, if you were to see Eddie Johns' truck, would you be able to recognize it?"

Herb Torrance looked at Estelle skeptically. "Last time I saw him was what, four or five years ago? Something like that? Always wondered what happened to him, but didn't care enough to ask. Last time I saw him, he was drivin' a fancy rig. Seems to be it was dark blue or black, maybe. Think it was a Ford. That's about as close as I can come."

Estelle beckoned, and he followed her to the Quonset. She held the door for the rancher and for Gastner, and shut it securely behind them.

Standing with his hands on his hips, Torrance regarded the mess on the floor. He shifted a step or two to the side, looked some more, and then said, "Shows some use, don't it." He looked up at the others in the room, as if seeing them for the first time. "Bobby, you fellas workin' to restore this? Your budget that tight, is it?"

"Just needs a little touch-up," Torrez replied.

He pivoted at the waist and regarded Estelle. "You're askin' about Eddie Johns? Does this have something to do with that?"

"Yes, sir. It does."

"This what's left of his truck? Is that what you're gettin' at?"

"Can you tell us anything about it, sir?"

Torrance's eyes narrowed a little, and he walked the length of the carcass, the expression on his face that of a rancher judging livestock. Estelle let him look without interrupting his train of thought.

"Couldn't really say," he said finally. "I guess this was black once upon a time, and I'd guess it was a Ford crew cab." He held up both hands in surrender. "That's my best shot, but then I guess you folks already know all that."

"Sir, can you tell us why Gus Prescott would have this wrecked vehicle at his ranch?"

Herb Torrance looked genuinely surprised. "Now wait," he said. "He did have a truck that belonged to Johns. Big old

three-quarter ton. Gus told me about that. The story goes that
Johns had it parked over at Giarelli Sand and Gravel in Deming
when a kid driving an ore truck screwed up royally and drove
right over it. Gus said he bought the wreck for salvage…wanted
the engine, I guess. Well, now. This is the one?"

"It might be, sir. Did the truck catch fire in the accident?"

Herb chuckled. "Don't think so." He chuckled again. "Ah…"
He shook his head in amusement. "I tell you, if Gus Prescott
didn't have bad luck, he wouldn't have no luck at all." He shook
his head again. "Let me tell you about that. I was drivin' to town
one day and saw this plume of black smoke shootin' up. Right
over at Gus' place. So I drove in, and by the time I get there,
he's standin' there lookin' at a smokin' wreck. See, he was tryin'
to cut something off the truck—one of the bumper supports,
I think. Anyway, before he knows it, the damn thing catches
fire. He had this garden hose stretched all the way over from
the house. That and a little fire extinguisher. He coulda set the
whole ranch on fire. Damn good thing it wasn't windy."

"And that's when he told you the truck originally belonged
to Johns?"

"Yep."

"When was this, Mr. Torrance?"

"Oh, hell, it's been a couple years. Three or four, maybe. He
just pushed the wreck over there in line with all the other junk
he's got. I guess," and Torrance paused to scratch his scalp. "I
guess he got out the engine and tranny. I know that he wanted
to put the diesel in his own truck. Wouldn't be surprised. He's
actually a fair hand as a mechanic."

Estelle looked across at where Bill Gastner rested against a work
bench. His arms were crossed over his belly, and he lifted both
shoulders in a helpless shrug, a tinge of relief on his broad face.

"What'd he pay Eddie for this piece of junk?" Gastner asked.
"Did he say?"

"He didn't. Wouldn't have been much, 'cause Gus ain't *got*
much. Maybe they made a deal for some work. Don't know.
Gus didn't say, and I didn't ask."

"I never got the impression that Gus cared much for Eddie Johns," Gastner continued.

A hint of wariness crossed Herb Torrance's face. "You'd have to talk to him about that. Johns was all right, long as you didn't have to be in the same county with him." His smile was thin. "I'd be curious to know how he come to end up stuffed in that little cave."

"Us too," Gastner replied.

Chapter Forty

After Herb Torrance had left, it was Bill Gastner who first voiced the confliction of relief and disappointment. "Well, I thought I had something. So where are we now?"

"One version," the sheriff said cryptically. He had his cell phone in hand, and walked off toward a dark corner of the Quonset. He spoke so quietly that Estelle couldn't hear him, and she turned to Gastner.

"We need to contact Giarelli's, *Padrino,*" she said. "It's not that I think Herb would lie to us, but it's a loose end."

"I can't imagine Gus making up something like that," Gastner said. "It's possible, I suppose."

"How long have you known him, sir?"

"Gus? Good God, sweetheart, just about forever. Well, twenty years, anyway. Before he bought that place, he worked for Burton Livestock, over in Deming. That outfit that supplies rodeo livestock? He managed to drive one of their livestock rigs into a bar ditch. Killed some stock, wrecked an expensive truck."

"Alcohol a factor?"

"Sure. He's never been able to beat it. Learned to harness it a little, maybe." He sighed. "Old Gus has his share of demons, that's for sure. I guess he's no different from the rest of us in that respect. Nice kids, though. I just love 'em."

"I'm surprised, though," Estelle mused.

"At?"

"Well, it surprises me, after what we've heard, to find out that Gus would associate with Eddie Johns enough that he'd buy his wrecked truck."

"Oh, come on, sweetheart. Where there's a possibility of making a buck, where wheeling and dealing is concerned, personalities go by the wayside. Johns could be a charmer when he wanted to be. Gus saw a possibility for a good deal, and snapped it up. You know what one of those big diesel engines costs new in a box?"

"A lot."

"A lot is exactly right. And the engine with a matching transmission? A whopper. Gus has himself an older Ford, and here's an opportunity to kick it up a notch."

"Why would Eddie Johns sell something he *knew* to be valuable for salvage for nickel-dime?"

"We don't know what Gus paid for it. On top of that, the insurance company might have already forked over to Johns for the loss."

"Did he strike you as the sort of guy who would just give stuff away, sir?"

"He strikes me as the sort who'd give Gus a good deal if he knew that he'd get something that he wants in return. Who knows…maybe he traded for a hundred hours of grader time. Something like that. You'll just have to ask him."

They both turned as Torrez approached. "Giarelli never had a wreck like Torrance was talkin' about," he said. "Doesn't know who Eddie Johns is. Never had any dealings with anyone by that name. Hasn't had a driver wreck a truck on the highway since 1969. Never had a wreck with anyone visiting the crusher plant."

"Son of a bitch," Gastner said wearily. "So who's lying?"

"Don't think that Giarelli is, but I got Gayle givin' Deming PD a call for a records check. We'll know soon enough. If there was a wreck, the insurance companies would require a report."

"But no word from Mears yet?"

"Nope."

"Where are we heading with all this?" Bill Gastner asked. "If we're thinking that Gus Prescott killed Eddie Johns…"

"I'd want to hear a reason," Torrez said. "Give me a motive." The room fell silent. "'Cause nothin' ties any of this together."

"Meaning the tie with Freddy Romero?"

Torrez nodded. "It ain't no secret that Gus didn't like the kid. He ain't exactly welcoming him into the family, is he. So he sees the kid ride by, and maybe follows him? Is that the idea? There's a dozen reasons that Gus might want to go through the canyon. Doesn't mean that he's lyin' in wait for Freddy, does it."

"Unless he knew why Freddy was snooping around that particular piece of real estate," Gastner added. "If Gus saw the article in the paper, he knew two things. One, that Freddy found the cat skeleton. Two, that the kid *didn't* find it where he said he did. That's kind of interesting, you have to admit."

"I want to hear from Mears after he talks with the Ford dealer in Las Cruces," Estelle said. "And then I want to hear Mr. Prescott's version of the Giarelli story."

Torrez nodded. "Don't be goin' down there by yourself." He turned and looked first at the silent Tom Pasquale, then at Gastner. "That goes for anybody just now. Not 'til we know what we're dealing with."

"How sure are you that someone took at shot at Freddy Romero's four-wheeler, Robert?" Gastner asked, and when Torrez didn't respond immediately with anything other than a raised eyebrow, the former sheriff added, "Because that makes a substantial difference. If someone *did,* then the threat may very well still be with us. If not, then the trail behind Eddie Johns' killer might be five years stone cold."

Torrez remained silent. "I mean, what have you got?" Gastner continued. "A little scuff mark on the ATV's front shield, a rock-shredded tire, and a tiny, amorphous bit of brass that could just as easily be the remains of a brass deck screw or from a bit of brass plumbing pipe that jounced out of someone's truck."

"I am one hundred percent sure," the sheriff said softly. "I know a bullet fragment when I see it. And so does Sarge. And the microscope don't lie, Bill."

Gastner nodded. "Then someone's still out there with a rifle, folks."

"That's all I'm sayin'," Torrez said.

"I need to talk with Casey Prescott again," Estelle said. "And I don't want an army with me when I do it. I know she's not in school today."

"You called the ranch?" Torrez asked.

"No. The school, earlier. I didn't want to call the ranch before I had to."

"I'm no army," Bill Gastner said, "and nobody's going to mistake me for one."

"I could use your fatherly perspective, sir."

"My 'fatherly perspective.' My own kids might argue about the value of that."

A few moments later, as they both settled in Estelle's county car, she looked across at Gastner. "I have a theory," she said, but he quickly held up a hand to stop her.

"I don't want to know anything that might color my 'fatherly perspective,' sweetheart. Besides," he said, "I have a few theories of my own. Unfortunately, none of them are worth a good God damn."

"Suppose that Gus Prescott disliked Freddy Romero just as much as he claims. Any Mexican who walks the earth. Suppose that he's just as much of a bigot as he likes to sound. He doesn't want a Mexican kid dating his daughter. His daughter might have let it slip that she was riding the four-wheeler with Freddy all over the place, and maybe let it slip that she was with the boy when he found the cat."

"Just suppose."

"So Gus sees Freddy ride by, and takes the opportunity to go talk with the kid. Maybe try to scare him away."

"Maybe. With a rifle shot across the bow? Got a little too close for comfort."

"That's more than likely. I mean, how easy is it to hit a fast-moving target for the average shooter? I don't know what kind of gun Gus might own, but it's apt to be your average ranch rifle of some kind."

"Plenty hard, no matter what."

"Exactly. For one thing, he's been drinking. He decides it would be a good thing to scare the boy, but when he tries it, he gets a little too close. One shot wings the front fender and tire, and startles the boy for just that fraction of a second that it takes to make a mistake. Pow, Freddy hits the rock, and over he goes."

"Or Gus *wanted* to kill him, *wanted* to hit him, and is a piss-poor shot."

"Either way the results are the same," Estelle said. "I vote for accidental discharge."

"And all that's if Gus is telling the truth about Eddie Johns' truck."

"See, that's the thing, sir. If he *isn't* telling the truth, then he has more reason to stop Freddy than just fatherly concern for his lovely daughter," Estelle said.

"'Fatherly concern' isn't a *just* kind of thing, sweetheart. People have killed for much, much less. Is Casey pregnant? You know what dads think about that, too. When my kids were growing up, there was a time or two when I thought I was going to have to shoot somebody."

"I don't think she is, sir."

"But you can't be sure."

"No...not until I ask her."

Chapter Forty-one

"I don't want you talking to her." Jewell Prescott stood squarely in the doorway of the double-wide mobile home, and there was no mistaking her posture. With one hand on each door jamb, she was an effective road block. As if picking up unpleasant intimations, the three dogs, at first so bumptiously gleeful, had retreated to a shady spot at the end of the trailer near a propane tank.

"Mrs. Prescott, I wouldn't intrude if I didn't think it was important," Estelle Reyes-Guzman said.

"Oh, *everything* is important," the heavy woman said. "And my two daughters are important to me. Listen, Casey's in just terrible straights right now. She doesn't want to go to school and put up with all *those* questions. And I see no reason to be dredging all this unhappiness up over and over again. You just go talk to someone else about all this."

"Mrs. Prescott," Estelle said, "When there's an official investigation, we talk with whomever the situation requires. I'm sure you understand that. I'm certainly sorry for any intrusion, but that's just the way it is."

"There's nothing Casey can tell you."

"That remains to be seen, Mrs. Prescott."

"Bill, you've known us for years," the woman said, and Bill Gastner nodded slightly, his expression sober. "What are we supposed to do? What are we supposed to *tell* you?"

"It's the simplest thing if you just allow us to do our job and get on with it," he said.

"I don't *have* to let you all talk with Casey, do I?" The question was directed to Bill Gastner, but Estelle saved him the trouble of being diplomatic.

"No, ma'am, you don't," Estelle said. "And if that's the route you and your husband wish to take, then two hours from now, we'll be back with a court order, Mrs. Prescott. You're perfectly welcome to be present when we talk with Casey. In fact, I encourage it. She'll probably feel more comfortable with you there."

Jewell Prescott almost smiled. "Oh, I'm not so sure of that, young lady. There's a number of things we don't see eye to eye on."

Estelle saw movement behind the woman, and both Casey and her older sister Christina appeared.

"Come on, mom," Casey said. "None of this is going to go away." Her mother didn't move her arms, and Casey leaned against her well-padded shoulder, rubbing her cheek on her mother's arm. "Come on." Her eyes were red-rimmed, but she managed a smile for Estelle. "Christine and I will talk with the sheriff."

"Oh, I just don't think..." Jewell bit off her words and shook her head vehemently, tears coming to her eyes.

"It'll be okay." Casey circled her mother's shoulders in a hug, and then as her mother turned, slipped past her.

"Is your father home?" Estelle asked.

"He went into town to get a part for the grader," Christine said. She hugged her mother as well, but Jewell didn't follow them out the door. She watched with sad eyes, as if she had every expectation of never seeing them again. She lifted a hand once as if she wanted to say something, then thought better of it.

"Thanks, Jewell," Bill Gastner said.

"I've always trusted you," she said, and it was an admonition rather than a compliment, as if to say, *"I've tried...I can't do it... now it's your turn."*

"I appreciate that, Jewell. You hang in there."

"Oh, boy," she murmured, and backed away from the door, closing out the intrusion of the outside world.

"Let's go look at the horses," Casey suggested, and she walked with her hands shoved in her hip pockets, heading toward the small corral and shed. Two horses stood like statutes, watching their approach, and the mare nickered as they drew near. Christine stooped down and scooped up a wayward treat of hay, a movement not lost on the mare, who crowded the fence.

"I always feel better with these guys," Casey said, stroking the young bay gelding's silky neck. "Sis and I were just getting ready to go for a ride. If you'd come ten minutes later, we'd be a dust trail on the horizon."

"I'm glad we didn't miss you." Estelle gently pushed the mare's head away. Still munching hay, the animal seemed fascinated by the undersheriff's cap. "Did your father talk to you about Thursday?"

"What do you mean, did he talk? About Freddy, you mean?"

"Yes."

"When I got home from school, he had the newspaper and had read the article about finding the cat's skeleton. The first thing he wanted to know was whether I'd gone with Freddy to Borracho. I don't know why he thought I *would* have, but parents seem to have this *radar*, you know? They always seem to know. He was real angry that I might have skipped school. I mean *real* angry."

"Did you tell him that you were with Freddy when he found the cat?"

Estelle could see a slow flush creep up Casey's neck and fan across her peaches and cream cheeks. "No." She glanced at her sister. "He'd been drinking, and he was upset. I don't know why the article ticked him off so, except he doesn't like Freddy, and here's this neat article and all. But I just said no. I didn't want to have another argument. I didn't say we'd been out there together on Sunday, or anything else."

"Sometimes it's better just to lie low," Christine added.

"Did he mention that he'd spoken to Freddy on Thursday or Friday?"

"No. He just saw the article. If he talked with Freddy about anything, he didn't say so." She stroked the gelding's neck with one hand while letting him nuzzle the other palm.

Estelle watched the two girls, both of them deep in the saddest of thoughts, but unconsciously communing with the horses, who sponged up the affection without judgment.

When he'd been sitting in the Broken Spur, listening to Freddy Romero blast by on his four-wheeler, Gus Prescott had been aware, if he'd read the article carefully, that the boy had fabricated the tale of where the jaguar's carcass had been found.

"Casey, did your father ever talk much about Eddie Johns?"

"Not to me."

"Christine?"

The older sister frowned. "I don't know what kind of case you're trying to build, sheriff. You asked me that earlier, and you also talked to my dad earlier. He told you what he knew."

Estelle gazed across the yard toward the spot where the line of old vehicles had rusted into the prairie. *None of this is going to go away,* Casey had said to her mother. None of *this.*

"We're just following pathways, Christine. At this point some pretty indistinct trails. I was curious about the circumstances that led to your dad buying that wrecked truck from Johns."

"I didn't know that he had done that."

"The one that burned?"

"Now *that* I remember. Dad said that he was cutting off some part and started a little fire." She smiled. "A *little* fire. Oh, sure. But it wasn't much loss. It was wrecked anyway."

"You saw it? Before the fire, I mean."

"I don't know if I did or not. It wasn't something that I paid attention to."

"I saw it," Casey offered. "I mean, before he burned it."

"All bashed up?"

"Well, kinda. It was shiny black, I remember that, 'cause after he lit it on fire, it was *ugly* black. He was really ticked."

"You remember the make?"

"No. Just a wrecked truck. That's all I remember. He sold a whole bunch of that old stuff so he can buy parts for the grader. But you already know that. You saw it go out this morning."

The buzz of Estelle's phone was startling, and the mare jerked her head back, ears pitched forward. Estelle stepped back slowly, and flicked on the phone.

"Guzman."

"Hey," Torrez said. "Borderland's records show a 2004 black Ford 250 crew cab sold to Eddie Johns on November 12, 2003. He got the VIN, but that ain't going to do us much good. The dealership don't keep a record of the engine and tranny serial numbers, but we don't have those anyway. Yet."

"That's good work, Bobby. They carried the paper on it?"

"Wasn't any. Cash deal."

"*Ay.*"

"Thirty-eight thousand dollar cash deal."

"Real estate was going well for Mr. Johns, apparently."

"Something was," the sheriff said. "Where you at right now?"

"Talking with Casey and Christine Prescott."

"Gus there?"

"No. The girls said that he went to town to buy some parts for his road grader."

"Okay. Look, this El Paso mess is gonna take Mears a while. He's got folks workin' for him at the bank, at the utilities... everything so far says that Johns just vanished without notice. He didn't close out any accounts, didn't clean up any of his mess. Didn't even clean out the fridge, the landlord says. He was there one day, gone the next. No notes, no nothing."

"That probably rules out any lingering notion of suicide," Estelle said, and Torrez grunted with amusement.

"He ain't no suicide. Suicides don't crawl back into caves and shoot themselves in the back of the head."

"I know he hasn't had time to dig into too many dark corners, but has Tom found any hint of a Mexican connection?"

"We're gonna find out. But my guess is that the Mexicans are just as much out of the loop as we are. They may have been plannin' something, or maybe were interested in what Johns had to offer, but there ain't no actual connection that I can imagine."

"We'll see what Captain Naranjo finds out," Estelle said. Tomás Naranjo, an ally in the Mexican *Judiciales,* sometimes cooperated with them so willingly that it seemed he considered Posadas County to be a small but obstreperous extension of his own state.

"You're going to talk with Prescott again today?"

"I think so. It bothers me that he lied to Herb Torrance about how he acquired the truck from Johns."

"Maybe he ain't lyin'."

"That would mean that either Herb concocted the tale, or the people you talked to at Giarelli's have faulty memories."

"Either is possible. Ain't likely, but possible."

Estelle had turned slightly, and now a motion from Gastner drew her attention. He pointed toward the south, where a roil of dust rose behind an approaching vehicle.

"We'll talk with Gus here in a bit. He's on his way in right now."

"You be careful."

"Oh, *sí*." She switched off and turned back toward the corral. Casey Prescott was still receiving a full dose of commiseration from the mare, but Christine had stepped away from the horses, standing close to Gastner's elbow.

"What's actually going on?" Christine asked quietly. She looked from Gastner to Estelle, and at the same time, Casey pushed away from the corral. The same question was in her eyes. Estelle had known both girls for years, and had had the opportunity to talk with Christine a number of times in an official capacity. She had long ago come to the conclusion that the young woman was not only strikingly pretty, but equally quick-witted, caring, and honest. The impulse to simply lay the case open before her was strong. But the cloud that hung at the moment over their father's head was more than just dust kicked up by a pickup truck.

"Whenever there's an unattended death," Estelle said, "we're required to follow up on every detail. Painful as it might be."

"Unattended," Christine said, taking her time with the word. "Are you referring to Freddy, or to Eddie Johns?"

Estelle hesitated. "Both. In both cases, we believe that there's a possibility that the two incidents were not unattended deaths."

Casey moved a step closer to her sister until their arms touched, but the younger girl didn't speak. Not an *unattended death*. The terminology—even the concept itself—was so familiar for a cop, yet so completely alien for a teenager who'd just lost her boyfriend. *Someone else was there*. And that changed everything.

Christine gazed at Estelle, her expression assessing. "Oh, my God," she whispered, but any other comment was drowned out by the sounds of Gus Prescott's pickup. The extended-cab truck pulled in a few paces from Estelle's cruiser, twenty or thirty yards away. The clattering of its gruff diesel engine died abruptly and Prescott got out, followed by a small white poodle who shot off toward the house. From a distance, Estelle could see a long gun in the rear window rack, well out of reach of the driver without climbing out of the truck and accessing the back seat.

"Good mornin'," Prescott said, affably enough. He seemed in no hurry to approach, and Estelle turned to the girls.

"Excuse us, please."

"I don't think so," Christine said firmly, and her response surprised Estelle. "I want to know what's going on."

Behind them, the little dog yipped as he was mobbed by the three larger animals, and Estelle heard the screen door of the house open and then close as he made it unmauled into his sanctuary. Jewell Prescott appeared to be perfectly content with *not* knowing what was going on outside.

"Find your grader parts, sir?" the undersheriff asked as she walked over toward the truck.

Gus Prescott watched her with feigned indifference as he got out and then crossed around the front of the pickup. "Had to order," he replied.

"Herb seems eager to get that road of his fixed," Gastner offered.

"I guess he might be," Prescott said. He wiped his face, dabbing at the corners of his mouth. From a dozen feet away, Estelle could smell the beer. "You girls get on into the house, now."

The order might not have sounded ridiculous had Casey been accompanied by one of her school chums instead of her sister. But Christine was in no mood to chirp, "Yes, daddy" and do as she was told.

"Sir," Estelle said, "we were interested in what you can tell us about the Ford pickup truck that belonged to Eddie Johns."

"What do you mean?" Prescott rested an arm on the hood of the pickup, as if feeling the need to protect it.

"Just that, sir. I was wondering how his black Ford three-quarter ton ended up on Cameron Florek's junk hauler. I was wondering how you happened to come by it." She glanced at the fender of Prescott's own truck, still decorated with the *XLT Triton V-8* emblem...not the diesel that was obviously under the hood.

For a long moment, Gus Prescott didn't answer. His gaze flicked first to Gastner, who stood relaxed but watchful, then to Christine and Casey, and finally back to Estelle. He looked her up and down, and Estelle could see that his eyes watered and wandered...he was so juiced that he would have a hard time passing a field sobriety test.

"I got to get me a beer," he said flatly, and looked over at Gastner. "You want one, Mr. Livestock Inspector?"

"Appreciate the thought, but no thanks. Too early in the day for me, Gus."

"Well...it ain't *ever* too early." He walked to the passenger side, opened the door, and Estelle could hear the snap of plastic as he pulled a can away from a six-pack. The firearm in the back window was a shotgun, very much like the one in her patrol car rack.

He didn't close the door, but circled around it, popping the can as he did so. "You're sure?" He raised the can to Gastner.

"I'm sure, Gus."

Prescott shrugged and glanced dismissively at the undersheriff. "So, what do you want?" No simple courtesy there, Estelle noted.

"Just to clear up some things, Mr. Prescott," Estelle said.

"There's nothing to clear up."

"I wish that were true, sir."

Prescott rested his can carefully on the sloped hood, and took his time lighting a cigarette. The blue smoke jetted out against the fender. "You didn't drive all the way out here just to waste county gas, lady. So if you got something to say, just say it and get it over with." He took another long pull on the beer. "You're just enjoyin' the hell out of all this, aren't you."

"Sir?"

"Comin' out here where you got no business? Stirring things up where you got no cause?"

"That's an interesting take on it, sir."

Prescott's lips compressed into a tight line as if he suddenly realized he'd said too much, and his head jerked to one side as if he were wearing a shirt and tie with the collar too tight.

"Is the diesel engine in this vehicle the one from Johns' truck, sir?" She pulled the small notebook from her pocket, and thumbed through the pages, not bothering to read the contents. The notion of documentation was not lost on the rancher.

"What, you got to check it now?" Prescott strode around the front of the truck to the driver's door, jerked it open and yanked the hood release lever. "There," he said, groping for the safety catch. The mammoth hood yawned up, and he held out a hand, presenting the engine. "Bought that engine years ago. Got a good deal on it. So there you go, *sheriff.*" His sarcasm was heavy. "And yeah, it *ain't* the motor that come with this truck. Sure as hell ain't. You check all you want."

"How did you happen to come by Johns' truck, sir? A 2004, I think."

"Do I got to put up with all this?" Prescott asked Gastner. "I mean, a man's got rights, don't he?"

"Indeed he does, Gus my friend. Indeed he does."

"Well, then?"

"Well, then," Gastner said calmly, "we'd appreciate some answers, Gus. And I guess you know that you can give 'em now or later."

"What do you mean by that?"

"Just what I said. Now or later, Gus. If not to us, then there'll be someone else." Gastner grinned warmly. "I'd sure rather talk with me than somebody else."

Prescott frowned as he tried to understand that. "Look, I sold that wreck to Florek fair and square. You ask him. I got his receipt right in the house."

"We did ask him, Gus. Seems like a good thing to be clearing out some old junk. A man kinda gets buried by stuff after a while. But there's a few little things that don't square up, and you can understand our curiosity, I would think."

"What's your interest in all this?" Prescott asked.

"Me personally? Well, now," Gastner said, "I'm just lookin' out for some old friends. I got a right to do that, don't you think?"

"This Johns a friend of yours?"

"Nope. Never was. And now I have this nagging suspicion that he had some friends south of the border I wouldn't have cared much for either. That's why we're curious how you came by his truck, Gus. Just want to make sure everything is in the clear."

"I bought it off him."

"From Eddie Johns, you mean?" Estelle asked.

"That's what I said."

"Pricey unit," Gastner observed.

"Not when I got it."

"It was one or two years old when you bought it?" Estelle asked.

"More like three or four," the rancher said, and wiped his mouth again. He regarded the truck's engine, setting his beer can on the radiator housing. "Took me three days to put that in here. Runs like a charm."

"Hell of a lot of work," Gastner said.

"Damn right." Prescott moved the can and reached up to grab the hood and pull it shut.

"So that's that. You satisfied?"

"Had the truck been damaged when you bought it?" Estelle asked.

"Hell, yes, it was damaged. Johns...well, he wouldn't say for sure what he did, but he rolled it down into an arroyo. That's what I think. Wasn't a body panel left that wasn't wrecked. Insurance wrote it off."

"Johns had the salvage as part of the settlement, and you bought it from him." Gastner made it sound as if the answer to that one question would put a period to the whole discussion, and Prescott nodded quickly.

"Sure. That's how it was."

"Giarelli had nothing to do with it, then."

Gus Prescott shot a quick glance at Estelle. "What makes you think that he—who's Giarelli?"

"One version of the story has an employee of Giarelli Sand and Gravel in Deming backing into Johns' truck right there in the company yard, sir."

"I don't know where you heard that."

"That's a problem, then, sir. If Johns rolled his truck into an arroyo, there'd be a police report on the incident—probably in our files or with the state police. Otherwise the insurance company wouldn't pay him. They wouldn't total it out without a report, and Johns wouldn't stand for that. He wouldn't get a cent." Prescott's mouth worked and he flicked a piece of tobacco off his tongue. "And if the accident happened at Giarelli's, there would also be an incident report, sir. They'd see to that. Otherwise, *their* company insurance wouldn't pay."

"Dig, dig, dig. It's like a *dog* scratchin' at a flea bite. You won't leave it alone." He licked his lips. "Look, I don't know about all this Giarelli business. All I know is what Eddie Johns told me. That he'd wrecked the truck and collected a shitload of insurance, and wanted to know if I wanted the salvage. Just a nuisance to him. Maybe he made up a story to tell somebody so he wouldn't sound like a simple son of a bitch. How the hell would I know."

"So Johns signed the truck's title over to you," Estelle said.

"I didn't get no title. The thing was wrecked. It was salvage."

"He removed the license plate?"

"Well, damn, I don't know whether he did or not. Or the insurance company. Hell, maybe his old aunt Minnie did. Who the hell knows. *I* don't have it, that's for sure. Never did." He huffed with exasperation. "And you know it ain't on the truck now. You checked thorough enough. That's what my neighbor tells me." He squared his shoulders. "Just what are you tryin' to prove with all this mumbo-jumbo?"

"Do you own a rifle, sir?"

The question took the rancher by surprise. He glanced toward the pickup, then at Gastner.

"'Course I own a rifle. Everybody in this county owns a damn rifle."

"Is that what you normally carry in the truck, sir? Other than the pump shotgun you have there?"

"Sometimes I do. Sometimes I don't. What, now you're going to accuse me of shooting Johns? Is that what this is all about? First I shoot him, then I steal his truck?" He managed a derisive laugh. Estelle watched as the color ran in splotches up his cheeks, as if he was fighting a fever.

"Mr. Prescott, Eddie Johns wasn't shot with a rifle, as I'm sure you know by now, neighborhood communication being what it is. So no…I don't think your ranch rifle shot him."

"So what's the point, then? What are you gettin' at, lady?"

"May I see the rifle?"

"A rifle's a rifle."

"May I see it?"

"Well, hell, I suppose so." He turned toward the truck, going again to the passenger door. Estelle watched him as he bent over and collected the gun, a short, angular weapon that had apparently been lying on the front seat or leaning in the passenger well. With the door open, she couldn't see exactly what he was doing, but it appeared he was fumbling out the magazine. She shifted to her left a step or two, away from Bill Gastner, circling so that the rancher would have to turn to face her. Prescott tossed the magazine on the seat and stepped back, his footing not all that steady, the muzzle of the carbine held skyward. She had not heard or seen the bolt drawn back, so if a cartridge had been chambered before, it was still in place. He thrust the weapon out toward her, holding it forward of the trigger guard.

"Ruger ranch rifle," he said. "Got to be a million of 'em around."

"I would think so." Estelle took the gun and turned so it was pointing off toward the distant hills. She racked the bolt back, and a cartridge spun out of the rifle. Bill Gastner almost caught it in midair, then bent to retrieve it and dusted it off before handing it to Estelle.

"Yeah, I shoulda done that," Prescott muttered.

"I'd like to borrow this firearm for a day or two," Estelle said. She pocketed the cartridge. "Would that be all right with you, sir? I'll bring it back out to you tomorrow."

"Well, no, I don't guess that would be all right at all. You don't just wheel in here and confiscate my guns, lady. I mean, just what are you up to?" He didn't wait for an answer, but turned to his two daughters, who'd remained silent though the entire conversation, watching the back and forth like spectators at a ping-pong tournament. "I'd kinda like some privacy here," he said, and his tone had abruptly softened.

"He's right," Estelle added, and Christine looked from her father to the undersheriff, eyes pleading. But this was no time for Gus Prescott to be dealing both with the undersheriff's questions and an audience as well. "I'll need to talk with both of you again, but if you'd give us a few minutes?"

For a moment it looked as if Christine would refuse, but then she nodded and touched Casey on the elbow. Estelle noticed that the two girls did not walk back toward the house, where their mother waited. Instead, they crossed the yard again to the corral and the horses. No wonder Christine had felt the need to hurry home from college for this mess, Estelle thought. All Christine's skills honed over years as a bartender would be needed for a family guided by a father who could always find the deepest rut in a mud hole.

"I don't think it's right that you come in here and upset everybody," Prescott said. "It's a hard time for Casey."

"I understand that." She turned the rifle this way and that, and passed the muzzle close by her nose. Turning the rifle, she looked into the dark recess of the chamber. The aroma was not one of bore solvent or oil. In fact, the rifle itself was grubby, the action speckled with dirt, lint, and dog hair. But it had been fired recently enough that the characteristic aroma lingered.

For an instant, she was tempted to hand the rifle to Gastner, who during his many years in both the military and law enforcement had inspected a myriad firearms, but she decided against it. Prescott was watching her as if he'd handed the rifle to a tourist who had never seen one before. His hand kept reaching out, an almost involuntary motion that said he expected her to drop the little Ruger any moment.

"Could use a cleaning," she said.

He almost sneered. "You'd know about that, would you, lady?"

"Well, probably not, sir." She smiled at him innocently. "Do you practice a lot?"

"No. You obviously ain't bought ammunition lately. God damn near have to mortgage the ranch to afford it. When they got any of it, that is."

"How about on Thursday?"

"Thursday what?"

"Did you shoot this on Thursday, sir?"

Prescott took a long time forming an answer, and Estelle watched a range of emotions on his face, as if he were trying to solve a really tough Sudoku puzzle.

"You ever seen the number of prairie dogs we got, lady? You let them run, and you won't have a stick of grass for ten miles."

"You don't poison 'em?" Bill Gastner asked.

"Sure. Some. It don't work. We try everything."

"Doesn't seem like there's as many as there used to be."

"Hopin' not."

"So you were out shooting Thursday?" Estelle was facing southeast, with a full view of the two-track that wound in toward the ranch. In the distance, without stirring dust, the county patrol unit had appeared around the end of the mesa and now idled along the road into the Prescott's. Still too far away for her to recognize which unit it was, she knew that it had to be either Deputy Tom Pasquale or Sheriff Robert Torrez. The sedate approach, like someone out ambling about with no real destination, suggested the Sheriff himself. The breeze, light and fitful, was to her back, and it would be several minutes before Prescott could hear the vehicle.

"Maybe. Maybe not. I don't keep track of things like that."

"Sir, we have reason to believe that at least one shot was fired at Freddy Romero when he was riding on the Bender's Canyon road."

"What are you sayin'?"

"Just that. Someone took a shot at him."

Prescott looked across the yard toward where Casey and Christina were standing, communing with the horses. Casey had been watching them, and for a long moment father and daughter's eyes met across the distance.

"Nobody told me that the kid got shot," Prescott said finally. "Enough people been out there that talk would go around. Somebody'd know. Nobody said nothin'."

"I said that someone shot *at* him, sir. He wasn't struck by the bullet."

"Then how do you know, lady?"

"His four-wheeler was hit, sir. We have bullet fragments that were found in the front tire."

"And you think I did that? Is that what this is all about?"

"You left the Broken Spur Saloon shortly after Freddy passed by, sir. You're not the only one who did, but you're the only one seen driving across the mesa toward Bender's Canyon Trail, the same route that Freddy took." Prescott didn't respond. "I'd have to wonder what it was that the Romero boy was doing that concerned you so much," Estelle continued. "I can't believe that it was just his courting of your daughter."

In the seconds of silence that followed, Estelle could hear the gentle whisper of the approaching Expedition patrol vehicle, and the rancher turned to look. By now, the vehicle was close enough that they could see the shield on the doors and the roof-rack of lights. The figure behind the wheel could only be the sheriff, large and broad-shouldered, one arm out the window as if trying to stroke the heads of the chamisa that passed by the door.

"Spit it out, lady." Prescott's voice was almost a whisper.

"I think that Freddy Romero found the remains of Eddie Johns when he found that cat skull, sir. He found Johns' hand-gun, and maybe knew exactly what was in the cave. He wanted to come back, but not with your daughter. Casey said that they had an argument about his reckless driving. You read in the newspaper about the discovery of the cat skull, or your daughter told you—either way, you wanted to warn Freddy away so you'd have time to cover up that little cave. You fired a shot at Freddy, and he panicked and crashed." Estelle watched Prescott, watched the set of his shoulders, the placing of his feet, the flicking of his eyes. The whisper of the Expedition's V-8 grew louder.

"That's what I believe happened, sir."

Prescott turned to watch Torrez's approach. "I don't know where you get these wild stories. You can't prove a word of it."

"Actually," Estelle hefted the rifle, "I think we can."

"You can't just come onto my property and confiscate my goods."

"If you're in the clear on all this, then maybe that rifle will prove it," Gastner said. "Think this thing through, Gus."

"That rifle don't have a thing to do with me and Eddie Johns," the rancher said.

"What does, Gus? You think we're not going to be able to trace that wrecked truck? Match up the damage to it with that old road grader of yours? Something like that?"

Gus Prescott looked down at the ground, then to his left as Sheriff Robert Torrez idled the county unit closer, coming to a stop a few feet behind Prescott's truck, angled so that it didn't block the sheriff's view of them.

"I always thought a lot of you, Sheriff," Prescott said finally. He looked up at Gastner, eyes sad.

"And we'll work through this, Gus." Gastner made it sound as if they were engaged in "working through" a simple neighborhood fence spat, Estelle thought. His mellow voice and grandfatherly manner could be a grand defuser, and she guessed that was his intent.

"That's pretty damn easy for you to say." Prescott looked as if he wanted to say something else, but it stuck in his throat. His gaze wandered off again toward his daughters, and Estelle saw a deep sadness there, more than the beer or rum-soaked depression of the chronic drinker during a moment of self-recrimination.

"Lemme get my keys," he mumbled, and turned to his truck. Estelle stood a pace or two in front of the right front fender holding the carbine, while Sheriff Torrez now approached from the right rear. As the rancher turned to round the left front fender, Gastner took a step toward him, a casual enough move that kept him close. Gus opened the driver's door and slipped inside, and did two maneuvers at once. The ignition key hung from the column, and instead of removing it, he twisted it forward, the big diesel starting with a sharp bark.

Without an instant's hesitation, he yanked the gear lever into reverse and swung the door first toward him as if to close it, but then banged it hard open, aiming for Gastner.

The older man pivoted back a step, almost losing his balance. With a spray of gravel and dirt, the truck shot backward, its massive back bumper crashing into the left front fender of the Sheriff's Expedition. Bodywork crumpled backward like tissue, jamming into the front wheel. Even as the crash resounded, Prescott yanked the gear lever into drive and accelerated hard, the homemade, welded iron grill guard catching the left front wheel, tire, and fender of Estelle's Crown Victoria.

The undersheriff dove off to one side, sailing over the sedan's hood to crash to the ground, the carbine skidding away. She felt more than saw the pickup swerve past her, and scrambled to her feet, yanking out her automatic.

Sheriff Torrez had reacted faster. As soon as the truck had driven clear of both Gastner and Estelle, he fired quickly, holding his .45 in both hands. The back window of Prescott's pickup dissolved in a shower of glass, and Estelle could see the holes punching down the side of the truck even as it sped away. One of the rounds struck a back tire and howled away toward the west.

Both girls had dived to the ground by the fence, and the horses whirled in panic, nickering loudly. Christine's arm was clamped around her younger sister, but Casey broke loose and dashed after the fleeing pickup truck.

"Daddy!" she screamed. Estelle twisted to yell a warning at Torrez, but saw that the sheriff was already holstering his weapon.

"Everybody all right?" Gastner sounded as excited as if somebody had dropped a box of books.

"Yes," Estelle replied. She stepped around the mangled front of her car. The left front wheel was jammed inside the crumpled fender, pointing off in a direction all its own.

"Give a hand here," Torrez shouted. He was yanking at the Expedition's bodywork, then backed away. "Need something to pry with." In a few seconds he returned with the handle from his handiman jack, and he and Gastner heaved at the stubborn sheet metal.

As they worked, Estelle watched the retreating pickup, heading out the same trail she had taken to meet with Casey at the windmill. There was no open road out there, no back trail to refuge. The undersheriff pulled her phone from her pocket and touched the speed dial. Gayle Torrez's response was immediate.

"Gayle, Bobby and I are down at the Prescott ranch and need assistance from a uniformed deputy ASAP."

"Pasquale is on the road just west of town. I'll have him swing down that way."

"We'll be apprehending a single male subject who is armed and may be dangerous." She hesitated. What did Gus Prescott think he could accomplish? Did he think the law would simply let him go? Did he think he could evade a manhunt? Judging by his effective performance as a truck driver, he wasn't as inebriated as might first appear. *Run,* she thought. *Panic and run.* "Tell Thomas to alert us when he swings off the highway at Moore."

"Affirmative."

She felt the hollow sensation in the pit of her stomach as she watched Bob Torrez take the heavy steel bar and thrash the fender into submission. His face was flushed with both effort and anger. For his part, Gus Prescott was not going to change his mind and drive meekly back to them.

"And Gayle, you might as well have an ambulance en route. Maybe we'll get lucky and it'll be a wasted trip for them."

"Affirmative. You want a heads-up to the state police? And Jackie Taber is in the deputies office doing paperwork. I can send her."

"Affirmative on the SP's, Gayle. And go ahead and send Jackie. This is going to be a confrontation thing, not a chase. There's nowhere the suspect can go."

"You guys be careful."

"Absolutely."

She snapped off the phone in time to see Torrez give a mighty heave that seemed likely to tip the Expedition on its side. Something cracked and the sheriff nodded. "Now we go," he said, panting with the exertion.

"Casey!" Estelle shouted. The girl had lugged saddle and tack out of the small barn, and was in the process of rigging the mare, who'd been wearing only the hand-woven rope hackamore. Estelle jogged over toward the girls. She could see that Christine was confronting her sister, and had taken the bridle from her. Their conversation was intense and private, their faces just inches from each other.

"Casey," Estelle said, "Do you know where your father is going?"

The girl was crying, and she waved a hand hopelessly, taking in the open country to the north and east.

"His favorite spots are the breaks over east, out beyond the windmill," Christine said. She reached out a hand and gripped Estelle's. "Don't let him hurt himself," she whispered.

"I'll try my best. You girls need to stay here with your mother." If Jewell Prescott had heard the gunshots and ruckus, there was no sign.

"The sheriff tried to *shoot* him," Casey cried.

"No, he only wanted to stop the truck," Estelle said. Behind her, the Expedition fired up, and she turned. "Promise me?" Christine nodded, but Casey was having none of it.

"If I can find him, I can make him listen," she wept, and swung up on the mare. She didn't wait for the bridle, but seized the hackamore and twisted the mare's head around, away from her sister's reach. The gate had been drawn to one side, and the mare made for it, the unsaddled gelding in hot pursuit.

Chapter Forty-two

Now that he was underway, Sheriff Robert Torrez drove with no particular sense of urgency. He let the battered SUV heave along the rough two-track out toward Lewis Wells, and occasionally in the distance they could see the dust cloud raised by Casey's mare. The gelding kept easy pace, no doubt reveling in free running with no human to kick his ribs or jerk his mouth.

"So what's he gonna do?" Torrez asked. "He don't have nowheres to go."

"We can hope just what Christine said…go out and find a quiet place to sit down and think."

"He's going to have a lot of time to do that," Gastner said from the back seat. "You have to wonder," he added, and braced himself as Torrez maneuvered over a short patch of slick rock bordering a small arroyo. "Is there a back road out of here?"

"Nope." The sheriff shook his head. "Unless he wants to try driving cross-country. The arroyos ain't going to let him do that."

The windmill appeared first as a speck on the horizon, then gently turning, the rudder swinging the blades to track into the fitful breeze. Lewis Wells sprouted out of a swale, a slight depression where the cattle had trampled the grass to dust.

"That well was drilled in 1951," Gastner announced as they approached the last slight rise before the swale. "I wish I could remember the homesteader's name. It'll come to me. Lewis bought the property, but he didn't do the drilling."

Torrez leaned forward as he drove, both arms on the steering wheel. To the north and east of the windmill, the country looked as if a giant had snapped folds into a tawny, rock-studded blanket.

"There she is." Estelle pointed. She pulled the binoculars out of their case and found the image. Casey was urging her mare up a rough slope, the gelding following close.

"Over to the left," Torrez added. She swung the binoculars and the pickup truck burst into focus. Prescott had pulled the vehicle near a copse of ragged, stunted elms, opportunistic little trees that responded to even the hope of water. They managed to tower over the sharp-spined acacias.

"Stop here," Estelle said suddenly, and Torrez looked at her, puzzled. "No. Stop here, Bobby. Stop." He did so, and she handed him the binoculars. "If we drive in on them, we're going to push him to do something. We don't want to do that, not with Casey over there. There's no point in forcing his hand. He has nowhere to go."

"You got that right," Gastner leaned forward, his fingers clutching the prisoner grill that separated front from back.

Estelle popped the door. "I'm going to watch from here," Torrez said. Estelle knew exactly what he meant even before he hefted the compact, scoped rifle from the rack that stood vertically beside the transmission hump. He could sweep the hillside four hundred yards away. "He ain't going to want to talk to me anyway."

"I think I should go," Gastner said.

The undersheriff slipped out of the truck and opened Gastner's locked, prisoner-proof door. "You're feeling like a stroll, sir?"

"A *stroll*, yes. I don't think Gus sees me as much of a threat."

They watched Torrez arrange a folded jacket on the hood of the truck, with a heavy bean bag in front of that. He settled behind the rifle, working this way and that so that weapon didn't rock on its short magazine. For a moment he visually roamed the hillside, eye close to the scope objective. The bolt of the rifle rode open.

"Casey's tied her horse to a stump behind the acacia grove," he said. "She's makin' her way up the slope." Estelle saw the barrel of the rifle tilt upward, then drift from side to side before freezing. "He's sittin' on a big slab of sandstone," the sheriff said. "Range finder says four hundred and twenty yards."

"He's in the open?"

"Oh, yeah."

"Then that's where we're going," Estelle said. Of all the people in the world who might be behind the rifle, she felt absolute confidence in Robert Torrez, but the ghost of apprehension still raised its head.

"He's got the shotgun with him," Torrez said. "He's holdin' it between his legs, stock down."

"*Ay,*" Estelle whispered.

"Pay attention," Torrez instructed. "I ain't going to wait this time." She knew exactly what he meant. It had been three years, and her side still ached on occasion where a nine millimeter slug had taken her through the margin of her vest. An instant after the pistol's trigger had been pulled, Sheriff Robert Torrez had fired, a hundred yard shot that the .308 rifle bullet had covered in a tenth of a second...an instant too late. "If he makes a motion to point that shotgun your way, he's a dead man."

There was no comfort in leaving the decision making to Gus Prescott.

Chapter Forty-three

The undersheriff kept her pace slow for Bill Gastner's benefit. The older man watched his feet instead of the hillside in the distance, but on occasion he would stop to look off toward where Gus Prescott sat in the sun, looking out across the peaceful prairie. No doubt he watched their progress. Whether he could catch the glint of sunlight on the scope that watched him from four hundred yards away was another matter.

Estelle tried to imagine the swirl of conflicting thoughts that must be torturing Gus Prescott at that moment. If he knew he was in the crosshairs, his pulse would be hammering in his ears, no matter how deep his depression or how rich the alcohol in his bloodstream. The father in him would react to Casey's presence, mixing worry for her safety with the torture of what she must think of him.

As they crossed the swale toward the ragged, low hills, walking under the possible trajectory of the bullet from Sheriff Robert Torrez's rifle, Estelle could come to no firm conclusion about Gus Prescott's intentions. He had ambushed Freddy Romero, rather than facing him eye to eye. If he had shot Eddie Johns, he'd done so in the back of the head, when the man was preoccupied. He hadn't confronted Johns face to face. In his own front yard, he'd recognized that he was outnumbered three to one, and fled…to this rock in the sun.

"Wait a second." Gastner stopped, hands on his hips, squaring his shoulders, sucking in air. "I should do this more often. The hiking part, I mean."

Estelle looked back toward where Torrez waited, then turned and surveyed the hill ahead of them. Casey had stopped a dozen paces below her father, and they appeared to be talking. The sound of another engine attracted her attention, and she turned in time to see Christine's little station wagon pull in beside the sheriff's department Expedition.

"*Ay,*" she breathed, and pointed. "Christine."

"She's got common sense," Gastner said. "She won't interfere."

"She can't just stand there and watch someone point an assault rifle at her father," Estelle said.

"But that's exactly what she's going to have to do," Gastner replied. "Nope, here she comes."

Estelle reached around and removed her radio, making sure it was set to channel three. "Bobby, he's not going to do anything while the girls are here."

The radio squelched twice as Torrez touched the transmit bar to indicate he'd heard.

"We hope he won't," Gastner added. "He's fresh out of choices." He took another deep breath. "I'm ready."

His deeds had, in effect, admitted to involvement somehow with two deaths, but Gus Prescott actually hadn't *said* anything incriminating. Estelle knew that whether he could actually bring himself to utter those words while he looked his daughters in the eye was another story.

She skirted a jumble of smaller boulders that had slumped down from the hillside, and when she was sure that Prescott had a clear view of her, she stopped, arms held out to the side.

"Sir, we need to talk."

"Just stay away," Prescott replied.

"Can't do that, sir. I'm concerned for Casey's safety." She could see the girl, now off to the side somewhat, still a dozen feet from her father. "Casey, are you all right?"

"Yes."

Estelle shifted position somewhat but Bill Gastner stayed well behind her, positioned to intercept Christine. Estelle could see that Prescott held the shotgun between his knees, the barrel pointed upward. If the rancher leaned his head to the left, he could touch the blued barrel with his ear. One hand was on the fore end of the shotgun, the other resting on his knee. The trigger guard was concealed between his knees, but it would take only a breath of time for him to drop his hand to the trigger, a few more second fragments to move the barrel so that it pointed somewhere other than into the open sky.

In her left hand, Estelle held the portable radio, and she pushed and held the transmit bar so that Torrez could listen in on the conversation. "Sir, will you put the shotgun down? Just lay it on the rocks beside you."

"It's okay right where it is." Prescott's voice cracked a little, and that was a good sign. He hadn't settled into the dangerous calm of a man who'd made up his mind.

"What do you plan to do with it, sir? I don't see that you have many choices. I hope you'll make the right one."

"I don't have to talk to you."

"No, sir, you don't. Do you have a cell phone with you?"

He laughed, and shook his head. "Cell phone."

"If you do, you might use that, sir. Call someone you *will* talk to."

"Well, I don't need to talk to nobody. I got myself into this mess all by myself. I guess I can get out of it, one way or another."

"That's what concerns me, sir."

"Don't care if it concerns you or not, lady." He nodded at the badge on her belt. "Wearin' that don't make you God."

"It also concerns your daughters, sir. I can't believe that you want Casey and Christine to have to live with this."

"It ain't *their* problem."

"Oh, yes it is, sir. Let me draw some pictures for you, sir. If you swing that shotgun around and point it at me or Casey…" and she held up the radio, the transmit bar still depressed. "You can see the sheriff across the way. He's watching you through the scope of his rifle, sir. And listening as we talk. If you make a threatening move, you'll be dead. Just like that. You won't even hear it coming."

She saw a flicker of anxiety on Prescott's face, and his eyes squinted, focusing in the distance first, then darting to his youngest daughter, then to Christine, who was just coming up behind Bill Gastner. The older man reached out a hand and stopped the girl, who nodded quickly and looked up toward her father.

"Is that what you want your daughters to see? To live with? I can't believe that. You want that image to be their last memory of you?"

"I…I ain't going to do you no harm."

"That's good to hear, sir." She smiled at him. "I've been harmed enough in the past couple of years."

"Yeah, well."

"That leaves some other choices. Are you planning to harm yourself, sir? Have you ever seen what a 12 gauge shotgun does to someone?" Casey whimpered something and out of the corner of her eye, Estelle saw the girl sink to her knees. "I have, sir, and I can't believe that you want the girls to witness that. To live with that?" Her thumb still held the transmit bar, and she shifted her grip a little. Turning away so she could look out across the open prairie, she shook her head. "So beautiful, sir. Your ranch is so beautiful."

Prescott stated to say something, but she cut him off. "I was out at the windmill earlier with Casey. She tells me that this is one of her favorite places. Yours too."

"That ain't your affair."

"Sure enough not, sir."

"Daddy," Casey said softly, but couldn't finish the sentence.

"Maybe you can imagine what this spot will mean to her if you go through with this."

"You don't know what I mean to do. Don't think you do."

"Well, sir, if you're not going to shoot *me*, and you're not going to shoot your *daughters*, and you're not quail hunting, then that leaves you. That's the way I see it, sir."

"You can just get off my land."

"Sir, that's not going to happen, and you know it." He looked at her for a moment, and she repeated herself. "That's not going to happen, sir. And I think that you're smart enough to know that. When there's an incident, we don't just 'go away.' In fact, more officers are enroute. My deputies, the state police. Even an ambulance. And you know what? I want it all to be a wasted trip for them."

"I ain't going to talk to them."

"You don't have to, sir. You can talk to me. Or Mr. Gastner, if you want. You owe it to your daughters now, sir. You owe it to them to clear the air. Years ago, you and Eddie Johns had an argument. What did he say to you, Gus? Did he want you to go into business with him? Is that it? To hook up with the Mexicans?"

"Nothin' like that. I had no dealings with him."

"He made some remark about Christine? Is that what it was?" When Prescott didn't reply, Estelle shifted the radio to her right hand, relaxing a cramping thumb. "We all know how Johns was, sir. Christine tells me that he made passes at her down at the Broken Spur. Is that where it started, sir? You were protecting her, is that it? Who could fault you for that?"

"That son-of-a-bitch..." he started to say, and cut it off. He closed his eyes, and the side of his head actually touched the shotgun barrel.

"He came out to talk to you one day while you were working on the road for Miles Waddell, didn't he, sir. Is that it? Things went from bad to worse after that?"

"I said it ain't your concern."

"How could it not be, sir. We recovered a body. The victim had been shot through the head, just like the jaguar. Now how would that not be our concern? And the *why* of it all is our concern, too, sir. Self-defense can come in many forms, sir. We know what kind of man Eddie Johns was."

"Shootin' somebody in the back of the head ain't self-defense," Prescott said.

300 Steven F. Havill

"Well, sir, that depends on what was said, what was going on. If you felt that Johns was a threat to you…" Prescott's eyebrow twitched. "Or to your family…" When he didn't respond further, she added, "I think that there's a lot of the story that will come out. You have to give it a chance. I know you had a reason for what you did, and you thought it was a good reason, sir."

"The boy," Prescott said, and he looked toward Casey, eyes pleading. "I just wanted to scare him off. I knew where he'd been, what he was diggin' into. I know the girl's sweet on him, and I don't care about that. I know you won't believe that, but it's true. But he found the cave. I know he found it. I didn't know what to do."

"How was shooting at him going to scare him off, sir? Wouldn't he just go to the authorities?"

Prescott actually laughed. "That little Mexican? I don't think so. He didn't want no one findin' out what he found."

"The handgun, you mean?" She watched Prescott's face carefully. If the rancher had known that Freddy Romero had picked up Johns' automatic, and in fact had it with him on the four-wheeler, why hadn't he just scrambled down into the arroyo and retrieved it after the crash? Did he panic? Panic so thoroughly that he had forgotten to go back and seal off the little cave?

"Maybe that." Prescott remained pointlessly cagey, as if he had cards to play.

"What difference would that have made? There was no connection between the gun and you, sir."

The rancher shrugged helplessly. "I didn't think it through."

"Sometimes we just act," Estelle said gently. "Like the Romero boy. He lied about the location of the cat's skeleton because he wanted to explore the rest of the cave, and find what there was to find. He didn't think it through."

"I didn't mean to hit him." Prescott cleared his throat. "Didn't even mean to *shoot*. It just went off…"

"That's what the evidence shows, sir. Let us help you," Estelle said, seeing him sinking into that easy sea of self-recrimination.

"Let Casey and Christine help you, sir. You did your job protecting them as best you could."

"That Romero kid gettin' killed was an accident," Prescott said, addressing Casey directly for the first time. "I didn't even mean to shoot. I didn't hit him, and I didn't mean to hit his four-wheeler. If you'd been with him…"

"But you knew she wasn't, sir," Estelle said.

"I just saw him comin', drivin' like hell's afire, and I didn't pay attention. God damn rifle went off without a thought."

"You didn't climb down to check on him, sir."

"Nope. I know dead when I see it." He drew a deep, shuddering breath. "I guess I got some things to answer for, ain't that right?"

"Yes, sir, that's right."

"Might be easier just to let the sheriff…" His gaze drifted out, across the valley where the sheriff waited. Estelle knew that the rifle's bolt would be closed on a live round, the safety off, Torrez's rock-steady finger close to light trigger.

"You think about your daughters before you take that road, sir."

"Daddy," Casey said softly, "let them help you."

For a very long minute, Gus Prescott said nothing. And then, with exaggerated care, he leaned the shotgun forward a bit and waited while Estelle stepped forward and took it from him.

Chapter Forty-four

Estelle Reyes-Guzman looked up from her desk as a vast, colorful form filled her doorway. County Manager Leona Speers regarded her with affection.

"Welllllll," she warbled. "Dare I ask you how things are going?"

The undersheriff leaned back in her chair. "The road ahead is a little straighter."

Leona's eyebrows shot up. "My, how philosophical we are this morning. How did the confab with his nibs go?"

"The district attorney is going for a second degree murder charge in the death of Eddie Johns, and criminally negligent homicide in the death of Freddy Romero. And everything is always open to negotiation and bargaining."

"That's all fair, isn't it?"

"Oh, yes. It's fair. Expected, and fair."

"Harvey will go with the Pat Garrett defense?"

Estelle looked quizzically at Leona. What Derrick Harvey, the public defender, would decide was always in question.

"You know…self defense. They claimed that Garrett was so dangerous that his killer felt justified in shooting from behind. Face to face, he wouldn't have stood a chance against Garrett."

"True enough. Prescott would have no chance face to face with Eddie Johns, and knew it."

"Mr. Johns' reputation is going to receive an airing in court, I can believe."

"I would expect so," Estelle said. "I've never heard it called that, though. The 'Pat Garrett' defense. Interesting."

"Oh, my, yes. You just ask Bill Gastner. He'll know."

"I may have to do that." She turned and found the appropriate folder. "I have two names for you," and held the folder of job applications out to the county manager.

Leona held up both hands. "Oh, I don't need to know, do I? Just that you hire *two*." She grinned and leaned forward eagerly. "Who are they?"

"If David Veltri will come work for us, that would be perfect," Estelle said. "He has military police experience, a perfect record, and is a home town boy. Married, one child. That's one. And I want to talk in person with Becky Hronich."

Leona's eyes grew wide with surprise. "The retired Chicago detective? My, I can't imagine."

"Well, neither can I."

"But she's older."

"Oh, just ancient. I believe forty-six."

"Family?"

"Husband retired from the military, and builds boats. No children."

"Something of a culture shock for them, I would think. Wait until she talks with Bobby. I'd like to be a mouse in the room."

"Well, as a matter of fact, she's had occasion to do that very thing on the phone. 'No nonsense,' is how he described her. She's willing to come out for an interview. Take a look at her file, and see if you have any questions."

"Oh, it's not *my* hire."

"I know, but I value your opinion, Leona."

"What did Mr. Bill say about the detective?"

"That if we didn't hire her, we should have our heads examined."

"There you are, then." She nodded brightly, then her expression sank into a frown. "I hear some disturbing rumor, by the by, and that's really why I stopped by."

"All rumor is disturbing, Leona."

"No, this *really* is. The Romeros? George and his wife? I heard they are planning to sue the department. Well, to sue the county, the department, *you,* my dear, the EMT's, and any other moving target they can find."

Estelle nodded noncommittally. "I heard rumblings of that too. *Padrino* talked to him a time or two, and that was the impression he got."

"My dear, on what *grounds?* For heaven's sakes, who could have done more than you did?"

"That's not the issue, my friend," Estelle replied.

"Whatever *is* the issue, then?"

"That he *can?* That it gives him something to focus on, maybe? Someone else to blame? I can't imagine his loss."

Leona shook her head slowly, lips compressed. "You're too sweet, dear. One son loses an eye, the other dead in a senseless crash? We could argue parental supervision until the cows come home, but that won't do any good."

She regarded the undersheriff, who didn't reply. "Maybe his lawyer will talk some sense into him."

"Don't hold your breath on that, Leona."

"I suppose not. But we have good lawyers, too, don't we. What fun they'll all have."

Estelle's phone rang, and she picked up the receiver, holding up a finger so that Leona wouldn't leave.

"Guzman."

"Ah, good," Frank Dayan said. "I was hoping I could catch you."

"How are you, sir?"

"Just fine. Any chance?" She knew exactly what the newspaper publisher meant.

"What works for you, sir?"

"How about right now?"

"Here or there?"

"I'll be right over."

Estelle hung up. "Frank's chance," she said. "He's finally going to scoop the big metro papers."

"He lives for that, the dear sweet man. Has Mr. Prescott explained himself? I mean, my goodness, if there *is* an explanation for what he did?"

"Eddie Johns was infatuated with Christine, Leona. He made crude remarks to Gus on a number of occasions—enough to get his fatherly blood boiling. Prescott was going to Waddell's property to work on the road, and Johns was there, so excited that he'd managed to shoot a cat so old, tired, or sick that he couldn't run. He crowed about being able to sell the carcass in Mexico...apparently there's a market.

"That led to an argument, and one thing led to another. Gus says that Johns was talking a blue streak about what *he* was going to do...with the cave he'd just discovered, with the cat, with the Mexicans who'd pay a fortune for the carcass, with the stargazers facility he and Miles Waddell were planning, and sure enough, even with Gus' daughter.

"He crawled into the cave a bit, and Gus was right behind him. The handgun's butt was right there near at hand, Johns was in an awkward position so that he couldn't react, and that was the opportunity. Gus took it. That's his story. He was really, sincerely, worried about Christine."

She reached out and tapped one of the folders. "If you read Christine's deposition, you'll hear some scary things about Johns. *She* was easy with it all, but her father overheard enough. Christine remembers her father telling her at one point that she wouldn't have to worry about Johns any more. She didn't think anything of it at the time."

"How terribly sad."

Estelle held up her hands in surrender. "Too much drink, too much lots of things. The trouble is that Gus panicked when it was all over, and then combined that with trying to be too clever. After the shooting, he had Johns' truck to contend with. He drove it home, stripped what he could use or sell, and crushed it by rolling it with that big old grader of his. Then he burned it to make it look old. Our interest in the cave discoveries prompted him to be just too clever...again. He'd been planning to sell the junk vehicles to make some money to fix the grader, but he hadn't gotten around to it—until the story about Freddy broke. And then he thought that he'd better get rid of the remains of Johns' truck."

She shook her head. "If he'd left it alone? If Johns' truck hadn't been on that load, if *Padrino* hadn't seen it, we might never have known."

"Oh, my dear, I have faith you would have made the discovery somehow. When people get too clever for their own good..."

"That's what we have to always hope," Estelle replied. She heard steps out in the hallway, and Frank Dayan appeared behind Leona.

"Good morning, you handsome devil," the county manager greeted, and Frank's blush was intense. He ducked his head and looked beyond the county manager as if the undersheriff was somehow going to protect him.

"Got a minute?" he asked.

"Come in, Frank," Estelle said. "Leona, I'll let you know when our hires sign on the dotted line."

"Just wonderful." Leona waved a cheery hand. She squeezed past Frank, which deepened his blush even more. She squeezed his arm. "Aren't *you* the lucky one, though."

To receive a free catalog of Poisoned Pen Press titles, please contact us in one of the following ways:

Phone: 1-800-421-3976
Facsimile: 1-480-949-1707
Email: info@poisonedpenpress.com
Website: www.poisonedpenpress.com

Poisoned Pen Press
6962 E. First Ave. Ste. 103
Scottsdale, AZ 85251